MAVIS

Brenda K. Marshall

FAWCETT CREST • NEW YORK

A Fawcett Crest Book
Published by Ballantine Books
Copyright © 1996 by Brenda K. Marshall

Grateful acknowledgment is made to Pabst Brewing Co., Milwaukee, WI, for permission to reprint a portion of the Hamm's Tom-Tom Jingle.

http://www.randomhouse.com

Library of Congress Catalog Card Number: 96-90979

ISBN 0-449-22571-2

Manufactured in the United States of America

First Hardcover Edition: June 1996
First Mass Market Edition: July 1997

10   9   8   7   6   5   4   3   2   1

"ENGAGING . . .

Marshall gives language to many characters. . . . Taking risks, she succeeds with ease."
— *Publishers Weekly*

"Each of these women is a bright and distinctive character. . . . MAVIS pulls us deep into the heart of her family."
— *The New York Times Book Review*

"Admirable . . . Marshall is a talented and promising writer with a precise, finely tuned prose style which is a delight to read."
— *Nashville Banner*

"Intense, dramatic, and complex relationships between sisters . . . As the dramatic events unfold, readers will enjoy her fresh, honest approach."
— *Booklist*

*For Mom,
and in memory of Dad*

ACKNOWLEDGMENTS

I don't know how many times I was convinced that *Mavis* was completed, only to have someone read a part or the whole of the manuscript and say, "I like it, but . . ." To each of these readers, many thanks: Michael Kreyling, Mark Jarman, John Casey, Susan Minot, Laurie Lynn Drummond, and A. Manette Ansay. I am also grateful to Dr. Marcia Montgomery of Nashville, and to Director Bill Broer and Jerry Kemmet of the North Dakota Bureau of Criminal Investigation for taking the time to answer my questions, and to Barney Karpfinger and Leona Nevler for believing.

Finally, all my thanks, all my life, to Valerie Traub.

PROLOGUE

July 1990

IF MAVIS DIDN'T THINK OF HERSELF AS A NORTH DA-kotan, it was simply because there was no other identity conceivable. And from what she read of the behavior of others with the misfortune or bad judgment to live elsewhere, she was grateful to be surrounded by sensible people. Certainly she had sympathy for victims of catastrophe and hard luck, but all her remarkable generosity was directed toward immediate family and community. And always, couched in her statements of concern, was the added moral: "If you live on a floodplain, you should expect the occasional flood," or "If you build your house on sand, you should expect it to slip out to sea someday."

Mavis's identity was that odd mixture of superiority and submission that constitutes the psyche of a farm people with little regard for anything that smacks of impermanence. Theirs was a constancy bred less by time than repetition, for the North Dakota sod had been broken little more than a hundred years earlier by relatives just three or four generations back. Nonetheless, when most of those generations have lived under one roof, have driven cattle in and out of the same barn, have shared in the cycle of spring planting, summer worrying, fall harvesting, and winter survival, that which is transient becomes trivial.

Dakotans expect the repetition of hot summers and cold winters. Along with their hot summers they expect the occasional hailstorm and maybe a tornado or two. Along with their cold winters they expect the occasional blizzard and maybe an ice storm or two. North Dakotans prefer not to be surprised at all.

Changeable weather is not simply accepted, but relied upon. Imagine the awkward moments of silence that would befuddle sunburned or windburned farmers with no mention of rain, wind, or sun to bridge their greetings into talk about crops, market reports, and local and state politics. How, for example, would one old Norwegian— his cap pushed back on his forehead, showing the demarcation between pale and tanned skin, consternation in the depthless Nordic eyes blasted by a prairie sun—begin to convince the young man wiping tractor oil from his hands with a dirty rag of the importance of sitting in on the next open school board meeting without first mentioning the weather's antics?

The farmland itself is as likely to be the origin as the excuse for clichés. From the sky, the patchwork quilt; from the land, amber waves of grain. Each mile is intersected by a crossing road, all ninety-degree angles and squares. Inside each square mile lie rectangles of gold and green and black: ripening grain, beans or corn, plowed fields. On the edge of several squares sits the neat farmstead, with house, a barn or two, silos, grain bins, Quonsets, outbuildings from various generations, perhaps some pens for livestock, and even some trees. Each carefully mowed yard is defined by a line of properly spaced evergreens or a hedge or a morning-gloried fence, always the attempt to check the seeming infinity of the plains, of the prairie which itself joins with the sky in a land that can be defined only in terms of space. A land so open and undisturbed by shifts in terrain that a steady gaze toward the horizon reveals the planet's curve.

It's late July, so it's hot. Mile after mile the grain ripens within the grid of intersecting gravel roads. Every now and then within a field, a thin line of weeds taller than the surrounding crop stands as an embarrassing reminder of a preoccupied farmer's moment of lost concentration in the spring as he sprayed 2-4-D Amine. Chemicals in this pristine land? To make a living otherwise would be impossible, the farmers insist, as they negotiate within the shrinking space of husbandry and survival.

Although the navy beans have begun to yellow, the soybeans are still a bright leafy green. Tassles beginning to burn atop eight-foot-tall rows of corn are causing suppertime consternation between husbands and wives who are nonetheless grateful for the same sunshine that daily lifts the faces of fields of sunflowers from east to west. By mid-September each browned head will be permanently bowed, held down by its own seeded weight.

The quintessential smell of summer permeates the countryside, released by the season's second cutting of hay. One man works each field now, cutting and baling the hay into huge cylinders. Only twenty years ago the laborers would have been two, one catching and stacking smaller rectangular bales swung upward by a mechanical arm attached to and propelled by the truck driven by his more fortunate partner. Forty years ago the crew was again doubled. Then the arms swinging the bales were human, hardened and tanned. At the ends of the iron arms were hands grasping metal hooks, one for each hand, one for each end of a bale snagged and swung onto the back of the hay rack, to be stacked by someone else. Someone smaller. A son. A nephew.

These days the figure inside the tractor, combine, or truck cab may wear a scarf over hair rollers, but farmwives are more likely to be at their jobs away from home—starting an IV, ringing up a purchase on a register, taking a summer school class at a nearby college for continuing ed teaching credits. Or they may be hanging out laundry, doing the dishes, taking the kids to swimming lessons, shopping in Fargo (not forgetting to pick up the part for the combine), baking cookies, trimming the hedge, mowing the lawn, changing diapers, balancing the books, watering the cattle, unclogging the drain, drinking coffee with the neighbor, taking lunch to the harvesters, picking chokecherries, canning tomatoes, making pickles, weeding the garden, painting the trim, or writing up a lesson on the new tax-law changes to present to the Homemakers Club (the lesson the month before was on yet another decorative use of Styrofoam balls).

And Mavis Schmidt Holmstead? What is she doing sitting in a public lavatory in a police station letting slow tears fall unchecked? Her husband, Frank, retired from farming six years ago, and shortly thereafter from life as well with a massive heart attack. Her oldest son, Glenn, and his wife, Peggy, run the family farm, and run it well it seems, even without her help. Her other son, Craig, does something arcane with computers at Boeing in Seattle. She could go home and find something to can, but her pantry already looks like a survivalist's. No need to ride around on the mower, the grass not growing much in this heat; besides, Glenn's girls do most of her yard work. A nice yard that her grandchildren mow for her. A nice house that she has lived in, alone, for five years, but not the house she lived in for the preceding fifty-five years, almost thirty-five of them with Frank, so not really her home. No real farm records to keep: what was planted where when, sold where when, contracted where when for how much. No men to feed. No livestock to think about. Retired, so no more papers to grade. Tired most of the time, and just beginning to admit to herself why, but not quite, because now she has one more thing to do, and it's the hardest thing so far. Thinking, Soon they will all be home, and must I spend the rest of my life lying to them?

1

ALTHOUGH MAVIS STATED CLEARLY AND OFTEN THAT she believed in God, her life suggested that she believed equally in Mavis. Comfortably imprisoned within her own design, her impatience was all for those less completely imagined, and this was certainly not the first time that she had been nudged into irritation by Janice's pauses, ellipses, and lapses into silence, which Mavis interpreted as indecision.

Mavis had followed her short knock that Friday directly into Janice's apartment to find Janice facing the door, her expression startled.

"What?" Mavis asked.

"I thought . . ."

"What?" Mavis asked again. "Is something wrong?"

"I thought you might be . . ."

"I told you I was going to be in town this afternoon for a doctor's appointment and you said 'stop over for coffee on your way.' Were you expecting someone else?"

"No. Well, maybe . . . I guess." Janice paused again, then her gaze focused as if she had just recognized her oldest sister. She also recognized Mavis's exasperation with her greeting, but was, for the moment, intrigued by her own anticipation of what she was likely to say next. For the first time in Janice's life, it seemed, she had become unpredictable. She held the name she had not intended to speak behind her tongue for a moment longer, tasting the secrecy, fear, and silence that once again were about to escape into anger.

"Jack." Janice spit the name as if surprised, then all but smiled at Mavis's grimace of revulsion in response. Janice turned and passed through the short hallway into her small living room.

Mavis was right behind her.

"You were expecting Jack now?"

Janice turned to face the family-famous "Mavis-look" that combined withering displeasure with genuine incredulity. Suddenly she understood that for the first time in her life she had in her power the words that could deflate that look, that could make Mavis see her, only her, and in a way that even Mavis couldn't have anticipated. And she didn't even need to say it all.

"No, not now, not Jack. We won't be doing that anymore."

"Won't be doing what?" Mavis spaced her words with unnecessarily clear diction, as if she were interrogating a child rather than her forty-eight-year-old sister.

"It, Mavis. We won't be doing *it*." Janice paused, then in that brief silence realized with dismay that she had actually stopped, that her emphasis had somehow punctured her rare resolve. Her shoulders dropped into the stoop that customarily resisted her Schmidt height as her gaze slid past Mavis's expression of disgust. She could feel Mavis willing her to go on, and resisted.

"Janice."

It wouldn't do any good to try to explain. There was no logic to unfold, no reason to clarify, nothing Mavis could ever understand. Janice wanted to say to Mavis: Our lives aren't always about making sense, we're not always in control, some things just happen. But Mavis would just look at her like she'd lost her mind. So Janice took a breath and started again, knowing that Mavis would not let it drop, gauging just how much information she would need to release before she could again be silent.

"Jack would be in Fargo, always half drunk. Each time he hurt me a little more. The last time he almost broke my nose."

"And Norton didn't notice." This spoken as a statement, Mavis's summation of Janice's husband.

"I told Norton I'd tripped over boxes in the back room at work." Janice hesitated. "He . . ." and stopped again.

"He what?"

"He called me Irene when he hit me."

Mavis looked into the eyes that should have leveled hers, noticed the tension sealing Janice's mouth into a weaker version of her own Schmidt jaw. For just a moment Mavis slipped toward the loss of their youngest sister, Irene, dead now for over a year. But already she was thinking well beyond what she had been told, wondering: What is it I must now make right? She took a deep breath, determined not to allow Janice to settle back into her signature silence.

"When was this?"

"Not long before the accident." Janice's voice had become a whisper.

Mavis waited, then dropped her words with quiet but unerring accuracy.

"I guess I knew that."

With a sudden intake of breath that further rounded her shoulders, Janice felt these words as a blow to her stomach. Mavis had known? But no one could have known. Janice was now paralyzed by the old confusion, her rage at Mavis's assumption at odds with a desperate need to have this sister make it all right. She didn't know which impulse tripped the release.

"You don't know everything."

It was a childlike assertion of independence, which broke down almost immediately as Janice began to weep, and Mavis recognized the plea behind the anger. She didn't have time to understand the anger and hadn't needed to hear the plea, because she was already waiting to hear something else she couldn't have known, but, of course, must know.

"Tell me."

"I don't know how."

"Tell me," Mavis repeated, but softened the command with an emphasis on the last word.

Janice sank to the sofa and spoke into her lap. "Finally I'd said 'No more.' I felt like I'd been inside some kinda nightmare. I'd made myself sick. Not because of me. But Irene. Jack said if I wouldn't see him when he wanted, he'd tell Irene about what we'd done. I said no, I was gonna tell her. Then he said no, he'd kill me first. You know how he talked. Big tough guy. Carrying that . . . that rifle around in his pickup. But Mavis, Irene was always there for me. She didn't just love me like the rest of you 'cause I was family. I didn't have to be smart, or pretty, or funny. She liked me. Me."

Something familiar about the impotent rage beneath Janice's despair opened a window to the past and Mavis was a child again, looking down on a silently weeping man pulling a dog's limp body by the hind legs toward a freshly dug grave. The dog's head bounced behind the body at an impossible angle. Flies gorged themselves on the thick blackness that was the neck. Mavis closed her eyes, shut the memory.

"Did you tell Irene?"

"No." Janice's tears stopped. "For two weeks after Jack said that, I tried to figure out what to do. I wanted to tell Irene just 'cause no one shoulda ever lied to her. No one shoulda hurt her. But I had. I didn't know why, and I didn't know how to tell her. It wasn't the kids. I was worried about Blair, sure, him still being at home with Jack and Irene. But I just didn't do anything. Janice never really does anything, you know. I just come when I'm called and do what I'm told.

"And then, you know, it was too late. And Jack, at the funeral. Comes up to me with all those bandages on his hands like he's some kinda hero for trying to open a door, and says, real low, 'Maybe this is really your fault, Janice.' Well, it took me a year, but I did something. Plain old, dumb, nothing Janice did something."

Realizing that she was now towering over her sister, Mavis lowered herself to the worn sofa that, like much of the furniture in this small apartment, had once been hers, and prodded Janice through a halting description of what was probably not, at first, an atypical day. Struggling to get Norton, his mood foul from the moment of waking with the morning's hangover, out of bed and drinking coffee before she was off for work. Standing on her feet all day long, forced to smile at customers half her age with twice her income as they complained about food prices. Her only conversation with twenty-year-olds who talked about movie stars and boyfriends. Mopping up broken jars of juice toppled by children of mothers who pretend not to notice. Fifteen-minute breaks in a dingy back room littered with cardboard boxes and heavy with stale cigarette smoke, where she feels, once again, a rush of blood into her panties after four months with no period, and wants to weep at the unpredictability of her forty-eight-year-old body.

When her shift was over, Janice had driven to the service station where she had scheduled her chronically overheating car for a tune-up, tired of hearing Norton say he'd get to it soon, and sat, this time for almost two hours, in another dingy room decorated by full ashtrays, until a young man, in clothes too clean to be those of a good mechanic, smilingly told her they'd just gotten to her car, that the fan clutch was shot, would cost her about one hundred dollars to replace plus another twenty for thermostat and gasket, and that they couldn't get the part until the following morning. Now, near tears of frustration, she explained that she needed to be at work a half hour before the shop opened. No problem, the young man had replied, studiously refusing to notice Janice's distress, she could have a loaner car and they'd fix hers first thing in the morning.

The young man's bright humor made her want to smash her fist into his smiling face. Instead, she took the keys for the loaner car and rushed to the repair shop in North Fargo where her vacuum cleaner had been fixed. It was 6:25 when she tried the locked door. A sign in the window read: OPEN 9:00 A.M. TO 6:30 P.M. MONDAY THROUGH SATURDAY. Now she was crying, and, wanting the drink she wouldn't take, got back on Interstate 29, but headed north out of town, instead of south toward Main Street and her apartment in West Fargo. She had driven the ninety-odd miles north in a stranger's car in tears and anger, and for no reason that she could explain, pretending that Irene would be there with a cup of coffee

and a listening ear. Had driven past the farmyard where
Irene could not be and saw Irene's son, Blair, doing
chores alone in the twilight. About two miles past the
farmstead, she pulled off the road onto a tractor approach,
parked in a stand of trees, and waited, she couldn't have
said for what, for hours, as the darkness thickened. A
dark night on a North Dakota country road. Not one
single car passed by.

Just after midnight a pickup pulling a horse trailer
came creeping along down the center of the gravel road.
Leaving her car, she crossed through the tall grass of the
ditch to the side of the road, shivering a little in the cool
evening of a hot day, and waved the pickup down. It was
Jack. It had never occurred to her that it could be anyone
else. He was drunk. He sneered when he saw her, and
said, "Sorry, lady, I don't do Schmidt cunts no more."

She was standing outside the truck with the passenger
door open. His head was nodding; she didn't think he
could focus very well. She still didn't know what she had
come to do, but she knew what she was about to do. Not
for her. For Irene. Reaching behind the seat, she pulled
out the deer rifle Jack always bragged about keeping
loaded. At first he didn't seem to be able to tell what she
was doing. Then he laughed and reached over, grabbing
the barrel of the gun. Said she must really want it bad.
And then his laughter exploded into red bits of skin and
blood and bone and she was running back to the car.

Janice finished speaking with a series of gasps, as if
the unusual length of her narrative had swallowed the
oxygen from the room. Mavis looked for a moment at
Janice's bowed head, then closed her eyes and, as an
afterthought to her intentions, asked her God for forgiveness. Dropping her hand from her chest where it had
rested as if to protect her heart from Janice's story, Mavis
began to ask questions, dragging numbed responses from

her sister. What were you wearing? Where are the clothes? The shoes? What kind of gun? What happened to it? Where? Think! Again, what time was it? Did anyone see the car? What make car was it? Did you wash it before going back to the garage this morning? Any stains on the upholstery? Describe the stand of trees. Where are you usually on a Thursday night? Where did you tell Norton you had been? On and on. More questions and more as the afternoon moved toward evening.

Around six P.M., when two policemen knocked on Janice's door with the news of a brother-in-law's death and questions about his lifestyle, friends, and enemies, Mavis and Janice were picking at TV dinners as they watched the Channel 4 news.

MAVIS

AS SHE DRIVES THE FORTY MILES FROM WEST FARGO TO her farmstead that evening as instinctively as a blind woman moves about the furniture of her house, Mavis is grateful for her body's numbing exhaustion. Once home, she completes her nightly toiletries with her mind determinedly blank, slips under the covers and into willed emptiness.

Seconds or hours later she is in the house of her youth, pulling pieces of shredded dolls from deep within the toilet bowl, in front of which she has discovered a child-like Janice stuffing and flushing, stuffing and flushing. Chastising the little girl, twelve years her junior, Mavis reaches in for sodden arms, legs, and tiny heads with shocked eyes and hair that clings to her wrist. Looking up as she works, Mavis asks her little sister the inevitable question, and watches as Janice's lips move but release no sound, then form a quiet smile. Suddenly, strong fingers lace about hers in the cold water and squeeze as Mavis frantically tries to shake loose the severed male hand that wears a wedding ring placed there by Irene.

With a gasp, Mavis is awake and holding her breath as she stares into the silence that seeps from her dream into the surrounding dark. The dresser facing her bed creaks, contracting in the increasing cool of the evening; the clock/radio to her right hums the tune of a missing rubber foot. Still it is the dream's void that swells into the bedroom.

Mavis coughs, and coughs again, as if to clear the dream's images. But they remain, insistent, now attaching themselves to the afternoon's horrors. Mavis sighs, sits up, and reaches for her glasses, and sees by the numbers that now replace the greenish blur to her right that she has slept for almost three hours. Knows she will sleep no more, and swings her feet onto the floor. She leaves the bedroom, crosses through the family room, and stands at the kitchen sink to fill a glass of water. The kitchen window directs her gaze into the distinct darkness of the country night, where certainly, she thinks, it must be easier to breathe. Pulling an afghan from the back of the couch, she again crosses the family room and passes through the front door into the prairie's silence, which is itself darker than the darkness is silent. Neither is still.

Mavis sits on the front steps of her farmhouse nestled in a stand of trees that breaks up the plains' expanse with the effectiveness of a picket fence in the surf. She leans forward, arms resting on knees, wrists crossed; leans into the summer midnight and into the silence that registers not as absence of sound, but as the abstraction of absence itself, and lets her breathing calm.

She had believed her midnight vigils were behind her. Wed for thirty-five years and widowed for five, Mavis had spent her first months of mourning refusing to distinguish between night and day, living on cereal, living in pajamas. Night followed night of waking in tears to spend the remaining dark hours reading *Reader's Digest*s, cleaning out closets, stoop-sitting in the moonlight. But grief, she had decided, is ultimately tedious business, and resolved that if she must miss Frank for the rest of her life, she would miss him during the day. At night she would sleep. Yet here she is, awake once more, and lonely in the dark. Because the decisions she must make are too big to be made alone. Because if not alone, she wouldn't be making them at all.

Wrapping herself tighter within the afghan slung over her shoulders, Mavis releases her dream's "why" into the evening. The question she puts to herself, however, has little to do with a sister's adultery with a brother-in-law—whom even dead, Mavis considers only with disgust—or with what should have been the inconceivable act of murder. That harvest, she understands, is complete. Rather, Mavis sifts through the afternoon's chaff of anger and loathing, searches for the seeds of Janice's despair, and wonders how, at sixty years old, she could be seeing this for the first time.

Mavis's gaze pushes past the hinted outlines of trees and outbuildings, into the darkness of a past beyond eyesight. She does not find herself immediately in the company of any of the four "little girls"—Judy, Janice, Isabelle, and Irene—but with Maxine, two years her junior, at thirteen years old. Blue eyes sparkling in excitement, cheeks rouged by the still-raw March wind, nose running and wiped on a sweatshirt sleeve, she is begging Mavis to sit for "just five minutes more" on that soggy blanket on sodden ground while she reads "just one more verse" of something or other.

Why they were sitting in the middle of a cow pasture by a muddy creek in early spring Mavis couldn't recall. She could remember later peeling out of her damp jeans in the entryway, and reminding Maxine to do the same before opening the door to the kitchen. And then, with the smell of freshly baked cinnamon rolls washing over them, even Maxine was willing to cease her running recitation of . . . Emily Dickinson. Of course. They had sat with their feet resting on the open oven door, letting what heat was left in its belly warm cold toes inside the clean socks they'd sent five-year-old Judy after. Mom would have been in a shapeless shirtwaist housedress, gray hair permed tightly to her head to be no bother, heavy shoes set down toe first to keep from making noise. What was she doing? Cleaning the baking pans? Making dinner? Feeding the twins? No, she and Maxine had Isabelle and Irene on their laps. Mavis watched behind her closed eyes, but couldn't bring her mother into the picture, sensing her only as a diminishing drone of activity in the background. And where was Janice? At three she must have been somewhere near.

Frustrated with Janice's absence within this tableau of six-sibling harmony, Mavis moves forward, into her own early adulthood. She is sitting on Frank's lap in the same kitchen, causing her mother to leave the room, embarrassed by their open affection, mumbling about mending to be done. How odd that her mother goes to the room she had once shared with Maxine, now in college, and that she and Frank had claimed her parents' bedroom as their own. But Frank just grins and puts his finger, covered with fine dark hairs, to his lips when she mock-struggles to get up, saying, "Don't wake little Glenn now that he is finally down for his nap." Then the school bus pulls in the drive and Frank makes his daily joke about getting more than he bargained for with her—a farm as well as a whole family of Schmidts, complete with mother-in-law and a handful of sister-children. As double exclamation points to his observation, Isabelle and Irene rush in with their nine-year-old school tales, Izzy clearly embellishing while Irene counters with less fanciful corrections. Judy, just turned thirteen, comes in mid-story, having waited outside for the bus to make its circle around the driveway in order to wave good-bye to one of the boys. Isabelle, her good humor already beginning to edge with anger, automatically switches to a litany of Judy's most recent offenses, and eleven-year-old Janice disappears around the corner.

Increasingly distressed, Mavis continues to search through treasured images, only to find this middle sister slipping quietly into another room, or standing silently in the background, or just not there at all. Until, there . . . there she is. This can't be Christmas because no tree ornaments hang by colored ribbon from the light fixture above the dining room table, Mavis's nod toward festive interior decorating, so perhaps this is Thanksgiving. Surely there must be a half-dozen children in the next room with the TV going. Janice holds her own child, and smiles that quiet smile of hers, next to her husband, Norton, who is evidently capable of sleeping sitting up at the dinner table. Next to Norton is Maxine, and she has her hand on her husband Charlie's knee and he's smoking that pipe, and Mavis knows Maxine thinks he looks so dignified in his tweed coat, but he looks as asleep to her as does Norton, and she'd sure like to cut those few long hairs he has swept up from the side to cover his bald head. Maxine holds a cigarette in her other hand, and passes it over Charlie to Isabelle, who looks at Frank, and then all three glance at Mavis, and Maxine says, "Uh-oh, the Mavis-look." So Mavis gets up to get more coffee, and Frank pats her fanny, which he says is supposed to remind her that he loves her, when saying so would be too personal. Irene is across the table, between Janice and Jack, waving away all the smoke and giving quick glances at her husband until she says, "Jack, if you want to watch football, just go in the other room, then." The room is suddenly, uncharacteristically, silent, until Isabelle pulls the tension away from Irene with a joke directed toward Judy, sitting between Jack and . . . which husband would it be, Butch? They all laugh, except Judy, who scowls, and Janice, who simply smiles.

With a shudder that has her tugging at the afghan, Mavis again sees the quiet smile of a little girl standing by a toilet, surrounded by dismembered and dripping dolls. And remembers, dimly, a story she had been told by one of the other younger sisters when she had returned for a weekend home from the nearby teachers college she was then attending. A story about Janice, about a rare but violent tantrum. A story certainly exaggerated, barely believed, easily dismissed, quickly forgotten. And wonders, were there others?

Mavis returns her gaze to the present and the pale moonlight beginning to break through the cloud cover. She does not expect the new light to distinguish foundation from firmament, knowing full well that such distinctions do not signify on the prairie, where the expanse of the land openly challenges the space of the sky.

She has looked so long and so steadily into the empty night, alone, that she is now able to see in the darkness the light that is its component. Her eyes begin to trace the outlines of the trees about her. To her left, beyond the farm buildings, she now sees that the stubble field is not as flat as a tabletop, which is how she herself has described this land, but that it gently ripples and heaves as she imagines an ocean in its calm must do in its own unimaginable space. In front of her, beyond the lawn and the hedge, just on the other side of the driveway, she sees the more common sight this time of year, a field of full-headed wheat, black now in silhouette against the light of the three-quarter-mooned sky.

She studies the distance, and realizes that she had not been seeing grain because she had been thinking field. Now the distance consists of thousands upon thousands of individual stalks, and she sees how each stalk must culminate in a bristling head of grain, and the clarity catches at her throat. And holds. For there is no husband's voice beside her, ready to deny her culpability out of love, no field of family to hide a singular growth of despair. There is simply the darkness of Janice's silence, which is no longer still.

"Her life had stood a loaded gun," Mavis says aloud to the night.

Slowly she reaches up to her left breast, remembers the doctor's appointment she had been loath to make and then failed to keep, and presses once again the hard irregular lump that makes her stomach churn with something much more than the slight pain this stone releases. And makes her decision: She had the power to kill; I have the power to die. This much I can do for her.

2

MAXINE SCHMIDT DOUGLAS ON A SUMMER SATURDAY morning did not look like the stylish, congenial, but aloof scholar she had developed as her academic persona. True, someone peering in through the windows of her breakfast nook in a small but tasteful house in the Chicago suburbs would see this fifty-eight-year-old woman, coffee mug within reach, respectably perusing the latest issue of the *Tulsa Studies in Women's Literature* through her trademark blue-tinted glasses. But the perfectly coiffed, impeccably dressed woman who would walk out her door was now quite comfortable with her hair flattened by the evening's pillow as she lounged in faded men's pajamas that sported a childish nautical motif.

Nor was Maxine actually reading the journal held open on her lap. She was not even pondering, for the moment, how radically literary criticism had changed in the past few years, now formulated within a vocabulary that she suspected should make her excited, but only made her tired. Rather, she was studying her feet propped up on a nearby chair, thinking, So this is the decade in which one's toenails begin to yellow. She was grateful for the telephone's interruption, and quickly crossed the room to answer.

Maxine knew no other voice as well as this one, and this one, she knew, had nothing good to tell her. With coffeepot poised over her cup, Maxine held the phone to her ear.

"What's wrong, Mavis?" she asked.

The line was silent for a moment, then Mavis answered with her own question, "Why do you think something is wrong?"

"I can hear it. What's happened?" Maxine thought car crash, farm accident, illness, child, sister, niece, nephew.

"Jack is dead."

"Irene's Jack? Jack Carlson?"

"How many Jacks do you know, Maxine?"

"A handful, actually."

"Well, this handful is dead."

"Good Lord. Car accident? When?"

"No. Maxine, he was shot. Shot and killed. In his truck, on the road a couple of miles from the farm. The night before last."

"Murdered? No! That's impossible. In Brickton? Jack? Who would . . . well, granted the man was an asshole, but . . . oh, those kids have been through hell already. Is Blair with you?"

"Blair will stay a few days with a neighbor friend and his family, where he evidently spent most of his time last year after Irene's accident. They're good people, probably why he managed to finish high school at all."

"And Jackie?"

Maxine felt a chill come upon her as Mavis hesitated in response to her question about this volatile niece. She repeated the question.

"Mavis, what about Jackie?"

"Well, she appears to have disappeared."

"What does that mean, to appear to disappear? To magically materialize for the purpose of dematerializing?"

"You pick the oddest moments to be pedantic, Maxine."

"And you are being a tad vague. Are you saying that Jackie is AWOL from the Hazelden? How exactly does one disappear from a chemical dependency treatment center? Does she know about . . . oh, Jesus, it doesn't get much worse than this, does it?"

Maxine stopped to take a sip of her coffee, and slowly realized in the ensuing silence that she had not asked a rhetorical question.

"What?" she asked, with growing dread.

"Well, actually it does get worse."

Mavis's tone dropped Maxine onto the kitchen stool by the phone.

"What?"

"I shot Jack."

There was no appropriate response to such a statement; it was ludicrous, so far out of the realm of possibilities that Mavis might just as well have added that she had taken up robbing banks and eating small children. And yet, this was certainly not in line with Mavis's particular sense of humor, which could be dry or deadly, but never absurd. Maxine waited for the words to follow that would make sense.

"Beg your pardon?"

"You could try, but I don't see what good it would do."

"You are being much too glib to be serious. What is going on?"

"Maxine, I will tell you this, and then I don't want to discuss it further. Jack Carlson was a bastard. He was a lousy father and a lousier husband. He was the one driving too fast with a bellyful of beer, and he's the one who should have burned in that car, not Irene. Well, maybe he's burning now."

Maxine was stunned, uselessly thinking, Mavis swears? Mavis said bastard?

"Maxine, are you there?"

"I don't understand what you're saying to me."

"Jack is dead. I killed Jack."

"I don't believe you."

"Nonetheless."

"Where are you calling from?"

"Home. Why?"

"Why aren't you in jail then, if you—"

"I haven't told anyone else yet. There didn't seem to be anyone to take care of the funeral arrangements, so I had to take charge. First thing Monday morning I'll go into Fargo to the police station."

Maxine could feel a totally inappropriate grin beginning to tug at her cheeks. Recognizing the attraction of hysteria, she said aloud, "You shot Jack and then you arranged his funeral. I have no idea what to say, other than you've never lied to me before, and now you are and I want to know why. What's going on?"

"What's done is done. There's no sense with asking why now."

Maxine sighed into the phone, temporarily defeated, having run up against a wall she had known for fifty-eight years.

"What do you want me to do?"

"I could use someone around me now with a head on her shoulders. Could you come home for a while?"

"I'll make my reservation this morning. Do you want me to call Izzy and Judy? I imagine you've already talked to Janice."

"Oh, Janice knows. And yes, call the others, but tell them they don't need to come home just yet. But you come now, Maxine."

Maxine wondered as she buckled into her seat if she should be congratulating herself for efficiency or bemoaning the lack of complexity to her life, either of which or a combination had allowed her to lock and leave her home for an unspecified length of time not much more than forty-eight hours after Mavis's summons. Or would Mavis say, "What took you so long?"

She's counting on me for something now, Maxine thought, remembering how in other summers, decades ago, she and Mavis had tied themselves to the iron radiators with bedsheets and then crawled out on the steep roof to sleep on those hot summer nights. The sheets were to keep them from rolling off the roof in their sleep. If Mavis woke first, she was sure to untie Maxine's sheet to pretend to let her fall. Oh, how we giggled then, Maxine thought, but I knew Mavis would never let go.

Maxine's chuckle prompted the woman in the seat next to hers to turn her way with a greeting. Maxine lowered her head and met the woman's hopeful look with piercing blue eyes over dark blue-tinted glasses, smiled slightly and nodded, then pushed her glasses onto the bridge of her nose and opened the Elizabeth George mystery on her lap. She'd gotten the glasses a few years ago on a whim, and was delighted to discover that her undergraduates would go away and leave her alone when they couldn't make eye contact.

Maxine turned the pages but did not read. They were all to be home, after all. Isabelle had already talked to Janice before Maxine called her with the news, and had insisted on taking an emergency leave from the hospital in the small California mountain town where she lived. She had scheduled her flight to meet Maxine's in Minneapolis so they could fly into Fargo together. And of course, once Judy had heard that all of the other sisters would be home, there was no keeping her in Indianapolis. She'd be showing up in a few days as well.

Maxine flagged a passing flight attendant and requested two scotches.

"Two?" The young woman smiled a smile that Maxine hoped had never fooled anybody.

"Two." Maxine held up two fingers to clarify what she hadn't expected to be a difficult request. Well, she thought, I don't suppose it's easy wearing all that polyester.

Maxine hoped the scotch would numb the headache that seemed to have begun with the ring of the telephone two days ago, but as usual expected less than she hoped for. Going home to North Dakota with her sisters had often been fun, riotously so at times; it could also be compelling, chaotic, and wrenching, but never, never calm. Even in the best of times someone would say something thoughtless, intended or imagined, someone would forget to ask about someone's kids, someone would mention the wrong ex-husband (Judy's, odds were, with four to choose from), someone would cry or stomp off, someone would drink too much and get defensive, or worse yet, honest. There would be a few serious talks (provided there were no more than three sisters in the room at one given time), but even these were unlikely to be calm. But we'll all laugh, Maxine thought, again shaking her head.

Mavis laughs and tells stories, too, but not quite as often. She drinks, but never too much. She plays cards, talks farming, brings us all up-to-date on people we grew up with—careers, kids, cataracts, and cancer. And if she is in the room when the emotional bombs go off, none land under her chair.

But, oh, good Lord. What do we have to laugh about now? And how do we talk to each other with Mavis making these claims and Irene gone? They've been our emotional bookends, Maxine thought: Mavis keeping us normal, Irene keeping us close. Are we, I wonder? What would we be with Mavis gone, now that Irene is just the

ghost we see laughing beside Isabelle? A ghost for
Isabelle. Maybe I should write children's stories instead
of monographs on Emily Dickinson. Or on *Clarissa*.
"The bitch got what she deserved." I actually had a student say that. What is a bitch? Am I? Are we? Is this
what we deserve?

Maxine lowered her head and slowly swirled the ice
cubes in her empty glass until a well-manicured hand
lifted it from her.

3

ISABELLE LIFTED HER HEAD FROM HER HANDS WITH A
deep sigh, but kept both elbows on the bar as she supported her chin on one fist. I have a sister who is a murderer. Well, good for her, she thought bitterly, raising her
glass in silent salute. I should have done it.

Isabelle took another sip of the Jack Daniel's she used
to coat the year-old pain of her twin's death as it continued to burn in her gut. She had spent the remainder of
that day last year after she had been told the news, trying
to phone Irene, knowing there would be no answer but
encouraged by the incessant ringing, because as long as
no one answered the phone, then perhaps Irene could be

just outside, running to the phone, about to pick it up on the tenth, or eleventh, or twelfth . . . Wanting to ask her twin if she'd ever had a heat rash like the one that had sprung up mysteriously and suddenly on her arms and legs earlier that day, probably in reaction to too many years in the sun.

Still, Isabelle thought as she returned to the present and her whiskey, a sixty-year-old widowed mother and pillar of the community is bound to get better treatment from our legal system than would a forty-six-year-old lesbian.

"Don't you think so?" Isabelle asked the bartender, who was washing glasses slowly but with no attendant thoroughness as he watched travelers pass by. Isabelle waited for her question to register.

"Beg your pardon, ma'am?"

"Whom do you think would be more likely to appeal to the sympathy of a North Dakota jury: an older, well-respected family woman or a smart-ass lesbian?"

"I don't know, which?" The bartender leaned forward, expecting to hear the latest North Dakota joke.

"Well, which do you think?"

"The older family woman, I suppose." The bartender was still waiting for the punch line.

"I suppose so, too."

The bartender found an opportunity to move to the other end of the bar, away from the woman who was obviously neither sixty years old nor a lesbian. Not with those legs. But maybe a little nuts.

There could be no insanity plea, Isabelle thought. Mavis crazy? That would be like calling Wilt Chamberlain short. It's a shame Judy wouldn't be the one going on trial. She'd just have to walk in the door, and the judge would tell everyone to go home. The woman's missing a button. I wonder if she'll still be wearing that

ratty mink coat this summer. Good Lord. Comes back to
Irene's funeral, to seventy-degree weather, wearing a
mink. Because it's new. What will be new this year? Not
the teeth, the nose, or the boobs. That was all done long
ago. Certainly a whole year won't have gone by without
a bit of cosmetic surgery.

Maxine says Judy brings out the worst in me, but even
Irene had her moments, referring to Judy before she
discovered plastic surgery as the Ur-Judy. It's getting a
little weird, like she's becoming inanimate. I can see
Judy with a glass eye with a Rolex inside it someday.
Wouldn't make her any more interesting, but at least
more useful to have around while we listen to her latest
pathetic fantasies. So I asked her when she called last
week (God knows why) how old this latest guy is, and it
takes her a while to come up with "forty-two." Forty-
fucking-two. How old are you, then? I asked, but she
didn't answer, exactly: "Men my age are all so goddamned old." Which means she's probably knocked
eight years off her age to match this latest dude's. Don't
you have any women friends? I asked, nice as you please,
which she took for an opportunity to trot out her ignorance: "Not your kind, that's for sure." And another conversation ended pleasantly. Oh, Jesus, Isabelle, she told
herself, think of something else. No need to start fighting
until we're at least in the same room. And no need to pretend that I don't smoke, either, as long as I'm by myself
in an airport.

Isabelle turned to the young man who was now sitting
on the bar stool beside her, quietly drinking a beer and
reading a paperback with a cover picture of two robots
flanking a redhead with big hair, wearing a miniskirt, and
sporting breasts that appeared to be supported by torpedo
casings. Circling this engaging picture were the requisite
asteroids and planets. Another young man reading soft

porn who thinks he's reading science fiction, Isabelle thought. A backpack was sitting beside his bar stool. He needed a haircut and could use a new pair of jeans. The T-shirt, however, was clean. That's how you can distinguish graduate students from the homeless, Maxine had once told her, years ago. Yet, not long ago on the phone Isabelle thought she'd heard a note of nostalgia from Maxine for those longhaired and Birkenstocked students, comparing them favorably with what she called "the influx of baby-yups," to whom "visionary" meant being able to picture the espresso machines they could buy with tenured salaries.

Well, Maxine would be pleased to know that all the Birkenstocks aren't in California, Isabelle noticed with distaste, giving in to the almost hypnotic repulsion she experienced upon seeing the toes of strangers close up. Linda, Isabelle's lover, had suggested that her reaction to bare feet was probably a sign of deep emotional distress reflecting some traumatic childhood incident. Isabelle rejected this theory as California psychobabble. What bewildered Linda, however, had long amused Isabelle's sisters, who kept a lookout for the ugliest feet to bring to Isabelle's attention.

At Isabelle's involuntary snort of amusement in recollection, the young man tucked his feet behind the stool, alerting Isabelle that this stranger was decidedly uncomfortable with the intensity of her gaze. She raised her gray-blue eyes, and smiled. "Could I bum a smoke?"

"Sure." The young man was startled to be addressed so pleasantly by the woman who had just a minute before been so intent upon his feet that she hadn't responded to his hello. Her concentration, however, had allowed him the opportunity to notice that she was about fifty percent tanned legs.

"Thanks, I'm not trying to quit. I'm just too lazy to walk over to the cigarette machine."

"Are you waiting for a plane, or just get off one, or waiting for someone, or ... uh ... Huh?" he finished, having stated all the possible reasons why someone would be in an airport bar.

"Yes."

He was determined to be friendly. "I'm on my way to Spokane. From Fargo."

Someone other than a North Dakotan would have thought it odd to fly east to Minneapolis in order to go west to Spokane, but Isabelle had not been gone for so long that she'd forgotten the erratic flight patterns offered to Fargo fliers.

"You're from Fargo, then?" Isabelle asked.

"Nope, outside of Fargo. Garden. It's just—"

"I know. I grew up near there."

Another woman, Isabelle thought, would now ask, Oh, where? The young man continued his story. "I'm a graduate student at—"

"NDSU," finished Isabelle.

"Yeah!" A big smile crossed the young man's face. "In horticulture."

"Well, you know what they say. You can lead a whore to culture, but you can't make her think." Isabelle snorted, a short blast of rather noisy air escaping a very fine, strong nose. Not very becoming, Judy had often told her. It was, however, the type of mannerism that her friends loved.

The young man laughed with her, pleased to be having a conversation during a layover with a pretty woman who obviously had an earthy sense of humor. Isabelle's snort, however, had nothing to do with her telling of a very old joke, but rather with the look of horror she imagined on her lover's face as she pictured her overhearing the joke.

Not an appropriate joke from a feminist, Linda would have insisted. Not even a funny joke. And Isabelle would have agreed. Indeed, as head nurse in the hospital's emergency room, she would have made the same speech to her staff upon hearing such a joke. Nonetheless, she had spent much of her life saying things she knew she shouldn't, for just that reason.

Isabelle and her new friend exchanged names and began an unsuccessful game of "Do you know," beginning with professors at NDSU that could have been there twenty-five years before, when Isabelle and Irene were students. The bars and hangouts had changed as well. When the young man resorted to listing some of the buildings on campus that they must have shared, Isabelle was feeling decidedly aged. But he was buying her another Jack Daniel's and lighting another cigarette and seemed completely incapable of asking any questions about her—which suited Isabelle just fine—and was energetically explaining his master's thesis on some sort of mushroom fungus, the mention of which had Isabelle once again staring at the young man's toes.

At the high point of this discussion (judging by how pleased the young man seemed to be with himself), Isabelle let her eyes drift across the bar to meet the eyes and the small smile of a young woman in her early thirties.

A hot fudge sundae, thought Isabelle, who, after a slight smile at the woman, quickly looked down, a lifetime of caution evidenced in a move that neither refused nor acknowledged the woman's interest. I'm scoring pretty low in my feminist reverie rhetoric, Isabelle lectured to herself in the voice she used occasionally with her male nurses. To have not only objectified another woman so callously, but to have had such little imagination in the process, continuing the chauvinistic association of woman with food, thus, dish, tart, hot fudge sundae, blah blah. But no, that's not what I mean at all, not at all what I've tried to explain. If you have a diet that is healthy and satisfying, then an occasional hot fudge sundae is not really going to do any harm. So, here's my point, Isabelle had cautiously said to Linda, an occasional affair wouldn't have to affect our relationship.

A lot of partners would have launched immediately into suspicion (Whom are you having, or want to have, an affair with?) or hurt (You're not satisfied with me anymore!). But Linda was a lot smarter than that, pointing out that for most people the notion of an affair calls up an emotional response a bit more complicated than that of a trip to the Dairy Queen, and adding, "I don't think either of us could have an affair just now without dramatically altering our relationship." Who said anything about "either of us"? Isabelle remembered thinking.

A change in the young man's inflection clued Isabelle back to his conversation, which was trailing off with a "Wow, look at the time. I'd better get to my gate."

By standing, Isabelle's new friend appeared to signal a scene shift. Suddenly everybody, except Isabelle and the largely immobile bartender, seemed to move. The young man pumped Isabelle's hand and told her to have a great stay in her "native land" and said good-bye again, while the young woman across the bar slipped off her bar stool, began to round the bar as if to walk toward Isabelle, then checked her step, smiled again, and walked out the door as a very tall woman wearing Isabelle's nose and cheekbones and a disheveled, albeit expensive, linen suit sat down beside her, letting blue-tinted glasses slide down her nose so she could look over them with Schmidt blue eyes.

"Well, he seemed like a bit much." Maxine smiled in greeting. "Graduate student. Engineering."

"More like not enough. Horticulture."

"Same thing."

"Looks like they made you ride on the outside of the plane."

Maxine nodded toward a trio of flight attendants passing by. "I had to arm wrestle the cherub-bimbos for drinks, which the situation certainly seems to call for." Maxine and Isabelle held each other's eyes for just a moment, before Maxine took the easy route. "Speaking of which, when some people say they'll meet you at the gate, they don't mean the nearest cocktail lounge."

"This would be a good place for a bar, wouldn't it?" Isabelle said in a louder voice to catch the bartender's attention. "I'll have another Jack Daniel's and my mother here will have a, what? Glenlivet?"

"Don't we have another plane to catch?"

"Late. Leaves in an hour, according to that very useful screen across the corridor. Time for one more before we head into reality."

"You don't have Glenlivet, do you?" Maxine spoke to the bartender, and then ordered a Johnnie Walker on the rocks when he grunted a negative.

"Would you like a cigarette?"

"Isabelle, I quit smoking about twenty years ago. I thought you quit, too."

"No, I just quit buying them. It appears that my new friend forgot to take his cigarettes with him when he left, possibly because I'd laid my purse down on top of the pack."

"I could lend you a couple of dollars if you think that would keep you from further petty larceny."

"I'll take your money from you when we play pinochle. And don't tell Mavis about the cigarettes or she'll make me fly to Spokane to give them back."

Another quiet moment passed between the women

with this direct mention of Mavis's name. The two sisters waited for their drinks and silently took stock of each other. Then, drinks in hand, they lifted them in a mute and ironic toast, but instead of drinking, smiled and leaned toward each other, the lips of each grazing the left cheek of the other.

"Have you been okay?"

"Yes and no. More yes, less no." Isabelle hesitated. "It's been hard, Maxine. I bet I didn't talk to Irene more than a dozen times a year, but I've picked up the phone I don't know how many times since the accident. With her gone, it's as if—well, not like losing a part of you like a leg or an arm or something, like people say death is, but like all of a sudden just being wrong or different. As if some organ inside me that I didn't even know was there had been removed and now I'm just different. I look the same. The world looks the same. But I can't breathe like I used to. And now this . . ."

"I know, I know. It sounds so trite and typical to say, but why Irene? Why someone good, someone so loved?"

The women were dangerously close to tears. They hadn't expected to talk like this so quickly, and certainly not in the exposure of an airport cocktail lounge.

"Why?" Isabelle was relieved to be angry. "Because Jack is a negligent, drunken, stupid, stupid, stupid fucking man."

"Was."

They were in danger now and they knew it. They both had had too much to drink, both hurt too much, and both were too vulnerable. And so they did what their family did best: joked their way away from an emotion that could leave them out of control. The direction to turn for the joke was clear to both.

"I suppose Ma Barker will be meeting us at the gate in Fargo." Isabelle snorted.

It was a weak joke, but had the necessary stabilizing effect. For the sake of form, Maxine added, "If Mavis goes to prison, she'll be warden in six months."

The mention of prison, however, immediately undid the sisters' attempts at jocularity, as Isabelle's face reminded Maxine that for the twins Mavis had been almost as much mother as sister.

"Mavis can't go to jail, Maxine. She's sixty years old, for Christ's sake."

"I don't know. She said she was going to Fargo this morning to . . . to . . . to confess, I guess. She said it as if she had some annoying paperwork to do. I have no idea what the procedure for such a thing is. I just know that if Mavis can't be at the airport, then Janice will pick us up."

"I wonder if Janice knows any more about all of this?" Isabelle mumbled as she placed some money on the bar.

"Oh, I don't think that's likely." The scotch, Maxine realized as she gathered her purse and rose to stand, had done little to soothe her anxiety—had, in fact, simply darkened the patina of unreality coating this trip home.

"Which way do we go?" she asked, hooking her arm into Isabelle's.

4

CONFESSING TO A MURDER, MAVIS DISCOVERED THAT Monday morning, was a bit more complicated than she had anticipated, and certainly more complicated than she appreciated. Much as if she were scheduling an appointment with her hairdresser or mechanic, Mavis had dialed the number for the Fargo Police Department and explained to the answering voice that she needed to stop by that day to confess to Thursday's murder of Jack Carlson up in Wash County.

Mavis was surprised at neither the slight pause that followed her announcement nor the information that she would be put on hold. She was somewhat taken aback, however, to be told by a new voice that the office she needed to call was the Wash County Sheriff's Department in Brickton. Would she like the number? she was politely asked.

Shaking her head in disbelief, Mavis dialed the new number, heard an older woman's voice identify the sheriff's office, restated her desire to confess to her brother-in-law's murder, and was once again put on hold. Then the line went dead.

"Good Lord," Mavis muttered as she redialed, prepared to put her foot down and insist on speaking with someone with some authority. On the first ring, the receiver was picked up.

"Wash County Sheriff's Department, this is Sheriff Hansen speaking."

Mavis used her schoolteacher's voice to explain, yet again, her purpose for calling.

"Where are you calling from?" Sheriff Hansen asked, and then, hearing her reply that she lived less than an hour west of Fargo, audibly sighed with relief.

"Here's what you need to do, Mrs. Holmstead. You get yourself to the Fargo police station this morning. That's located at the City Hall . . . you know where that is? And you ask for agents Heyerdahl and Madsen with the North Dakota Bureau of Criminal Investigation. You got that? Heyerdahl and Madsen. They'll take care of you. Okay?"

Sheriff Hansen hung up the phone and looked out the window, across the street to the hardware store he had inherited from his father and had run for almost twenty years. What the hell had ever convinced him to run for sheriff? And who the hell got himself murdered in Wash County? He looked over at his deputy, who had been on his way out when the phone conversation brought him back to stand by the secretary, who completed the staff of the Wash County Sheriff's Department.

Sheriff Hansen shrugged at his deputy and nodded him out the door with a reminder that Agent Heyerdahl would be expecting that information from the courthouse he'd requested by this afternoon. When the door closed, the sheriff turned to the older woman who was still watching him.

"Lila, get one of those BCI agents on the line for me. They should be halfway to Fargo by now anyway."

Let the state agents run with the ball, he thought. That's just fine with me.

It was mid-morning when Mavis walked into the Fargo police station and repeated the names the sheriff had given her. This time there was neither hesitation nor confusion, and she was quickly ushered into a small room where she was joined by a man in his mid-fifties and a woman Mavis judged to be in her early thirties at best. They introduced themselves as agents Heyerdahl and Madsen of the North Dakota Bureau of Criminal Investigation, which was assisting the Wash County Sheriff's Department in its investigation of Jack Carlson's death.

"Mrs. Holmstead," Agent Heyerdahl began after the introductions, "you understand that you are under no obligation to answer our questions at this time and that you have the right to have an attorney present?"

Mavis kept her gaze steady on Agent Heyerdahl as he spoke. He was a nondescript middle-aged man whose gray crew cut reflected the fashion of the fifties, not the nineties. His sansabelt polyester pants and neat short-sleeve shirt spoke of Sears or JC Penney. A slight paunch was beginning to wrinkle his waistband. The blue eyes behind horn-rimmed glasses were unremarkable, suggesting no particular intelligence or personality. He could be a feed salesman, extension agent, or insurance adjuster, Mavis thought, although there was nothing of the softness about him that she associated with "city," and thus found easy to discount. It was this inordinate ordinariness that she found most unsettling.

"I am here precisely to answer questions," Mavis replied, "and I do not wish to have my attorney here." Then, with the tape player rolling, she systematically explained how this Thursday past she had driven north to her late sister's farm, waited in a nearby stand of trees until about midnight until her brother-in-law drove by, flagged him down, and shot him.

The room was silent for a moment when Mavis finished.

"Let's get some of these facts straight, then, Mrs.

Holmstead, if we could?" began Heyerdahl, who pulled his chair a bit closer to hers and then posed a series of questions that Mavis was quite sure she had already answered: What time had she arrived at the stand of trees? What car was she driving? Did she have the car with her now? What time had Jack Carlson driven up? What did she say to him? What did he say to her? At what point did she shoot him? Where had she gotten the gun? The bullets? What did she do with the gun after the shooting? What had she done then? Where had she gone? What time had she arrived home? And she had left home at what time that night? Had anyone seen her—other than Carlson—from the time she left her home near Crow to the time she returned? Where were the clothes she had been wearing?

Heyerdahl continued to ask his questions as if he were inquiring into the moisture content of a load of barley, occasionally nodding at his partner, who was busy writing on a small pad. Mavis noted the precision with which Agent Madsen's summer suit, belt, shoes, and jewelry were coordinated, but thought she could use a better haircut. Agent Madsen also appeared to be holding her body unnaturally still, perhaps in emulation of the older man, but her eyes reflected the tension within her pose. Mavis brought her own gaze back to Agent Heyerdahl, who was silently but steadily studying her.

"Mrs. Holmstead—" He hesitated, reaching to his left shirt pocket to replace a pen in the plastic pocket protector there. "—could you tell us just one more thing, please?"

"Certainly."

"Why?"

"Why what, Mr. Heyerdahl?"

Agent Heyerdahl missed the slightest of beats, and continued, "Why did you shoot your brother-in-law?"

Mavis was again quite certain that she had already answered this question, but once again provided the summary she had prepared.

"Jack Carlson killed his wife, my sister Irene, in a car crash. He was drunk, he was negligent, and he was never charged, never made to pay for what he did. I could no longer live with that knowledge."

"So you drove up to his place to murder him."

"That's correct."

"And you didn't take a weapon with you, but expected to find one, loaded, when you found Mr. Carlson."

"That is also correct."

"And you wore gloves while you handled the gun."

"Yes."

"Um-hum. Why did you wait almost a full year?"

"I was hoping the police would do their job."

"I see. An eye for an eye and a tooth for a tooth?"

"If you want to put it that way."

"How would you put it, Mrs. Holmstead?" The investigator leaned just a bit closer and held her eyes.

Mavis did not blink as she replied, "I would put it this way. I have recently become an old woman. My sister is—was, still young. This I can do for her."

"But your sister is dead."

"Yes, Irene is dead."

Heyerdahl glanced briefly at his partner, who had begun to rhythmically drum her fingers on the table. Mavis fought the urge to reach over to still the young woman's drumming. Finally, the older agent nodded at Madsen, who silently rose to leave the room.

"Mrs. Holmstead—" Heyerdahl sat back and studied the tired but composed woman in front of him. "—Agent Madsen will need a little of your time now. We'll need your fingerprints, your signature on a statement, and your patience for a few more questions. Would you be willing to undergo a polygraph evaluation?"

"A lie detector test?"

"Yes."

"Of course."

"In the meantime, with your consent, we'd like to take a look at your car. You can make yourself comfortable in the cafeteria on the first floor after Agent Madsen is finished. We'll send someone in to let you know when we're done."

"And that's it?"

"For now."

"I'm free to go?"

"For now."

"Until?"

"Well, Mrs. Holmstead, I'd suggest you get a lawyer. And don't leave the area. We will be in touch."

"But . . . have I been charged?"

"No, ma'am. Not at this point."

"I don't understand."

"Mrs. Holmstead, trust me when I say we will be in touch."

Within the hour agents Heyerdahl and Madsen were studying a sheaf of papers a third officer had spread before them.

"How unusual." Heyerdahl let a rare note of sarcasm enter his voice as he stood back from the table on which he had been leaning. "Our polygraph results appear to be inconclusive."

"Well, actually," the third officer pointed out, "there is very little suggestion of deception characteristics in response to the pertinent questions. The results, in fact, suggest that Mrs. Holmstead is telling the truth." When neither agent responded, the officer shrugged and left the room.

Madsen turned to her partner. "I understand that you find the usefulness of polygraphs to be limited, but how do you explain those results?"

"Perhaps Mrs. Holmstead doesn't perceive the shooting of her brother-in-law, no matter who did it, as a crime."

Madsen allowed herself a moment to study the man with whom she had just begun to work, then continued, "We'll get the lab results from the car in a couple of days. We took photos and a cast of her tires, but with no rain for a couple of weeks now, there were no clear tracks to speak of at the scene. We have the prints to check on the gun, but I expect we'll find it covered with that old farmer's who found Carlson and the rifle. Nonetheless, that will give us a start." The young woman looked up and shrugged. "But . . ."

"But what?" Heyerdahl prodded.

"But I don't believe she did it."

"No, I expect not. Nonetheless, it looks like she's going to show us who did."

Downstairs in the drab cafeteria, Mavis was irritated by the wait and by her own creeping anxiety, which stemmed from this unexpected lack of closure. "I would like to know what happens next," Mavis had finally insisted to the younger agent, who had directed her to the cafeteria following the lie detector test. Madsen had simply shrugged and said, "We'll let you know."

Well, if they were going to be coy for no good reason, she would use the time well. Of course she would be seeing her lawyer. There were a great many decisions to be made now. Decisions about land yet to be deeded over, about CDs and bonds, about savings. There was the will to be updated. Now she must think about what she would leave to her son Glenn and his family, and to her younger son, Craig. She hesitated with this last thought. Leave Glenn and Craig.

Mavis put her hand to her cheek and was startled by the moisture on her fingertips. Standing quickly, she spotted the door to the women's rest room. Once inside the empty room, she entered a stall, covered the seat with toilet paper, and sat down. Leave Glenn and Craig. With the phrase echoing in her head, Mavis cupped her left breast in her hand, looked straight ahead at the green metal door, and finally, finally allowed the slow tears to fall.

5

"A FAMILY REUNION, MAVIS? A FAMILY REUNION?" Maxine was incredulous. "Have you really and truly lost your mind, then?"

The two sisters had been taking turns bending, standing, and stretching as they picked tomatoes and cucumbers in Mavis's vegetable garden. In the distance they could hear the muffled roar of the lawn tractor where Isabelle, no doubt, was extending the yard into the scattered trees that hid Mavis's house from the road, going where no mower had gone before. At Mavis's for less than forty-eight hours, already Isabelle and Maxine had begun to claim this farmstead as home through their labor. They would cook and clean and mow and garden next to Mavis without giving the effort a second thought, because they would not be guests in Mavis's house. They were family.

Maxine waited for a response, fists on hips, as she watched Mavis's back. When that response was silence, Maxine continued, "Now? With Aunt Emma and Aunt Alice and Big Dan and Gloria and all the other first and second cousins and nieces and nephews and all their families and oh, good Lord, Mavis, don't you think the timing is a bit peculiar?"

"You and Isabelle are already home." Mavis spoke into the soft black dirt. "Judy will be here this coming Monday. I wouldn't be at all surprised if Craig is on his way. It's pretty short notice, but don't you imagine everyone will just be dying to come?" She stood, smelled the large ripe tomato she had in her hand, and passed it to Maxine, who took note of her older sister's wry smile, which had nothing to do with good humor.

"That's one vegetable I never get tired of." Mavis was bent over again.

"A tomato is a fruit, not a vegetable."

"Botanically speaking, it's a berry."

"And a berry . . . Mavis, a reunion is not a good idea."

"Yeah, uh-huh."

The dreaded "yeah, uh-huh" of Mavis, which could mean "I'm listening to you but I don't think what you are saying calls for a response," but often enough simply meant "I'm not listening to you at all." Maxine was not to be so easily dismissed.

"Don't 'yeah, uh-huh' me. Over the years, I've

whined, cajoled, and argued with you. Now that we're middle-aged, I'd like to think that my opinions are of some import here."

"Unless you're planning on the two of us living until we're one hundred twenty years old, God forbid, I think we're a bit beyond middle age."

"That's hardly the point."

"Which is?"

"Well, how would it look for one thing? What, precisely, would we be celebrating?"

"We've never needed an occasion to have a family reunion, Maxine. And who knows when we'll all be together again." Mavis walked away a few steps to bend to the zucchini, leaving Maxine to consider Mavis's reasoning silently. Because they never would all be together again, not with Irene gone. Or was this one of Mavis's oblique references to her claim that she had killed Jack? The shudder that raised goose bumps along Maxine's bare arms had nothing to do with the late-morning temperature, which had already moved well into the mid-eighties. She waited for Mavis to look up.

"You are absolutely determined, aren't you?"

Brown eyes, still sharp in an ever softer face, met Maxine's blues, unprotected by the tinted glasses forgotten on the kitchen counter. Mavis's voice was steady:

"What will we do with all this zucchini?"

"What will . . ." Maxine sputtered, then followed Mavis's gaze to the cardboard box filled with vegetables. "Give it away, I suppose."

"You know what they say—North Dakotans only lock their cars during July and August, to keep neighbors from filling the backseats with bags of zucchini." Mavis smiled, and, having temporarily derailed the conversation, brought it around to a parallel track.

"Let's not invite agents Heyerdahl and Madsen to the

reunion, even if they are doing their best to become part of the family. What, by the way, did they want from you this morning so early?"

"They weren't really interested in talking to me at all. It was Isabelle they wanted."

"What, specifically, did they ask?"

"What did I know about Jack. Did I, too, hold him responsible for Irene's death? Did I think you killed him?— which I do not."

"Go on."

"They wanted to know why you would say you shot Jack if you hadn't."

"And?"

"And I said, quote, Lord knows."

"No doubt. Is that all?"

"They seemed quite concerned about finding Jackie, which I was glad to hear."

"What did they want from Isabelle?" Both women followed the sound of the tractor mower to Isabelle, where she was now winding her way around the trees in the house's side yard. As they watched, Isabelle lifted her right arm in a sweeping gesture as punctuation to the conversation she was having with herself. The older sisters allowed themselves a brief, shared smile.

"Much the same, plus questions about Jack's relationship with Irene and the kids. They also asked if Irene had talked about Jack and some neighbor. Thorburg?"

"Thorson."

"Who's he?"

"Oh, Jack and old Ivor Thorson have been at each other's throats for years. Irene said it was a feud that had been handed down to Jack by his father, who was evidently just as charming."

"So the lawsuit had been going on for some time, then?"

"What lawsuit?"

Maxine shrugged. "Detective Heyerdahl—"

"*Agent* Heyerdahl," Mavis interrupted with a correction, then added, "and he doesn't seem to like being called *Mister* Heyerdahl at all."

Maxine began again. "Agent Heyerdahl asked Isabelle if Irene had ever mentioned Jack's intention to file a lawsuit against this Thorburg."

"Thorson."

"Something about some ditching *Thorson* had done which Jack claimed put some of his property underwater much of the year."

"That happened a couple of years ago, although I hadn't heard anything about a lawsuit. In fact I never did hear a clear account of the argument, not from Jack anyway, and Irene always did her best to change the subject before Jack could get his bowels in an uproar. There was Thorson's ditching, but there was also something about the land that was flooded being some wetlands Jack's father had reclaimed."

"Wouldn't that put Jack in the right, then?"

"Depends on how you look at it. Not if Jack's father hadn't gone through the proper governmental channels necessary to drain off wetlands. So maybe Jack had the moral high ground—"

"To use an inappropriate metaphor," Maxine interrupted.

"—but perhaps Thorson had the government on his side, what with ducks more highly valued than productive farmland. A lawsuit certainly would have irritated that old Norwegian. But no, Agent Heyerdahl, that dog won't hunt."

Mavis stood again and leaned back to stretch, leveling her eyes on the horizon. Maxine looked up from the short rows of beans she had begun to hoe, noticing that

Mavis's face was shining with sweat. She looked exhausted, which, Maxine supposed, was to be expected. There was no use asking about her health again. Mavis had admitted to being chronically tired, but ignored Maxine's suggestion that she get a checkup.

"No offense to Heather," Mavis had said the night before, referring to Maxine's only child, a physician at Johns Hopkins Hospital, "but doctors never really know what's going on until they do an autopsy, which isn't much use diagnostically."

Now it was Maxine's turn to press her hands against the small of her back. Looking straight into the solid blue above her, she stumbled against the dizzying space and felt Mavis's hand upon her arm. Reminded that the overwhelming design of the plains is to be without design, to be impossibly full of a vertiginous emptiness, she breathed in deeply, and found herself telling Mavis the old truth.

"I left North Dakota almost forty years ago, and yet this is the only place that feels like home. Something about this sky makes me feel both safe and overwhelmed. It's peaceful, but not necessarily friendly." Maxine laughed at herself. "Is that what you see when you look up?"

Mavis raised her chin to take in the sky, and did not stumble. "We could use rain, and we're not going to get it. Not today anyway." Then, with eyes leveled to her sister's, she added, "I know I am worrying you. I am sorry, but I'm just glad you're here now." Mavis stooped a last time to pick up a box of vegetables with a grunt, and began walking to the house, leaving Maxine to follow.

6

THE TISSUE-THIN SHEETS JANICE PULLED OVER THE
mattress in the guest room were soft with wear. Squaring
the corners and pulling the fabric tight, Janice took pleasure in the repetition of motions she had learned as a
quiet child from a quiet mother. Her slightest of smiles
evaporated with the slamming of the apartment door.
Standing in the bedroom doorway, Janice listened to
Norton's footsteps go directly to the refrigerator, believed she could hear the hiss of pressure escaping the
aluminum can.

"Christ, what a day," came his greeting from the dining room that was equally a part of the kitchen. "Christ,
what a day!" he repeated, louder, unfolding the paper
Janice had placed on the table for him. Janice waited,
unmoving, in the bedroom for the still-louder question.
"You home?"

"Yes, back here."

"Christ, what a day." Norton almost looked up as
Janice walked through the kitchen to the utility closet
to drag out the newly repaired vacuum cleaner.

"How was your day?" Janice asked as she began to
vacuum around Norton's feet, occasionally looking up to
watch his mouth move. She was pulling the canister
around the corner into the small living room when she

realized by Norton's raised eyebrows and set mouth that she had been asked a question.

"What?"

"Do you have to turn that damn machine on the minute I get home?"

"Mavis will be here with Isabelle and Maxine for supper in about an hour. You know I just got home from work myself, so this is about the only time I've got." Janice spoke over the roar of the machine.

"A man should be able to have a little peace and quiet when he comes home from work. Is that too much to ask, then?"

"Today."

"Today! Every day! Every day I come home you're chasing that damn machine, or running the dishwasher, or the washing machine, or you're banging pans around. Or babysitting that brat from upstairs. There's never a moment of peace."

"Norton . . ." Their eyes met for the first time. "It's called housekeeping. I'm doing the best I can with the time I've got."

"And what about me?"

Norton did not expect the direct look Janice gave him as she switched off the vacuum and returned the room to quiet. He pushed his lower lip out a bit more and reached a hand out for his beer. When she remained silent but did not shift her gaze, Norton grunted in disapproval and returned to his paper.

Janice continued to stare at her husband, marveling for at least the hundredth time how her vision had clarified in the past ten days since she stood outside a pickup truck on a country road in the middle of the night and made a decision. What had once been dimples, she now noticed were creases of fat that vertically split each cheek. A daring pompadour had thinned into a small bump of hairs carefully gathered at Norton's forehead. And when had the lip lifted out of a laughing smile and into a sneer? She had been twenty-five, slipping quietly into her life as an "old maid" when she had first seen that smile and those dimples on a face that didn't reflect a care in the world. She was four years Norton Berg's senior and amazed that this thin-hipped muscular young man could even see her. He made her laugh, and she fell in love with the new sensation. But not, she supposed, with him.

Nor did she suppose there was anything unusual about how their relationship had progressed through the years. His dreams never materialized, not through any fault of his, of course. Jimmy and Tina came quickly, and she soon found herself mothering a husband along with two children. This he both insisted upon and resented, and so the clichés set in. His regular drinking became excessive, and although Janice recognized the attraction of simply bowing out, she doggedly kept herself in the traces, determined to do the kids as little damage as possible. Now they were grown and gone, and she slept next to a man who had not been her lover for years, who was sometimes belligerent in his booze, but not attentive enough to be abusive.

"What *about* you?" Janice spoke aloud, causing Norton to start at her voice.

"What? What the hell, Janice?"

"What about me, rather?"

"What are you talking about?"

"Be careful, Norton. I am very tired."

"Jesus Christ." Norton pushed his chair back, paused for a moment with both hands on the table as he looked into Janice's rare direct stare. "Jesus Christ, what the hell has gotten into you lately?"

"That's a good question. Thank you for asking."

"Christ Almighty, I don't need this today." Norton

stood up, reached for the pack of cigarettes on the table, and turned to leave.

"Oh, Norton. There's no need to storm out of here. You know Isabelle will be fixing drinks the minute she walks through the door. You can wait that long."

Norton turned with his hand on the doorknob and started for the second time at the half smile he hadn't expected to see on his wife's face. "What the . . . I'm going 'round the corner," he muttered and stepped out into the apartment hallway.

"And I'm going 'round the bend," Janice muttered to herself in the empty apartment.

Within the hour Janice was again at the door, dust rag in hand, welcoming three sisters for a visit. She'd had time to put a pork roast in the oven and to wipe out the tub and sink before they arrived. She'd almost finished her dusting pass through the apartment, but there'd been no time for a shower.

"Well, it's Suzy Spotless," Isabelle spoke in greeting as she walked through the door in front of Mavis and Maxine. "You were dusting last week when Maxine and I got into town. But—" Isabelle held up her hand and changed her voice to mimic Judy's higher, softer tones. "—I do hope you have my room ready? Although I didn't specifically state where I wanted to sleep. I hope that didn't inconvenience you?" This, as each sister well knew, was in reference to a call a few days back from Judy, during which she had reminded Mavis that she preferred to stay in the basement bedroom with its own bathroom when she visited. It was the room Isabelle had been occupying, but Isabelle was quite happy to spend her second week in North Dakota with Janice, and more than ready to get out of the house where Judy soon would be.

"Pushed from sissy to sissy, Isabelle . . . unwanted." Maxine added, "It's so sad."

"It is. Maybe a drink would help."

"Where's Norton?" Mavis asked as she took down a coffee cup from the cupboard. "Anyone else?"

"No thanks. I might make myself a drink, though," Isabelle said, raising her voice a level.

"He walked down to The Office to get out from under my feet while I cleaned," Janice answered Mavis as she opened the cupboard over the refrigerator to show Isabelle where they kept the liquor.

"How long ago?" Mavis turned to Janice.

"An hour, more or less. Why? What difference does it make?"

"Where do you keep your cards, Janice?" Maxine asked from the dining room table, looking from Janice to Mavis and back to Janice again. "We must have time for a couple hands of whist before supper."

"In the drawer under the phone. I just need to peel some potatoes. Supper in less than an hour."

Mavis moved to the drawer Janice had pointed to, but instead of opening it, placed the heel of her palm on the counter above, using her fingers to keep the drawer closed. "Maxine, why don't you and Isabelle drive around the corner to Main Street and get Norton. Then the four of you can play whist. I can peel the potatoes."

Maxine and Isabelle directed much the same quizzical look toward Mavis.

"Norton's a big boy, Mavis," Isabelle said. "I think he'll know when it's time to come home."

"Actually," Janice entered the conversation, "that's a good idea. But maybe you should have a drink with him there so he doesn't think the Schmidt women are telling him what to do."

"You go ahead, Isabelle," Maxine said. "It doesn't take two."

"No." Mavis and Janice spoke in unison, Mavis covering the chorus with a laugh. "We'd just have to send you later to get those two."

"Thanks a lot." Isabelle was headed for the door. "They don't want to play with us, Maxine. Is The Office on the same block as The Lariat?"

"What are you up to, Mavis?" Janice turned to her older sister the minute they were alone. " 'Don't say anything,' you said. 'I'll take care of it,' you said. And then you do this! Walk into the police station and say that *you* killed Jack. Why? Why?" Janice was shaking her head as she shook off the hand Mavis attempted to place on her arm. "And now you're planning a family reunion? Just what am I supposed to be doing now, Mavis? Have you thought about that?"

"Actually, I've done a lot of thinking . . . about a lot of things." Mavis let herself sink into a chair at the table and continued, "About why any of us do what we do, about the bad things we never have to account for, about the good things we never get credit for, about the guilt we carry around one way or the other."

"I have no idea what you are talking about." Janice picked up the dust rag she had slung across the back of a nearby chair and turned her back to Mavis.

Mavis sighed and stood to follow Janice out of the dining room. She watched as Janice dropped to her knees to dust the base of a living room end table that Mavis had handed down when she had redecorated her own living room some years before.

"It doesn't really matter. But Janice, I want you to let me do this. It makes sense."

"Of course it doesn't make sense. None of it makes sense. You did not kill Jack, remember? I did. Me. Not you. It was *mine not to tell*." Janice tapped her chest on each of these final four words, looking up at Mavis now with wide eyes.

Mavis's brow furrowed at Janice's words, less in anger than confusion. She was increasingly uncertain about how to talk to this sister. Someone she thought she knew had disappeared ten days ago in the midst of an impossibly tawdry story, and there was no time now to go back to find that sister, no time to find out who this was, now kneeling in front of her. No time for blame or apologies or fresh starts. Just time to mop up.

"It couldn't stay a secret—"

"It has to stay a secret!" Janice's voice was desperate.

The room was silenced by Janice's plea. The women looked at each other. Then Mavis caught the thread of Janice's fear. And tugged. "No one needs to ever know about what you . . . you and Jack did. But a man is dead. The police will look for his . . ." Mavis searched the room for a word she could possibly use, then started again. "They will look for someone until they make an arrest."

"Things can stay a secret, Mavis. Things aren't always discovered."

"That's not how it works. But I can make this work."

"How? How will your going to jail make it work? How am I supposed to live with that?"

"I won't go to jail. I promise. It doesn't make sense yet, I know. But please, Janice, just let me do this for a while and you'll see. Just give me some time."

"Time for what? It won't work. Whatever you're up to, it won't work. It just won't work." Janice looked down with surprise at the now-broken ceramic ashtray she had set down with unintentional force on the end table.

Both women stared at the broken dish that had been dusted around in over a dozen living rooms since the weekend some twenty-three years ago when Janice and Norton had honeymooned in South Dakota. The gold lettering, almost rubbed off the edge by now, had once read, FAMOUS BUTTS: THE OTHER SIDE OF MT. RUSHMORE. The picture of four naked butts, now split in two at the bottom of the dish, was equally faint.

"Can you mend it?" Mavis reached out her hand to take the ashtray from Janice.

Janice ignored Mavis's question and reach, passing by her into the kitchen. As she was about to drop the dish into the wastebasket under the sink, Janice noticed a red fingerprint on one of the butts.

"Teddy's, do you think?" Janice surprised Mavis with a small smile, holding the dish over so her sister could see.

"I can't remember the order." Mavis spoke slowly, as if asking a question. "And it is from the back, remember. Certainly too chubby to be Abe's. Are you okay?"

Janice lifted her left index finger to reveal a small red slit at its tip. This time she did not move when Mavis reached for her hand. Mavis squeezed the finger, and both women watched, fascinated, as a bright red ball replaced the slit, then slid onto Mavis's thumb.

"I'm going to take care of it, Janice."

7

WHEN MAVIS AND MAXINE DROVE INTO MAVIS'S YARD that evening after a night of supper, coffee, and cards at Janice and Norton's, every light in the house was burning. That was odd, since Mavis habitually left just the kitchen light on, and there were no cars in the driveway, but it wasn't terribly disturbing. Locked doors were common enough these days in the country, but still not the norm. Mavis locked her doors to humor her son, Glenn, when she left in his company. Typically, she would secure the front door and the seldom-used back door, but leave the side door into the attached garage unlocked. It was a pattern repeated throughout the area, probably a vestige of the days in the not-too-distant past when garages were separate buildings. Lights on in the house probably meant that one of Glenn's girls had been dropped off for the evening, an indication that there had been some type of dispute between Becky and Janie over what would be watched on TV. In these cases it was easier to take one of the girls the five miles to Grandma's for the evening. Mavis's TV ran well into the night every night, and she paid little attention to what was on.

So Mavis actually was surprised when the garage door opened on what appeared, under a coating of dust, to be a light blue Mercedes convertible. The sisters took but a moment to say, simultaneously, "Judy."

"I thought she drove a Lincoln?" Maxine wondered out loud, but then, again in unison with Mavis, answered her own question with "Boyfriend."

"A Mercedes. This Junior must have some money," Mavis pointed out to Maxine, with the combined frown and raised eyebrow that actually meant she was amused.

"And a mother fixation," Maxine added. "Pretend that we think it's a Chevy."

The women hauled the groceries they'd picked up at Hornbacher's earlier in the day from the trunk of Mavis's pine-green Cadillac through the garage and into the house. As Mavis paused to wipe her shoes, which weren't dirty, on the welcome mat, she caught sight of the back of Judy's head as she sat motionless in the family room, refusing to acknowledge that someone had walked in the door.

Mavis directed a tired smile toward Maxine, who had let her opaque blue glasses slide down on her nose in order to gauge Judy's hair color. Red? she mouthed to Mavis.

"Judy," Mavis called out, walking into the kitchen that joined the family room. "When did you get here? How long did it take? Is that your Chevy in the garage?"

At this Judy turned, wide-eyed in disbelief, startled out of her pout. Seeing their smiles, she recognized the bait, but was unable to resist it.

"Chevy, my ass. That's a Mercedes 450 SL. A very expensive sports car. A convertible, in fact. And thanks for the welcome. I've been here since six; I drove twelve hours today, and get here to find no one. . . . Where were you?"

"It's nice to see you, too." Maxine crossed to Judy and they touched cheeks. "We did some shopping in Fargo and then went to Janice's for supper. And now we're pooped." With the last word, Maxine sank into the easy chair across from the couch where Judy sat with her feet propped up on the coffee table.

"You're pooped! Try driving across the United States and stopping about a million times to keep the car from . . ."

As usual, Judy finished her sentence on its penultimate word. Although new acquaintances and strangers were confused by such ellipses, sometimes waiting futilely for her to finish a sentence, people who knew Judy well knew there was no need to wait. More often than not the unspoken word was clear through the context, and her hesitation provided the opportunity for someone else to get into the conversation.

Mavis and Maxine, who were ten and eight years old, respectively, when this next sister was born, had unwittingly set the pattern in motion. Both, bookish and impatient as children, quickly got in the habit of finishing the toddler's, then the child's, sentences, rather than wait for the word they knew was forthcoming, just as, in time, they would finish her housework and homework. Whereas Judy grew comfortably, if lazily, into a pattern whereby all closure was brought about by her older siblings, Janice's response to the same interruptions was simply to remain silent. As the girls grew, the older two occasionally added variety to their sentence completions, manufacturing several possible endings to Judy's conversation, until Judy made a selection. Thus, Maxine stepped in, and on, Judy's sentence with:

"Stalling?"

"Overheating?" countered Mavis.

"Blowing up?" Maxine raised her eyebrows at Mavis.

"Running out of gas?"

"Overheating," Judy chose.

"Did you?" Mavis asked, setting down the air pot with

coffee and mugs on the kitchen table, drawing the other sisters into the kitchen.

Judy brought her feet off the coffee table and rose with a small groan meant to reemphasize the tedium of her day. Whereas the years had packed solidity into Mavis's and Maxine's tall frames, Judy's carriage remained statuesque. The impressive height, fine bone structure, clear skin, and startlingly blue eyes she had inherited were the raw materials she had dedicated her life to perfecting. She was artist and artwork, and for years the results had been nothing short of stunning. Even now, at fifty, as cosmetic surgery began to shift away from enhancing toward corrective, there were few who would agree with Isabelle's opinion that although Judy was spectacularly photogenic, her effect in person was somewhat less successful.

"Did I what?" Judy asked as she crossed into the kitchen, bent slightly to Mavis, and once again performed the ritual of kisses just missing left cheeks. Something different about this action nudged at Judy, but just what it was she couldn't immediately identify, and almost as immediately forgot.

"Keep the car from overheating."

"No. And I'm here to tell you it was damned hot out there on I-29 today."

"Were you by any chance wearing a coat?" Maxine asked as she winked at Mavis.

"I see Norton was serving drinks. Is that where Isabelle is?"

"Um-hum," from Maxine.

"Did she come home alone?"

"Yeah, uh-huh."

"Good. On the other side of Watertown. If this is such a friendly goddamned part of the country, why did about a million cars pass before someone stopped to . . . ?"

"Help. Who stopped?"

"A very nice Fargo businessman. Gave me a ride in to Watertown, to a service station. They towed it in, fixed something or other, and then overcharged me, I suppose. Seventy-five smackeroos. Now there would be a lovely place to have to live."

"How long were you there?" Mavis asked.

"Hours. But John and I had dinner, so the time passed quickly enough."

"John?" Again Maxine and Mavis spoke in unison.

"The gentleman who gave me a ride." Judy was exasperated explaining the obvious. "His name is John Conway. He and his brother have some type of business."

"That's pretty specific," Mavis pointed out.

"I was stranded on the side of the road in the middle of nowhere in one hundred degree heat, Mavis. I didn't know how to get a complete résumé and set of references for the person who stopped to . . ."

"Help. It was nice of him to buy you dinner."

"I didn't say he bought me dinner."

"Did he?"

Judy's response was rolled eyes and a sigh. "I'm meeting him for drinks at The Granary, whatever that is, in Fargo on Saturday night. I said I would bring all my single sisters along."

Maxine, who had been on the verge of dozing over her coffee, instinctively pushed her glasses up off the tip of her nose and disappeared behind the lenses. Mavis was smiling. "Your sisters? I thought surely we would be your aunts by now."

"Ha. Ha. Well, Maxine will go with me, won't you?"

"Right now I'm going to call Heather, and then I'm going to bed. I'm so tired I can't see straight." Maxine stood and headed toward the basement door.

"You haven't taken the downstairs bedroom, have you? Mavis, I specifically said that's where I would like to be, and you said . . ." Judy stopped when Maxine turned around, winked again at her sisters as she walked past them, and turned into the hallway to the guest bedroom separated from Mavis's room by the bath.

"Everybody's a comedian," Judy said, and turned to Mavis, who had begun rinsing out cups at the sink. "What about Craig? Is he coming . . . ?"

"Home. I'm not sure. We'll know if Craig is coming if we see him at the dinner table. He can sleep on the couch or at Glenn's." Mavis turned from the sink with a sigh, gave Judy a half smile, expressing her own fatigue. "I'm pretty tired, too. I bet you are as well."

Judy refused the dismissal. "Mavis, if you'd like to talk about it all, I'm not too tired. I mean, are you ready for the . . . ? Do you have a good . . . ? What happened, anyway? It doesn't make sense. I have a good friend in Indianapolis who says . . ."

"A trial, if there is to be such a thing, is a long way off, and I have a fine lawyer," Mavis broke in. "And there's nothing to talk about. Really," she added as Judy began again. "Let's just go to bed."

"I just wanted to help."

"Yeah, uh-huh."

"That's right. You never need any help, do you? Well, it doesn't look like that now from where I'm standing."

"Judy." The tone was final, a bit ragged, the older sister's voice of control resonating familiarly if not necessarily pleasantly back through years. "Where you are standing is in my kitchen. I appreciate your concern. I really do. And I'm glad you're here. But there's nothing you need to do."

Judy equaled Mavis's look for a moment, then dropped the challenge.

"Good night, then."

Mavis was just about inside her bedroom door when Judy called back, "Is it okay if I park my Mercedes in the garage?"

MAVIS

MAVIS STANDS IN FRONT OF THE FULL-LENGTH MIRROR mounted on her bedroom wall. She hears Maxine moving about in the bathroom next door. In the kitchen Judy is evidently taking inventory of the refrigerator before going downstairs. Once again she reaches up to palpate her left breast.

It is growing inside her, daily. This, too, a loaded gun, death taking on life. There is something familiar about her simultaneous fascination with and dread of the invader. But always the determined resignation. She supposes others will call it acquiescence, or simply giving up. But that's not it. Take what the world gives you, and use it.

Something familiar, though, remembering a hip-high Glenn, thick dark hair in a crew cut, freckled face made even more open by the spaces replacing missing teeth.

Legs set apart solidly in dungarees. The striped shirt completing the picture of the five-year-old inquisitive farm boy.

"Tell me a new thing, Mom," his persistent request. His mother a fabulous creature, owner of all knowledge.

So she'd tell him. Did you know that where we are standing right now was once a lake? So big that even if you stood on the top of a hill on one side you couldn't see the opposite shore. Before we started to count years in this country. When the land was still growing up. And beside the lake lived the ancestors of the people who would one day be the Sioux Indians. Ancestors. The people in our family who were on the earth long before we were born. Older than grandparents. Much older. They lived in Crow a long time before we did. Yes, even before Fletcher had the grocery store.

"Tell me a new thing, Mom."

And on. And on.

But never this.

When you were growing inside me, I despaired. I cried, grieved, mourned toward the time I would have to share your father with you. Your father, the first thing in my life I hadn't had to share. Always in my life there had been children: Maxine reading my books while I washed and ironed Judy's things, helped Janice with homework, held and fed the twins.

Never this. Glenn, when you were inside me, I felt like you were a tumor.

8

MAXINE WOKE THE NEXT MORNING TO THE SOUND OF junky coughs coming from the bathroom between her room and Mavis's, and wondered which irritating memory was about to trip forward. Of course. Charlie's morning phlegm ritual. That, at least, I don't miss, Maxine thought, looking out the window at yet another morning of endless blue. Maxine brought her focus in to the bird feeder where a number of wild canaries were flitting about, the males slimmer and more distinct than the females—the black blacker, the yellow yellower. "Dapper," she said aloud, and then realized that this was the second time this morning that she had been disturbed by the thought of her ex-husband, and she'd been awake for less than five minutes. She turned her attention back to the bird feeder and worked to pry free the word that was forming at the back of her mind. Charm. A charm of goldfinch.

By stacking the pillows behind her and sitting up a bit, Maxine could see the large plastic pan filled with water that Mavis kept under the cherry apple tree in the front yard for the birds. A flicker, she was delighted to see, was making its way down the tree, sideways, toward the pan, which was, as it had been all week, the site of a great deal of unpleasant squawking in the form of at least a dozen blackbirds. "Those damnable blackbirds," she muttered in Mavis's voice, and smiled.

Now attuned to the birds, Maxine tried to separate their calls. The almost constant gentle cooing of mourning doves smoothed the edges of the harsh cries of the blue jays, which every now and then surprised her with their musical tweedle. Somewhere out of sight a woodpecker was hammering on a tree. She listened for, but did not hear, the juggled notes of the meadowlark's song that she rehearsed in her mind on those days when she wondered how she had come to be a city dweller. There must be birds in Chicago, other than pigeons, she thought. I should put up a feeder, she considered, and then immediately dismissed the idea, knowing that once emptied, it would stay empty too long, inspiring more guilt than pleasure.

Maxine's attention next moved, as it had each morning upon waking in Mavis's house, to the assortment of family photographs that lined the wall facing her bed. Reflecting Mavis's notion of interior design, they were hung in no particular order, but were nonetheless lined up and spaced evenly: Glenn and Craig in high school graduation poses; Mavis and Frank on their twenty-fifth wedding anniversary; a collage of decades-old family photos with a heavy emphasis on pets, pasted on tagboard by a young Craig and enclosed within a rough frame made by Glenn, a Christmas present to their parents. If asked why these photographs were tucked away out of sight in a spare bedroom, Mavis would reply, Maxine knew, that she saw them every time she dusted, and who else would want to?

Maxine kicked the light covers off her legs and moved to sit at the end of the bed to study the two family portraits that held her own figure. The portrait on the left was an enlarged color photograph of six tall women, an imitation of the older brown studio portrait next to it, taken when some of the sisters were still little girls.

By the time of the color photo, Maxine noted, we had all moved into the same age bracket of adult women, but in the original portrait Mavis and I, seated in front, are clearly a separate generation from the little girls clustered behind us. Mavis looks properly professional, having just finished school with her two-year teaching degree. Her head tilts slightly to the right and one eyebrow is lifted, suggesting a habitual, if controlled, impatience. Her smile is slight, lips meeting. There is nothing left of the girl in this young woman. Her eyes, unaffected by the smile, are the only eyes in the photograph to translate into black.

I had just graduated from high school and was still carrying some baby fat at seventeen. I look so serious behind my wire-rims; I'm sure I must have looked at Mavis for a cue as to what shape my mouth should take before the flash. Judy, behind me, practices the perfect smile. She had been able to convince Mom and Mavis that at the grown-up age of nine her hair should be let out of the braids that were still pulling the faces of the other three girls to attention. Eyes bright and laughing, she is the only one of us to show her teeth. She is, as usual, a contrast to Janice beside her, whose seven-year-old eyes seem unmediated by the photographic process as she looks directly out of the picture at me. She has Mavis's eyes, only in the Schmidt blue that the rest of us inherited from Dad. And then there are the twins, barely able to contain their excitement at the novelty of being in a professional photographer's studio, sneaking arms around each other at the last moment, fat cheeks and braids, Tweedledee and Tweedledum.

We'd laughed and laughed at the portrait one summer at a reunion and decided to update our memories with a

new picture. Colorized and more relaxed, Mavis is never-
theless the center of the grouping, even though I am once
again sitting right beside her. She wears glasses now, too,
as does Janice. Mavis and I are back to being brunettes,
although we both appear to have instructed our hair-
dressers to let the gray through around our temples, as if
we are once again just beginning the graying process.
Judy is in her blond phase, her dreams of being a beauty
fulfilled. She stands to the right of Janice, who provides
the buffer between Judy and Isabelle to her left. If I don't
have my reunions mixed up, this was the one where Isabelle had infuriated Judy by insisting that she let everyone squeeze her new, improved breasts to see how they
felt with implants. Judy, Janice, and Isabelle are so close
to the same height that you could level a board on their
heads.

Isabelle is smiling broadly, softening the scowl that
now permanently creases her forehead, and instead of an
arm around Irene, she's placed a hand on Mavis's
shoulder. She is turned just slightly toward Irene, so that
in some way Mavis and the twins form their own
grouping. Oddly, Irene and Isabelle, the babies, are the
grayest of us all, Isabelle equally salt and pepper in her
cropped cut. Irene's permed shoulder-length hair softens
those chiseled features she and Isabelle share. Irene's
smile is as gentle as Isabelle's is broad, and this time
only she and Janice do not part their lips for the camera.
And it was Irene, after all, who didn't quite reach the dramatic height the rest of us had taken years to get used to.

Only ten years ago and we were so much younger.
Mavis had Frank. I had Charlie. Judy? Judy still would
have been married to Rusty. And we all had Irene. Mavis
has been alone for as many years as I have, but she, at
least, has an excuse. Well now, that's a new low, Maxine
chastised herself, to accept the cultural superiority of the

widow over the divorcée. Where, on your scale, then, she asked herself, does a tired college professor fit in? And while we're at it, when did I get tired?

Maxine slid back onto the bed and crossed her arms behind her head. When did I decide I'd published enough, read enough, attended enough conferences for one lifetime? When did I stop "keeping up"? My vote in departmental meetings increasingly determined by gut feelings and allegiances, and less and less a reflection of intellectual or philosophical grounding. I look around at my colleagues, most of them still men who are evidently incapable of seeing the humor in their uniforms of pipes, tweed sport coats with leather elbow patches, and pseudo-British accents, despite their hometown being Trenton, Toledo, or Tuscaloosa, or bearded Marxists in wire-rims trading references for cleaning ladies, or men who call themselves feminist because they invite the sec-retarial staff to the department Christmas party. When I mentioned this to a female colleague, she asked me how long I thought I'd be mad at Charlie.

Oh, the good old boys, the good old boys, who think that if, somehow, a woman manages to still be in the pro-fession, a full professor, at fifty-eight, then she must psy-chically be male. So that I'm expected to find some sort of sense in the explanation given by that old fart Bailey, sitting smugly in his chair's office, as to why a colleague, known to have had sex with a student during a "private tutorial" in his home, only had his hand slapped: "Dr. Thomas erred, of course. Seriously. A grievous error. Not to be condoned. No, no. Of course not. Certainly not. But neither is it an error that we cannot understand, of course." He was actually smiling at me. "Dr. Thomas lives and breathes the passions of his texts. Obviously, ah-hem, some of the appropriate barriers broke down during an intense moment." Good Lord, that's what he

actually said. Not a word about the abuse of power, about
the embarrassing position the inappropriate actions of
one colleague put the rest of the department in. And my
response somehow too easily dismissed: "By your reasoning, then, we would excuse an anthropology professor
if, in the course of a passionate discussion on the proofs
of cannibalism, he chopped up and ate a student?" The
old coot was actually relieved: "That's why we need you
here, Maxine. A sense of humor always helps maintain
perspective."

Twenty years on one campus and it becomes a small
town. I know everybody well enough to know there's
nobody for me. At least with Charlie there was occasional, if not passionate, sex. Maybe I'll never have sex
again. Good Lord, that just might be the most depressing
thought I've ever had.

When Maxine walked into the kitchen twenty minutes
later, Mavis was sitting at the table with a cup of coffee
and a plate with a piece of toast getting cold in front of
her. She looked up from the *Fargo Forum* and smiled.
"Good morning. How'd you sleep?"

"Perfectly ... the sleep of the damned." Maxine colored, and added, "Like a log. I heard you coughing earlier. Do you have a cold?"

"Just a little congestion in the morning."

"Want more coffee while I'm up? Any sign of Judy yet
this morning?"

"I've heard some noises from the royal suite below,"
Mavis answered, pushing her cup toward Maxine.

"I've been watching the bird show. You're cultivating
quite a flock of blackbirds out there."

"Those damnable blackbirds. If I had a gun, I'd shoot
them." And then, to Maxine's wide-eyed astonishment,
Mavis said "Oops!" and began to snicker.

"Well, I suppose it's just as well that you don't have a gun, then," Maxine responded slowly, and added after a moment of confused silence, "It looks from the bedroom like there's something in the pan of water?"

"A couple of bricks for the birds to stand on. Otherwise those stupid blackbirds manage to drown themselves."

"You're not very consistent, you know."

"Keep 'em guessing, Maxine."

"You're not doing the crossword, are you? Judy will have a fit."

"Oh, dear, you're right. I'll stop now."

Mavis and Maxine drank their coffee and continued their week-long talk about community and family. Mavis had begun a list of area relatives to call about the upcoming picnic.

"I called Heather last night to see if she could come to the . . . reunion," Maxine said, stumbling uncharacteristically. "But Alan can't get away from work, and they don't want to take separate vacations."

"That's too bad." Mavis's response was sincerely regretful. "Glenn and Craig, if he shows up himself, would have liked to have seen her. Our Dr. Heather. Not bad when you think that neither Mom nor Dad finished high school."

"So you think Craig will be here?"

Mavis smiled and sighed. "Craig is here when he walks through the door. Beyond that nothing is certain."

Maxine read the end of that conversation in Mavis's tone and made the shift. "Glenn's crops certainly look good."

"They do. It's been a bit dry, and Frank would probably say that Glenn doesn't work hard enough, but he's a good farmer. And Peggy's sharp as a tack. She knows the farm programs and tax laws as well as anybody in the county, and she brings in a steady salary. I help out now and then, although my income from investments and whatnot isn't huge. But then what do I need, anyway?"

Coming dangerously close to discussing her own future, Mavis took a detour to the picnic. "Did you hear Janice say that Tina and the baby will be at Glenn's for the picnic on Sunday, with her new boyfriend, Alex, who, Janice says, actually seems to have a brain. The baby's a doll and Janice adores her. And Jimmy and Pam and the kids, all one hundred twenty, or however many there are now, will be there. Tina doesn't think anything about raising the baby by herself, Janice says, but you know Janice is going to help. None of Judy's kids will be home, of course."

"What about my kids?" Judy came through the door smiling, but ready to be offended.

"We were just counting who would be at the picnic, and said that Nick, Chad, and Beas—ur, Chrissie and their families wouldn't be here," Maxine reassured her. "There's coffee over there," Maxine hurried on, hoping Judy would choose to ignore that she had almost used the family's cognomen for Judy's youngest: Beastie. It hadn't been that many years back, when all the sisters were home and had gotten into an unusually virulent argument. None of them could reconstruct the conversation that had gone from playful banter to more pointed criticism, and then to what was assumed by all to be attacks on mothering methods and children. Certainly none of them remembered the conversation the same way. But it ended with Judy in tears, insisting that names like "Beastie" could cause a child permanent psychological damage, ignoring the fact that her little Chrissie was already in her twenties and that any damage was probably already done, as well as conveniently forgetting that it had been the nickname Judy herself had given her daughter as a baby.

"I'm not sure I blame them," Judy said, mug in hand. "Not everybody wants to come to North Dakota for a vacation, even at an exciting time like this."

"What are you eating for breakfast these days?" Mavis's look was direct and long at Judy.

"I'll make myself some toast, thanks."

"Put in a slice for me, please," Maxine asked.

"The women are having coffee this afternoon at Ruth Monroe's. I said the three of us would stop over."

"That will be nice. Ruth never changes," Maxine said.

"Nothing ever changes here," Judy said.

"Oh, I wouldn't say that," came Mavis's measured response. "I'm going out to the garden to pick some vegetables to try to unload this afternoon. Anyone want to help?"

"Sure," Maxine offered, rising from her chair to rinse the coffee cup. "Hold that toast. I love working in a garden that's planted in alphabetical order."

"I'll stay here and finish my coffee and do the crossword," Judy said. "Who's an Egyptian sun god with two . . ."

"Ra!" the sisters yelled back in unison as they walked out the door.

Judy filled in a couple of answers to the puzzle, looked up and watched Mavis and Maxine cross the yard, each carrying a cardboard box. Mavis's garden was evidently between the barn and the wheat field that defined the edge of the farmyard and rolled toward the horizon and the fringe of trees that marked a neighbor's farmstead. Judy was a little peeved at being left alone so soon. Suddenly, Mavis and Maxine broke into a run, or rather, something that resembled a trot, as if a starter's gun had gone off. Judy watched wide-eyed as her gray-haired sisters rocked into a stiff and slow version of a sprint to the corner of the barn, Mavis with her free hand holding her breasts to keep them from bouncing. Judy chuckled as Mavis reached the barn and slapped it with an open palm a good three feet in front of Maxine. The two stood there panting and grinning, and Judy saw them again as teenagers, paired up by their father for the first race. Janice and she would run a much shorter second, Irene and Isabelle just babies passed back and forth between the sisters. It was always close between Mavis and Maxine, both acting as if they couldn't care less who won, but neither able to resist competition. And always close between me and Janice, Judy thought. Janice and me. Janice and I. She didn't seem to mind losing. Then, after Dad was gone, all of a sudden Irene and Isabelle grew up and no one could touch them.

I'd forgotten that Dad wasn't always a bastard, Judy mused. He played kittenball with us, too. Started off fun, but then it was always, Choke up on the bat, put your other foot forward when you throw, lead with your elbow, get down to the ball, bend over, stand up, do this, do that, and always, watch Mavis. Do it like Mavis does. Until I'd get mad and he'd yell at me, Janice would cry, Maxine would pick up the bat and gloves, looking like she was tidying up, but all the time headed for the house to find a quiet place to read. And Mavis still there, offering to play catch for just a little while longer.

Brown nose. That's what I thought. Now I know that she was just trying to keep him from getting angry. Don't make him mad. Just don't make him mad, she'd say.

Another drunk.

Mavis doesn't talk about him much, and gets mad when I tell the truth. A weak man. When things didn't go right, he headed for the bar. So what if they were hard times. They were hard times for everybody. Mavis says Dad read to her, laughed a lot, was handsome. Her father maybe, not mine. Things worked out fine for her, though. Dad on his last legs, about to drink away the farm for good, when she marries Frank and they take over.

Not that anybody else really cared, about the farm, that is. I sure as hell wasn't going to stay in this godforsaken . . . Mavis always saying, "There's no such thing as being bored unless you choose to be bored. Want something to happen? Make it happen." Well, it's not boring around here now, for sure.

Damn. Five, six, seven words left and I don't have a clue. Oh well, Mavis can finish it.

9

SPEEDING OVER THE GRAVEL ROAD TOWARD THE Monroe place, Mavis soon encountered a cloud of white dust left hanging in the air by the last vehicle to travel this way. Probably someone also going for coffee, but no telling how long ago. On a hot windless day road dust could suspend indefinitely. There will be no ladies missing the opportunity to coffee this afternoon, Mavis thought wryly. But then, even close friends have a right to curiosity, and it's not every day you get to coffee with a murderer.

Driving these gravel roads, intersecting others at every mile line and at sixty miles per hour, brought the ongoing harvest into full view. Yellow swathers, green combines, red trucks. Giant Tonka toys in motion. Men carving out geometric patterns in fields with their machines. Trucks empty, then full, then empty again, making the trip from grain bin to field to elevator to field to grain bin, many eerily seeming to pilot themselves until a closer look reveals just the top of the head of the driver barely visible over the steering wheel of the two-and-a-half-ton truck. Children hauling a year's worth of hope down the road. This was the time of year when the men slept poorly despite their exhaustion, broke out in rashes, and found themselves constantly looking upward. God became rain. Not too much, not now, just enough, soon enough. How about a nice rain now and then a week of sun? Not too much to hurt the wheat, but enough to help the row crops. These the prayers of busy, overwhelmed, preoccupied men, who nonetheless never failed to raise an index finger off the steering wheel in salute to a passing vehicle, or to lift an arm in a wave from the tractor, or to stop the climb up the ladder to the combine cab to identify the car full of women passing by.

That evening in the early dark, as corn on the cob was buttered, tomatoes sliced and salted and peppered, hamburgers turned, fried potatoes served from the pan, one of these men might say to his wife, "Saw Mavis doing her usual Indy 500 best toward Monroe's this afternoon, with what looked like Maxine there in the front seat, and couldn't tell who in the back. Not at that speed. The ladies must have had plenty to gossip about today." Waiting for the story. Only the men able to distinguish between gossip and discussion as determined by whether it took place in someone's kitchen or the general store.

A couple of miles down the road in another large farmhouse sitting under yet another mercury vapor light and also surrounded by several outbuildings—barns, shop, machine shed, granary, silo, bunkhouse, garage—perhaps a balding neighbor asks his wife, simply, "What's new over coffee, then?"

Less than fifty yards away, closer to a stand of trees, which gives the newlyweds a sense of privacy in their one-bedroom mobile home, his son may pull his new wife onto his lap to ask the same question as she dishes up the Tater Tot casserole, but chooses his words less wisely: "Wish I had time to sit over coffee and cake for a couple of hours during the afternoon. Who all was there?" And the difference in the phrasing means that the son does not get his answer as quickly as the father, because first he hears his wife's litany of daily chores: of laundry, canning or pickling, cooking, and lawn mowing, of bills paid and book work brought up to date.

Then begins the information transfer and analysis that takes place each evening in hundreds of country homes across the Great Plains at the supper table. How many bushels Ginny Hart's husband says he's getting per acre on that quarter section of his west of the railroad tracks. ("Subtract ten," he says, "and that's more like it.") Preparations being made for the Hansens' daughter's wedding in two weeks. ("I don't go to weddings during harvest." He would.) The new minister's wife has two wigs—one for daily wear and the other for special events. (This news prefaced with the phrase "family talk," alerting any children present that something interesting is about to surface and that they are not to repeat what is about to be said outside of the home. They would.) More talk about a particular farm loan program and what papers have to be filed when.

Because many of the supper table combinations include babies, toddlers, small children, or teenagers, the conversation is supplemented with comments on fevers, bumps and bruises, baseball practice, 4-H camp, Bible school, the county fair, pierced ears (this decade it is the sons horrifying parents with the suggestion), or requests for the car for the upcoming Friday night. Most of the teenage boys are finishing a long day's work beside their fathers, just as dirty, not quite as tired, but twice as hungry. The boys have been calmed and worn by the rhythm of large movements—combines sweeping up and down forty-acre fields, trucks driven back and forth on straight, level country roads, grain shoveled into pulsing augers that twirl and push their loads upward into grain bins. Their sisters are more likely to have been driven to petulance by smaller motions—sterilizing jars for canning, packing cucumbers into the brine, picking weeds in the garden, hanging laundry on the line, and finally, picking up the supper dishes as the "men" sit back after their dessert of peaches, halved and flopped butt up on a scoop of cottage cheese decorated with paprika.

Only rarely is the hair that falls out of the removed seed corn hat long, and then a teenage girl sits by her father at the dinner table trying to explain the new noise the baler now makes. Her father feels guilty looking at the dirt under her fingernails, and her mother worries about the sun lines around her eyes. Later that evening the parents talk once more about going into Fargo later on in the week to the mission to find some temporary help. The next morning these plans will be pushed aside when their daughter bounces down the steps for breakfast, nails clean and polished, young face fresh and unlined from a night's rest.

With the supper meal completed, the smaller children are excused from the table, and the teenagers disappear, replaced by pulsating music. Then, to the background of Metallica or Garth Brooks, the women add, "All the Schmidt sisters are home." Opinions on the significance of this news varies, depending on the teller and her relationship to the Schmidts. Some of the women had grown up with Mavis and Maxine, some with Judy, Janice, and the twins. The women who had married into the community knew Mavis well, but the younger sisters only in passing. Thus, Maxine was perhaps "still beautiful," "the same as ever," or "much older"; she was "comfortable as an old shoe," "a breath of fresh air," or "as snooty as usual." Judy was "in great shape," "dressed to kill," or "painted up like an Indian on the warpath"; she was also "as goofy as ever," "who knows, who's ever been able to figure that one out," or "more fun that all the other Schmidts put together."

And how was Mavis? Mavis was Mavis.

Proof of this was that despite a full two hours of coffee and strawberry shortcake, more coffee, and nonstop talk among ten women, no one came home the wiser concerning Mavis's alleged shooting. More to the point, the subject had only been introduced once, and then by Judy. Perky Jane Sorenson had said how nice it must be to have all the sisters together, and asked, exhibiting her legendary lack of tact, when had they all been together last? Nine memories around the table clicked through a series of events at about the same speed: Irene's death last year, the flocking of family for the funeral, and the equally rapid dispersal. Maxine had explained over a scotch to a friend that she doubted if the sisters knew why they had fled each other's company so quickly, but for her part she believed that somehow individual grief was magnified times five when they were together. "None of us has ever known how to be separate from the others," she had explained. "So instead of being able to help, we just breathed in each other's misery. We were suffocating."

Jane Sorenson was typically the last to click into synch with the collective memory, and was, of course, the first to burst out with her embarrassed "Yes, oh my, yes, yes, dear Irene, of course, oh dear. And now, here you are again in such odd, I mean, unfortunate, well, let's say . . ."

"Let's not," was Mavis's smiling response.

Even Jane Sorenson could recognize this as more command than request, but it was not an opportunity Judy intended to let pass.

"We really are a close family." Judy's tone was solemn. "So when we all thought that Mavis might need our support, we dropped whatever we were doing and dashed up here. Times like this, family should be together."

The table was silent. Several hands reached for coffee cups. A few of the women watched Mavis, waiting, anticipating. If any news was to be had, it would come now. Most of the women, many of whom had known each other and Mavis for several decades, lowered their eyes, embarrassed at the intimacy of Judy's statement in the company of nonfamily. Maxine pushed her glasses up, disappearing behind blue lenses. Mavis was directing a Mavis-look toward Judy, who was holding up remarkably well with her own stubborn look in return of "well-why-not" with raised eyebrows and firm mouth. It was Peggy, her eyes on a mother-in-law she loved and respected, even if she didn't understand, who defused the silence and dissolved the matrix of stares with a statement directed toward Grace, the wife of Mavis's first cousin, Bobby. "What we really need is someone to bring another pan of bars to the family picnic on Sunday. Is there any chance you'd have time to throw something together, Grace?"

"Of course. I've been meaning to ask what I could bring. Lois Jakes made that seven-layer chocolate bar dessert for Sylvia's shower last week and it was so good. Thought I'd try her recipe."

During the following discussion comparing Lois's seven-layer bars with Eva Smith's, Mavis's contribution was a series of "yeah, uh-huhs," while Judy pouted. She was back into the conversation in no time, however, when one of the women asked which nieces and nephews would be at the reunion, giving Judy the opportunity to talk about her children and—"Can you believe it!"—her grandchildren, none of whom, unfortunately, would be there.

Maxine closed her eyes behind her glasses, silently thankful that Isabelle wasn't present to give her opinion of Judy's children, who really were just fine, even Beastie. But Maxine's glasses slid down on her nose quickly enough, eyes smiling over the frames, when she had the opportunity to talk about her own Heather. Soon thereafter Mavis was back in the conversation with stories about her grandchildren. Grandchildren and children, from toddlers to forty, timeless common ground for conversation.

Peggy began the day's exodus, excusing herself with the need to pick up some groceries at the store and get home in time to take lunch to the men, meaning Glenn, Donny Nordstrom, the young man who helped Glenn six months out of the year, and Norton, who was helping drive truck this week. Judy decided to go with Peggy for the rest of the day, and Peggy was relieved to see that Mavis and Maxine were evidently sharing a joke as they, too, drove away. Mavis had noted, certainly not for the first time, that Jane Sorenson was just a little dumber than a fence post, to which Maxine added the expected, "Jane has an element of blank." Then they drove on in amused and comfortable silence to a cool, quiet house: Mavis to take a nap, Maxine to read, then more coffee while they made supper.

MAVIS

MAVIS SHUTS THE BEDROOM DOOR BEHIND HER, LIFTS her hand, and releases the restraint that keeps her from touching her breast in public, that keeps her from saying to her sisters, "Oh, by the way, I have this large lump on my breast. I haven't had it checked. But I know it's cancer." She can see the looks that would cover their faces in the moment before control. She knows, with neither pride nor guilt, but with simple understanding, the fear that would accompany concern.

They've all wanted to be held. Who holds me?

She slips her shoes off and climbs onto the bed, sinking into the soft floral coverlet made out of the same silky material as the drapes. She hurts and she needs to rest. She needs to think into the past.

Who holds Mavis? She reaches her hand over to the

right side of the bed. It's a fifty-fifty chance that the thought of Frank beside her as she sleeps will bring some relief. But not this time. This time his absence once more brings its own familiar but separate pain that lodges behind the now-constant ache in her chest.

She must go even further back, to a time before. To safety. To be held with nothing asked in return. To a father.

Surprisingly, not that tall. Not much over six feet. Hair slicked straight back. Strong teeth. Powerful forearms. Sitting in front of the coal stove, holding me on his lap and reading stories at night. His hands cold, the room cold, but I'm warm in my blanket on his lap. Mom sewing, cleaning, cooking, doing. He stands and swings me onto his shoulders, then bends at his waist, pretending to let me fall. I'm not scared. In winter and summer I see the world above everyone else, special on my perch. The ceiling fan is dusty. There are three large silver coins on the top shelf over the kitchen sink. The barn swallow eggs have hatched in the garage. He calls me his meadowlark while we do the chores. Puts me down to race. Teaches me to throw. His "number one" daughter.

But then, sometimes so suddenly, the thunder. His voice a changed thing, cursing, angry. What did I do? What did I do? Tools thrown, animals beaten, and an old pickup truck roars out of the yard. I can't eat and I'm afraid to make any noise. There's something about Mom's face that makes me look away. I go to bed early, and keep Maxine quiet, too. Finally I sleep.

But I'm awake again. I hear Magnus barking and barking and then a sound I don't recognize and the barking stops. Heavy steps begin to climb the stairs. A shoulder rubs the wall all the way up to the landing. That other door squeaks, warped in its frame. I hear Mom's voice, muffled, and it sounds scared like my heart. I put my head under the covers.

The next morning I stay in my room. I know he can't see me today, but I see him out the window behind the garden, digging. Magnus is beside him as usual, but he lies so still. Dad pulls Magnus by the back legs and Magnus's head falls back. Too far. The neck opens up. It's a blackened hole. He drops Magnus into the hole in the black dirt. Everything is black.

Later I sit on the swing. Push my toes into the crusted dirt, silky dust beneath. Still no rain. I watch him cross the yard to the burn barrel. He lifts his hand to his waist, then drops something in and looks at the barrel for the longest time. He wipes his nose the way they tell me not to. Now he can see me. He comes to the swing and puts me on his shoulders. His knife holster is empty. "Can my meadowlark sing for me today?" It's hard. I can.

10

GLENN AND PEGGY'S GIRLS, BECKY AND JANIE, WERE just about to climb the fence between the machine shed and the feed lot that separated farmyard from pasture when their mother's car came into distant view. Janie cradled a .22 rifle carefully, trying to find the right balance between armed and independent swagger and near-paralyzing caution. She had listened intently to Glenn's instructions about gun care, which he had learned not from his father, but from his aunt Janice, who, only eight years his senior, had sat beside him at least a dozen times on the quiet pasture hillside, scanning the area for unlucky gophers. Added to Glenn's program of gun safety was Janie's own vivid imagination, through which she frequently visualized the scenes of familial horror and grief that would accompany an accidental shooting. Although death remained an unreal abstraction for this ten-year-old, the horror of causing any type of scene was quite real. She rechecked the safety latch and passed the rifle over to Becky, who had just hopped down on the other side of the fence.

Janie hesitated as she swung her leg over the top board, registering the cloud of dust speeding toward the farm down the road that formed the boundary on one side of the pasture. Not waiting for the cloud to materialize into the family Buick with her mother inside, she hurried to jump down and get out of sight, following the unspoken maxim that directed most of her actions: if they can't see you, they can't put you to work. As she landed she turned to look back at the car between the top two fence boards. To her surprise, Grandma Mavis's sister Judy stepped out of the passenger side. Janie quickly turned back to Becky to motion her away from the fence, knowing full well that if Becky were to see Judy, she'd be lost. And there was no telling when Becky, who daily became more incomprehensible, would be bored enough again to hunt gophers with her. But it was already too late, for Becky had seen the car with Judy in it, and was just waiting to hand the gun back to her little sister before she headed back over the fence.

"Where are you going?" Janie protested.

"Aunt Judy's here. Come on."

"Becky, you promised. You said you'd shoot gophers with me."

"Yeah, but Aunt Judy's here now."

"She'll still be here later. Come on. You promised."

"I promised I'd shoot gophers with you, but I didn't say when." Becky was striding away.

Janie was dumbfounded by the treachery of this logic, and left with little but ten-year-old eloquence, "Liar, dumb bunny, jerk," hurled at Becky's back. With Becky's desertion, the afternoon of fun on the pasture hillside, waiting for gophers to peek out of their holes, was lost. Still, not to lose face and capitulate totally to her older sister's whims, she'd have to spend at least forty-five minutes out here by herself. Probably wouldn't be any old gophers out anyway, not in the middle of the afternoon, just some darn flies and mosquitoes.

Becky, however, was all flashing braces as she ran across the yard toward Judy, who was, of course, wearing the newest tennis shoes.

"Are you going to stay here?" was Becky's first question.

"No, I'm up at your grandmother's. Came here to see you and Janie for a while. Where is Janie?"

"Down in the pasture pouting because I don't want to shoot gophers," Becky answered, quite deliberately not looking at her mother, who could easily picture the scene that led to the parting, but decided to stay neutral. Clearly, upon noting Judy's arrival, Becky's emotional pendulum had swung toward the urge to be a young woman and away from being a child. How, Peggy wondered, had Janie's dogged and hopeful requests finally convinced Becky to "hunt" with her in the first place? At thirteen years old, Becky was less and less often moved by Janie's entreaties to lapse into preteen fun. Peggy had watched with some sadness as Becky steadily increased the emotional distance between the two girls, but reminded herself that soon enough Janie would be getting her own regular deliveries of adolescent hormones, making her equally difficult. Peggy studied her oldest daughter, feeling far more sympathy for her than Becky imagined at that moment.

"Do you think she'll be back soon?" Judy asked.

"About a half hour is my guess." Peggy smiled. "Becky, help me carry the groceries in. Has your dad been in since I left?"

"Nope."

Good, that means nothing's broken down today, Peggy thought. She was pleased to see that Becky was going to monopolize Judy's time. She didn't feel like being pumped for information about Jack's death just now. Not that she knew anything. But ignorance never got in the way of a discussion around here. Peggy looked at the ragged lawn as she walked to the front step. Only weeds had managed to grow without rain in the past almost two and a half weeks since Janie had last mowed. She'd have to get Becky or Janie to mow before Sunday's picnic, which would, of course, be here. Mavis had moved five miles and built a new house on the old Stromm place after Frank died, allowing Peggy and Glenn to move to the farm from their rented house in nearby Rippon. That only made sense. Neither Peggy nor Mavis was interested in repeating the pattern of multiple generations under one roof, and thanks to smart farming, wise acquisitions, and seasons of good weather and good grain prices in the 1970s, Mavis was financially able to turn the farm over to Glenn and move. Nonetheless, when family came home, it was to Mavis *and* to this farm. Peggy and

Glenn might live there now, but each of the sisters laid claim to the farm as home.

Thus, in a ritual that had already been performed by both Maxine and Isabelle, Judy needed to walk around the house and remark, again, on how it had changed. The one inviolable, never-to-be-moved item, it seemed, was the piano in the living room, still bearing Judy's name carved clumsily into one of the legs by a five-year-old Isabelle in the hopes that Judy would get both the credit and the spanking. In this house, the piano was an instrument of torture, for the listener as well as the performer. Generations of children with little or no musical talent had suffered greatly in the living room, forced to practice in the cold mornings when they'd rather sleep, or after school when they'd rather play. Of the sisters' generation, Mavis, Maxine, and Janice took their lessons and played dutifully for five years from the fifth grade through the ninth. Then, released, they never went near the piano again. Judy also took lessons for five years, learned as many songs by heart, and played those five songs every time she was near a piano. Irene and Isabelle had taken advantage of their mother's fatigue and their father's absence, and escaped the lessons completely.

The next generation in this house was more fortunate. Glenn made a deal with his parents early on, promising to be a trombone virtuoso if only he didn't have to take piano lessons. Glenn's music teacher soon suggested to Mavis and Frank that perhaps a young athlete as gifted as he shouldn't be taking so much time from his sports. Craig was the only exception, loving to play and barely begrudging the responsibilities that accompanied his interest. Because the talent pool in a small farm community is often shallow, he was necessarily the church organist as well as the pianist for his high school choir. The latter experience he now blamed for the recurrence of "Cherish" as the music accompanying his not-infrequent nightmares.

Glenn's girls, however, had revived the tradition of morning complaints and afternoon rationalizations away from piano practice, much to the same effect. So when Judy finished her five-song repertoire and asked Becky to play, Becky produced her thirteen-year-old sigh and obediently and heartlessly played the easiest song she could get away with. Finished, she asked if Judy would show her how she made up her eyes.

In the kitchen, Peggy was laying out slices of Sweetheart bread, spreading Miracle Whip, and slapping down cold cuts as Becky's song began. Moving to the sink to wash the lettuce, she scanned the farmyard through the kitchen window, noting that Janie had capitulated more quickly than she'd expected and was headed back with rifle in hand. Peggy smiled as Janie came to an abrupt halt, head cocked toward the house. Suddenly the ten-year-old made a surprisingly graceful ninety-degree pivot on chubby legs and headed for cover, slipping into the garage. She had evidently heard the piano. Whereas Becky would roll her eyes and get the playing over with, Janie would simply stay away from the house as long as she thought there was a viable threat of required performance. If she had the misfortune to be trapped inside when requested to play a song for company, she would go from embarrassed excuses to pleas to angry tears when Glenn or Peggy changed the request to a command. All to no avail, of course, since most of the family simply considered this a part of the timeworn ritual that preceded a child's recital.

Peggy bagged the sandwiches and cookies—oatmeal rocks, hard, large, dry, and Glenn's favorites—took the water jugs half filled with ice from the freezer and added water, and headed out the door. As she passed the garage she met Janie's mournful eyes with a smile.

"How'd it go, Annie Oakley?"

Somebody in a movie, Janie knew this one. "Nothin'."

"Is the gun empty?"

"Yeah."

"How about putting it away, then, and driving me out to the field with lunch?"

"All right!" Janie's face lit up as she started to run, remembered the rifle, and quickly strode to the house.

It's nice to know that we can make our children as happy as we can make them miserable, Peggy mused, hoping they both would survive Janie's second time behind the wheel.

The ride out to the field was without incident, despite a brief game of slow-motion chicken with Newt, an old retired farmer who had always driven down the middle of the road, slowly. So that for about a quarter of a mile Newt's ancient pea-green Chevy pickup and Peggy's Buick, driven with wide-eyed intensity at about fifteen miles an hour by Janie, crept toward each other, both in the middle of the road, so slowly and inexorably that Peggy was hard put to stifle her giggles. Just when she was beginning to worry that Janie had been hypnotized by the near-motionless progression of the vehicles, Peggy watched her lift a pudgy index finger from the steering wheel in imitation of her father's farmer's salute, as she pulled far to the right to let Newt pass, who answered the salute with a short nod as he moved the stub of the most disgusting cigar in the county to the other side of his mouth. Janie's developing skills were not further tested before she was able to safely turn onto an approach and then into one of the broad ditches that served as a tractor path for machinery moving from one field to another.

As they bumped along, Peggy watched a dust cloud approaching on the county road paralleling the ditch. Judging from the speed, that would have to be one of the Jackson boys. Odd, Peggy mused, you'd think they'd be helping in the field at this time of day, and then returned her attention to Janie, who was nudging the Buick out of the ditch and down the side of the field toward the truck where Norton sat smoking, waiting for the hopper on Glenn's combine to fill.

"Well, hey, if it ain't Barney Oldfield!" Norton shouted as Janie got out of the car, trying not to act like the drive was any big deal.

Barney Oldfield. Who's that? Janie was about to ask, but Norton was already talking with Peggy about how he would have to put in a day of sales in his Fargo territory tomorrow and so wouldn't be able to help out driving truck. He'd talked to Glenn, who'd said Peggy would be able to take over.

"Of course," Peggy answered, "although the weatherman said there's a slight chance of rain tonight and a fifty percent chance tomorrow."

"That's what I told Glenn, though it don't look like it now. Still, we'll probably go as late as we can tonight. Make hay while the sun shines. Not that your beans couldn't use some rain."

Janie listened, fascinated. This was the same conversation she heard among adults all season long, no matter who talked, and it always sounded so important. So grown-up and smart. Sometimes when she played with her dolls—Pete and Mr. Beasley (an old bald doll of her mother's which had undergone a gender transformation through hair loss)—she would have them compare the amounts of rain they each got the night before and talk about what soybeans were selling for according to the market report. Ever since she'd given Becky's Barbie a haircut some years ago, Becky had laid claim to all the girl dolls, and for the life of her, Janie couldn't think of what else boy dolls could talk about.

All three stopped and watched Glenn approach in the three-year-old John Deere 8820 combine, straight-cutting the wheat with its thirty-foot-wide head and feeding it into the guts of the machine to be winnowed and separated. These machines were different beasts than the ones his father had pulled back and forth across the fields, sitting on a tractor in the scorching sun, his face blackened by fine North Dakota dirt, his neck aching from being cranked around to watch the swaths his tractor straddled as they were licked up by the combine behind. Now Glenn sat in the air-conditioned, glass-enclosed cab of this self-propelled giant, surrounded by controls and gauges. Now, the farmers joked, we can worry in comfort. The combine was a beautiful machine, an absolute necessity to the farming operation. Peggy and Glenn had stared into the computer screen while figuring on the handheld calculator for many a long night before applying for the loan necessary to make this eighty-thousand-dollar purchase, and when Glenn had finally driven it in the yard and climbed down out of the cab, Peggy knew as she kissed him that she was also kissing a new house good-bye.

Glenn brought the combine to a halt and backed down the half-dozen ladder steps before jumping the final three feet to the ground. It was unusual in these parts to stop the combine at all during a good harvest day, except to change drivers, especially with rain in the forecast. But when Peggy brought lunch out, Glenn stopped. They had discovered long ago that in the midst of mid-harvest stress, these fifteen-minute breaks were more important to their marriage than getting in fifteen minutes more of combining before the evening dampness called a halt to the work.

Between bites of sandwich, Glenn asked Janie, "Say, Parnelli, was that you driving the car out here? Looked pretty professional."

Janie beamed, but this time asked, "Who's Parnelli?"

"Parnelli Jones. Someone on your mother's side of the family." This in reference to Peggy's second speeding ticket of the summer.

Peggy ignored the comment, smiling at Glenn and wondering why she thought it was somehow almost sexy to watch him put an entire cookie in his mouth when he was out here in the field, under the sun, a little dirty, when it made her want to scream when he ate like that in her kitchen. No matter. The look that passed quickly between them caused her to make a mental note to be sure to shave her legs later this evening when she took her shower.

"Supper is at your mother's. I'll tell young Donny when I take him lunch. Is he still swathing on the other side of the pasture?"

"Um-hum. He should be done in a couple of hours, then Norton here can eat and get back to Fargo. All you women will terrify young Donny."

"Well, I know that more than two Schmidt sisters in one room scares the bejesus out of me. Young Donny'll probably break down now, just so he can sit out supper in the field," Norton added.

"That's why I packed extra sandwiches for him. Do you two anticipate similar attacks of insecurity, or will you be able to make it to supper?"

"I grew up with Mavis—" Glenn smiled, then put his hands on his hips and changed his tone. "—and I ain't afraid of nothin'." Glenn looked up at the cloudless but increasingly leaden sky. "It might rain tonight. I gotta get goin'."

"Do you think?" from Peggy.

"No, not really, but I could be wrong." Glenn was striding back to the combine. "Say," he turned, "speaking of scary women, how was coffee with the ladies this afternoon?"

"We talked about how crabby our husbands are these days. I'll tell you about it later. Judy came back with me. She's teaching Becky the finer points of makeup."

"Oh Lord, this will cost us," Glenn muttered as he climbed in and shut the door.

"Here, Peggy." Norton held out an uncallused palm. "I can take young Donny's lunch to him. I'll pass by there with this next load."

"Oh, thanks, Norton. See you later."

"Can I drive back, too?" Janie asked.

"May I. Just be careful when you leave the approach to the road."

Janie was intent on her driving while Peggy planned out what she could get done in what remained of the day. By Monday she needed to finish a proposal for the superintendent to take to the school board, requesting more funds for a sex education program that she, as Rippon's elementary school principal, agreed with the school counselor should be instituted in the curriculum. The chances of getting the funds were zero to none, she expected. This was not a particularly liberal community, there were serious shortfalls in educational funds throughout the state (with no relief in sight now that the state's voters had soundly defeated by referral the legislation's latest tax package), and the school board had its quota of old men who made thoughtful comments such as the one she'd heard last spring: "Everything a kid needs to know about sex he can learn on the school bus like the rest of us did. Har. Har."

Into her plans and worries came Janie's voice. A question.

"Mom?"

"Um-hum?"

"Do you think Judy would show me how to put on makeup, too?" Janie was beet-red asking the question.

"I'm sure she would love to, sweetheart." Peggy reached over and touched the round pink cheek of her long-lashed daughter. "But you're so pretty, you probably don't even need to bother," she added, and then realized that sometime soon, during the girls' next argument, Janie would reinterpret this to Becky as something like "Mom says you're ugly, so that's why Judy showed you how to wear her makeup."

Finally, Janie brought the car around the corner and into the driveway in the slow creep so consistent with her usual caution. There in the driveway was a dust-covered red Bronco that Peggy could now see whiz by her as she and Janie had turned into the wheat field. The screen door banged and out strode a tall, thin man wearing shorts and hiking boots and a grin as wide as Glenn's.

"Well, it's A. J. Foyt behind the wheel!" the man exclaimed, bending his lean body for a hug and winking at Peggy. Janie blushed with the contact and decided to not even bother with this strange name business. Probably just another relative.

"Craig! Why didn't you tell us you were coming? It's so good to see you. And look at that, what, is that a beard?" Peggy and Craig hugged.

"You look like George Michael," Janie piped up.

Craig laughed. "That's who I'm trying to look like."

Peggy had already closely scrutinized her brother-in-law without seeming to do so. Tall like Glenn, he didn't have Glenn's bulk, and now he seemed thinner than usual. And there was a tiredness around the brown eyes that he, like Glenn, had inherited from Mavis, the anomaly in a family of blue eyes. In fact, it was Craig who most obviously carried the Schmidt genes. With that angular face, he had often been mistaken for Isabelle's brother.

As Craig held the screen door for Peggy to pass through, he touched her arm.

"I know we can't talk now, but is Mom okay?"

"I think so. She seems so. But nobody, and I mean nobody, knows what happened or what's going to happen next. I'm glad you're here."

As they entered the kitchen, Becky turned a face toward her mother as grotesque and self-satisfied as only a thirteen-year-old's wearing the makeup of a fifty-year-old trying to look thirty can be. The wares of five Avon ladies appeared to be spread out on the kitchen table.

"Hello, gorgeous," Peggy said, imitating Barbra Streisand's Fanny Brice, to no one's recognition. "Who's this beautiful woman?" Peggy asked, and then motioned Judy with her eyes toward Janie, who was sitting at the table staring mournfully at the tubes and bottles.

Judy was quick to catch on. "How about Janie? Would you like to go to my fashion school today, too? The first thing to remember is to always start with a clean face."

Well, Peggy thought, that should lose her right there.

"So Judy, when you're done with Janie, can you give me some tips?" Craig winked at the giggling girls.

"I can give you one now. You need a shave."

Craig laughed as he bent to Judy's kiss. "That's probably a good idea, and a shower. I've been driving straight for eight hours. Then I'll go on up and see Mom. Was that Glenn combining I passed?"

"Um-hum. We'll all be up to Mavis's later on for supper. You know where the towels are."

"The family towels are in the back of the second drawer down, and the company towels are in the front of the drawer, so it looks like you only use the best towels always."

"Wrong," Peggy replied. "That's one Mavisism that's been successfully done away with in this house. Holler when you're out of the shower so I can start the dishwasher."

11

WHEN CRAIG DROVE INTO HIS MOTHER'S YARD LATE that afternoon, he was pleased to find Maxine in the hammock stretched between a box elder and an anchoring post. For years the sisters' kids had been, if not interchangeable, then easily exchangeable. Janice's Tina and Jimmy had spent entire summers on Mavis and Frank's farm. As a teenager, Judy's Chad had been shipped to Irene and Jack's farm to spend the summers with Jackie and Blair, in the hopes that the demands of farm work would sweat out a rebelliousness that was manifesting itself through a fascination with drugs. Glenn had lived with newlyweds Janice and Norton his first semester of college, when at the last minute he decided to go to North Dakota State instead of joining the Army, only to find that he hadn't applied in time to get a dorm room.

Glenn was eighteen and it was 1969—a good year to enter college instead of the service, if that was an option. The entire year before his graduation from high school, Glenn had decorated his bedroom with recruitment posters, and Frank and Mavis could hear him doing sit-ups at night before bed while Craig hovered nearby, in equal parts anxiety and fourteen-year-old awe. Then Mavis made Glenn's decision: "If you get drafted, you go. If you don't get drafted, you don't go. Right now, you're eighteen years old and you're going to college. If, at twenty-one, you want to join the Army, then that's your business."

Craig, who'd gone to school at U.C. Berkeley, had spent most of his vacations and summers with Isabelle in Greenview, in the Sierras, and still spent the occasional holiday with her and Linda. As a result, he and Maxine's Heather, who as a high school and college student had also spent a couple of weeks each summer in California with Isabelle, had become close friends. None of this was very confusing, for each nephew and niece quickly realized that the rules of the house he or she entered were remarkably similar to those they'd just escaped.

Although each Schmidt sister's husband must have entered into marriage carrying his own baggage of family rituals and personal idiosyncrasies, other family traditions, rules, and daily expectations withered in the presence of Schmidt truths. Such truths were often trivial: butter dishes were never refrigerated, but always covered and placed on the shelf above the toaster, which was always in the corner; shoes were never allowed past the kitchen, but could be dumped in any fashion in the entryway; no one would eat the last cookie, brownie, or piece of cake that slowly petrified on the platter. Their truths were just as often sublime: children and adults were to attend church each Sunday, where they would learn to pray for forgiveness and give thanks for blessings, but on weekdays their destinies were their own responsibility.

Each sister could easily (and readily) recite a dozen ways in which another sister's household could be improved, whereas nieces and nephews passed from one house to the next as if stepping through a mirror. Only the occasional exception was experienced in the house-hold of Jack and Irene, where Jack's personality would sporadically erupt: a gun hanging on the wall in a living room otherwise decorated with unremarkable landscape paintings purchased at the furniture store along with the couch; the odd nights away from home on generic "farm business"; a calendar, provided by a tool company, on the garage wall, picturing a big-haired blonde with huge breasts and a miniskirt. For years Isabelle had snorted over Jack's horror when he discovered that she had clipped out the screwdriver the big blonde was holding so proudly and replaced it with a cutout of a hatchet.

More typically, the husbands unthinkingly abandoned former rituals as they entered into their wives' routines and assumptions. They gave their children hair color, chins, shapes of eyes, and the occasional nervous man-nerism, but basically the children's habits and neuroses were their mothers'. And the mothers' were the sisters'.

Craig motioned Maxine back into the hammock and they kissed, full on the lips, in greeting. No missed cheeks for him. He kissed people he liked and kept others at arm's length.

"Where are you buying your perfume these days, Maxine? The local feed store?" Craig asked, wrinkling his nose from the kiss.

"Deep Woods Off." Maxine held up the can. "Damned mosquitoes keep trying to lift me off the hammock."

"Chemicals for a better life." Craig took the can to spray his legs. "Where's Mom?"

"Taking a nap, so bring that lawn chair by the house over here into the shade and talk to me." Maxine closed her Patricia Cornwell murder mystery and lowered her head to study Craig over her glasses as he crossed the lawn.

They made small talk about mysteries (a favorite vice of both), about Craig's drive home, and about Craig's job. He was unlikely to be laid off during the current Boeing purge, he assured her. He was a Berkeley boy, he said, and smiled. "We're charmed." Maxine admitted to looking forward to retirement but being more than a little terrified of not having anything to do. She was a little lonely, yes. He was a little lonely, too, and no, he answered his aunt with a rueful smile, there were no new women in his life, and all the old ones were relatives. Then it was her turn for the smile.

"Heather called me, I guess it was a little over a week ago, when—when all this happened," Craig said. "Will she be coming home?"

"No, she can't get away. None of Judy's family will be here, either. It won't be much of a reunion."

They both raised their eyebrows at the word.

"Of course Irene and Jack's kids . . ." Maxine hesitated.

"What about Jackie and Blair? Where are they? How are they taking all of this?"

"Only Blair was at Jack's funeral, which must have been a very interesting event. I've gotten almost no information about that day from Mavis, and Janice didn't even go."

"Where's Blair now?"

"On the farm. He'd been staying, off and on, with a friend's family up there in Brickton for most of last year. Isabelle tried to talk with him, but he's not having anything to do with any of us. And to tell the truth, I don't suppose we would know how to act around those kids just now, considering." Maxine paused for just a moment at Craig's gesture of impatience, then continued, "He's saying he wants to farm now instead of go to college, but I'm sure there must be liens on the place. Actually, I wouldn't be surprised at all to see him enlist."

Maxine stopped and looked across the driveway to the golden field of wheat, ready now for harvesting, still in the breezeless afternoon. "It's all so sad," she went on. "Blair was so close to his mother, and he's been just lost, absent I guess, all year, and now, well, he's just completely adrift. And Jackie . . ." Maxine widened her eyes. "Do you ever talk to her?"

Craig shrugged his shoulders and shook his head. "It's probably been years."

"I don't know who does. I don't know if any of us really know her. I was relieved when she agreed to go to the Hazelden. It's supposed to be one of the best chemical dependency treatment centers in the Cities. I'm pretty sure your mother's footing the bill for that, too."

"Why wasn't she back for her dad's funeral?" Craig shifted in his chair and reached down to slap a mosquito at his ankle, then studied the blood on his palm. When Maxine didn't answer, he looked up to find her staring at him.

"Hasn't anyone told you?"

"What?"

Maxine took off the glasses that had been perched on

the end of her nose. Rubbing the bridge of her nose and keeping her eyes shut, she related the bits of information she knew. "I guess it was Janice who called the Hazelden to tell Jackie about her father. Just who did what those first days after the shooting is a bit difficult to unravel. All I know for sure is that Mavis was busy taking care of the funeral preparations. Good Lord . . ."

"I know. But what about Jackie?"

"She wasn't there."

"Where was she?"

"Where *is* she, you mean. She went AWOL from the treatment center the Tuesday before the murder."

"And the Hazelden didn't contact anyone? Unless . . ."

"Exactly. I suppose they called Jack. But that's the end of that phone tree."

"And no one knows where she is now?"

"No, but agents Heyerdahl and Madsen—"

"Who?" Craig interrupted.

"The agents from the North Dakota Bureau of Criminal Investigation who are in charge of Jack's murder. Don't worry, you'll meet them. Anyway, they seem pretty interested in finding Jackie. Whereas—" Maxine shook her head and looked up into Craig's dark eyes. "—your mother just goes about as if nothing has happened, except she seems a bit put off at the police for not seeming to take her 'confession' seriously."

"Why does she think they aren't taking her seriously?"

"Well, Craig, she hasn't been arrested."

"I talked about that to a good friend who's a cop. He says there may be lots of reasons why Mom's not in jail, most of them to do with the time involved to complete certain procedures, but that it's unlikely the investigators on the case wouldn't take a confession seriously."

"What kind of procedures?" Maxine asked, shifting in

the hammock and picking up her murder mystery as if it were a reference book.

"Well, there's the fingerprinting, which my friend says may have been sent to the FBI to be ID'd, and that can take weeks. There's some sort of crime index computer that prints go through. Also, he said the police would need to show probable cause as well as something beyond circumstantial evidence in order to get a judge to sign for a search warrant, or to get an arrest warrant."

"But would they need all that? She confessed, remember?"

"Hey, I don't know. My friend also suggested that maybe the police would have some doubts about Mom's sanity."

Maxine's response was to throw her head back and laugh, and Craig was relieved to be able to join her with a chuckle.

"Next to Mavis's claim to have killed Jack, that is the most ludicrous thing I've heard."

"I know. The final suggestion my cop friend had was that perhaps, in digging through Jack's past, the police had come up with a better lead."

Maxine looked away from Craig and the two were silent for a moment. When Craig took a breath, as if about to speak, Maxine raised her hand as if to show Craig her palm. "Don't say it, Craig."

"I'm not saying anything. But we both know Jackie's carried a lot of pain around for a long time."

"I'd hate to think why."

Craig was looking at the ground between his knees when he asked, "Do you really not know why?"

Maxine breathed a sigh against the fist she was holding against her mouth, and answered, but not to Craig, "I don't know what I don't know."

Again they were silent. Craig reached over for the

empty glass of ice cubes left over from Maxine's iced tea, pulled one out of the glass and played with it in his mouth, until he could say, "We're a family of talkers. We can start in the morning and talk all day long. We can tell stories and make jokes with the best of them. Anything, a trip to the grocery store, is fodder for a story, a dentist appointment material for a joke. But we're not so good with a few pertinent questions, are we?"

Maxine studied Craig as he spoke. When had he grown up so? There was an integrity about this man that she trusted. He had Mavis's loyalty and determination, without her defensiveness or mania for self-preservation. He'd also seemed to have lost that devil-may-care attitude that he'd shared with Isabelle and Judy, God forbid that the two should be mentioned in the same breath. Now she could see Frank's patience, which came out as stolid in Glenn, but looked more like introspection in Craig. He was only thirty-six, three years older than Heather, but as he spoke, Maxine couldn't help but wonder what he had seen to age those dark eyes. A chill crept under the shadow of yet another question she had not asked, and probably would not ask this nephew. About friends, about lovers. And for the second time in their short conversation Maxine faced her own cowardice. *"Mene, mene tekel upharsin,"* she muttered.

"Beg your pardon?"

"You're right, of course," Maxine said. "We all snap to in a crisis, there with all we have to offer. But anything less than a crisis we can ignore. Not very efficient, I suppose."

"And what crisis is Mom directing now?" Craig asked.

"Meaning?"

Craig began to sketch out his question, putting things in order, in a logical path, as if he were explaining one of his computer programs. "I expect that Mom is completely capable of killing to protect something of hers. She could also maybe kill to protect herself. And maybe she could kill to protect an ideal—God, country, home. That sort of thing. But"—and here Craig hurried to finish his sentence as he heard the screen door clap shut, stood and smiled at his approaching mother, who was smiling in return in surprise—"but"—he looked back at Maxine— "she's not vindictive and she's not a vigilante. She could never walk out the door intending to shoot someone. You know that, too. So here are some of those pertinent questions. What's she doing? Whom is she protecting? Why?"

Craig closed the distance between his mother and himself with three long strides, and to the echo of Craig's "Why?" Maxine watched Mavis kiss and hug her youngest son. It was an unusually long hug for Mavis, an embrace of unasked and unanswered questions.

12

THAT EVENING AT MAVIS'S WAS LIKE A THOUSAND other evenings, familiar to every family member there, regardless of the shifting role he or she played: sister, son, mother, father, uncle, aunt, brother-in-law, sister-in-law, niece, nephew, grand-aunt, grandmother. In this family there were few uncomplicated relationships, but far fewer uncomfortable ones.

Had he been in his own home, Craig would have been busy at the counter and stove. But on this first evening in his mother's house, he slid easily into the male rural ritual of watching women work in the kitchen. So as Maxine made Bisquick shortcakes and cleaned and cut up peaches for dessert, Mavis cleaned and chopped beans from her garden. The potatoes were peeled and set in water. Packages of pork chops had been thawed in the sink. Meat would begin frying when someone drove in the yard, and if the boiled potatoes were cold by the time the men got there, then Mavis would slice and fry them, too.

Maxine and Mavis gave their joint report on Judy, who, as usual, came in for a certain amount of loving abuse. Their amazement with this sister was constant. All four of the younger sisters, "the little ones," had comprised a separate set from the older two; in fact, Mavis and Maxine were both convinced that the mother and father they had known were simply not the same people who parented the younger girls. Somehow, in the second decade of that marriage, hope, optimism, and laughter had been replaced by anger and silence, then alcohol, then absence. None of this, however, completely explained Judy. They loved her, but they were hard put to understand the choices she made, the concepts she privileged. As usual, Craig spoke in Judy's defense. Although Judy and Isabelle were the two sisters whose actions most consistently confused the others, albeit for widely disparate reasons, they were also the two most quickly championed by the next generation, especially by Glenn and Craig, whose youngest years had been spent in the company of the four youngest sisters.

Craig felt the conversation wrap around him, hold him, soothe him with easy talk. Family talk. About neighbors and children and grandchildren and weather and crops, and, as always, North Dakota politics. When Peggy, Judy, Becky, and Janie drove in the yard, they brought with them more talk, more laughter.

Supper was informal. Mavis served the girls and Craig the chops as they were done. Peggy pointed out that Becky and Janie didn't need their grandmother to wait on them: this directed at the girls, not their grandmother. Janie wondered if since there were enough people for a slimly fielded game of work-up, could they play softball after supper. It wouldn't be *that* dark. There were no takers, but lots of promises for Sunday at the picnic.

Norton showed up around seven-thirty, grinning and pleased with himself as only a city man can be after a day in the field. Young Donny had sent his excuses after all; he would go straight home when the day's combining was done. He had just finished swathing the north pasture field and was taking over the combine from Glenn when Norton passed them in the truck after dumping a load at the elevator. The second truck was standing empty at the end of the field so young Donny could unload the full hopper while the others were eating. It all seemed like an intricate dance to Norton, who relished relating these details and switches. To the women, who let him talk away, it was simply the age-old rhythm of farming.

Soon Glenn drove in, bringing Norton's car so that Norton could head back to Fargo. Glenn and Craig shook hands, grinning. Again, comments about weight. Here too little, here a little too much. Glenn took the beer Mavis offered, ate as if he were starving, asked if anyone had watched the weather on TV, finished with coffee and peach shortcake, winked as he got off the kitchen stool at Janie, who was standing quietly but strategically by the

door with her softball glove and ball, played catch for ten
minutes in the near dark with his youngest daughter, and
was back in the truck Norton had brought up within the
hour. With weather this dry, harvesting would go on well
into the night.

Becky and Janie did dishes while Mavis, Maxine,
Judy, and Peggy played whist, keeping Craig in the conversation, which was mostly about Judy's current boyfriend, Jed, and related problems, meaning his kids.
Feeling less threatened than usual, probably bolstered by
the presence of Craig and Peggy, Judy was able to relax
into her own brand of humor, which included a little self-
mockery, remarking at one point that Craig would soon
be older than she was.

Tonight no one would ask any questions harder than
why someone hadn't played back someone else's invite.
No one would make demands more difficult than Mavis's
request that if Judy knew she had all the rest of the tricks,
then why didn't she just lay down her hand. And the only
major disagreement would take place in the kitchen as
Becky and Janie argued over who was the cutest: Jordon,
Donnie, Joseph, Jonathan, or Danny.

When Peggy and the girls left for home, Mavis stepped
out the door behind them, standing alone for a minute.
Children, grandchildren, sisters all here now. Except
Irene, she thought, looking up, aware that these days
when she looked to the sky, it was more often her husband she spoke to than God.

God.

Oh yes. I know I'm being obstinate, as usual, she
prayed, but I don't really feel like I'm doing wrong. Is it
wrong to choose one fight over another? To try to give
more life instead of trying to have more life? Am I guilty
of too much pride, like they've all said at some point?
Am I meddling? Taking on too much? And then, in a

quintessentially Mavis moment, she finished her prayer with "Help me to be right."

Mavis stared a bit longer at the sky and the clouds, now quickly moving the twilight to darkness. A much cooler breeze than she'd felt for days was disturbing the trees that surrounded the house and tinkling the wind chimes in the corner, which she had put up to scare away the swallows with their muddy nests, and that had soon become a favorite perch. She turned to go in as Craig walked out the door, letting out strains of Budweiser music from TV into the evening air.

"I think it just might rain after all," she said to her son, reaching up to touch his cheek as she passed back through the door, leaving him to study the clouds on his own.

13

SHERIFF HANSEN WAS THINKING ABOUT THE STORY HE'D heard long ago of a distant relative who'd been knocked off her chair by the current of a lightning strike that had passed through the phone line as she chatted away. What bothered him most, he supposed as his attention drifted from his phone conversation toward the sheet lightning lifting the early day's gray, was that there was nothing in the story about her getting back up. It sort of gave him the willies, so he tilted the receiver away from his ear to deflect potential lightning bolts.

He had an irate old lumberyard owner on the line, a businessman who'd supplied Hansen Hardware's own lumber side business for years, but whose services now, he'd just been informed by the sheriff's son and current store owner, were no longer needed, and wasn't that a fine howdy-do. The sheriff was about to say something that would sound as silly to himself as it would to his caller, something about needing to let the next generation make its own decisions and its own mistakes, when his eyes were drawn to the slightest of motions from across the room.

"Hold on a minute, Roy," Sheriff Hansen interrupted his caller. Ten feet directly in front of him the doorknob had begun to slowly, silently rotate. The stealth of the knob's turn circled the sheriff's curiosity into alarm until the small, sharp click of the door's unlatching brought him bolt upright in his chair. The voice near his ear asking, "You still there, Art?" was now faint behind the drum of his heartbeat as the door began to inch open.

"I'll call you back," the sheriff said in a tone between a growl and a whisper, but did not lower the receiver he held in his left hand. A hiss from without stopped the door's progress and brought the sheriff's right hand to his belt as the room suddenly vacuumed into still deeper silence. Sheriff Hansen slowly released the breath he'd been holding as he realized that what he had registered was the ceasing of muffled voices from within the storeroom to his right. Seconds later his secretary stepped through the doorway from the storeroom, a list held in her hand as if it were someone else's used Kleenex, to find her boss staring at the exterior door, which was once more creeping open. The sheriff's posture brought Lila's own stare around to see first an elbow, then a shoulder, then the profile of Agent Heyerdahl backing around the door he'd been nudging open with his butt. His glasses were blurred by raindrops and his shirt stuck to his shoulders. In his arms he held a cardboard box on top of which balanced two large plastic cups of coffee. A small stain steamed against his chest, coffee high.

Heyerdahl paused when he cleared the door to find both the sheriff and his secretary in positions of waiting, the sheriff with phone receiver to his ear in one hand, his other hand resting on what appeared to be an empty holster.

Sheriff Hansen cleared his throat and spoke into the hum of the disconnected line: "Yes, yes, that will be fine. 'Bye, then." He forced a calm smile toward Heyerdahl.

"I see you've found Rosie's."

"Homemade cinnamon rolls." Heyerdahl looked down in appreciation at either the box in his hands or his belly. "I can't resist. There's plenty here if you'd like some."

"Maybe later."

"Lila?"

The older woman shook her head and held up her list as if there were something on the sheet of paper that forbade cinnamon rolls. Heyerdahl recognized Madsen's small, neat, square handwriting, and nodded in sympathy. He was impressed with his partner's efficiency and agreed completely that many of the rather tedious phone calls and requests for records be delegated to the sheriff and his small staff. He also knew that just a few questions regarding the photographs of babies in a plastic cube paperweight on the secretary's desk, or even a comment or two shared about the weather, would have left Lila eager to please. Instead, she'd clearly been put off by Madsen's brusque approach. His young partner

probably considered her own demeanor to be professional, but part of this job, she would soon learn, consisted of putting others at ease. And if he didn't miss his
guess, Lila was privy to most of this small town's gossip.

Heyerdahl raised his eyebrows in question, and Lila
replied with a head shrug toward the storeroom behind
her as she reached back to open the door for the laden
agent. As Heyerdahl stepped through, he heard the
sheriff address his secretary.

"Well, let's see what's on that list today, Lila."

The small, windowless room Heyerdahl entered was
lined with metal shelves that held manuals, newspapers,
magazines, clothing, fire extinguishers, oxygen tanks,
first aid supplies, ammunition, and several neatly labeled
boxes that gave the space a sense of controlled clutter. A
brand-new conference table filled the remaining space in
the center of the room, so that the two new chairs, one of
which now held Agent Madsen, could be pushed no more
than a foot from the table. The agents had made the
sheriff's office their center of operations, although the
limited facilities made frequent trips to the Fargo police
station a necessity. So far, contact with the home office in
Bismarck could be handled by telephone and fax.

Heyerdahl moved aside some of the folders Madsen
had spread across the table and set his breakfast down.
The younger agent reached over to move the coffees farther away from the notebook computer she was studying.

"Have you been jogging?"

Madsen looked up at her partner, saw that he was
joking, then looked down at her outfit to see if she could
find the occasion for his jest. She wore a neatly pressed
beige washable silk shirt, beige linen slacks lined with
silk to keep them from wrinkling, and a woven belt that
matched her woven leather shoes. Her costume jewelry

was simple, yet tasteful. She had been determined not to let her partner's relaxed sense of style influence her own dress, and she knew this morning as she studied the full-length mirror that she passed muster as both professional and fashionable.

Or did she? Madsen furrowed her brow, remembering her decision not to add the matching cropped jacket in anticipation of the afternoon's heat. If she were starting her career as a state agent somewhere with more high-profile investigative activity and thus more prestige, would she be making different choices? She looked back up at Heyerdahl, who was studying her with a smile.

"Why?"

Heyerdahl tapped his forehead, and Madsen reached up to touch the lace handkerchief she'd forgotten was tied around her head.

"Oh, this." She pulled the headband off, setting free curls that immediately tumbled into her eyes. "I have given up on finding someone in Bismarck who can cut my hair, so I'm letting it grow out. In the meantime, it's driving me crazy, so . . ." She stopped and lifted the handkerchief.

"And when it gets longer will you put it in a snood?"

"A what?"

"Never mind. How's it coming?" Heyerdahl asked as he opened the box to offer her a roll.

Madsen gave her partner a quizzical stare. She hadn't worked with him long enough to recognize his humor, so she didn't know if he was teasing or if he really thought she would eat one of those things. She shook her head no, but accepted the coffee with a "Thanks . . . I think," then began to point to various piles in front of her as she spoke.

"Jack Carlson's business affairs, though pretty shaky, were unremarkable. He carried some heavy bank notes, but that's not unusual for farmers in the area, owed on some cattle he'd picked up this spring, was behind on payments to the local implement dealer, but only by a couple of months, and the manager there says that's not unusual. There's a lien on one hundred sixty acres, but—"

"But we've ruled out suicide," Heyerdahl said, nudging Madsen forward.

"I've been able to get a look at the county register of deeds, property tax records, insurance information. I've talked to local businessmen and bankers, and there's not much respect, but nothing really amiss."

"And . . ."

"Ivor Thorson's statement checks out. Carlson's death hasn't raised the old man's opinion of his neighbor." Madsen changed her accent to mimic the old man's. " 'Hees yust a bad one, that Carlson,' but not only does Thorson's wife say he was snoring next to her the night of the nineteenth, just as he has been for the past forty-five years . . . Well, not exactly . . ." Madsen hesitated.

"Not exactly?"

"No, the snoring seems to have gotten much worse since he retired from farming some years back."

"I see." Heyerdahl smiled. "Well, we'll certainly have to remember that. There was something else?"

"Thorson's prints were quite specifically on the stock and the barrel of the murder weapon only."

"As we expected. What about Carlson's social activities?"

"I haven't had a chance to study the phone records yet, but his credit card bills are a bit unusual."

"How?"

"Well, in the first place, all the other bills are still under Mr. and Mrs. Jack Carlson, but there's also an American Express account that he's had for years under his name only."

"A corporate card?" Heyerdahl asked.

"No, and I've just started going through the records, but the bulk of the charges are for motels." Madsen hesitated, then added, "And not for places that far from home—Grand Forks, Mayville, Fargo, Cooperstown, Crookston—not places a person couldn't drive home from."

"Some professional obligation, perhaps? Something to do, say, with the Soybean Association or the Cattlemen's Association?"

"No, Rod and Gun Club and the American Legion, that's all."

"Do the overnight stays continue after his wife's death?"

"Yes."

"Any pattern?"

"Not yet, but I have a feeling that there's something here."

"Did you get Mavis Holmstead's phone records?"

Madsen tapped a separate pile.

"And?"

"And I haven't looked at them yet," Madsen answered, then quickly took the offensive with a question of her own: "What about the daughter?"

"Nothing." Heyerdahl moved a half step back from the table where he'd been leaning with elbows locked as he looked at the papers Madsen had spread before him. "And it's past time to change the way we're handling that. Nothing against the Minnesota Bureau of Criminal Apprehension, mind you, but finding Jackie Carlson doesn't seem to be a top priority for them." He looked at the boxes stacked on the shelves in front of him as he absentmindedly patted his belly.

"Let me see Carlson's credit card bills and phone records. I'll correlate the trips with phone calls made from his house, see if I come up with something. Why don't you take a trip back to your old stomping grounds?"

"The Cities?"

Heyerdahl nodded. "Jackie Carlson has been missing for almost two weeks. Her father's been dead for eleven days. A murdered father and a missing daughter, and we're going to look pretty silly if we don't find her soon. See what the BCA agents have been doing, then do it better, but let's not ruffle any feathers."

14

IT WAS ONE OF THOSE SLOW, EASY, ALL-DAY RAINS THAT wash the prairie with the sighs of hundreds of farmers. Bedroom doors in farmhouses across the county closed as couples made love to the patter of rain against the window in the near background, and the chatter of children farther away, downstairs enjoying the novelty of being inside on a summer morning. For Glenn and Peggy, making love this morning seemed like a continuation of their lovemaking the night before. As usual, they'd spent the night huddled together in the middle of the bed (it was his turn to spoon her), so when Peggy woke, she really couldn't tell what she noticed first, the sound of rain or the feel of Glenn curling into her, his hand sliding up her side to feel the heft of her breast. She welcomed both equally.

Married for fifteen years, with two daughters, Glenn and Peggy had what others called a "good marriage," and they believed that to be the truth. Glenn frequently acknowledged their good luck in finding each other, and Peggy allowed Glenn this theory of luck while quietly but persistently teaching him to share in the emotional work of keeping their marriage from slipping into tedium. Peggy knew Glenn would probably walk through fire for her, as long as the word "work" wasn't mentioned. He was a man who could, and usually did, labor strenuously from sunup to sundown, to be happily bone-tired at the end of the day, simply because he did not associate that dreaded word with what he did. But he could just as easily be mulishly stubborn when the physical or mental requirements involved something he did not enjoy. So as Peggy encouraged him to listen to her, really listen, without formulating responses while she was speaking; when she helped him to see that her tears weren't to be met with immediate assurances hastily spoken in the hopes that she would stop making him uncomfortable; when she created an emotional space within which his own rare tears were safe; when, in short, she helped him to join in on the emotional work of their marriage, he didn't think of it in those terms. Glenn was more likely to put it this way: as long as they really didn't mean it on those seldom occasions when they said "fuck you" to each other, they were okay.

Both believed implicitly that good sex was an integral part of a good marriage, so both worried about how the intervals between lovemaking increased as the years passed. They made promises to take on fewer commit-

ments, to try to worry less about their future and the
future of the girls, and to find more time just to relax
with each other. And both found themselves, more often
than they cared to admit, exhausted by the time they
reached bed, silently grateful for their spouse's fatigue,
and satisfied by the reassuring hand-on-thigh as they fell
asleep. Thus, making love the morning after making love
the night before reminded them both of earlier years
together, years before children, years when the choice
between sleep and sex was no choice at all. It was going
to be a good day.

A day to go to town for parts—a family joke shared by
most of the area's families. Sometimes going to town to
get parts meant just that: a drive to nearby Rippon or to
Fargo to get a belt for the combine, or blades for the
plow, or hydraulic hose for the sprayer. But sometimes
"going to town for parts" meant picking up the combine
belt and stopping off at The Nestor or Stockyard for a beer
or two or three with the other farmers who were taking
advantage of the wet weather to relax.

But today Glenn and Peggy would go together for
parts, and together they would do some shopping (having
finally agreed to buy Becky a small television for her
room, with the understanding that it would be removed,
pronto, should her grades suffer in the fall), and together
they would meet Isabelle, Glenn's favorite aunt/sister
and senior by only six years, for a drink. Except that
no one had ever had *a* drink with Isabelle. And that was
fine with Glenn, and okay with Peggy; with harvest in
full swing, Glenn had seen little of Isabelle since she
got home.

A little before three P.M., Glenn and Peggy pulled into
the driveway of the apartment house in West Fargo
where Norton and Janice lived, parked the car, and went
in to say hi to whomever was home. Isabelle answered

the door on one knock, windbreaker in hand, talking: "I am dying of boredom here all alone. Please take your aged auntie out for a drink! Oh, Glenn, it's so nice not to have to bend over to say hi for once. I can manage one more time, though, Peggy. Mavis called this morning and said Craig's home, but he was going to spend the day with her. How's he look?"

Isabelle kept a running commentary going as she traded quick hugs and ushered them back out the door before they'd even gotten all the way in.

"Norton and Janice still at work?"

"Yup, I left them a note saying we waited here for a good forty-five minutes just in case someone got home early, and that I didn't know where we were going or when we'd be back."

"You don't seem to be too busy here?" Peggy said.

"Good Lord. I wanted to spend a few days with Janice, but, hell, she works all the time. Two days of crossword puzzles, solitaire, and a dumb novel, and I'm ready to go nuts."

As they drove from West Fargo through South Fargo on Thirteenth Avenue, Isabelle studied the passing housing complexes, condominiums, and shopping centers through her rain-splashed window.

"Fargo is really changing. Most of this was open field last time I was here."

"You haven't been back in a long time."

Neither of these statements was accurate. South Fargo development had been in full swing for years, and Isabelle had been home a little over a year ago for the least amount of time possible for Irene's funeral. Had Glenn forgotten? Isabelle wondered. Or did he, like everyone else in the family, simply not accept that occasion as a homecoming? Was there something in his simple statement that could be interpreted as a reference to her personal life in California, which was so separate from the life she'd known in North Dakota? Was Glenn saying that she was like a stranger to him?

You're paranoid, Isabelle, she thought to herself. The tension behind this reunion is affecting the few brain cells you have left. Glenn may be Mavis's son, but he has never had her rather eerie way of loading up the simplest statements, and of leaving others maddeningly empty. She met Glenn's eyes questioning her silence in the rearview mirror.

"Well, I'm here now," Isabelle said with a shrug, and added softly, "of course." And then, "So, where are we going?"

"There's a fairly new bar called The Fabulous Fifties near here. You'd like the music. I think they're open in the afternoon. And there's a Ground Round down the street with an okay bar. Or we could go somewhere else? What do you want to do?"

"I want to go somewhere where the men wear seed-corn caps and cowboy boots, and the young women wear jeans that are too tight, and the middle-aged women wear jeans that are too tight, and the bartender is a woman with a bad dye job, in a polyester pantsuit, and where it isn't so bright you need sunglasses, or so loud you can't hear each other. And where the only neon sign is a Miller's sign in the front window."

"Bub's," Glenn said as he took the left that headed them downtown. It had been a college haunt, a nonde-script bar small enough to always feel full, where an older classmate's ID was always welcome as proof of age.

The three ran together from the car to the door, passing from the grayness of the rainy day into the artificial dark of the bar. Here, all at once, was that assault of dismal sensations that signaled the waste of daylight hours in a neighborhood bar: the smell of stale cigarette smoke, the feel of shoes sticking to a wood floor that can never be clean, the sight of red vinyl chairs and benches, the sound of an AM radio station in the background. Isabelle felt her mood brighten immediately.

"So Peggy, why aren't you home whipping up some Rice Krispies Jell-O or a casserole with crushed corn-flakes on top for the picnic, then?" Isabelle asked, mocking the singularly midwestern culinary insistence on incorporating breakfast cereal into all meals.

Peggy redirected the banter. "Because anything that's to be eaten outside the house needs to be finished five minutes before we walk out the door or else *all* the children at my house make short work of it." She reached over and patted Glenn's stomach, and then rested her hand on his thigh.

"That's true," Glenn agreed. "Right now the girls are probably perched on the freezer in the basement eating frozen cookies. That is, if there's room in the freezer for anything other than bags of rolled-up clothes waiting to be ironed." These were three-generation jokes. Isabelle had grown up in the same house as Glenn and Glenn's daughters, and all of them were notorious frozen cookie filchers, and even Peggy had come to appreciate Mavis's laundry day strategy of rolling up damp clothes and storing them in plastic bags in the large compartment freezer toward the day when there was time for ironing.

It was small talk and it was necessary. The first pitcher of beer would go quickly as they joked about a front-page story in the *Fargo Forum* about a Northwest Airlines pilot who had been grounded after it was discovered that he'd had at least seventeen rum and Cokes and not much sleep the night before flying from Fargo to the Twin Cities. But soon Glenn and Peggy were talking about Becky and Janie, their school, their sports, their friends; Peggy's work as principal of Rippon's grade school; and this year's crops, because they looked good so far. On bad years, the conversation would be limited to a hopeful "We think we'll be okay."

Isabelle felt as if she were in a dark cocoon, safe, with moods good and about to get better. She excused herself to go to the bathroom, and when she returned, by way of the attached liquor store where she bought a pack of Winstons, there was another full pitcher of beer on the table.

Glenn smiled sheepishly as he took a cigarette. Peggy took one, too, her signal that she was going to make no complaints this afternoon. It would be her only cigarette, and she would drink much less and more slowly than the other two. She knew that Glenn knew just how rotten he would feel tomorrow, and that he probably wouldn't smoke again for another year. She also knew how much he enjoyed having his a-little-bit-too-wild aunt all to himself. Despite Isabelle's and Glenn's closeness in age, the hierarchical division between them was distinct, as it was between all the sisters and all their children. Thus, the opportunity to be friend to friend, as opposed to nephew to aunt, was to be savored.

During the second pitcher of beer, Peggy asked Isabelle about Linda. What she actually said was an uncharacteristically muddled "How are you and . . . Linda doing? Uh, I mean, well . . ." and then finished quickly with a shrug and "So how's it going, then?"

That, however, was not the kind of question likely to get an elaborate response from Isabelle. The choices as she saw them were "okay," "been better," or "been worse." She and Linda had talked at some length about whether it would be a good idea for Linda to come home with her, finally. Actually, Linda presented this suggestion, noting that they had been together for almost nine years, that the family all "knew about" the two of them, that Izzy had often admitted to feeling alone without Linda when she was back in North Dakota, as well as angry at her family because they didn't seem to recognize her relationship. And, added Linda, they never would as long as Isabelle herself encouraged this image of herself as a single woman.

Isabelle had responded sincerely about how wonderful, of course, it would be to have Linda with her, but this probably wasn't a good time, with "Mavis's crisis and all," as she was calling it. And besides, maybe her family wasn't ready for their relationship yet.

To which Linda was less patient in pointing out that she couldn't remember when someone in Isabelle's family had not been in some type of crisis (although this certainly did look like a hard one to top); that if Isabelle were less hooked in to her siblings' opinions, then what they thought of her lifestyle wouldn't be such a big deal, but since Isabelle *was* so close to them all, it was probably time for her to do some work changing the way they thought; and that since Isabelle was forty-six years old and her oldest sister was somewhere around sixty, if she waited much longer, everybody would be dead.

Somewhere in all this, Isabelle had heard her family insulted and decided to solve the situation by escalating the discussion into a fight. With all this in mind she answered Peggy with "Fine. Real good. Yeah, uh-huh."

Two pitchers of beer allowed Glenn and Peggy to break into a chorus of their own "Yeah, uh-huhs." They had always thought that particular evasion or negation was Mavis's alone. But here evidently was another Schmidt who spoke the same protective language.

"It's a shame Reagan and Bush didn't speak Mavisese during the Iran-Contra scandal," Glenn said, laughing. "Then instead of hearing over and over again, 'I don't remember,' we could have heard 'Yeah, uh-huh, yeah, uh-huh.' They would have both sounded so much more intelligent."

"Why, Glenn! How dare you speak so blasphemously about Republicans? Surely Mavis doesn't allow that?"

Peggy laughed. "Even Republicans who get elected President are fair game."

"Especially when their first order of business is usually screw the farmer." Glenn's tone was serious for a moment. "Bush may be smarter, but he's no more help."

"I heard an interview with Reagan the other day where he was asked what he thought of Lithuania. He replied that he thought it was fine and was down to two hundred milligrams a day." Isabelle laughed.

Glenn leaned forward for his turn to tell a joke. "Isabelle, did you hear about the Norwegian who moved from North Dakota to California and the mean IQ of both states went up?" He laughed at his own joke and added, "Tell that one to Norton. Norwegian jokes really piss him off."

"Glenn, why would a Californian tell that joke?" Isabelle asked.

"Okay, say a Norwegian moved from North Dakota to Texas."

"Who do you know from Texas?"

"Nobody."

"Then it's not funny."

They were all laughing now, and Isabelle took the lead telling stories of things that had happened to her on the trip home, including the man who sat next to her on the airplane who, after finishing his dinner, rolled up his napkin, dipped it in catsup, and ate it. Stories. Telling stories. It's what these people did. It's how they talked.

"Okay, how about this." Glenn was determined to tell a good joke, and went through his entire repertoire of Ole and Lena jokes, retelling the Norwegian jokes that North Dakotans, many of whom are at least partly Norwegian, share.

As the third pitcher arrived, Glenn had, with Peggy's prompting, wound down on the jokes.

"Sweetheart, have you ever heard a joke that wasn't a Norwegian joke?" Peggy asked. "Or rather, remembered one?"

"Yup. At the elevator yesterday Monty Jakes told one. Let's see. I remember the punch line, but how'd it start?" It wasn't hard to believe that he was losing concentration, the hat advertising a local implement dealer pushed far back on his forehead, his face beginning to flush. "Oh, yeah, that's it." He stopped and looked pleased with himself.

Peggy and Isabelle began to laugh together.

"What?" they said in unison. "What's the joke?" Peggy prompted again.

"Oh! Well, Rock Hudson walks into a gas station and—" Glenn stopped suddenly and frowned at Peggy, who was directing her best principal's gaze toward him.

"What?"

"Maybe you'd like to select a different joke, Glenn."

"No, this is good. I'll get it right. Rock Hudson *drives* into this gas station, and says to the attendant . . . Peggy, for Christ's sake! That's my leg!"

"What makes you think that's Peggy kicking you?" Isabelle asked, but was still smiling.

"Oh Christ, Isabelle. I'm sorry. That was stupid of me."

Isabelle put her hand on his arm as he reached for his glass, forcing him to look at her as she spoke. "Not stupid because you were going to tell that joke to me. Not stupid because you were going to tell that joke to a gay person. But stupid because you were going to tell the joke at all, whatever it was. It's just not funny. Shouldn't be, to anyone." Isabelle was uncomfortable chastising Glenn. Her role among the sisters was that of the any-thing-goes good-time Charlie. But Glenn was too smart not to be any smarter than that.

"Have you lost many friends?" Peggy quietly asked. She was protective enough of Glenn to take the heat off him, but wise enough not to change the subject.

"Surprisingly few, considering our community and how close we are to San Francisco," Isabelle answered, now comfortably slipping into the first-person plural that set Linda down beside her. "We've known two young men who have died. An E.R. nurse with me and a young man I played tennis with when I first moved to Green-view. We have friends who are living with AIDS. Linda has a coworker, a young woman, who was just recently diagnosed. And I see more cases in the hospital, of course. But Greenview isn't really that large."

Glenn nudged Isabelle. "Do you realize you actually mentioned Linda's name?"

Finally relaxed by many beers, Isabelle began to talk about Linda and her work as an acquisitions editor for a small publishing house, and how really good at it she was. As she talked she realized how much she longed to have Linda make up a fourth at this table. "And we're fine. Nine years. Looks like it might work, although it really is a lot of work."

"That's the truth." Peggy looked at Glenn. They'd been a little uneasy as Isabelle talked about her life with Linda. It still seemed just too unreal to have a lesbian in the family. Peggy had done some work toward educating herself about homosexuality, but Glenn, despite a surplus of brains and goodwill, was inclined to be intellectually and emotionally lazy. If something wasn't in his experi-ence, it simply didn't exist. Isabelle had often used that definition to describe the entire North Dakota culture, but only after a preface covering the honesty, loyalty, community, and general superiority of North Dakotans.

Whereas the first two pitchers of beer had been drunk in the midst of laughter, the third was stripping away layers of self-protection and baring more serious concerns, even if the conversation frequently skidded off track as Glenn and Isabelle swerved and swooped through topics. When that pitcher was empty, Glenn announced that he *had* to eat soon. Where should they go? Isabelle, as expected, suggested that whenever you had to make a decision, you should have a drink and think about it.

Peggy was directing a meaningful look at Glenn which he was steadfastly ignoring. Isabelle had a reputation for refusing food and choosing to go on drinking once started. But Glenn was all Isabelle's today, and grinning, hollered, "Okay, summon the wench."

Peggy and Isabelle exchanged groans.

"It's a joke!" Glenn said.

"Glenn, don't tell jokes." Isabelle shook her head. "You're terrible. No good. Inappropriate. Not funny." But she was laughing. "Do you get it?"

"Yeah, uh-huh."

Isabelle had, as a matter of fact, taken quite a notice of the waitress, who, in return, hadn't noticed Isabelle at all, and never would. This is the problem with drinking, Isabelle thought. Makes you blur distinctions.

"Okay, one more beer apiece. Not a pitcher. Then we eat. Agreed?" Peggy had taken charge, just as Glenn and Isabelle had expected. "I'll get the waitress on my way to the can."

Isabelle and Glenn were silent for a minute after Peggy left the table. Then Isabelle finally brought up the subject they had all avoided, but which was clearly why they were together.

"Glenn—what's going on with Mavis? Did she do it?

Do you know? Has she, what's the word I'm looking for—condescended to talk to anyone other than her lawyer? What's happening, for Christ's sake?"

"I don't know, Izzy. I swear I don't know. But Christ Almighty it's a mess. And Mom just doesn't seem to have much to say on the subject, and she doesn't seem too concerned. She's got that I-can't-be-bothered attitude. Like . . . did we ever tell you about the time Elmer stopped her for speeding and—"

"Elmer is still around?"

"He retired just last year. Anyway, Elmer stops Mom for speeding one day. She's doing her usual sixty-five to seventy miles per hour down the gravel road—"

"I never understood how Mavis justified driving that fast on gravel. You know how she used to get after us about speeding."

"She says she never goes any faster than she knows she can control."

"But the rest of us would be out of control at those speeds."

"I think that's the general idea."

"So . . . ?"

"So what?"

"So what happened . . . with Elmer?" Isabelle prodded.

"Oh! This is great. So Mom's speeding down the road, hell-bent for leather, and Elmer pulls her over just before she hits the blacktop. Mom stops, rolls down her window, and says, 'Not now, Elmer, I'm already late,' and takes off, leaving Elmer standing there with his mouth open."

"But Glenn, how could she have done it?"

"Oh, Elmer didn't mind so much, I guess. And I suppose she stopped in at the station on her way home to get a ticket."

"No. I mean how could she have done *it*? Mavis

murder? Mavis? The pillar of the community? Mavis the Perfect?"

Glenn bristled a bit. "She's human too, you know. I mean, I can't believe she'd kill somebody, but it's not fair of everybody, of all of you, to think she's perfect all the time, you know. That's like she doesn't have feelings like everybody else or something. You know. She does."

"Yeah, yeah. But hasn't she talked to you or Craig at all? I get this totally unbelievable phone call from Janice that Jack has been killed. I think, good, the son of a bitch. And then she says that Mavis is saying that *she* did it, and she's so hysterical that I can't tell what's what."

"I don't think she's ever been hysterical."

"She was hysterical on the phone."

"Mom was hysterical?"

"No, dummy. Janice. All she could say was Jack's dead and Mavis says she's responsible. That much I can believe. Mavis is nothing if not responsible. So I called Maxine because I figured if anyone can talk to Mavis it's Maxine."

"And?"

"And nothing. Maxine had already talked to Mavis, and she still didn't know anything."

"Oh, she knows something."

"Maxine?"

"No, Mom."

Isabelle snorted. "I mean Maxine. Maxine said that somehow Mavis had made her feel like she was prying into Mavis's personal life. Said she got off the phone feeling silly."

"I can't imagine Mom ever feeling silly."

"*Maxine* got off the phone feeling silly. And then thought, wait a minute, my sister calls to tell me that she's murdered her brother-in-law, and I get off the phone feeling like I've done something wrong. Mavis is a wonder."

"Yeah, she's a wonder. But it's not funny. Those two investigators have been out talking to her a couple of times, and to me, and to everybody, and well, who the hell knows who. And Mom doesn't say much of anything. We're all waiting, but we don't know what for. Hell, on TV she'd be in jail or something, or, I don't know. I don't know what's going on. And when we ask if she killed Jack, she says, 'Yeah, uh-huh,' and changes the subject. 'Yeah, uh-huh.' That's what you say if someone asks if you ate the last piece of fucking pie! Not if you've knocked off your lying, cheating, son of a bitch of a brother-in-law."

Peggy had returned to the table during this exchange and was sitting silently, looking down at her cup. With Glenn and Isabelle as designated drinkers, she'd been sipping coffee for the past hour. At the end of Glenn's last speech, she had made the family "you're talking too loudly" motion, a hand lifted and floated downward, as if to soothe the words themselves into coming out more softly. Glenn paid no attention.

"The son of a bitch was as responsible for Irene's death as if he'd shot her. I'm glad he's dead." Glenn's face was beet-red and his words were slurring.

"I never thought anything could happen to her. She was always the one who made it smooth when I fucked up. It's been a year, and every day I still picture her trapped in a burning car while that drunk, Jack, crawls out with scratches. I just can't believe she's gone. She was so ... so, well, shit, just so good." Isabelle was about to cry, and Glenn, too, was getting teary-eyed.

This is the damnedest family, Peggy thought. They steadfastly refuse to show tears or pain, unless they're drunk. Knowing how horrified these two would be to find

themselves crying in Bub's Pub, Peggy took hold of the
conversation and steered it away from Irene.

"To tell the truth, we don't know much more than the
papers tell us, which isn't much, because it seems too
simple. On that Thursday night, Jack was drinking at the
Too High Bar in Brickton. He'd taken a couple head of
feeder cattle to market, and although he probably didn't
make much of a profit with those sorry animals, he had
money in his pocket and was buying people drinks,
which, I imagine, is the only way he could get people to
talk to him. Irene was real popular there and he never had
been, especially not, I guess, after the accident. I guess he
was pretty drunk and was crying on people's shoulders
about what a rough life he'd had, etcetera. You know
how Jack can be."

"Asshole." Glenn and Isabelle spoke simultaneously,
then, startled by their timing, lifted and clicked glasses.

"Yes, well, it seems that he finally managed to irritate
some potato farmer to the point where there was an argument and then almost a fight, but Jack was so drunk that
the bartender and a couple of guys tossed him out. That
was about midnight. Sometime late the next morning old
Ivor Thorson, a neighbor of Jack and Irene's, was driving
by and saw Jack's pickup a couple of miles from the
farm, there in the middle of the road. He was just going
to drive by, figuring that's all the farther Jack had gotten
before passing out. But when he slowed down to get
around the pickup, he noticed a rifle laying on the road
by the ditch. So he gets out and picks up the gun and goes
around to tap on Jack's window to wake him up. I guess
up to this point he didn't think anything was too odd. He
just figured that fool Jack had been up to some nonsense,
probably shooting at a rabbit caught in the headlights and
then forgetting the gun before he passed out. But then
this Thorson gets to the window and sees—sees all that

blood, I guess. Goes to the other side, starts to open the door, changes his mind, and goes for the cops.

"That's Friday morning. Friday afternoon we get a call from someone from the Wash County Sheriff's Department doing his darnedest to find someone who cares that Jack is dead. Jack's brother—you remember Ted, he was at Jack and Irene's wedding—well, he's supposedly a ranch hand somewhere in Montana. No one's located him yet. Or Jackie . . . but you know that part of the story. Just Blair, who'd been out drinking beer with friends till the wee hours." Peggy stopped, looking for but not finding the right words. "He's only eighteen years old.

"Well, anyway, the upshot of this call is that they're looking for *somebody*, some relative, to start taking charge of arrangements once all their—whatever it is they do with . . . murdered people, is done. Glenn was in the field, and I knew Jack didn't have family, really, and I knew Mavis would be at Janice's so I told them to call there.

"Evidently they did. Sent someone from the Fargo police to ask all the questions you see them ask on TV, I guess. Did Mavis or Janice know if Jack had any enemies? When had anyone in the family talked to him last? After all the questions, Mavis says they're supposed to give the body to a local undertaker who should call Mavis, and she'll pay for the burial and all. Isn't that rich? So on Saturday afternoon Mavis comes down to our place and sends the kids outside. They loved that, you can imagine. And says she'll be going to the police station in Fargo on Monday, because she wants to tell them she killed Jack. We thought she'd lost her mind, except, you know, she's Mavis. She's not going to lose her mind."

"Could she have done it?" Isabelle asked.

" 'Course not," from Glenn.

"I mean, logistically," Isabelle said, unintentionally adding a few syllables to the word. "Is there some reason why the police would believe her? Could she have gotten up to Brickton and back without being missed? And he was shot, right? They have tests for prints and gunpowder burns or whatever, don't they?"

"I don' know. S'pose. Who knows? We'd been up to Mom's for supper that Thursday night. Looking back, I can't remember anything different, 'cept that she seemed really tired, but she's been tired a lot lately, and kinda pale. Says she just needs to take iron pills and forgets. She'd called earlier and said she had a roast in the oven and did we want to come up. We ate supper, drank coffee, talked about this and that, watched some sitcom, and went home—"

"About nine-thirty," Peggy finished.

"She'd said she was going into Fargo the next day, Friday, to run some errands, and if she had time, stop over t'see Janice after she got home from work."

Peggy took over, retracing some ground. "Friday night we called Mavis just to touch base and see if she knew any more. She told us about talking with the police at Janice's, but didn't say much else. Then Saturday she drops this bombshell. Tells us that she's going to 'give herself up.' She actually said that. Mavis used a cliché."

"But she's not in jail," Isabelle said, crunching up the now-empty cigarette pack, then lighting the last cigarette. "How come? If they think she done did murder?"

"That seemed odd to us, too. It's like they don't believe her, either, but you just don't expect Mavis to lie. They took a set of her fingerprints. We know that much. And then Mavis told them—isn't this right, Glenn?—that she was wearing gloves that night. Gloves? In the middle of summer? Either way, she . . . wait." Peggy held up a hand. "Glenn, you're being paged. Shall I get it?"

"Nope, I think I can still rec'nize a phone." Glenn ambled toward the bar.

"So now what?" Isabelle turned to Peggy.

Peggy returned Isabelle's question with a shrug. And then added, "But something's got to happen. He's dead, for sure. Murdered, for sure. And Mavis says she did it. Something's got to happen, and soon, I would imagine."

"And in the meantime Mavis is planning a family reunion picnic for Sunday. At your place. And what's better, we'll all be there." Isabelle snorted. "They should lock us all up. In padded cells."

Glenn was back at the table with a grin. "That was Judy. She just knew we were out having fun and couldn't stand not being part of it. So she and Maxine came in to Janice's. We're supposed to get our butts over there. Janice has supper."

"How'd they know we were here?" Isabelle asked.

"Process of elimination. They've evidently called about five other places. I've been here with Norton before."

"Judy's just afraid we're talking about her. Well, let's go, then." Isabelle was digging in her purse and leaving way too much money for the waitress. "Peggy, buy me a pack of Winstons while I go to the bathroom. Good Lord, Glenn, why do you get so short when you drink?"

"Don't know. Something happens to my knees."

"Well, you're too short to drive." Peggy smiled as she opened the door for one drunk and watched the other stop to talk to some strangers on the way to the bathroom.

15

WHEN PEGGY, GLENN, AND ISABELLE ROLLED INTO Janice's, Glenn and Isabelle were still snorting over Isabelle's departure from Bub's. Having forgotten what Glenn and Peggy's car looked like, she'd stepped into the closest vehicle, looked at the startled older man behind the wheel, and said something to the effect of, "Christ, Glenn, you look terrible." That led to Isabelle's story about how a few summers back she and two friends from the E.R. had gone to a Giants game, drank all day and most of the night. While she was gone, Linda and a couple of landscaping friends had planted a small hedge beside the walkway, causing Isabelle to exclaim as she and her friends drove into the yard late that night, "Jesus, how long have we been gone?"

By the time they reached Janice's door, the others were well aware of the trio's approach, as well as of which story was being told, for it had been told a few times before. Inside the apartment, Janice, Norton, Maxine, and Judy were playing whist and having drinks. A tray of ham sandwiches on homemade buns sat on the counter.

"Look at all the sissies!" Isabelle yelled as she romped in the door. Glenn went for the sandwiches and Peggy stood back and smiled as Glenn and Isabelle coursed once again through their story about Isabelle's mistake at

Bub's. Already, in this first retelling, the story's delivery had become quite an elaborate affair.

Judy and Isabelle were the only two sisters present who had yet to greet each other this visit. A personal history fraught with years of meanness and misunderstanding made any greeting an embarrassment. The obligatory hug was brief; there were no missed kisses.

"You look like you've been having fun," Judy said.

"Sure, we've been playing bar games. You know, name the seven dwarves, Santa's reindeer, the muses, Judy's husbands, things like that."

"Well, you're pretty drunk. Some things never change."

"Couldn't find my butt with both hands," Isabelle agreed.

"You've had your hands full, looks like." Maxine smiled at Peggy. "Have these two been behaving badly?"

"Perfectly appropriately for Bub's, I guess. Isabelle, eat some of these sandwiches."

"In a minute. I have to pee so bad my eyeteeth are singing 'Anchors Aweigh.' "

"Glenn, play my hand while I refill some drinks." This from Norton, who was ignoring his wife's look, which quite openly asked him not to refill his own. "Maxine?"

"Not yet."

"Judy? Another scotch and soda? Peggy? Glenn?"

Both Peggy and Glenn declined as they played Norton's hand together, Glenn sitting, Peggy leaning behind with her arms wrapped around his neck.

"Isabelle," Norton called, "what can I get you to drink?"

"I'm so full of beer," Isabelle said, coming around the corner zipping up her jeans, "I just couldn't take another swallow. So how about something to sip. Got any Jack Daniel's?"

"J.D. coming up."

"Where's Mavis?" Isabelle asked, directing the question to Maxine.

"Home. Says she's beat. Craig's there, you know," Maxine answered without looking up. "Sweetheart, play your seven of hearts." She smiled at Glenn, who had the lead to her right but was hesitating.

"What makes you think I have the seven of hearts?" Glenn was smiling back.

If someone were bluffing here, it was likely to be Glenn. All the sisters were excellent whist players, with the possible exception of Judy, who was just very good because she didn't quite concentrate well enough to talk, trade jokes, and count cards at the same time.

"Of course you have the seven. There are only two hearts out. Your seven and one more. Judy and Janice are sloughing, so you know who has the other one, but you don't know what it is, do you?"

"Maxine, you are as pompous as my mother at whist, but I think you're just taking advantage of my weakened condition. Okay, what do you have?" Glenn asked, laying down a seven of hearts.

"I have an eight," slapping it down and tapping it with her index finger, "and the rest are mine."

"Peggy, take my hand before I lose the whole shooting match for Norton and Judy." Glenn got up and walked into the connecting living room, switched on the TV, and lay on the couch.

Peggy smiled. "We've lost him. Whose deal?"

"Mine," Janice said. "And the seven dwarves are Happy, Dopey, Doc, Sleepy, Bashful, Grumpy, and Sneezy. Mavis gave Tina and Jimmy a little record player with that record and storybook for Christmas about a thousand years ago and they drove me nuts with it."

"Well, there's Sleepy on the couch." Isabelle walked in from the kitchen, where she'd been talking with Norton, pointing to Glenn, who was already snoring. "And we've got our own Doc," she said, laying her hand on Maxine's shoulder. "Speaking of Dopey, Judy, I hear you trashed your car on the way here."

"Well, you heard wrong, then," Judy replied, glaring across the table at Peggy, who responded with a wide-eyed shake of the head and a shrug. "It simply over-heated in this godforsaken weather. That's all. And I met a very nice man who helped me out."

"Okay, I was wrong. I should have said Grumpy. Was this man single by any chance?"

"Hmm."

"Uh-oh, number five coming up."

"At least I can get a man."

"Play your cards, Judy," Maxine urged. "We can have arm wrestling and fistfights later."

Isabelle, however, was not about to let the comment lie. "Getting a man to drop his trousers just may be the easiest thing to do in the world. What you haven't figured out is how to keep them around after they zip up."

"Isn't it nice to have us all here together again," Janice intervened. "I wish Irene were here to somehow make you two behave. Judy, it's still your turn. To play a card," she hastily added.

"So much for the dwarves," Isabelle said, Irene's ghostly introduction in the room enough to make her back down, at least temporarily. "The muses are a little harder. Unless, of course, Dr. Douglas here knows them?" eyes arched toward Maxine.

"Get ready to be impressed, then. My profession, as you have pointed out many times, has made me a fount of useless information: Clio, Calliope, Urania, Erato, Melpomene, Euterpe . . . oh, oh."

"Clytemnestra and Ukelele!" Isabelle threw in.

"Big deal," Judy muttered.

Maxine shook her head at Isabelle, who was ready to pounce.

"Did Mavis give your kids presents every Christmas?" Judy asked Janice. "She didn't ever send mine Christmas presents. Not like she couldn't afford it. That doesn't seem fair. Their feelings could have been hurt."

"Judy . . ." Isabelle was exasperated. "You and your kids lived in fucking Indiana, and saw Mavis every couple of years, at best. Janice's kids spent weekends and summers with Mavis and Frank on the farm. They helped with harvest. They worked in the garden. They're closer. That's all. It's not a matter of keeping score. Do you send Christmas presents to Glenn and Craig?"

"Glenn could use some new underwear," Peggy suggested.

"Family should treat everybody the same. That's what I think. And Mavis has more money."

"That's crap. Different people have different relationships. Besides, I wouldn't be keeping a list if I were you."

"And just what is that supposed to mean?" Judy bristled.

"Well, hasn't Mavis ever helped you? Every time you decided to go to college—before you yourself realized that you are terminally stupid—didn't Mavis make it possible? Who helped you get set up after about a dozen of your divorces? Me, me, me. That's all you think about."

"Oh, fuck you, Isabelle."

"Makes me want to get together more often, you two." Maxine sighed. "Judy, it's your turn. Play your ace. It only takes one trick, you know."

Suddenly it was Janice speaking. "Mavis this and Mavis that. Mavis does this for my kids and that for your kids. Mavis in control. Mavis on a white steed. Mavis in charge. Well, sometimes I just wonder who she thinks put her in charge."

Everyone was silent, staring at Janice, amazed at the venom with which she had spoken. It was as if she had thrown up a huge toad that squatted on the table. The sisters could look away, pick a new topic, but for the rest of the evening it would be hopping around the table, showing its warty butt at every turn of the conversation.

"I think I'll make myself that drink now," Janice said, getting up from the table. "Maxine, do you want another yet?"

"No, in fact I could use a cup of coffee. I'll make a pot."

"The air pot is full."

"Get me a cup, too, please," Isabelle asked Maxine.

Maxine threw the cards in the middle of the table, took off her glasses, and stood. The game was obviously over.

"You know, Mavis could use our support now. Isn't that why we're all here? Isn't that what we should be thinking about? We sit here and drink and laugh and talk, but not a word about what Mavis is going through. And she's not looking all that great, either. She's lost a lot of weight."

"Don't kid yourself, Maxine. Mavis has never needed any of us." Janice was looking into the sink, her voice quiet and angry. She lifted her glass to take a drink, stopped, looked through the doorway at Norton, who, having moved from the table to the easy chair facing the television, was already asleep, his glass empty beside him. With a sigh, at once defeated and stubborn, she emptied her own drink into the sink and said, "I'm going to bed. There's plenty of room to sleep here for anyone staying. Good night."

The room was silent until Judy spoke. "Well, what do you think of that?"

"I think it's time for us to go," Peggy said, moving toward the couch to wake up Glenn.

"Let's do a switch," Isabelle suggested, her head already aching in anticipation of the next day's hangover. "I'll go back with Glenn and Peggy. You two stay here with Janice and Norton."

"We're a step ahead of you, Izzy." Maxine smiled wanly. "Our suitcases are already in the guest room."

Isabelle carelessly restuffed her suitcase and led Peggy and Glenn out the door. Getting into the backseat of the car, she put her head back on the seat. Before getting in on the passenger side, Glenn finished a yawn and asked Peggy over the roof of the car, "What happened? Why was everyone so quiet?"

"You have the damnedest family," Peggy answered. "Let's just go home."

MAVIS

SHE WEARS NAVY-BLUE POLYESTER PANTS WITH A crease, and a white cotton sleeveless blouse, and the kind

of tennis shoes bought at the Federated. The arms
growing out of the sleeves are aging but not infirm, the
skin around the elbows discolored from years of leaning
on kitchen counters. The hands growing out of the arms
show veins and brown spots. Still, they look like a safe
place to put a baby, a hammer, a pie.

She stands alone in the living room looking out the
picture window. It's dark outside, but the living room is
brightly lit. She is looking at a woman in blue polyester
pants and a white cotton blouse. An old woman, it seems.
She brings her hand to her left breast while studying her
face. A deep sigh and she turns.

She walks into her bedroom, hers only for so many
years now. Opens the bottom drawer of the dresser and
pulls out a man's work shirt. She backs to the edge of the
bed, sits, brings the shirt to her face. And breathes.

16

THE ROAR OF THE VACUUM CLEANER MET ISABELLE AS
she opened Mavis's front door the next morning.
Uncanny, she thought, turning to wave at Peggy, who
had just dropped her off and was on her way to Rippon
for a meeting with the school's guidance counselor to

talk about their sex education proposal. Only Mavis could sense a hangover coming down the road in time to start the vacuum cleaner. Thank God at least I'm old enough now to refuse to do the actual vacuuming. I think.

Siblings, children, nieces and nephews grew up knowing they could count on cleaning house the morning after if they were silly enough to debauch while under Mavis's purview. Years ago, when Isabelle was a teenager in Mavis's house, Frank had once murmured to her in passing as he escaped quietly outside, "Just be grateful she doesn't own a jackhammer." Isabelle allowed herself a moment to miss the quiet man they all missed quietly, then stepped into the house. She went immediately to the refrigerator for a Coke, and then headed for the family room couch next to the kitchen. With the one eye she could keep open, Isabelle tracked Mavis's determined and rhythmic approach—two steps forward, a tug at the reluctant canister behind, a series of stabs in a semicircle with the carpet attachment, and then two steps forward. Inexorable, Isabelle found herself repeating over and over to herself. The roaring machine moved closer, closer. Isabelle closed the eye and willed Mavis to stop.

Craig came around the corner, dust rag in hand. "It's my horizontal old auntie. Does Glenn look this bad?" He bent over the back of the couch and they kissed. "Or smell this bad?"

Isabelle groaned. "I didn't actually see him this morning. I've only been up for an hour, and he was already outside. But—" She smiled. "—Peggy left a note for him to vacuum while she was out, seeing as it was too wet to be in the field."

They laughed, and Mavis, noticing that her racket wasn't making Isabelle very contrite, and actually being finished with the floors, shut the machine off, put it away, and joined the others. Coffee cup in hand, she sat in the easy chair and asked, "How long did the party go on last night?"

"At Janice's, not that long, really. But Glenn and I and our chaperone, Peggy, spent a little time at Bub's before we went back to Janice's."

"Bub's!" Craig laughed. "And you got Glenn out before closing time? That, in itself, is pretty amazing."

"Well, he was getting hungry, and then we got the summons from Judy, so we moved on. By the by, Mavis, what's up with Janice?"

"What do you mean?" Mavis's voice was icy and still, and the quizzical half smile she added as she finished did nothing to thaw the tone.

"I don't know. She seems really stressed out. She flew off the handle for no particular reason last night, though I can't remember this morning what it was all about. Is Norton drinking again?"

"I thought that was pretty much under control," Craig threw in when Mavis's response to Isabelle's question was a shrug and raised eyebrows, followed by a heavy sigh.

"Janice doesn't talk about that part of her life with me, and since it's her business, I don't ask."

Isabelle and Craig traded a look that included a smile, even though their expressions didn't change. Mavis's claim to her own privacy was legendary. Although she had shared her life with a troop of siblings, children, nieces and nephews, to the extent that there wasn't a relative in the bunch who couldn't name at least one occasion (usually more) when Mavis had been available, with time, with money, with advice, with love, to help them out, still, the unspoken bottom line was that the time, money, and advice were to be given on Mavis's terms. Only the love was unconditional. As for privacy, everyone deserved it and everyone could demand it;

nonetheless, what everyone knew was that Mavis knew all. Thus, if Mavis didn't know if Norton was drinking again, then it was because Mavis chose not to know.

"Well, whatever it is," Isabelle put in, "she had a burr under her saddle last night."

Craig smiled at his mother as he suggested, "Maybe all of you had taken her away from housecleaning. You know how your sisters just love to vacuum, sometimes more than others."

Mavis didn't change her expression, but her voice held a returned smile as she answered. "A clean house is simply a sign of respect for the guests."

"Does Linda vacuum when you have a hangover, too?" Craig asked Isabelle, and pretended not to notice his mother's back stiffen as she leaned forward for the TV remote control.

"Oh please, no, not *Wheel of Fortune* or *The Price Is Right* or whatever comes on now," Isabelle begged. "That could kill me today."

Mavis put the control down and picked up the newspaper Isabelle had brought in from the mailbox.

"Did you see the headlines?" Mavis asked Isabelle.

"No, why?"

" 'Iraq Invades Kuwait,' " Mavis read, then continued, " 'Tank-led Iraqi troops invaded Kuwait before dawn today, and the Revolutionary Command Council of Iraqi President Saddam Hussein announced the Kuwaiti government had been overthrown.' " Then, spoken over Isabelle's "They what?" and Craig's "Oh, Jesus," Mavis moved on to a front-page news item of greater importance. "The House passed the farm bill limiting commodity subsidies."

Craig and Isabelle waited for Mavis's next comment, until they realized that she was now reading the paper to herself. Isabelle smiled at her nephew and returned the conversation to an earlier topic.

"Linda's behavior modification program is even less subtle than your mother's, if you can imagine." Isabelle winked at Craig. "But for the longest time now she's just ignored my, how shall I put it, occasional lapses. I think she has a new program brewing." Isabelle didn't mention that Linda had started going to Al-Anon meetings, having met with little success in trying to convince Isabelle to try AA or, at least, ACOA meetings. Isabelle was about to relent from her "Not me" to a "Not yet" stance, but that was her own business.

Mavis had put on her tight-lipped, eyebrows-raised look, accompanied by sighs, as she read the paper. Both Craig and Isabelle knew that her expression was as likely to be in response to their topic of conversation as to what she was reading. Being open-minded, Mavis had been known to say, isn't the same as wanting to hear the details.

Craig had longed to speak more frankly with his mother about his life, and last night with everyone else in Fargo, he'd thought he'd have the opportunity. But somehow, despite their obvious pleasure in each other's company, their evening of quiet talk was filled with gaps, lurches of conversation, and questions evident though unasked, and safely unanswered.

Just once had Craig asked about the shooting, saying that he knew she hadn't done it. Mavis's response was ready: what she had done and was about to do was her choice. Someday it may make sense to them all. They would have to wait for that day. Until then, she did not care to discuss it. Don't think about it, she had said. I'm the only one who needs to think about it.

Oh, Craig knew, there were so many answers to that, not the least of them being "Why, why must you always

be in control? Why can't we help?" But he knew that
control was as essential to her as the air she breathed. So
when she asked him not to ask questions, she was asking
him to allow her that control. Yes, he thought, like his
aunts had thought before him, yes, I owe you that much.
But still he asked himself the question he doubted his
aunts could ask: Is it our need to believe that she's in
control that fuels her own need? Is that what she sees
in us?

He had asked about her health, and she answered that
she intended to make an appointment soon to see a doctor
to find out why she was so tired. She'd let him know
what she found out. Craig assumed that his mother's discomfort around the topic of health reflected her fears for
him. Although Craig knew that Mavis had to know that
he was gay, neither of them had spoken the word aloud in
the presence of the other. In fact, Craig was quite sure
that his mother had never spoken the word at all, for all
things displeasing were more easily borne if not enunci-
ated. Surely now was the time for clarification, he
thought, for she was likely to be accepting the terrifying
association between being gay and having AIDS that
occupied the troubled territory between history and
homophobia. Now was the time to simultaneously claim
his identity and deny her fear.

Craig waited for the right moment to move the conversation away from the safety of crops and weather, away
from neighbors and relatives. And waited. And watched
his resolve diminish beneath the force of Mavis's
unspoken request that he not label her assumptions. So
he talked about his work, and she talked about her grandchildren, his nieces. Often they didn't talk at all. But that
didn't mean they didn't love.

Craig shrugged his shoulders in Isabelle's direction.
They could talk later.

"What time is your appointment in town?" Craig asked his mother, who frowned at him, evidently because he had mentioned this in front of Isabelle.

Her appointment, with her lawyer—her expression clearly warning that neither Craig nor Isabelle were to ask further questions—was at one o'clock. In fact, she would take a shower now and get ready to go. She had a hair appointment and other errands to do as well. No, she didn't need anyone to go with her.

"Your-mother-my-sister is a bit uptight today," Isabelle commented, a groan behind each word, once Mavis was out of the room.

"I think the fact that the rest of her family turned out to be human irritates her sometimes," Craig said, slipping off the kitchen stool behind Isabelle's couch. "Are you going to stay on that couch all day? If you are, I want you to know that you're not my idea of a good time."

"I'm well aware that I'm not your idea of a good time, which is, if I remember, something slight, blond, blue-eyed. The Richard Thomas look, you know, John-boy. Am I right?" Isabelle opened first one eye, then the other, when Craig didn't return the banter. He had turned his face away from her and was looking out the picture window.

Isabelle recognized that particular clench of the jaw and with a small groan berated herself for her hangover-induced thoughtlessness. Rather than call further attention to her gaffe, she hurried on, "And no, I'm not going to stay on this couch all day. I'm going to lie on the couch in the porch, where we can open all the windows and I can smoke without getting that Mavis-look from your mother when she comes home. And you're going to sit out there with me. We'll solve everybody's problems but our own, because we don't have any, and we'll trash all the people in our lives who drive us nuts. I'll tell you about the self-improvement programs Linda has me on. We'll trash those, too. Okay?"

"Okay." Craig looked back at Isabelle. "And maybe we'll talk about why Linda isn't with you on this trip after you vowed to never come back for a family 'vacation' "—he clawed the quotation marks around the word—"without her."

"Okay. And then we'll talk about certain discussions it seems like you haven't had yet with your mother."

"Okay."

"Okay."

They smiled at each other, looking forward to the afternoon. Isabelle had a reputation for no-holds-barred discussions. Craig was capable of making cool, deadly incisions into the conversation. They loved these talks.

"In the meantime—" Isabelle groaned as she assumed the vertical. "—let's do something useful until Mavis leaves, so she'll like us again."

"Peel these peaches." Craig placed a large paper bag in front of Isabelle, who was sliding onto a kitchen stool, having successfully, if not painlessly, walked a full six feet. "I will show you how to make a lattice-top pie."

"Cherry pies have lattice tops, not peach pies."

"Says who?"

"That's what pictures of pies 'say.' "

"Just watch and learn."

"I already know everything I want to know."

"You could surprise Linda."

"I surprise Linda all the time."

"Yes, but this could be a pleasant surprise."

Dressing in the bedroom, Mavis listened to the sound of banter and laughter from the kitchen and smiled to herself. For the hundredth time since her family had begun to gather, she wondered if just maybe things could work out somehow. Then, wincing as she put on her bra, she thought, maybe not.

"So tell me, why isn't Linda with you?" Craig, not Isabelle, was stretched out on the porch couch. Isabelle was no less comfortable, slouched in the overstuffed chair set at a right-degree angle to the couch, which, with its accompanying dingy and lumpy ottoman, completed the porch furnishings. It was the kind of old furniture that is so unattractive that no one who sees it can imagine ever buying such items, but too comfortable to throw out. Two pairs of high-topped Reeboks had been kicked off and dropped in the corner created by the couch and the chair. Isabelle had agreed to Craig's request to leave the cigarettes elsewhere.

"She had reservations to come, too, but then I had some reservations of my own. Get it?"

"Oh, please."

"Well, actually we had a sort-of fight. Or to be more to the point, when it came right down to the wire, I chickened out and picked a fight, which as you know can be a damned hard thing to do with Linda. I think I said something to the effect that she was just being selfish and thinking only of her own agenda—she always listens when I use the word 'agenda'—and that she'd just be in the way if she came home with me."

"Oh nice, Isabelle."

"I know. I know."

"But you haven't told me yet *why* you didn't want her to come back with you. Are you two okay?"

"Better all the time, really. So as usual, I loved being alone and independent for about two days, but now I'm lonely and feel like hell. I can't make sense to anybody about who I am without her here, and I miss her. And I feel guilty. And blah blah."

"So why, then?"

"Well, I suppose I just figured that it all would be easier for Mavis if I didn't complicate her life with mine."

"I wonder how many times we take the easy way out and then put the responsibility on Mom. It's like our lives are one long conversation with her while she's out of the room."

"Yeah yeah."

"Blah blah. Yeah yeah. I'm not saying that having her baby sister bring her lesbian lover home would be the high point of her day, but I mean, let's be real here, it sure wouldn't be the hardest thing she's done lately." Craig stopped to readjust the pillow behind his neck without taking his eyes off Isabelle, who had been staring out the line of opened windows paralleling the couch as Craig spoke. She turned and lifted one corner of her mouth in a smile without humor.

"Craig, you know how homophobic this whole community is. Hell, the whole damn state is, and—"

"Why stop there, why not mention the country, the world, while you're at it? Listen, Isabelle—"

"No, you listen for a minute. It's not the world we're dealing with here. But it is a community that's—that's—well, that is important here. If not to me, then to Mavis." She hesitated. "And this family. Everybody thinks they should get a medal for open-mindedness just because they can fit their tight lips around the word 'gay' now and then. But that's the extent of it. That's all the further they can get."

"I know that, Isabelle. But isn't it also true that you've got an entire life that you don't let these people in on? Why should they acknowledge your life with Linda when you do such a good job of secreting her away?" Craig paused, watching Isabelle's face register her displeasure at being confronted, and wondering how hard he could push before Isabelle's famed stubbornness kicked in and overrode her pleasure in his company.

"Is that a rhetorical question?" Isabelle asked Craig after the pause had become uncomfortable."

"No."

"I don't parade her around when I come home, because I don't feel like taking the abuse. How's that?"

"Not good enough. Bringing your spouse or partner home isn't 'parading' someone around. That just shows how much you've bought into the homophobia around here. And secondly, you already feel abused or you wouldn't be so angry. Linda is a beautiful, articulate, charming person. And I've seen you for too long together not to know just how much happier and, forgive me, 'centered' you are when she's around. Why not let the family see that?"

"Just that easy?"

"What did easy ever have to do with anything?"

"Well, you're a fine one to talk. I don't remember ever hearing about you bringing Rob home."

"That's what makes me a fine one to talk." Craig held Isabelle's eyes and then explained what she already knew. "I didn't bring him home when we were delighted, joyful, thrilled even, with our lives. When I could have said, hey, look at how happy I am for the first time in my life. So. Now he's gone. And now if I mention my love, I have to mention my loss, and that will just confirm Mom's fears."

Isabelle started. "Craig, are you saying—"

"No, no," Craig cut back in quickly. "I'm fine."

"You look like you've lost weight."

"Isabelle, I'm negative."

"Thank God."

"Perhaps, but some days I don't feel too damn thankful."

"I'm sorry, sweetheart."

"Yeah. Me, too." They were silent, both staring out into the prairie sky, which so often seemed vast and limitless with possibility, but for the moment seemed only empty. "So here's the moral of this story—I know you love it when people wrap things up for you—I had the chance to show Mom and Glenn and everybody here who could see just what a special life I had with Rob. I wouldn't have had to 'parade' anything. And we shouldn't underestimate my-mother-your-sister. I don't think anything is as important to her as seeing that the members of this Weirdo Theater family are happy. But I missed that chance. You, however, can show everybody now. Bring the lovely Linda on down." Craig smiled. "The only criticism you'll probably get around here is that you've brought home a pigmy. What is she? Only five-seven or so? People will probably be relieved that she won't be able to introduce dwarfism into the Schmidt bloodlines."

"Five-eight. And you're right, of course. I know that. Next time, Linda comes with."

"Girlfriend, you are as dumb as a post. No. A box of rocks. Go. Call her now. Tell her to get a one-way ticket here. For tomorrow. We could use another softball player for Sunday's picnic. Then you'll cash in your return plane ticket if you can and you two can help me drive back to the coast. I'll spend a couple of days with you both in the Sierras and then drive back up to Seattle."

Isabelle was open-mouthed. "I can't just call her up today and say, 'Hop on a plane tomorrow.' Besides the expense, she hates quick decisions."

"No, dear. You hate quick decisions. Linda, I expect, would love the spontaneity. Go. Call. But first bring me Maxine's murder mystery from the end table in the family room. And a Coke on your way by. And when you're off the phone, we'll solve everybody else's problems. Go."

17

"THAT JUSTIN IS REALLY A JERK," JUDY COMMENTED ON the television's voices from behind her *Fargo Forum*, folded to Friday's crossword puzzle.

"I thought that was Lance."

Judy looked up with disbelief at Janice. "Lance is dead. He's been dead for three months. Now Justin is trying to get Tiffany in bed, but she doesn't love him. She's still in love with Lance."

"Who is dead?"

"Who is dead."

"I guess I haven't seen this one for a while. I'm not home much in the afternoon." Janice pulled a plaid cotton shirt from the basket beside her and began to look for the seam Norton had complained about pulling apart.

"I'm usually too busy to watch these things, too," Judy quickly added, "what with all the hours I've been helping out in the office at Jed's . . ."

Janice held the needle in her left hand and, nodding her

head slowly as if agreeing to something very serious, attempted to locate the needle's eye through her new bifocals. It occurred to her, after a moment of silence, that she didn't know how Judy's sentence should end.

"Jed's what?" she asked.

"Dealership."

"Hmm."

Hmm, what? Judy wondered as she reached for her Diet Pepsi on the coffee table beside the sofa where she had been most of the day, and where she had slept during what was left of the previous night, after returning from her date. She had planned to meet John Conway, the man who had come to her aid when her car over-heated on the drive home, the following evening, but had quickly become bored with the company of women, first at Mavis's and then at Janice's, and hadn't stared at Conway's business card for very long before making an early call.

Both Janice and Maxine, she hadn't failed to notice, had limited their questions this morning to "Did you have a nice time?" Prudes. Judy's attention was drawn back to the TV by the swelling of dramatic music.

"Something's going to happen today," she said, bringing Janice's focus up from her mending and back to the TV, where the camera was zooming in on a young woman's angry expression, directed toward the man who had just grabbed her arms. "Something always happens on Friday."

Judy waited for Janice to take up her part of the conversation. When she didn't, Judy began to fill the silence with the details of this particular soap opera, the affairs, the illnesses, the business deals, doing so in remarkable detail, Janice thought, for someone too busy to watch daytime TV. In the background, commercials for Excedrin and Cascade dishwashing detergent boosted the

TV's volume. Pain and drudgery, Janice thought to herself, the reality behind the fantasy.

When the picture of a woman smiling proudly in front of her sparkling toilet blacked into a long kiss between a man and a woman, Janice wondered aloud, "Troy and Monique are back together again?" and then answered her own question with, "Evidently."

"I like those two." Judy reached for the dictionary to check a crossword guess. "They know how to have a good time."

When once again Janice failed to pick up the conversation's thread, Judy was left to her own thoughts. Did you have a nice time? they asked. Well, as a matter of fact, I had a very nice time, thank you. Sitting across a table from a good-looking man, just the right amount of gray around the temples to look distinguished, but no belly flopping over his belt. Enjoying dinner with a man who knew how to talk about something other than crops and rain, knew how to listen to my opinions, how to question or agree without being condescending, how to keep the conversation going while looking longer and longer into my eyes. Finishing the wine with a man who knew when to stop talking, when to reach over to touch my hand, when to let his gaze fall across my breasts for just a second, making his interest clear, but not insistent. Standing up to leave the table as he pulled out my chair and leaned toward me as I rose so our bodies made the slightest contact, again a request, but not a demand.

Did I have a nice time? they ask, but don't really want to know. Oh, better than nice, much better than nice. Sitting on the balcony of his condo overlooking the swimming pool. Still talking and talking, no judgments made. Separated, he said, not divorced; I smiled, hadn't asked. Feeling the kisses begin, slow, no rush, no games, no resistance, no regret. All the crap of the world about to disappear for at least a little while.

He leads me into the bedroom and we stand in front of each other. His smile looks, I imagine, a lot like mine. Slowly we undress, article for article, item for item, not touching. He looks, watches, until I unfasten my bra and feel him move toward me as if tugged by the weight of my released breasts. He reaches for me but I put his arms back by his sides, slide my hands down his arms, and say, "No. I want to feel you." He looks just a little surprised, but nods as he holds my eyes. Glancing my hand lightly from the inside of his thigh up and over his hip, just grazing the still-dark thick hair with my nails, I move behind him and press my body to his. My breasts fit beneath his shoulder blades. I slide my hands up over his sides, cover his chest, thumb his nipples, and reach down to hear the long intake of breath. He understands the pace I have set, turns to me and begins the jawline kisses. He knows now that he must use his whole body to make love with me, may not feel his pleasure separate from mine. Reaching over, he pulls the covers off the bed. I can see that the sheets are freshly laundered and smile to myself. I lie down. He lets his tongue lead him past ankles and calves to the insides of my knees, journeys up, letting his tongue split my pleasure and briefly linger, crosses my belly with his lips, releases his second sigh as he bends his head to take my breast into his mouth. Then looks at me. Sees me, hears me, wants me. It's all that simple.

Did I have a nice time? Oh yes indeed. I had a nice time for a very long time. With a man, a sweet, sexy, gentle, passionate man I may or may not see again.

"Judy?"

"What?"

"I said, why are these two fighting now?" Janice gestured toward the two women now on screen, heads close together as they sat at a restaurant table, directing soft tense words at each other. "Andrea and Adriane, right?"

"They don't like each other."

"Never have, but why are they fighting now?"

Judy put the newspaper down and listened to the television conversation for a minute.

"I never pay much attention to them. Why they went into business together is beyond me. Two bitchy women. Who cares?"

"Why do you and Isabelle fight?"

Surprise, irritation, then disinterest crossed Judy's face in rapid succession. Jesus Christ, a thousand possible questions to ask, a million things to talk about, and she asks me something like that.

"We don't fight that much," Judy stated in a tone meant to end the conversation before it got going. As the sibling closest in age to Janice, Judy knew that although this quiet sister was least comfortable with conflict, once she bit into an idea, it could be hard to shake her loose.

"You fight all the time."

Terrier. "Oh, I doubt that. But I guess we just don't have much in common."

"Other than family and background."

Judy shrugged at Janice, turned her attention back to the TV, and repeated, "I guess they just don't like each other. Let's get to the good stuff."

"That's probably not what you had in mind." Janice smiled at Judy as two women in a commercial strolled through a meadow of daisies while talking about douching.

"Yeah, right. There's a realistic mother-daughter conversation for you. I've had some whoppers with Chrissie, but none that I can remember about which flavor of douche I prefer."

"I think they refer to them as 'scents,' Judy," Janice said, finally laughing.

"Can you imagine Mom talking like that with one of us? Not likely. It's a wonder we figured anything out at all."

"Well, we had those pamphlets Mavis gave us."

"What Mavis gave us couldn't save us." Judy chuckled at her rhyme. "Me, anyway. Oh good, it's going to end with Justin and Tiffany. I knew it would."

Janice looked up from the button she was sewing onto a pair of pants just as the young woman slapped the young man, then winced with the woman as the young man's hand crossed her cheek in return, felt the slap, and again heard Jack's voice: "I said, keep your eyes shut." Janice felt the old rage in her gut. Rage at his words, but more than that, a self-loathing fury at her own physical response to the blow, at the thrill accompanying the sting. She knew Jack could be counted on to help her with the flat of his hand, knew that all she had to do was look at him working on top of her, and there, again, would come the slap to the cheekbone that was for her alone.

It was the slap she had felt just once as a child, after the aging man with a chronic cough had asked her to hand him a wrench. But she didn't know the names of the tools before her, made the wrong choice, and suddenly was sitting, knocked aside by a rough hand. Her father had stared at her, then at his hand. Said "Christ Almighty," and shuffled to an old pickup truck to roar away. The little girl could feel her heart pounding, thrilled by the surprise, by the sensation for which she had no words, a mixture of pain and elation. Because now she had a secret that was hers alone, attention that was hers alone, not shared, not handed down, not to be compared. And it didn't matter at all that it had hurt.

It never happened again, was never mentioned, and soon thereafter he was dead. The intensity of the moment slowly dimmed until years later a brother-in-law, a predator, sensed what she no longer knew. Reminded her of the only thrill she'd known that she could call her own, of the equation that was equal parts secret, pain, shame. So she had opened her eyes to invite the slap that would take her over the edge, and he had not disappointed her, and her reply was the tug of her orgasm, and then his was accompanied by the word intended to deny her even this pleasure.

And did she whisper "Irene" to him, she wonders, when she pulled the trigger, as he whispered "Irene" to her when he pulled away?

18

ALTHOUGH WEDNESDAY'S RAIN HAD BROUGHT A MUCH-appreciated reprieve from the early August prairie heat, by Saturday afternoon the temperature gauges attached to windows on the west side of farmhouses showed a climbing mercury under a hazy sky. The rain had been a godsend for the row crops and had only taken the farmers from their grain harvest for a couple of days. The humidity that remained acted as an adhesive, pasting shirts to backs, bare legs to car seats, and bad moods onto a generally pleasant people.

Peggy had managed to make her kitchen about ten times as unbearable with a number of steaming kettles as she grudgingly went through the process of putting up pickles. She hated pickles, she hated to can, and she hated the humidity. By the picnic tomorrow afternoon she somehow needed to have her house cleaned (Glenn had conveniently not had time to vacuum) and her lawn mowed, and a tub of potato salad made. And her summer was as good as over. School started in a little over three weeks, but she would have several full days in her principal's office in the interim. Too soon. And too hot. Her bra itched, her bare feet were sticking to the kitchen floor, and if Mavis showed up with one more goddamned box of cucumbers from her garden, she swore she'd take them out and throw them into the trees.

Peggy stood at the top of the stairs that descended from the kitchen entryway, strewn with dirty tennis shoes, into the dank basement below. Her expression registered her distaste for the cement steps that were slick with the humidity. She would not touch the sweating cement walls, which gave her the creeps. Goddamned old house. Character. Don't give me character. Old and damp. Old and hot, then old and cold. "Walls that sweat, for Christ's sake," she muttered as she headed down for yet another box of Ball jars.

The bottom turn of the steps opened onto a cavernous room with a packed dirt floor that was lined with appliances and machines: a portable generator, water pump and softener, chest freezer, washing machine and dryer, a large free-standing, two-basin sink, and a sump pump in the corner. Peggy passed quickly through the next small room, patting the new furnace which alone out of everything in the basement gave her pleasure. It was a metallic green boxlike item with none of the heavy iron apertures and handles that had made the aged and fickle furnace it replaced totally incomprehensible to her.

Peggy crossed through the "potato bin," which hadn't seen a potato for several decades, and which, under her tenure as homemaker in this house, had been neatly shelved to hold plastic file boxes filled with financial records, dated and alphabetized. In the adjacent pantry the shelves were lined with labeled and dated jars of canned peaches, pears, and cherries, pickles, and toma-toes. Gone were the web-enclosed mystery boxes that might contain empty Ball jars and lids, but were just as likely to hold a cast-iron frying pan, an ancient handheld egg beater, and a couple of heavy irons that predated electricity. Gone were the coffee cans filled with ball bearings, nuts and bolts, skate keys, and unrecognizable parts of machinery now rusting at the local dump. And gone were the shelves lined with paint cans, solvents, tur-pentine, putty, caulking, and endless half-full spray cans of fake snow used for stenciling Christmas scenes on windows.

Stretching for a box of jars above her, Peggy hesitated as she heard a noise in the next room, which connected with the first, appliance-lined room and completed the circular pathway through the basement.

"Janie, is that you?"

"Um-hum," came the swallowed reply. A moment later Janie appeared in the doorway, inhaling deeply to capture the smell she loved. More dank than damp, it was a smell to cover the roof of the mouth, a smell with a history.

Peggy wrinkled her nose in reaction to Janie's satisfied sniff.

"What are you doing down here?" Peggy's voice verged

on cross, although she'd decided to ignore the walnut crumbs Janie hadn't thought to wipe from her chin, remnants of a frozen thumbprint cookie left over from the last community wedding reception and pilfered from the huge cabinet freezer.

"Looking around the coal room," Janie answered, naming the large storage room in the basement's far corner, filled with dismantled bicycles, ice skates, unlikely pieces of furniture, clay planting pots, a milk can, an ice cream churn, a treadmill sewing machine, and dozens of items long forgotten. Although Peggy had done some significant cleaning and arranging there as well, it remained a room that lived on in the past, with a logic of its own. As a whimsical tribute to her mother-in-law's surprising legacy of what seemed to Peggy to be an impenetrable clutter, she had left the Glo-Grow plant light, sans bulb, hovering over long-dead but strangely preserved geraniums.

"Looking for what?"

"Anything. There's nothing to do around here," Janie replied, her last words swallowed when she saw, too late, Peggy's face darken.

"Oh, I think there's plenty to do. For starters, how about mowing the lawn, and then how about weeding the petunias."

"I mowed last time. It's Becky's turn. Becky never does her share." Wrong again.

"Becky is helping me put up pickles. Would you like to trade jobs with her?"

"No, I'll mow." Janie had her put-upon look as she turned to go, but Peggy knew that with the threat of work to be done in the house, she could count on Janie to mow, weed, trim, and keep busy in general, outside, all day long.

She also knew that she could count on Becky's mood

being as murderous as her own, but that was just too bad. They'd get the pickling done and out of the way by mid-afternoon. Then she and Becky would clean the house just well enough to escape comment tomorrow. It was a picnic, after all; people should stay outside. Then maybe she'd have a couple of hours to herself to do her own work. Fortunately, the men were harvesting across the road from Mavis's, who had offered to feed them. And thank goodness Glenn's aunts were nowhere in sight today. She could use some time alone.

Five miles up the road at Mavis's, the atmosphere was greatly improved, in large part by central air-conditioning, in lesser part because there just wasn't all that much to do, except, perhaps, talk on the phone. When the sisters were in their respective homes, weeks, even months, could go by without a phone call or a letter. Now that they were all back in North Dakota, each morning began with a report of the day's planned activities. Maxine had called to say that she would be lunching in Fargo with old friends. Judy had gone shopping with Tina and with Jimmy's wife, Pam. And Janice had a headache and hoped to spend the day on the couch. In fact, she didn't know if she'd feel well enough tomorrow to come to the picnic.

When Mavis got off the phone with a "Good Lord," Craig mentioned that he thought perhaps his mother had broken her all-time record for the number of "yeah, uh-huhs" in one phone conversation. Mavis answered by continuing the conversation she was having with herself, saying that she thought Janice should be able to pull herself together like everybody else and have a good time.

Craig shrugged his shoulders and held his hands up in front of his chest, as if to remind his mother that if she were in the middle of an argument with someone, it

wasn't with him. He was on his way out the door to help
drive truck, giving Glenn's man, young Donny, the
chance to get off early today as he'd asked. He'd be back
to work again the next morning with the rest of the men,
who would harvest until around noon. By one o'clock on
Sunday, relatives could be expected to begin to show for
the picnic, arms laden with baked beans, buns, coleslaw,
Jell-O, Rice Krispies bars, seven-layer chocolate bars,
and Gloria's dreaded spice bars.

Today, however, Mavis would be alone, and grateful
for it. Isabelle had taken Mavis's Cadillac into Fargo
to pick up her . . . her friend, Linda. Why not? Mavis
thought. Bring them all on. But only men today. She
lifted her eyes as if to speak with God, and spoke to
Frank instead. Only surround me with men who will
talk about how the grain is running, about which elevator
is paying what price, about how full the grain bins are at
home. They will ask me if I heard the market report and
the weather report. They will ask me for more meat loaf,
more potatoes, more coffee, another piece of Craig's pie.
I will want to hear all they have to tell me, and I will have
all the answers they need.

19

ISABELLE ORDERED A LEMONADE AND SETTLED IN AT the table with a scowl. The two parallel and vertical lines on her brow that merged into a strong nose dissected the bottommost of the three horizontal frown lines that creased her forehead. Lines deepened partly by too much California sun, but more so by unrelenting disappointment in the rest of the human race. Linda had traced these lines early on in their relationship, saying they looked like a hieroglyph: what was the secret behind her frown? A sign of character, Isabelle had maintained. Not much later Isabelle's response was seemingly confirmed as the two watched a television special on cosmetic surgery, equally fascinated and appalled at the possibilities of self-mutilation. One of the women interviewed explained how she'd simply had one little nerve snipped so that she wouldn't get that terrible crease above her nose. "See," she beamed, somewhat blankly, "I couldn't frown if I wanted to," wiggling and squinching the lower part of her face, while the mask above her nose remained eerily static. "I wonder if she got the lobotomy at a discount," Isabelle had commented. At this moment, however, Isabelle's disdain was not, surprisingly enough, directed toward anyone in particular, but rather encompassed the entire building she was in. She was mad for the second time in less than two weeks at Fargo's new airport.

She was disappointed at yet more mauve and gray, although she supposed she should be grateful to be spared the by-now-ubiquitous green and brown and brass furnishings that an anthropologist of the contemporary would find had signaled the yuppie invasion. But now ferns were giving way to philodendrons, palms, and dumbcane, and green and brown to the mauve and gray that Isabelle associated with top-of-the-line caskets. And all these windows, all this openness. Why bother with a building at all if it makes you feel like you're sitting in the middle of the runway?

So what had been wrong with the old Hector Airport anyway: a little cramped, a little dirty maybe, but mostly just worn and familiar. And a great bar, dark and intimate, about the size of a bathroom in a fancy hotel. Hidden in the corner of the three-room airport—big waiting room with ticket counter and luggage dock, cafeteria, and cocktail lounge—the bar had to have been the darkest place in Fargo aboveground. Three booths with lumpy seats, a few small round tables with molded plastic chairs, and the bar practically cutting the room in half diagonally, maybe fifteen feet long.

Fargo was getting away from her. She intended to resist that surest sign of aging—the resentment of change—but still she wasn't happy with Fargo's . . . what? Not modernization, exactly. It had never been in the dark ages according to her, although it was far from the cutting edge. But it was this—this unfamiliar chi-chi-fication, gentrification, yuppyization. Isabelle just didn't feel coddled here anymore. In a land so open that the gently curving earth always met the sky in the infinite distance, a land so flat that the vantage point for any area was a highway overchange, Fargo had provided dark, enclosed relief. Small dark movie theaters, small dark restaurants, small dark bars. Isabelle closed her eyes and remembered the cool relief she had always felt walking in out of the sun, into one of those places. Escaping the horrible beauty of the expansive plains—the relentless sun or the unhindered wind—by burrowing into the dark of The Empire or Ralph's.

Standing in the sun and looking across the seeming limitlessness of the open land had always made her feel brave and strong and pleasantly alone. We must be a strong people, she had reasoned to herself, to be able to tolerate this exposure. But even a strong people must occasionally give in to their smallness in all that space. Then they would slip into the safe, private relief of the enclosed dark. Cool if they were coming in out of the summer sun. Warm if they were escaping the bite of a winter wind sweeping unchecked over a snow- and ice-encrusted flatland. That's when they would need to find the places with finite boundaries. Where do the people in this city go now to feel safe and secluded and simultaneously communal? The latter still a compelling need for the scattered people of a primarily rural state. Not to a fern bar, for Christ's sake, Isabelle thought, the scowl lines deepening.

And this certainly isn't the answer. Isabelle's baleful look once again swept the new Fargo International Airport lounge. Cute little neon squiggles for signs; glass and mirrors everywhere. The wall on one side was simply a long window that separated the lounge from the gate areas. They can see you. You can see them. On the opposite side of the room there was no wall at all, so that travelers who leaned over the second story railing could watch people entering and leaving the airport, picking up luggage and buying tickets. And while we're at it, Isabelle thought, this isn't even really a lounge at all. It's a restaurant that serves beer with barely an excuse for a bar. A six-seat number set out there under a light so that anyone bellying up is on display.

Who designs these things, anyway? Where are the distinctions? Here you eat. There you drink. That's what this place needs, fewer squiggles and more distinction.

Isabelle looked at her watch, put some money on the table, got up, and rode the escalator down to check the arrival board behind the Northwest counter. Linda's plane was on time and would be on the ground in less than ten minutes. Isabelle recognized the unpleasant tension cramping her stomach, and acknowledged to herself just how difficult she must be to live with. I call her up and ask her to rearrange her schedule so she can be with me for the rest of my trip, and now that she's almost here, I wish I could turn her plane around and send it back to San Francisco. Together for nine years and I'm afraid of commitment. Isabelle savored her last moments of independence. Alone in an airport. Nobody cares who I am. Nobody cares what I do.

The waiting area had slowly filled as people moved toward the gate, wanting to see their passenger come off the flight as soon as possible, but not wanting to risk rubbing shoulders with a stranger. You could swing a dead cat by the tail between family groups and not hit anyone. Isabelle found a cleared space toward the back, to be spotted easily enough, but sure to see first. It gave her the seconds she needed to prepare, to adjust to the presence of the someone else who would make her two instead of one.

Isabelle felt her face flush as the tall, slim woman walked through the gate. Dark hair, shoulder length and layered softly away from her face, framed the darkest, most intelligent eyes Isabelle had ever looked into, a nose that, it's true, angled just a tad to the right, and full lips which parted over one of those smiles that makes the smiled-upon feel simply grateful. Then, for just a moment, that smile slipped a fraction, as she hesitated, her own brow furrowed as she looked for Isabelle. But not for long. It would be hard to miss a close-to-six-foot woman in a small area, harder still to miss Isabelle ever. Holding herself in a pose just caught in tension between an athlete's leisurely stance and a wild animal's readiness to bolt, giving off her customary contradictory messages—"Come here; go away"—Isabelle's chiseled features suddenly softened into the smile that all her adult life had allowed friends and lovers to forgive her her misanthropy. Mixed with delight was an awe that allowed Linda to break back into her own smile. Isabelle's was the look she'd been going for when she dressed this morning, choosing the new flowered and tailored cotton wraparound skirt that left an inverted V pointing straight up the middle of her left thigh. A loose cotton tank top tucked in and sandals completed the outfit.

Too moved to be distant, Isabelle walked toward Linda and met her with a kiss on the mouth, stopping the question that began, "Is something—"

Linda stepped back and smiled. "We kiss in the Fargo airport? Can North Dakotans tolerate such unabashed affection?"

"Lovers don't kiss in public in North Dakota." Isabelle smiled. "Too personal. People might wonder how we're related, but we certainly won't be taken for lovers."

Linda knew by a few of the stares that she and Isabelle had drawn that Isabelle was wrong, but evoking any kind of public display of affection from Isabelle was a small victory not to be questioned.

"What exactly do you have on underneath that skirt?"

"What exactly would you like to be under there?"

Isabelle began to consider which of Linda's panties would be prettiest.

"Darling—" Linda laughed after a moment of silence. "—let's not stand here and run through a mental inventory of my underwear. Truth is, everything's new. A welcome present for you."

Isabelle looked down at Linda in grateful amazement. For so many years she hadn't even dared to dream about a life with another woman, and then to have the smartest, prettiest, sanest woman she would ever meet fall in love with her, well, it was something she never intended to get used to. And then for that woman to buy underwear especially to please her. Surely there was a God.

"Is there a baggage ramp here, or do they just toss our suitcases out on the tarmac?" Linda prodded Isabelle out of her reverie.

"Haven't you noticed? This is a brand spanking new state-of-the-art, run-of-the-mill airport. And here's a tip. North Dakota jokes are all the rage in Montana, but North Dakota bashing here is no way to win friends."

"That was it. I promise." Linda hesitated. "Actually . . . I'm a little surprised to be here. Are you all right?"

"I'm always all right." The quick reply, and then, seeing Linda's impatient grimace, the truth. "I'm more all right now that you're here." Now their look was longer, open. They moved together to the escalator and rode down in silence.

Waiting for her luggage to wind by, Linda took stock of the small crowd scattered throughout the area, and indulged in one of her favorite pastimes, eavesdropping. It wasn't intrusive, she had often explained to a shocked Isabelle, for whom the greatest good was always privacy; rather, it was an insatiable thirst to know the lives of all those around her. "This is wonderful," Linda said to Isabelle with a smile, "everybody has your accent. And the people here are so handsome. No, that's not it. Everyone looks so—so . . ."

"Healthy."

"That's it! Everyone's so healthy."

"There's a difference between looking healthy and being healthy. I think what you're noticing is size."

"It's probably from not breathing in pollution all day."

"I wouldn't overromanticize if I were you. They're no strangers to a pretty impressive array of pesticides. And the diet . . . Just don't suggest a correlation between red meat intake and cancer. That theory is considered here to be just another strategy to ruin the ranchers and farmers." Isabelle smiled. "Being a lesbian may be suspect, but vegetarians are beneath contempt."

"I promise to eat all the dead animals placed before me. There! That's my suitcase. I can't believe it. It never arrives at the airport the same day I do. Or at least not at the same airport."

"Baggage never gets lost coming into Fargo."

"And the rain never falls till after sundown?"

Bags collected, Isabelle and Linda passed through yet another wall of glass and were immediately slapped by the blanket of humidity.

"It's hot," Linda noted with surprise.

"North Dakota has a summer during which it gets hot. Were you expecting snow?"

"Of course not." Linda smiled. "But kind of. And oh, look how flat it is. This is where you grew up." Linda studied Isabelle. "Where's the city?"

"Down the road a piece," Isabelle replied, affecting a country accent she had never heard in the country. "Over yonder is where we're headed. And this is Mavis's car. It's like parking a Greyhound bus. Look at the dash. This car does everything but wipe your butt."

"One of your more charming expressions, Isabelle."

Isabelle started the Cadillac and turned on the AC, which, after an initial furnacelike blast, began to spread cool air throughout the car. Isabelle moved her right hand to the steering column to shift into reverse, then stopped and leaned toward Linda for a kiss. Running her hand up Linda's left thigh, under the skirt, she heard what had to be the sexiest sound a woman can make: the unexpected and unplanned quick intake of breath at the touch of a lover.

Isabelle and Linda were not unfamiliar with dry spells in their relationship when work, anxiety, and fatigue made them forget the level of their own passion. And then there were the times when a simple touch on a warm thigh, a touch that had been repeated a thousand times, shocked the lovers with its intensity, burning forgotten nerves and setting their hearts to pounding. Linda put her hand over Isabelle's and moved it up between her legs and smiled at Isabelle's quiet "Oh" in return. Isabelle looked at Linda, her head back, eyes closed, and lips parted, brought her hand back to the steering wheel and put the car in reverse.

"There's nowhere we need to be right now . . . except with each other." Isabelle cleared her throat. "I know the Town House is still the closest motel. We'll go there now."

"Are you sure?"

"Oh yes."

MAVIS

SUNDAY'S BREAKFAST DISHES WERE STACKED IN THE dishwasher. Craig, showered and changed after spending the morning driving truck for Glenn, had backed his father's old pickup out of the empty barn and driven into Crow to collect some long tables from the schoolhouse for the picnic. Isabelle and Linda, who had shown up at Mavis's in the early evening the night before, had followed in Craig's Bronco to help. Mavis was alone. It was time to prepare.

First, the shower. A bath is to relax, after the test, after the battle. A shower is to brace, to prepare. The water streams and burns, pellets of fire scald away the earthly, the ordinary, the vulnerable. The sound of hail drums on the clear plastic helmet protecting hair perfected on Thursday and miraculously unchanged by Sunday. The washcloth relentlessly scours the face and the neck, for clarity of thought, for quickness of wit, ready for scrutiny. Then back again with more soap—arms, strength; underarms, calm; back, surety; and then, cautiously over breasts (to have pain is not to be weak); belly, fortitude; crotch, privacy; legs and feet, sturdiness.

And now. Cold. Pure cold. More pellets of fire, now icy. To be awake, to be new, to be alive. I choose the heat. I choose the cold.

Are the legs that step out of the shower younger,

muscles well-defined from calf to crotch? Is the belly flatter? The breasts . . . to have pain is not to be weak. Arms with firm flesh and defined biceps reach for the towel, bringing it up to a face sculpted in marble. The eyes are black with pure determination.

Mavis smiles as she brushes her teeth, and allows herself a short self-conscious snort. Then these teeth must have tips of diamond; that would explain the cutting remarks. She reaches for the partial bridge and rinses it under cool water. Titanium, no doubt. She covers her body with protective potions. Replaces the glasses with newly sparkling lenses on the nose always angled away from the ground.

She takes the new pair of Olga underwear from the Dayton's bag and bites off the ticket. How odd, she thinks, with everything else, to take such pleasure in new panties. With her back to the full-length mirror she lifts herself into the jogging bra she's discovered provides the most comfort. Her hand rests for just a moment on the left side of her chest, and she thinks: this is my Achilles' tendon. The rose-colored tunic blouse she takes from the closet reminds her of a day shopping at West Acres with Janie, a day in the early spring over a year ago, a day of ease and intergenerational camaraderie. Before the first death that led to the second, before eternity began knocking at her own chest. White cotton slacks with just enough polyester to keep the crease neat, footies and Grasshopper tennis shoes, and she is ready.

She turns to the mirror watching her progress and sees the nod of approval. Then the last touch, the indication that she is indeed going out: lipstick the only artifice to her being. Her lips take on a pinkness and softness to lull the inattentive. She strides to the kitchen, tall and strong, picks something up without

feeling its weight, and exits. She moves so surely it's as
if the doors open and close for her.

What do you see when you see Mavis? A sixty-year-old
woman losing her height to a curving back, carrying a
pot of beans out the door? Do you see a woman with
lines carved into her brow and dug into the loosening
skin of her neck, glasses slipping down a nose already
sweating with the humidity? Do you see a short-sleeve
shirt over white slacks, neither hiding the rounded belly
of an aging woman?

Do you see pain, worry, hesitation?

Then you don't see Mavis.

20

IT MADE NO DIFFERENCE THAT FOR THE PAST FORTY
years the land had been farmed by a Holmstead, first
Frank, then Frank and Glenn, now Glenn alone. The farm
remained "the Schmidt place." Within each carload of
relatives that rounded the corner of the driveway Sunday
afternoon, gravel crunching under the tires, someone was
bound to remark on the changes to the old place. Most of
these changes had been remarked upon before. Some

would notice a new fence that had actually been there for several years but was newly repainted, others the flower garden that far exceeded what Mavis's patience had allowed. Aging lilac bushes had been cut down and new shrubs planted. A bunkhouse had been converted to a workshop; the biffy behind was gone, but the peonies planted where it had once stood were the size of small trees. Feedlots had been converted to field space, and the house was a different color, with a new bay window in the kitchen.

The series of aluminum storage grain bins that had sprouted almost two decades ago between the old granary and the machine shed were no longer deserving of comment. Most of the farmyards across the state held similar excrescences. For years the giant silver warts multiplied, containing a percentage of the season's harvested grain, first stored toward the day that must surely come when the sale wouldn't represent a loss, then stored in reflection of a government farm program that essentially paid farmers not to sell their grain—a form of marketing through storage. Now that particular farm program was long gone, replaced by a series of others: commodity subsidies, payment for keeping less fertile land out of production, all of which looked like handouts to the city folk who got their information from Johnny Carson monologues. But not the answer evidently to the steady decline in the number of family farms.

For two weeks now area farmers had been chewing over statistics reported in a *Fargo Forum* story, statistics they felt they knew before they heard the actual numbers: in 1935 North Dakota held 84,600 farms; now there were 33,000. A congressional report suggested that an expected squeeze in farm income could cause one in four farmers across the nation to get out of the business within the next five years. Now there was the threat of a subsidies freeze in the midst of rising production costs and low grain prices.

So? comes the counterargument, read from a paper or a magazine, but sometimes voiced by a more successful neighbor. Why should taxpayers support farmers if they can't support themselves? Why should farmers receive subsidies of twenty billion dollars a year? Why should the government pay as much as forty percent of a farmer's net income?

An angry response is already waiting: that twenty billion represents less than one percent of the federal budget. Is that too much to maintain a plentiful supply of food?

But then comes the question that is less easy to answer. Who benefits most from the subsidies? Doesn't the lion's share actually go to the larger farm operations with net farm incomes of over $100,000, whereas the average net farm income for a North Dakota farmer is closer to $23,000?

But numbers, dollars, and figures aren't really what the arguments are about. Because for these men and women the notion of farming as a way of making a living is inseparable from the notion of farming as a way of life. It's more than what one does; it's what one is.

Sure, the relatives reassure themselves, the home place pretty much looks the same.

Like farm after farm interspersed across the eastern Dakota plains, this one, too, has a house that appears to be nestled into trees on the north and the west sides. Actually, the house preceded the trees, or more accurately yet, the tiny house first built where the present house now stands came first. The Schmidt house, however, is an original. One hundred years old two years before the state reached its centennial, it has been added to, remodeled, reroofed, and re-sided countless times, resulting in a sort of architectural schizophrenia.

Only the basement, with its dirt floors and ancient must, reveals the secret of the house's age. But it's a secret well kept, since, in one of those peculiar aberrations of northern plains' privacy, only individuals living in that particular house are allowed into the darkness below. Upstairs, out of the darkness of the house's past, light floods the rooms from east to west. The windows to the west look out on a thickness of trees. Evergreens, box elders, cottonwood, oak. But a child who escapes from the house and inside responsibilities by running into these woods finds herself under the full prairie sun before breaking a sweat. Any trees in sight then line up in straight rows every quarter mile, shelterbelts disproving the insistent old saw about a few barbed-wire fences being the only hindrance to the arctic winds that sweep into North Dakota from Canada. Windows to the east and south look beyond the farmstead into the uninterrupted space of flatland and open sky.

As the cars roll to a stop on the lawn and the shade available between the shop and the garage, the occupants separate, first by age, then by gender. Children immediately move away from parents, but don't move too far, standing by a sibling, watching to see how the groups will form. It's a moment of anxiety, for this could be the year when the group defines itself through the exclusion of one particular cousin, second cousin, sister or brother. But there doesn't seem to be that many children at this reunion; this is mostly a gathering of grown-ups.

The boys are handed a basketball by Peggy and head for the barn and the remembered hoop in the now-empty, and sweltering, hay mow. Janie watches suspiciously. Her basketball. Her barn. And she's stuck with the girls. Still, she is the oldest of the girls, with the exception of Becky and an older second cousin who have formed their own exclusive club and have already disappeared into Becky's bedroom. With age comes authority, which means that Janie will direct the little girls toward tree climbing, creek exploring, and bumper bikes, while the dolls will be left to heat up in the backseats of cars. If there's a mutiny, Janie has a contingency plan that still solves most of her problems: saddle her pony and ride away. And if she can make it to the late afternoon with these shrieking ninnies, there's always the softball game. And everybody plays softball.

The children's ritual of settling in is repeated—and probably originated—by the adults. Within minutes of greetings, the men find their way to the machine shed, where a cooler of beer waits by the door, and where relatives and in-laws will look over the new pickup head attached to Glenn's combine, which takes up well over two-thirds of the large building.

There they begin to talk about Wednesday's rain and the harvest thus far as they all open beers and a few tap out cigarettes. Glenn sets an empty coffee can next to two smokers, one of whom just grunts in dismissal as he taps the ash from his unfiltered Camel into the cuff of his Match-Me trousers. This is a picnic, a day off, supposedly, from farming, so the talk shifts to abuse of the Minnesota Twins and their last place standing in their division. Soon the conversation turns to that "goddamned Saddam" and includes words like "Hitler" and "embargo," as well as a quiet disagreement about the United States' role as world police. The word "army" causes one of the men to free-associate to a concern about army worms. His extension agent suggested Dylox or malathion, but a neighbor was using Penncap-M . . . and they begin to farm again.

Back at the house, the women pass between the

kitchen and the front yard, dropping off bowls and pans, picking up an iced tea or a beer, handing around Pam's eighteen-month-old baby (and patting what Maxine has referred to as Pam's "always already" pregnant stomach), and then choosing to sit in the shade beside either Aunt Alice or Aunt Emma.

Alice and Emma provide both a cautionary tale and inspiration to the women of the family, for their independence is as laughable as it is legendary. Most of the younger relatives would be hard put to explain where these "aunts" hang on their family tree, but the aged two are, quite simply, first cousins, Aunt Alice the unmarried sister of Mavis and her sisters' father, and Aunt Emma the unmarried daughter of their father's uncle. Although both women had reached the age where their own memories of a long-past youth occupied them more and more, they were equally ready to hold forth on tax laws, market prices, and foreign policy (as it affected farming, of course). Occasionally they asked questions of others. Then they ignored the responses because they couldn't hear much of what was said and were uninterested in the rest, made up the information they missed, and continued the conversation on that basis.

Although the two actually got along very well, family reunions historically were battlefields for allegiance. For days before such an event, Aunt Emma and Aunt Alice would make phone calls and plans designed to get each on the scene before the other. Nephews and nieces, whoever was responsible for giving the aunts a ride, saw to it that picnic after picnic, Easter after Easter, Christmas after Christmas, the two women arrived at about the same time. And it was easy to tell from the kitchen window which car pulling in the drive held an Aunt Emma or an Aunt Alice, for it would be the one with the passenger door opening well before the car came to a halt. It would be the one with the driver sprinting around the car after an abrupt stop to get to that door before an octogenarian toppled out onto the gravel in her hurry to exit. The sisters' cousin, Big Dan, once said he thought maybe he had a tire going flat coming over, but it just turned out to be Emma dragging one foot out the open door.

Once free of the cars, the aged aunts would position themselves well apart from each other and then study carefully which relative went to greet which aunt first. Thus, after laughing, but intricate, planning in the kitchen, relatives would enter the aunts' arena in pairs, followed by a ceremonious split, one to Aunt Alice, one to Aunt Emma, in what Craig had once called "the dowager dance." Fortunately, once food was set out, these two could be hoisted from their chairs and ushered through the line—they steadfastly insisted on filling their own plates—and resituated in a new, neutral grouping over which they could preside jointly.

When Judy arrived from Fargo with Tina, her baby, and Tina's new boyfriend, Alex (and with the information that Maxine would be along soon with Janice and Norton), Craig had just finished helping Isabelle and Linda set up lawn chairs and long tables in the front yard. This would be the hub of the day's activities. From here could be heard the crash of the screen door each time the kids passed through the house, accompanied by an adult's—usually Mavis's—call, "Don't let the screen door (bang) bang." From here the yard was in full sight, so when a mother asked, "Where did the boys get to?" someone else could point to the general vicinity where that group of adolescents had last been sighted. From here the bathroom, the beer, the iced tea, and the coffee would be handy. And from here the yard space across the driveway where the softball game would be played was in full view.

Craig and Judy were soon trading observations. He liked her with red hair; she was glad to see he'd shaved, now he needed to start eating. Judy believed that Craig was the one relative as cosmopolitan as she, and Craig knew that to Judy "cosmopolitan" meant knowing which fifteen-dollar bottle of wine to order, wearing the currently fashionable jeans, and seeing the touring versions of blockbuster, albeit aging, Broadway plays. But Craig also knew that taken out of the mysteriously threatening environment of her sisters' company, Judy could be a delightful and charming companion.

Isabelle and Linda stood by as Judy and Craig bantered. Isabelle had been introducing "my friend" to the nieces, nephews, cousins, aunts, and assorted in-laws, but to the immediate family Linda was a known, if unmet, item. Craig defused the situation before it became one by taking control of the introductions, thus keeping Isabelle from including an insult to which Judy would need to respond in kind.

"Judy, this is Linda." Craig was smiling at Linda and bringing her into the conversation with a hand on her elbow. He noticed that Isabelle's expression was protective, indicating her readiness to be provoked. Because of the twice-daily phone calls that the sisters' visit had generated between Janice's and Mavis's households, Judy already knew that Linda had arrived. Nonetheless, her face clearly registered surprise. Judy looked quickly at Isabelle, perhaps to confirm that the two were actually together, perhaps to see what expression Isabelle would be wearing at this moment, perhaps in wonder that a woman of Linda's beauty would have anything to do with her sister. Isabelle's look in return was steady, but her posture was defensive.

"It's nice to meet you." Judy's gaze returned to Linda with a smile that appeared genuine, although, as Isabelle was known to say, a genuine smile was one of Judy's more practiced artifices. "I'm sure you've heard a great deal about me. But then you must remember to consider the source." Her smile dimmed a bit.

Isabelle was beginning to bristle, but Linda was as determined as Craig that she not be an excuse for the sisters' bad blood. "I'm really happy to be able to meet *all* of Isabelle's family." There was a short pause, so Linda continued, "Craig was telling me earlier this morning that you're quite a skier. Maybe we could find some time later to compare notes. I've only skied once in the Rockies, but Craig said you'd know the places to go."

"Oh, I haven't skied for a couple of years now. But maybe I'll get out to Colorado this . . ." She turned to Isabelle. "Are you skiing again? I would have thought that knee operation would have put an end to . . ."

"If you can call it that. We go a couple times a year. It's a much more timid sport now than it used to be."

"I haven't skied for years," Craig put in. "To tell the truth, I never really liked being cold all the time. The only thing I miss is the après-ski in the lodge."

"I miss those lovely young men on the ski patrol, with those tight pants," Judy joked, getting more of a laugh from the other three than she expected, having managed in her requisite mention of her own heterosexuality in the company of lesbians to fill in what Craig had politely left out.

"On that note, I think I'll get a beer," Isabelle said. "It is, after all, well after noon, is it not? Can I get anybody else anything?" she asked as she began to disengage from the conversation.

"Not so fast, Isabelle. You promised to show me around the farm first." Linda caught her by the arm and steered her toward the farmyard, where Isabelle would give Linda pictures to go along with the stories she had told of growing up on this farm. They would walk past the tree which, with its many huge limbs, had been declared the best climbing tree on the farm, and a fall from which had given Isabelle her first broken bone. They would cross over to the silo by the granary, where their eyes alone would climb the narrow ladder to the top, a one-hundred-foot ladder that each child who spent a day or a summer on the farm had been forbidden to climb and that each had climbed at least once in that eternal ritual of adolescent clandestine independence.

It was when they walked into the barn with its smell of dry hay and animals long gone, however, that Isabelle felt the first real moment of return. Her eyes adjusted first to the dark, bringing into focus the line of cattle stanchions, then to the past as she watched a dozen dairy cows file in and compliantly put their heads through the bars of the medieval-looking machine, less out of obedience than out of habit reinforced by the hay on the other side of the bars. Then would come the metallic clatter as a strong arm pulled down a bar at one end of the contraption, locking all the heads in place.

Isabelle idly reached over to Linda to keep her from leaning into a corner covered with a translucent spiderweb centered by a spider, harmless but approximately the size of a child's thumb. She smiled absently at Linda's look of horror, and with an arm around her lover's waist, inhaled deeply, as if she were in a flower garden. She smelled the coolness of the cement, the sweetness of the remnants of hay in the loft above them, the dryness of the dust motes angling down from the small, dirty windows. She was also smelling a memory: the pungent, moist, almost spicy smell of fresh cow's milk, with the background smell of manure and cow piss which she had

never found offensive. The picture accompanying this
scent came from an elevated viewpoint, as she remembered sitting on the back of Miss Babbs, the aged and for
the most part immobile Holstein which was always first
in line to be milked. A wry half smile accompanied her
"hmmm" as she realized that the head of the man leaning
into the side of the cow he was milking next to her was
Frank's. It was Frank who had lifted her onto the back of
Miss Babbs, Frank whom she could hear singing, "Who
kicked Nelly in the belly in the barn."

It was this same gentle man who had occasionally
cracked the handy two-by-four across the butt or along-
side the head of any one of Miss Babbs's cronies who
refused to understand the concept of herding. And it was
Frank who finally admitted that he hated "fooling with
those damned beasts," strong words from this man,
brought out only by the recalcitrant bovine. Thus, the
dairy side of this barn had stood swept and empty for
many years.

Isabelle came out of her reverie when she realized that
Linda had asked a question.

"Sorry?"

"If their heads were stuck in this contraption, why'd
they need to be tied, too?"

"They weren't." Then, following Linda's motion,
Isabelle noted with pleasure that once again there was
twine hanging from some of the bars on the old cattle
stanchions.

"Becky or Janie must have tied those there," Isabelle
explained, smiling at what was evidently the recurrence
of a game she and Irene had played for hours, in which
the curved steel pipes that separated each cow's space
had become an imaginary horse. Part of the locking
mechanism then became stirrups, and a piece of twine
tied to a pipe in front, the reins. Day after summer day,

Isabelle and Irene had ridden in place, side by side, planning the next bank robbery, dividing up the loot from the last holdup. The next generation on the farm, Glenn and Craig, had shown no interest in this game. Animals, real or imaginary, lacked the attraction of balls to be hit, thrown, kicked, tossed, and served. Isabelle was surprised but pleased to see that her imagination had galloped through another generation, even if the rides were already, for Becky, at least, a thing of the past. I'll have to come out here with Janie, Isabelle thought, swinging her leg over the pipe and quickly rethinking the idea, finding no way to comfortably seat her bony bottom.

Beside the milking stanchions were two square ten-by-ten-foot pens, also made of the same gray pipe, and each also containing a single stanchion where a calf could be held securely while being vetted, or where a cow could be secured while her calf was being attended to. Here, Isabelle recalled for Linda, the twins had graduated to rodeoing when they tired of riding the range on pipe ponies. They would herd a young steer into the pen in the barn, and get it secured into the stanchion with a bucket of oats as bait. One of the twins would then get on the animal's back while the other lifted the release bar, setting the wild beast free. Most of the time the steer would quietly continue to munch at the feed, while the twin standing on the outside would play the role of announcer, energetically providing commentary unmatched by the steer's immobility, until both girls, overwhelmed by their own silliness, collapsed in giggles. Sometimes the steer, when released, would walk about the pen, its hide shivering as if irritated by flies, until it managed to rub the rider off onto the side bars. Still, the anticipation in this game was always high. Because there was always the possibility that this would be one of the very few bona fide rodeo steer rides. Short rides they were, the last ride of all ending with Irene's concussion at ten years old. Isabelle remembered wishing sincerely that she were the one unconscious and bleeding in the corner and not the one who had to set the steer free and run to the house for her mother. (Or was it Mavis?) At least Irene had the good sense to be apologetic for ruining what had been a very fun game. Maybe, Isabelle suggested to Linda, her grin disappearing, Irene had suffered a head injury far beyond what the doctor had thought at the time. Maybe that explained Jack.

The barn was partitioned in two, lengthwise, and as Isabelle and Linda slid the separating door open onto the other, larger side, with its open and swept cement floor, they came upon Janie in the process of explaining to three bewildered girls the contest rules of bumper bikes, which had something to do with 360-degree turns around the supporting beams, and a set number of allowed bumps into the other biker before crossing the finish line. It sounded a lot like a good way to get hurt, and Isabelle quickly ushered Linda through so that they wouldn't have to witness the game and thus be called upon to intervene in the name of adult caution. As they walked through the far barn door, Isabelle pointed out the names painted above what once had been the stalls of work-horses: Don, Prince, Erie, Jerrie, Pedro, Bill, Chub, Fannie, Nellie, Ethel, Dandy. Already cryptic references to a motorless past by the time of Isabelle's youth, the names written in the air had become mythical as succeeding generations pointed to the painted names with much the same mixture of reverence and curiosity directed toward the Lascaux cave paintings.

And the tour continued. Here would have been a haystack where they played king of the mountain. Here where a neighbor, Bernice Langdahl (now Johnsruud), and Mavis tied up Maxine in a game and then forgot about her, and when their mother released her three hours later, she wasn't even mad because she'd had her pocket copy of *Little Women* with her. There the hay mow windows they'd jumped out of while running away from cousins, resulting in Isabelle's now-chronically-sprained right thumb. There the creek with muskrats, turtles, crawdads, frogs and toads. There the cattle shed, which, with its long, sloping, icy roof, provided the perfect post-blizzard surface for sliding on a piece of cardboard, the two-foot drop to the eight-foot snowdrift below the highlight of the slide. The six sisters had formed their own, self-contained little community. Sometimes the girls were three units: Maxine and Mavis, Janice and Judy, Irene and Isabelle. Sometimes they were two: two older girls and four little ones. Sometimes their defining characteristic was Mavis as mother hen watching over her mischievous brood. As they grew older, however, each sister spent more and more time alone. But always, Irene was nearby.

"I miss Irene," Isabelle said suddenly. They were walking toward the house, across the yard space that would become a makeshift softball diamond by the end of the day. Isabelle had stopped and was watching the family members move about, and sit about, telling stories with their hands. In particular she was watching a newly formed group of Mavis with Maxine, Janice, and Norton, who must have just arrived. Odd. Mavis and Janice were hugging closely. This was the type of family that traded kissed cheeks in greeting and short hugs in parting. Other physical contact was restricted to funerals. Since Mavis and Janice saw each other weekly, there was no reason for them to ever kiss or hug.

"Maybe we're all just getting old," Isabelle said out loud.

Linda had no idea how Isabelle's last two statements were related, but didn't doubt that some series of recollections and observations tied them together for her lover. She watched Isabelle intently as Isabelle surveyed her relatives. And she watched Isabelle take a big sigh and set her shoulders, which she knew meant that Izzy was saying to herself something like, "Well, let's do this, then, and do it the best we can." It was a gesture Linda knew well, and she smiled in grim recollection as she pictured Mavis rising from her chair the evening before to greet her.

Isabelle abruptly started to stride across the yard toward her family.

"Darling, don't forget about me," Linda quietly called, walking behind Isabelle for the moment.

Isabelle turned to face Linda with a look Linda had seen often enough but still found unsettling. It was almost as if Isabelle were looking at someone she didn't recognize, as if the trip into the clarity of the past had blurred her vision of the present. With a shake of her head, Isabelle reached over to touch Linda's cheek with the backs of her fingers. "Haven't you noticed? We can't forget anything here."

Isabelle and Linda joined Mavis, Janice, and Maxine. Norton had paid his respects to the great-aunts with a wave and a hello directed toward anyone in the vicinity and was headed for the machine shed. This time introductions were easy. Maxine had met Linda some years back when she had spent a few days at Greenview following a Modern Languages Association convention in San Francisco. They had quickly become friends. Janice was quietly gracious, as usual, perhaps the only one of the sisters, besides Irene, who thought it worthwhile to get to know someone before forming an opinion.

The older sisters had been laughingly trying to figure out who should go talk with which aunt first. Mavis had already spent a good deal of time with both, so she didn't count. Simply sending Janice to one and Maxine to the other wasn't the easy solution it first appeared to be. Janice saw the aunts five or six times a year at least, whereas Maxine only saw them during her infrequent returns to North Dakota. Clearly, Maxine's choice was more important.

"We could just wait here until another nobody shows up," Janice suggested, "and then he or she could be part of my party. Surely two locals are worth one Maxine."

Mavis doubted it. Besides, she added, everyone who was coming was already here. Along with the five sisters, there were Glenn and Peggy, and their girls; Craig; Janice's son, Jimmy, with his wife, Pam, and their three kids; Janice's daughter, Tina, with her baby and her boyfriend Alex; Aunt Alice; Aunt Emma; the sisters' first cousin Bobby and his wife Grace; Bobby's sister, Evie, a widow who had brought their mother, the sisters' Auntie Lucy, from the Rippon nursing home. A recent stroke had frozen Auntie Lucy's face into a mask of cruel venom, which the relatives found disconcerting on the woman who had lacked the temerity to say "boo to a goose." There was another cousin, Big Dan, with his wife Gloria; their grown son Gary and his wife Susan and their four children, plus the two friends their kids had brought along. Rounding out the group was their second cousin Louise, a recent widow, with her unmarried daughter, Marge, who at forty still lived at home.

"Oh no, everyone isn't here who's coming," Maxine stated, eyebrows raised, lips purposefully prim, suggesting some mysterious implication.

"That's right," Janice added, with her own quieter version of the Schmidt snort.

"Who?" Mavis and Isabelle demanded simultaneously.

"Remember the kind man who helped Judy with her

car when it overheated in Watertown? Well, Judy tells us this morning that she's given him directions here and that he'll be joining our picnic this afternoon."

"Good Lord," from Isabelle.

"Now, he may be very nice," Janice cautioned. "Judy says he's nice-looking and charming. And what was it she said, Maxine? He's . . . what's the word she used? Urbane. Whatever she means by that."

"To Judy, it probably means he lives in a town," Isabelle said, drawing a reluctant laugh from Linda and a willing laugh from the others.

Mavis noted that Peggy was beginning to set out food, and she was about to go help when she saw her sons walking together toward the inner yard. Big, handsome, good men, she loved to see them together. Both well over six feet, Glenn had added bulk to Frank's frame, while Craig was all lean angles. Mavis assumed, correctly, that they were talking about farming. Whereas Glenn was either unwilling or unable to visualize Craig's life to the degree necessary to sustain a conversation in that direction much beyond "So how're things going?" Craig slipped easily into Glenn's world. Although this farm was no longer Craig's home, this was a land whose lessons Craig carried within; lessons of openness and self-sufficiency tempered by the constant awareness of a nature and a power bigger than anything human. It was not the symphony, not the coffeehouses, not the jazz bars, not even Mount Rainier off in the background, but this land well over a thousand miles away that allowed him to breathe deeply, that brought him calm when he began to shake with fear, or anger.

This wasn't something he could actually describe to his big brother: say Glenn, when I think about thousands dying young, I close my eyes and put myself in a tractor pulling a wagon filled with just-picked corn. I look back at that mound of hard yellow and then I slowly, so slowly, Glenn, turn my head and look at the fields, and the fences, and the shelterbelts, and the road, and then more fields and the railroad track, until I'm looking back at that mound of corn again over my other shoulder. Or this: Glenn, sometimes when I hear the voices of hate telling me we all deserve to die, I close my eyes and lie down in the snow next to you in those big parkas with the fur-trimmed hoods, and we make angels in the snow, and then I just lie there as the cold starts to seep into my butt and legs, and it's so quiet, Glenn, so quiet with the day darkening, and the only sound is a crack coming from somewhere in the trees. A branch breaking under snow? A ghost's footstep? You always went in first. And Glenn, so many times I just lay there, looking up, up into the dark, the quiet, the space.

No, this isn't what he could say, or needed to say. It was enough that Glenn was here tending the land, was the caretaker of this place that held Craig's looking-backward dreams. So they talked about farming. About ditching. About the machinery, the farm programs, the costs. Craig, grateful, and Glenn, unaware that there were other conversations worthwhile.

Craig stopped to scratch the old dog that would lie in the shade all day but would occasionally make the heavy effort of ambling over to put his nose against Glenn's pant leg. Craig felt a lump on the dog's chest and pulled away a fat ripe green berry of blood, dropped it to the ground and felt more than heard the satisfying pop as the tick exploded under his shoe. His attention was pulled away from the spot of dark red blood on the gravel driveway by his mother's wave, and he and his brother crossed the driveway into the yard.

"Glenn, is that really a Hamm's? I didn't know you

could still get that beer. It's been years . . ." Maxine wondered out loud.

"Dan's contribution."

"From the land of sky-blue waters," Maxine began to sing, and the rest quickly joined in:

"Comes the beer refreshing. Hamm's, the beer refreshing!"

"Oh Lord," Janice said, "now we'll be humming that song all day long."

"You know, it was years before I realized the 'Hiawatha' intertextuality," Maxine muttered.

"Say what?"

"*From* the *land* of . . ."

"Trochaic pentameter," Mavis threw in.

"Tetrameter."

"No, count them: On the shores of Gitchee Gumee . . ." Mavis hesitated as she topped the fourth finger of her left hand with the counting index finger of the right. "You're right, tetrameter."

"Who cares?" Isabelle threw in, smiling at her pedantic siblings.

"Well, it is an interesting advertising angle. I suppose we were being encouraged, subliminally, to associate drinking beer with the pristine freshness of a new world, validated by the background meter of a wholesome poet."

Suddenly Janice began chanting:

> *"On the shores of Gitchee Gumee,*
> *Of the shining Big-Sea-Water,*
> *Stood Nokomis, the old woman,*
> *Pointing with her finger westward,*
> *O'er the water pointing westward,*
> *To the purple clouds of sunset."*

Isabelle rotated Janice's extended arm about thirty degrees to the left. "That's westward, Nokomis."

"Good Lord," Mavis remembered, "you wore that grimy headband with its sorry feather for a week after your school program. You and Lucy Gentry."

"Minnehaha."

Suddenly the four sisters were chanting and, inexplicably, hopping and bobbing, in unison:

> *"Minnie-Minnie Ha-Ha*
> *Went to see her Pa-pa*
> *Pa-pa died*
> *Minnie-Minnie cried*
> *Minnie had a newborn ba-a-by*
> *Wrapped it up in tissue paper*
> *Threw it in an elevator*
> *First . . . floor . . . stop!"*

And just as suddenly the women were still, although there were a couple of hands on chests and some resultant heavy breathing.

"All this from a Hamm's beer," wondered Glenn, smiling broadly. "And all I remember is the bear. I really loved that bear. I used to pretend in Bible school that my Fizzies were Hamm's Fizzies."

"Fizzies!" the sisters crowed in unison.

"Now that's something I haven't thought about for years," Maxine said.

"Nothing very poetic about Fizzies, I guess," Isabelle teased.

"I just said it was interesting, that's all."

Mavis added her own teasing: "I see a new book developing. Say, perhaps no one has done a significant study on the Burma Shave sayings."

"Don't laugh," Maxine said, laughing herself, "it's a whole new world of scholarship out there."

"Well, here at least, some things don't change," Craig said. "For example, Glenn and I have a problem."

"Just one?" Maxine asked.

"Well, two actually," Glenn explained. "Aunt Alice and Aunt Emma. If we split up to say hi, whoever gets me is bound to feel like she got the shitty end of the stick."

The solution was obvious. Glenn and Maxine would head toward one aunt, Craig and Janice to the other.

"But someone better go help Judy start the barbecue," Janice said. "She's sending some nasty looks our way."

"Full of wrath was Hiawatha," Maxine chanted.

"A pain in the ass was Hiawatha," Isabelle added. "I'm going to go talk farming with the men," she announced, meaning that she was headed toward the machine shed and the beer. "I'll tell them the food's almost on." As she turned to go, she noticed that Tina was setting down a full pan of bars on the long table. Isabelle stopped, caught Mavis's eye, and with a small nod of her head, led Mavis's gaze to the pan of bars.

With a barely disguised smile, Mavis answered Isabelle's look of mock horror, picked up the pan, and said to a surprised Tina, "Let's put these bars on that pretty tray I gave Peggy for her birthday," adding, under her breath, "I'll explain in the kitchen." Mavis's smile included Linda, who followed them inside.

Isabelle, grinning to herself, crossed the yard thinking of Gloria's spice bars, hard, dry, and tasteless, with a cracked caramel frosting. They were legendary, not because of their flavor, but because of their probable age. The sisters had learned years before that if a full pan were set on the table in the afternoon, with a fork nearby for serving, that sometime during the day the fork might disappear, but the pan would remain unmolested. At the end of the occasion, Gloria would sweetly comment that people evidently hadn't been very hungry. Then, the sisters were convinced, she would take the pan of bars home and freeze it, to be resurrected and thawed for the next potluck. Isabelle even insisted that once, many years ago, she and Irene had forced thumbprints into the frosting to test their theory, and that that same pan had been identified at a wedding shower a full six months later. Thus began the strategy of chiseling out a dozen or so bars to be placed on a plate, which in this form would even be approached by a few unsuspecting children. To their further delight, the sisters noticed that Gloria's reaction to her newfound culinary success was clearly disappointment.

The kitchen was the scene of an intricately coordinated dance of women pulling pickles, catsup, and mustard out of the refrigerator, placing bars on plates, bringing beans out of the oven, mixing lemonade, stacking buns, taking the Saran Wrap off bowls of Jell-O, cutting pies, and stirring potato salad. Tina and Mavis deftly entered the dance, while Linda stood uncomfortably by, listening to nonsense conversations until she gratefully accepted a slobbering baby from . . . ?

"I'm Pam. He just wants someone to move with him. Are you sure you don't mind?"

She didn't. In fact, she welcomed the opportunity to escape the hustle and bustle of the kitchen and the four-way conversations that only she seemed incapable of following.

Just outside the door, Judy had begun to grill hamburgers and hot dogs, accompanied by the advice of Glenn, who now made up the fourth hand of whist at the card table nearby. His partner for the moment was Auntie Lucy, who, although largely immobile, was able to maneuver her right hand well enough to pluck out the appropriate card from the selection fanned out in front of her and held by her daughter Evie, who made up the fifth in a four-handed game, and who used her free hand to tug at her bangs in a nervous mannerism that Judy insisted was the result of years of pulling at those tight perms Auntie Lucy gave her all through high school. Just now it was the only card game in action, but by the time the grill cooled, there would be at least three tables of whist going nonstop, with most likely Janice and Mavis holding court at the winners' table.

The smell of grilling beef caused a troop of sweaty and dirty children to appear. They would eat first and fast. A few of the older children would sit in with parents, playing a couple hands of whist themselves, but they'd tire of this quickly and with their parents' encouragement would get the softball equipment and play their own version of quarrelsome coed workup.

In the meantime, no longer separated by gender, the men and the women formed groups over card tables and paper plates with talk and banter about the usual. There would be the comments about "enough food here to feed a threshing crew," which would precede some general remarks about Saddam Hussein, but the conversation would quickly settle into matters of more immediate import: state politics, grain prices, someone's auction, someone's wedding, someone's new car, new tractor, new ideas, old habits. A few Norwegian jokes would be passed around as well as a few racist jokes that only Craig, Maxine, Linda, and reluctantly, Isabelle, would recognize or admit as such. At some point a brave youngster would sidle up to Dan, an older man with an easy humor quite at odds with his closed, craggy face. Why, the youngster would ask, was Dan's right index finger like that, knowing full well the answer he would get. Dan would frown, and look down at the shortened digit he was born with as if it were the first time he had noticed the thing, too. Then he'd hold up the finger topped by a tough narrow ridge of horned nail that sat like an eraser on the tip of his finger, and answer, as expected, "Well, when I was about your age I was picking my nose one day, and sneezed. So I wouldn't be picking my nose if I was you."

This particular youngster was Jimmy and Pam's six-year-old Sam, already known for brave, if not always respectful, rejoinders. "Why would I be picking your nose, anyway?" Sam squealed, finishing with his own hiccuping laugh, which he had learned long ago allowed him to get away with just about anything.

"Okay, Sam, beat it," came Pam's voice as she jerked a thumb toward the other kids across the road playing softball. She swatted him playfully on the butt as he passed, mother and son exchanging smiles.

It wasn't long until the talk among the adults returned to the weather, which had refused to settle down this past week. First hot and dry, then the needed rain, and then the heat was slapped back to the earth by this enervating humidity. As the afternoon progressed, the heat and the humidity remained constant, but the sky, which had begun the morning as a dingy blue, was steadily graying, too early to be due to a setting sun. Earlier, the men in the machine shed had been listening to the weather report, which had forecast a windy evening, possibly accompanied by severe thunderstorms. There had been no mention of a tornado watch, but watch they would.

Rain in the forecast made the men feel uneasy about taking an afternoon off this time of year, even though it was Sunday. Although no one had said it out loud, most of the relatives here had felt summoned, in some way, by the timing of Mavis's call for a picnic. And although no one would ask questions directly of Mavis, they were all hoping that she would finally say something that would help them make sense of this shooting business. So they thought a little about murder and talked a lot about the weather, and waited.

The relatives who weren't playing whist were sprawled on blankets or on lawn chairs, trying to get comfortable following the picnic meal that never exactly ended but tapered off with Rice Krispies bars covered with a chocolate and peanut butter cement, when a Volkswagen van that looked like it had just driven out of a time machine pulled into the driveway.

"That must be Judy's new beau," Isabelle proclaimed in a mock delighted voice, to no one in particular, as she held up a five of diamonds and showed it, smiling smugly, to her second cousin and old high school classmate Gary, seated to her right, before sliding it under the other cards to show that she had successfully ducked the trick in this low hand.

The Volkswagen was the shade of gray that each vehicle must be at some point before it is painted and to which it would eventually return if not for rust. There was little doubt as to which end of the life cycle this vehicle, weather-beaten and dented, was closest. The compartment door over the rear engine, however, had been recently replaced or repainted a bright pinkish-red color, giving the van the look of one of those cherry-assed baboons that draw the largest crowds of awed spectators at zoos. It carried the requisite dozen or so bumper stickers plastered around its backside, suggesting the need to save whales, dolphins, and your mother (earth), supporting gun control, and documenting a series of elections lost: a Mondale/Ferraro sticker next to a *Lick Bush '88*, and a new, forward-looking *Bush/Noriega 1992* sticker. Above them all was the incongruous *I Don't*

Believe the Liberal Press message, frayed at the edges with an unsuccessful scraping. As the van rolled to a stop, the relatives smiled as the small percussion unit performing inside the van's engine compartment came to a belated halt some seconds after the engine had evidently been shut off.

Despite the fact that she knew she was being baited, Judy, at the picnic table next to Isabelle's card table, tugged at Isabelle's line. "That's not John, that's not his car. John drives a—"

"A red car," interrupted Isabelle, eyes still on the van. "A red car with one of those long protruding fronts. So where is he?"

"Something must have come up."

"More likely something came down," Isabelle muttered, shuffling the cards and ignoring Linda's look, which registered both surprise and dismay at Isabelle's venom.

Judy had a good excuse not to continue the conversation, for no one was paying either of these sisters any attention. Instead they were watching a young woman, tall, thin, and tanned, with hair cut brutally short, step out of the passenger side. The young woman stood quietly beside the van, hands by her sides, slowly scanning the gathering. Then, looking toward the house, her gaze stopped suddenly at the kitchen window. The only movement in the yard was the swaying branches and the flapping tablecloth reflecting the steadily increasing breeze that brought with it yet more heat and little relief. Some of the relatives may have had something appropriate to say, or at least the presence of mind to greet the newcomer, but something in her stance and in her blue eyes set deep into the strong, familiar cheekbones dictated the terms on which they would all meet.

Abruptly, the woman turned, reached behind the front

seat for a large backpack, and said something to the woman waiting behind the steering wheel. She then turned and walked, with backpack in hand, toward the house and toward Mavis, who had just opened the screen door, and letting it fall gently shut behind her with a clack, stood with her hand to her chest. Then Mavis dropped her hand, and the women walked slowly toward each other, eyes locked and watchful, but somehow expressionless. Linda would later retell this moment through the imagery of the western showdown, for each woman seemed to be weighing the decision of action or reaction. When the women were face-to-face, the younger one dropped her backpack, raised her hand as if to resist something unspoken by Mavis, and spoke herself. Her voice was insistent, as if she were in the middle of an argument.

"No." Then she hesitated and her voice softened. "I've come to stay for a while, Mavis. With you." A hesitation. Then, "Please, Mavis."

If hope is that thing with feathers, then pain is the void into which it flies. Only through pain is infinity understandable, because even people who grow up on the prairie can see the horizon. If the expressions of these women remained empty, it was because of a pain beyond representation. Mavis opened her arms and grimaced as the young woman moved into her embrace.

They stood together without moving while the others looked on, wondering what exactly they were watching. Into this moment entered a troop of children, marching two by two and led by Janie pumping a bat up and down like a drum major's baton. Together, as they snaked through the gathering, they chanted "Softball, softball," and placed the ball, bats, and the few gloves they had into the hands of the seemingly dumbstruck adults who could only be released into motion by the actors in the drama taking place before them. By Mavis or Jackie.

It was Jackie who signaled the next move, clapping a delighted Janie on the back and saying, "Of course, soft-ball! Everybody, softball."

The relatives who could got to their feet, some to greet Jackie before quickly moving to the makeshift diamond the kids had set up. Isabelle, Maxine, and Judy formed a core group with Mavis around Jackie. Janice stood behind Mavis, at once joining the group and holding her-self back. No one knew what to say. Jackie held on to Isabelle's hand, her eyes clouding for just a moment as she touched cheeks with her mother's twin.

"Listen, we all know that there are things that need to be said. But not now. I'm okay. Really. With all of you."

Jackie's statement was met with the silence of relief mingled with disbelief. This was Irene's volatile daughter, a young woman whose wildness had seemed more fren-zied than carefree, whose determined independence of the rigid moral codes of chronically conservative North Dakotans had spiraled quickly into a dependence on alcohol and cocaine following her mother's sudden death. Now this was also the daughter of a man recently mur-dered, evidently by one of the aunts she included in her welcome. What words could possibly make sense?

"Listen," she said again. "It doesn't matter where I've been. I'm sorry if I worried anybody. I've been keeping in touch with Blair, and he's been fuming about this family reunion. But I thought, well, hey, that's a good idea—celebrating my father's death. No, wait." She held up a hand to check the chorus of protestations. "I'm not being flip. I mean, I really thought, well, you know . . ." She began to sing: " 'Ding dong the witch is dead.' " She stopped with a short humorless chuckle. "Oh, I'm not making sense, and no I'm not drunk or high. It's just this—" The absence of expression that suddenly cleared her face of family recognition brought a chill to the sisters in the mugginess of the late afternoon. "I'm glad he's dead. I'm sorry for almost everything else in the world. But I'm glad the bastard's dead. I'm just glad it's over. Really."

Jackie spoke to the ground during most of this speech, embarrassed perhaps by its length as well as its content. Isabelle, Judy, and Maxine were studying her intently as she spoke. None of them noticed that Janice had moved forward beside Mavis, and the two were holding each other's eyes.

It was Isabelle who broke this silence. "Jackie," she said in a solemn voice. "There is one thing, at least, which we must know now."

The seriousness of her voice brought concerned looks from the sisters and the beginning of a head shake from Jackie.

"We must know," and here Isabelle's voice lightened, "who is that bohemian with the fashion disorder who brought you here and who is going to be constipated for a week if he actually eats all those beans and that many peanut butter Rice Krispies bars?"

The women swung their gazes to the driver of the van, who, it turned out, was not a woman, but a longhaired man making a serious run at the remaining food on the picnic table. Probably in his mid-forties, he was wearing a T-shirt advertising mustache rides for a nickel, tie-dyed sweat pants, and a kerchief on his head. Feeling their eyes on him, the man smiled and waved the Jell-O spoon in greeting.

"Oh, that's George. But he told me he prefers being called Alpha-Omega, or just A.O. I've been hitchhiking around for a while," Jackie answered vaguely. "He picked me up just outside the Cities. He's on his way to

Idaho and isn't exactly on a strict time schedule, and since this is so close to the interstate, he said he'd bring me here directly. I promised him gas money and food in return."

If he were planning on staying for any length of time, Mavis suggested, perhaps he could be convinced to change into another T-shirt. The sisters laughed, choosing not to recognize that Mavis was dead serious and could be counted on to personally see to his costume change before any of the kids decided to take a closer look.

"I'll take care of him and send him on his way," said Craig, who had quietly joined the women, slipping an arm around Jackie's waist. "If he's going through Montana, I should tell him about the construction on I-94 around Miles City."

"Aren't you going to play?" Isabelle asked.

"In a minute. In the meantime, the teams could use some more players, so get going, ladies."

"Women," Isabelle added automatically, and then, turning to Jackie, asked in a stage whisper as they crossed the driveway, "Is George single?"

"Well, his history seems a little complicated. But that's the impression I got." Jackie looked quizzically at Isabelle.

"There you go, Judy. Another hot one for you," Isabelle called as the women split up, three to each team already formed.

What next took place looked very much like a softball game in spite of the idiosyncratic ground rules. Anyone who hit the ball too far into center field, and thus over the fence and into the pasture, was automatically out. With only one softball available, chances of losing it couldn't be taken. There was one exception: if the batter hit the ball over the fence and into a fresh cow pie, that was an automatic home run. Since Glenn's few remaining beef cattle hadn't been anywhere near this part of the pasture all day, however, that particular ruling was unlikely to come into play. The boys and Janie were all duly informed that throwing the ball too hard around the bases was strictly verboten—an important rule since few of the fielders had gloves and a few of the players hadn't touched a softball since the last family picnic.

The bases weren't regulation distance apart, whatever that would be, but were about equidistant, although first base could be counted on to "float," depending on the talents of the particular first baseman. Glenn would be stationed there for his team, having taken over his father's role as the first-base clown. A fine athlete, he could seemingly fumble a catch indefinitely, keeping the ball bouncing in the air, off his hands, off his knees, waiting for the last possible second to pull the ball in for the out. Unless, of course, the runner was very young. Then there was the chance that the runner would touch base just a split second before Glenn finally took control of the ball, usually to the loud groans of the other youngsters on his team.

And since the teams were always short a few players, some of the older relatives choosing to nap, play whist, or continue their armchair farming, each batting team provided its own catcher, making for some questionable calls at home plate. Mavis's team had one more player, but Mavis said she was just going to hit and field, that Sam would be her runner, and somehow that logic satisfied everyone.

All in all, with the restrictions on hitting, throwing, and sliding, this should have been a fairly mild game, but never was. For this, too, was a game of words, softball banter taken to a higher plane of abuse.

The end of the game, determined by the whims and aches of the adults, and followed by the pleas of children for "just one more" inning, signaled the beginning of the end of the picnic. Mothers told their children to start thinking about going home, giving the kids a half hour to get used to the idea while the adults had their last cup of coffee or beer in the now, they noted with surprise, almost still twilight. Despite the scattered jokes and self-mockery concerning the declining athletic ability of aging adults, lapses into silence were frequent as their attention was drawn to the approaching darkness from the north. With the laughs a bit strained and the pans and plates gathered with barely concealed haste, no one needed to identify the urgency that was steadily knotting each chest. The stillness and the leaden sky were promising a storm, soon. The men began to discuss hail insurance.

"Your Lone Ranger is gone, Jackie," Isabelle remarked as Craig came to stand by their side. "That reminds me. Where's your new dude, Jude, in his red Trans Am?"

"I don't know and I don't really care. He didn't say he'd be here for sure. I just said he was invited and he said he might show up." She hesitated. "And he drives a Z."

"Well, hey man," put in Craig, "I mean, like wow, two strangers in one day would be, like hey, just too crazy. Do ya dig?"

Jackie shook her head. "Give it up, Craig. You are obviously not, and never were, hippie material."

"So what did you two talk about, then?" Glenn asked Craig.

"Fashion. And his passion for the color purple. I quote: 'Purple is the perfect mix between two essential states: blue, which is the spiritual and peaceful expanse of the soul in its quietness; and red, which is tumultuous emotion, completely embraced within the worldly. When I wear them both, as one, I am complete.' "

"That's really queer. What did you say to that?"

Craig hesitated, then smiled. "I said I liked his earring."

Aunt Alice and Aunt Emma, who had been watching and commenting upon the approaching weather all afternoon, were giving the impression of hens nervously stirring and settling back onto their nests all during the ball game. They had no intentions of being out when the storm broke. Their movements suggested that if their rides didn't get on the stick, they would set off down the road themselves on foot and cane. Dan and Gloria took the cue and gathered up Aunt Alice, who still lived by herself near their farm. Susan and Gary were ready to take Aunt Emma home, although now she seemed to be weighing the horrors of a twenty-mile walk in a storm against a return ride in a station wagon with six children. Glenn solved her dilemma, saying that he and Craig had planned on taking a drive "around the section" before the storm, and they'd be happy to give Emma a ride home. Children and elderly riders were gathered and cars quickly pulled out of the yard into an atypical dusk, early and deep.

The remaining women settled into the kitchen left clean by the same hands that had cleared the picnic tables during the softball game. Norton, the only male on the place now and a bit unsteady on his feet, made his way to the living room, to the TV, and to sleep.

Mavis, Maxine, Janice, and Jackie were at chairs on three sides of the kitchen table, which was pushed up against an interior wall on one long side. Judy and Peggy sat on the counter, a sight Janie and Becky would have loved to see, as they were consistently denied that perch themselves. The two girls were up in Becky's room

watching her new TV, having been reminded to first
make sure that all the windows were closed. Linda was
sitting on a stool next to the telephone by the kitchen/
dining room door, and Isabelle was positioned by the
refrigerator, making drinks.

The talk was still light, jokes made about the aunts
Emma and Alice which always ended in, "God willing,
I'll have half their brains at that age," complaints passed
around about sore knees or hips in reference to the
slowing gaits and reflexes seen on the softball field, and
comments about the threatening skies and the stillness
that seemed to pressurize the atmosphere. This was
throwaway talk, in preparation for what the women now
believed to be the meeting that had been called by Mavis,
the reason they were home.

Jackie declined a drink, choosing another Pepsi, much
to everyone's barely hidden relief. She had yet to explain
her AWOL status from the Hazelden. Isabelle, too,
decided she'd had enough beer for the day, telling herself
that Linda's presence didn't prohibit her from heavy
drinking; it just seemed less important. Linda, in turn,
had accurately gauged the tenor of this moment and was
in the process of excusing herself. She had been welcomed genially today, if not warmly, which made her
optimistic concerning her place in the family. But optimism looks to the future. At this moment she knew she
was an outsider, and whatever was about to happen
among these women wouldn't happen as long as she was
present. So, referring to some work she had brought with
her, and secretly looking forward to the time by herself,
Linda said her good-byes for the day and left, grazing
Isabelle's hand with hers. The women in the kitchen listened to her drive out of the yard in Craig's Bronco.

"She's a lovely person, Isabelle," Peggy said a minute
later. "I'm glad we got to meet her finally."

"She really is," Judy added incredulously. "Absolutely amazing, Izzy. How you can fall into a pile of shit and come up smelling like a rose, I don't know," she added.

Isabelle felt her face redden, partly from the attention to her personal life, partly in anger at Judy's comment. Judy was rarely subtle, but this was an open insult, regardless of its basis in ignorance. With unusual restraint, Isabelle turned from Judy without speaking, and smiling at Peggy as she set Mavis's first drink of the day, a vodka–grapefruit juice, in front of her, said, "I'm glad you got to meet her, too."

Mavis reached over and patted Isabelle's hand twice, setting the seal of approval.

Soon each woman had something to drink in front of her. Isabelle was on the stool Linda had left empty. Then there was that most unusual of circumstances for these women—silence.

A waiting silence. A silence as heavy as the stillness outside the window.

And then it began. The fat drops falling singly, one, two, then more, then more, quickly, splatting on the glass panes of the window. They fell faster and faster, accompanied by the audible rush of the returning wind, bringing with it the storm. Soon the rain was battering the windows. Then came the lightning, briefly displaying the outbuildings through the bay window, the silently counted seconds, and the clap of thunder.

Slowly each woman realized that she was also listening to a voice that had begun with the rain. Slowly the drops transferred to cheeks throughout the darkening room as the voice went on. And on.

MAVIS

"I HAVEN'T ALWAYS DONE THE RIGHT THING," MAVIS IS saying, "but I have always tried. Maybe too hard. Maybe not enough, after all. But I'm doing the best I know how, and I must, I will, do this thing my way."

Mavis listens to her own voice, soothing for once, even to herself. She knows she is about to tell the truths she needs them to hear, not the facts they may want to know. There are no words in her now about murder, about cancer. She has nothing to say about adultery or betrayal or envy or disappointment. She has nothing to say about death. Now she speaks of life, her life, their lives. This is how she says good-bye.

Four sisters, a niece, and a daughter-in-law listen in a farmhouse kitchen that darkens steadily with the night and the building storm. Lightning interruptions occasionally pierce the bay window to illuminate the increasingly youthful voice of the senior woman. Now and then a hand reaches across the Formica tabletop to tap out a cigarette from a package, and a lighter brings into relief a sister's face, a face no longer in a farmhouse kitchen, but now inside another's voice.

Mavis begins her tale of duty done, of care given, of wounds and underwear washed, of homework and dates reviewed, of dresses sewn and prides mended. One by one she picks her sisters up and hands them cookies as they run out the door to play, puts them behind school desks in clean, pressed dresses, gives them books to read—on pioneer women, on birth control. She places the younger sisters in their cribs, places balls in their hands, places curlers in their hair. One last time she holds the baby twins close.

Each sister is embraced, cherished, loved as she becomes a gift, a present, to Mavis, to the others, and then back to herself. Ragged strikes of lightning outline Mavis's awe as she lists the early accomplishments of her closest sister. Thunder punctuates Mavis's words, the elements growling agreement with her soliloquy.

"When Maxine was in the third grade she could already keep up with me in my reading book. By the time I was in high school she was helping *me* with *my* homework."

As Mavis speaks, Maxine feels her own schoolgirl hand slip into her sister's grip, and together they yell, "Red Rover, Red Rover, let Bernice come over"; together they collect eggs, hang out the laundry, read poetry, write essays. Sitting in the dark, Maxine feels, once again, encouraged into the world, trusting and trusted in her abilities, her intellect.

For just a moment that intellect catches on Mavis's pride, which lays claim to Maxine's accomplishments. Then, in the momentary day of a lightning flash, Maxine finds Mavis's eyes smiling on her. And bids her intellect relax as she renders unto Mavis that which is Mavis's due: a gratitude that costs so little in the giving.

Maxine lets her body fill with a sigh, then finds herself grinning as Mavis now leads three sisters back in time, to a weekday morning in a chilly farmhouse where the two oldest sisters, now teens, help a wide-eyed five-year-old Judy into her prettiest dress, tie her hair up in a new ribbon, and lead her to the breakfast table so charged with excitement that their mother hasn't the heart to say no to their plans of taking Judy to school with them, a walking doll to be coddled by teenage girls, winked at by teenage boys, and tolerated by teachers.

Judy hungrily stares into the mirror Mavis holds up to her youth, to ringlets and ribbons and afternoons of experimenting with Mavis's makeup. Although she faces the kitchen window, she does not see the rain that pelts the panes because she is fascinated by the picture that Mavis draws with generous strokes, a picture of a pretty little girl developing into a beautiful young woman. A sudden flash from the storm replaces Judy's picture with the Dakota night and lights up Mavis's wry laughter.

"Of course, I've never quite forgiven myself for lying to poor Fred Stanner. Him standing there as red-faced as a stood-up teenage boy could be, and me just as embarrassed, an adult telling a bald-faced lie to a kid, and you wriggling and giggling under the kitchen tablecloth where you'd ducked at the last minute when you decided you didn't want to go out with him."

Judy, too, laughs, tickled to see Mavis in the role of accomplice. Neither notices that the chuckles of the other sisters are slight, Isabelle reluctant to add to Judy's pleasure, and Maxine resisting a new awareness of the degree to which Mavis's tolerance, if not encouragement, of Judy's youthful capriciousness may have contributed to the less attractive self-absorption into which she grew. Janice's silence has nothing to do with Judy. Her heart pounds with anticipation as she waits to be seen, while her stomach tightens in anger as she expects to be minimized back into childhood by Mavis's portrayal. We are middle-aged women, for God's sake, not children, she thinks, hands clenched in her lap.

Then suddenly, to her surprise, she hears herself laugh out loud as the chair she sits on becomes a swing that flies into the air, propelled by the same hands that later lift from her eyes to reveal a birthday cake; she feels relief as the mysteries of long division clear under the influence of a patient voice; she breathes in the calm of busy and shared household tasks. Before Janice can relax into the seduction of Mavis's obvious love, however, an uncertainty clouds her recollections, for the face that dampens with the effort of bluing a tub of clothes, that leans over her chair with explanations, that looks over a bedsheet drying on the clothesline, is now Mavis's, now her mother's, now she cannot determine which. A series of electric strokes of light in the far distance translates the kitchen's darkness into pulsing shadows and outlines, and Janice looks up from her lap to meet Mavis's words, and sees Mavis see her not as a child, but as a mother with a child of her own.

"When you put Jimmy in my arms, I thought perhaps I had never seen a baby so beautiful, or a mother so happy. Nor, do I think, I had ever seen you so determined to do your job well. Perhaps I haven't told you often enough how much I respect that in you. It's a hard thing to do— to give something our all. It's harder still to know when to let go."

Mavis stops, as if this is to be the enigmatic note on which her discourse into the past will end. For a moment the skies are silent and the night holds its darkness. Into the quiet comes Isabelle, no longer forty-six years old, but once again the demanding baby of the family.

"What about me?"

"Izzy, Izzy, Izzy." Mavis replies in a bolt of light, and the women laugh aloud as a three-part rumble of thunder follows, echoing her repetition. "You have never been boring, I'll give you that."

Mavis now races to keep up with the pace that Isabelle set as a youth. The sisters wince as Mavis cleans and bandages knees and elbows shredded by falls from bicycles onto gravel; chuckle as Mavis gives Izzy books that she immediately sets aside, only to find them more quickly still replaced in her hands; marvel along with Mavis as she watches Isabelle's long legs carry her across finish line after finish line with no competitor near.

A startling clap of thunder directly overhead suddenly rattles the old farmhouse, the bay window frames a jagged bolt that forks over the barn, and Mavis opens her heart wider still.

"When Frank died, I found out what a terrible thing alone can be. I was lucky, I guess, to be fifty-five years old before I knew." Mavis hesitates, then blesses Isabelle's love. "I would not want you to be alone."

Then, in the dark, Isabelle speaks once more.

"And Irene?" Needing to hear, from Mavis, the words that will bring her twin into the room to once again sit beside her.

Mavis looks beyond the curtain of rain that clings to the window, into the static light that shimmers in the heat of the storm.

"Out there in the yard, buried and forgotten under a dozen trees, there must be a dozen shoe boxes filled with birds or mice, and Frisky, of course. Mom would just hand Irene the spade and tell me to ignore her, but I worried that she was becoming obsessed with death. So one day, I suppose she was seven or eight, I suggested that she didn't need to bury every dead animal she found. Irene just looked at me in utter amazement, like how did I get to be an adult and still be such a complete simpleton. Then, I'll always remember her words, she said, 'Why shouldn't I make it all right, if I can?' So she buried whatever was dead, and smoothed out the dirt, and made it 'all right.' " Mavis's sigh was deep. "She just wanted to make things all right."

"Don't we all? Don't we all?"

Maxine's voice holds a sadness, and a smile, and a question. It is the question each has been trying to ask since the moment Mavis claimed the impossible. It is the question each has expected to hear answered within this kitchen, within this storm, this evening. But Mavis is not taking questions. Hers is a litany of family, a ritual casting into a form of her choosing, a form into which she can neatly press their lives. Perhaps even Mavis is not aware of the extent to which she sloughs off that which is too rough for her narrative, tightens up that which is too inconsistent for her taste, and smooths out that which threatens to tear her tale, editing reality as naturally and as insistently as she draws breath.

The incessant crash and blaze of the storm, Mavis alone notices, is moving into the distance, leaving a light but steady rain in its place. Mavis feels herself weakening as well, but holds at bay for just a bit longer the fatigue that leans against her resolve. For only the sisters' parents remain to be cast into a final mold. She feels a moment of uncharacteristic hesitation, because the figures she wants to bring forth, she knows, will fit less easily within the framework of the younger sisters' recollections. Her father and mother had been young, not without hope; theirs had somehow grown so much older; one despairing, the other resigned. Beginning with the old love for a flawed father, she pulls her parents' shadows into the room.

The sisters tense with apprehension as their father enters. Mavis allows, for the moment, his deeper voice of frustration and anger, allows their discomfort. Then she begins to calm the man and the children as she lays bare his pain in order to sing it into silence. Slowly, a peace replaces the fury that had just for a moment cut from the past into the night. Mavis brings silence not by shutting a door, not by closing a window, but by soothing the memory itself. "He loved us," she says, "but his pain wasn't something he could understand, and it wasn't something we could see. We just saw the anger. But it's okay to have loved him. We were never wrong to love him."

Then, just for a moment, behind Mavis's voice, in the silence left by a father's vacuum of pain, the sisters hear the thin, quiet and steady hum of a mother's movements. They taste the food set down by finely wrinkled hands with fingers beginning to gnarl with arthritis; they slip into the dresses sewn late into the night; they step carefully over the newly scrubbed floors.

As Mavis brings her mother back into this house in which the sisters now sit, she notices that there is something about the busy woman's countenance, which looks neither forward nor up but is always focused on the mundane task at hand, that signifies a determination that moves well beyond drudgery, a determination not for herself, but for those who will eat her food, wear the clothes she mends, live in her spotless house. And Mavis feels a new kinship with this long-dead mother who perhaps also knew that the relationship between hope and resignation need not be one of opposites, who knew perhaps that by fading into the background, she was enabling her eldest daughter to come into a strength that would propel her generation forward. Mavis marvels to see, at this late date, her mother develop into a figure of respect who also knew how to inhabit a life that was both ending and looking forward to a future through the eyes of those who yet lived. As Mavis speaks, Maxine sees her mother toiling most clearly. Judy and Isabelle strain a bit harder for the pictures Mavis provides, then relax as their mother's hum begins to recede, to once again disappear behind Mavis's voice. And Janice shifts, imperceptibly, in irritation.

21

JUST AS THE WOMEN HAD ONLY SLOWLY BECOME AWARE of Mavis's voice, they slowly noticed that it had stopped. Shaking themselves as if they'd been asleep, each looked up at Mavis, who was once again drawn, tired, much older than sixty. But smiling.

No one needed to break the silence, interrupted only by Isabelle blowing her nose. The minutes ticked on as each woman continued her own private conversation with Mavis.

The telephone's peal came as a violation, and Isabelle jumped up from her seat to break the first ring. Nonetheless, her "Y'ello" came out in the tone of pleasant interrogation each Schmidt sister brought to the phone, regardless of what the ring had interrupted: tears, laughter, anger, sex. It was Glenn. He and Craig had stayed for a cup of coffee with Aunt Emma, who was somewhat unnerved by the swiftness and the violence of the storm. There had been about ten minutes of hail there. Then came the anxious

question: Had it hailed at home? Isabelle repeated the
question to the room, and the women, roused now, sheepishly shrugged their shoulders and admitted that they
didn't know. They didn't even know how long they'd been
sitting there in the dark. The women could sense Glenn's
amazement through Isabelle's end of the conversation. He
and Craig would stop by Mavis's to see if the storm had
done any damage there, then they would drive around the
home section, not that they were likely to be able to see
anything in the dark, Glenn added.

The spell broken, Isabelle reached for the light switch,
bringing the women back to the present.

Maxine spoke first. "I do miss Dad sometimes. I've
wondered what he would think of me now. Sometimes
when people are saying 'congratulations' and 'well
done,' I stop and try to imagine what he would have said.
Like when I held my first published book in my hands, I
went outside on that little stoop Charlie and I called a
patio and stood alone in the dark, and said out loud, 'So
what do you think of this, Dad?' And in my imagination I
had him say he was proud of me." Maxine cleared her
throat and changed her tone. "But then I thought it was
more likely that he would say that this would be a good
time for a drink and a smoke."

"I don't remember him ever saying one nice thing to
me," Judy said. "It was always 'don't do this and don't
do that.' " She hopped down from the counter to make
the second round of drinks. Mavis held her hand over her
glass, giving Judy the Mavis-look.

"What? Can't I say how I feel, too?" Judy asked.

"Of course you can, Judy," Maxine said. "You should.
There's precious little of saying what we truly feel
around here . . . usually. But let's be fair. He was sick.
Alcoholism is a disease. We couldn't know that then, and
that's neither our fault nor his."

"Don't talk to me like a . . ."

"Schoolteacher. I am a schoolteacher."

"Well, I'm not your student."

"Judy, don't you understand?" Isabelle couldn't contain herself. "That's what we're trying to do here. Trying to understand what's happening, what's happened. Oh, shit, if Irene were here, you'd listen to her."

"Yes, I would. Because she never thought she was too smart to talk to me. She was never putting on your goddamned airs, Izzy."

"My goddamned airs! My goddamned airs! I can't believe this. Where do you get off? You with your mink, your Mercedes, your this and that. Your 'I, me, and my.' Always acting like you belonged in someone else's family."

"Well, I never got much encouragement from any of you for being in this family," Judy shot back, and then immediately looked uncomfortable, having just been reminded of some of the manifold encouragements she'd received from Mavis. "Well, no, okay, so that's not exactly true. But you," looking at Isabelle, "you act as if you're so much more intelligent than I am. Why?"

"Because you're so stupid."

"Come on, you two," Maxine interrupted. "Where do you get this stuff? How can you not see each other from year to year, and then come out scratching and spitting like cats?"

Judy's voice was hard with hurt. "I'll tell you where it comes from. I'm tired of being treated like an outsider by my own family. I'm always the last to get a phone call with news, the last to hear that people are coming home, the last to know anything. And I know you laugh at me behind my back."

Isabelle's voice was soft and deadly. "You want to be treated like family, act like family."

"What the hell does that mean?"

Isabelle stared out the window, red-faced and tight-lipped, into the reflection of the overhead light.

"Well?" Judy insisted. "When haven't I acted like family?"

"Never."

"Bullshit. When haven't I acted like ..." Judy repeated.

"Oh, Jesus. I wouldn't even know where to start. When we were growing up, Judy. When we were growing up. And it's too late to change that now."

"What are you talking about?"

The rest of the women had been silent during this exchange, but now the silence deepened as each wondered what fresh horror Isabelle was about to reveal.

"Judy, whenever you've wanted something, you've expected people to jump-to, but if someone needed something from you, you disappeared faster than a fart in a Jacuzzi."

"Could you be more specific?" Judy's tone was icy.

"When we were kids, in grade school, for example." Isabelle was speaking reluctantly, resenting herself, Judy, the situation. "You were the one who got new clothes. I don't know why you didn't get hand-me-downs from Mavis and Maxine, but you didn't. Probably 'cause you were such a pain in the ass. So Janice got your hand-me-downs and we got hers. You probably don't even remember how the kids at school teased Irene and me about our clothes that didn't match. Making a ring around us, calling us Raggedy Anns, laughing. Irene cried and cried and I kept tearing into the ring to get a handful of hair or to twist an arm, but the ring just changed shape and moved away from me. And Irene cried and cried. I can see her like it was yesterday. Maybe she was wearing a new barrette she'd hoped someone would notice, or maybe she'd gotten a new pair of shoes. But all the kids were laughing at us, laughing and teasing."

"Well, shit, Izzy, is it my fault the others picked on you? What was I supposed to do?"

"You were older, all the little kids thought you were so special, so pretty. You could have made them stop. You could have claimed us. Or at least you could have done nothing. But you did something, Judy. I remember. You joined hands with the others and laughed and teased. You had to be in with everyone else, even the little kids. You chose them. But we were your sisters. We were your family. You should have taken care of us."

"I don't remember that."

"You don't remember what you had for breakfast, but that doesn't mean you didn't eat." Isabelle was sullen now, mortified that she'd just admitted how important Judy had been to her, allowing the others to reevaluate all the years she'd held this sister in contempt.

No one knew where to go from here. Isabelle had opened up in anger, but her anger had nowhere to go, and remained, heavy, in the room.

Then Judy said the impossible. "Maybe I didn't know how. I'm sorry."

"Too late." Isabelle spoke automatically, then added, "Besides, how are you going to say you're sorry to Irene?"

Isabelle's blow was on target, and Judy looked stricken.

"No, Isabelle," Mavis spoke. "Not too late. Never too late."

Again there was silence.

"You know, Isabelle, Mom told me that story, too," Jackie said quietly, after some minutes of emptiness. "But she told it different. It wasn't a story about Judy. It was about you. About how you two used to take care of each other."

"A paradigm shift," Maxine murmured.

"Beg your pardon?" Isabelle asked, now wearing a faint smile.

"What we call truth depends on where we are located individually in terms of, say, a particular historical or cultural . . . or familial context." Maxine stopped, aware that the women around her were either grinning at what they perceived as pedantry or furrowing their brows at what they saw as an introduction of nonsense into an important conversation.

"Thank you for sharing that, Dr. Douglas," Isabelle said.

Nonetheless, Maxine's brief speech had broken the tension of the moment. Maxine laughed herself, but insisted, "Perhaps my language is abstruse, but I think you know what I mean."

"Right, that we can never agree." Isabelle's tone was wry, but the nod she passed toward Judy was not unpleasant.

"No, I don't think that's it." Peggy spoke for the first time. "Exactly, anyway. I think Maxine is saying that instead of thinking of one way of looking at things as right and another way as wrong, so that we're always arguing, we need to understand that there are just going to be lots of different ways of seeing things."

The women listened, some nodded, but in general they looked unconvinced.

"I came around in a circle. Let me try again. Mavis is always saying what a boring world it would be if we all saw things the same way. So instead of those different perspectives being reasons to fight, maybe we need to use them as explanations as to why things don't always go the way we would . . . would . . ."

"Script them," Maxine finished.

"Right, so it seems like if we could somehow find a way to hear or at least be aware of other possible responses or viewpoints, then we'd be less threatened by notions, or even memories, that are different from ours." She stopped, unsure not only of the value of what she was adding to the conversation, but of her right to participate at all. She'd been married to Glenn long enough to be "family," but feared that at least in this situation her place was to be silent.

For a couple of moments the only sounds in the room were a few sighs as the women shifted in their chairs. Finally Janice, who had been even quieter than usual, spoke, with a question directed to her lap: "Does that mean, then, that there is no such thing as right and wrong?"

Everyone looked from Janice to Mavis, as if this were a question she had to answer for all of them. Only then did they notice the line of sweat on her upper lip, her ashen color.

"Mavis, are you okay?" Maxine asked.

"Yes, but I am tired. I'm going to lie down for just a minute upstairs." She stood and walked to the sink, running a glass of water. Then she walked to the door leading to the next room and the stairs. At the door she turned.

"I can't say what right or wrong is for any of you. I only know what I think I have had to do."

MAVIS

MAVIS CLIMBS THE STEPS HEAVILY, LEANING JUST A BIT against the railing beside her as she ascends. At the top of the steps she automatically turns right, and just for a moment is disoriented when the room she expects to walk into isn't there. She does not, however, feel the old blow of loss once more, because her physical pain demands her attention. She moves to the night table beside the bed, looks at the aspirin she's pulled out of her pocket, shakes her head in wan self-mockery, and swallows the pills. With trembling hand she sets down the water glass. Slowly she settles onto the chintz bedspread, feeling as if she's trespassing on the privacy of her daughter-in-law. Not because she's lying on the bed Peggy shares with her son, the bed shared with Frank for almost thirty-five years, but because there's nothing about Peggy, or the rest of her house, to suggest a taste for chintz.

She doesn't expect to sleep. She's just trying to hold in check the discomfort that yesterday seemed so much more manageable. Slowly she works her mind away from the pain in her chest and around the table downstairs. Methodically she passes subjects through her brain to rehearse, eliminating anything that catches at her heart with a ragged nail. She leaves the women in the kitchen, refuses the logic of the future, and begins to walk backward in her mind, toward safety, toward certainty, toward the known or the safe fantastic. Her eyes closed, her right hand slides from her chest to her side. Her face clears a fraction as the breathing slows. She walks toward what has always been the center of her universe. Crow, North Dakota. There, in front of her, it perches less on a hill than on a ripple in the prairie's rolling expanse. The town's line of demarcation is the end of the gravel road and the beginning of blacktop. Within three minutes, at thirty-five miles per hour, the gravel road takes over again as Crow's grain elevator rises in the rearview mirror.

The trip Mavis takes, however, is on foot, on an early summer day. She steps onto the pavement, and there to her right is the Crow Methodist Church. Here in Crow and its surrounding farm community, the world is divided into Methodists and not-Methodists. Most of the not-Methodists are Lutheran, and they, as well as other Protestants, are perfectly respectable. Other not-Methodists are Catholic. There are no Jews. Perhaps a few Jews live in Fargo, but nobody from Crow knows any. Muslims and Hindus live in India and Buddhists live in China, and atheists are people from the East Coast who only know what they read in books, which is to say, they don't know much about much.

The sign that reads CROW METHODIST CHURCH includes no Bible verse, no quote, no admonition; there's no way to get saved by driving by. Mavis walks inside, through the entry that can comfortably hold at least four people, into the church proper, which is one cool, dark, quiet room. A door directly ahead opens into the furnace room, which is also filled with crayons, hymnals, sheet music, and a flannel board with figures scattered willy-nilly. A shepherd's crook hangs precariously to the bottom of the board, the sheep it evidently meant to catch lie in the dust at her feet.

She backs out of the close room, turns to her right, and faces the altar from behind the pews. It's possible to get seventy-five worshipers sitting here comfortably, but not likely. Up front and to the left is the platform for piano and organ and room for the funereal Crow church choir. (Not "funereal" because they sing that badly, although badly enough, but because they only sing at funerals.) She shifts her gaze just a bit to the right, to the altar. Behind the pulpit two Jesuses flank a rough wooden cross attached to the wall. The Jesus on the right looks uncomfortably swarthy, neither German nor Norwegian. He stares, beatifically, she supposes, at the left Jesus, who stands and knocks, still, at that door covered with brambles. From somewhere within both pictures comes a beam of light, much like the soft beams coming through the windows on the south side of the building, high-lighting suspended particles of dust. Mavis walks back down the aisle to check the bulletin board by the door to make sure it isn't her turn to clean the church.

As Mavis closes the church door behind her, she places her hand on the warm metal of the railing and looks across the road, beyond the fields, to a train approaching Crow, but still several miles in the distance. She circles behind the church and walks north about a hundred feet, toward the two-room schoolhouse. In between the two classrooms, the Little Room for grades one through four, and the Big Room for grades five through eight, a third room holds two parallel long tables yoked to form a U on one end by a small table. Mavis is now one of the two adults monitoring the noise of lunching schoolchildren, but is much younger than her companion, Edna Olson, who has taught for too many years in the Little Room. She looks down the table at her "kids," catching Glenn's eye and shaking her head no as he clowns by trying to put an entire pancake in his mouth.

Mavis rises from the table, and as she slides the partitions back separating the three rooms, the children disappear, replaced by a handful of ladies, all dressed up and moving about in the kitchen toward the back of the center room. Mavis joins them in setting out dishes on the long table that separates the kitchen from the rest of the room, where men in interchangeable dark suits talk and laugh. Covered dishes are uncovered to expose tuna noodle hot dish, scalloped potatoes with ham, green beans topped with canned fried onions; foil is removed to reveal red Jell-O with canned fruit floating within its solidity and covered with whipped cream; homemade rolls, pie, and lemon bars crowd the table. There is coffee and Kool-Aid. Is it the Harvest Festival? A potluck dinner? Someone's twenty-fifth wedding anniversary celebration? Not a bridal or baby shower, for then the men would be dismissed.

Mavis brings a coffeepot over to a nearby table in one of the side rooms where school desks are pushed back along walls lined with blackboards that actually are black. As she asks, "Who needs more coffee?" her hand rests for just a moment, in a gesture proprietary but not yet familiar, on the shoulder of the man who has just recently become her husband.

It is a teenage Mavis, however, who pauses on the schoolhouse steps as she leaves, taking a moment to study the small building to her right. A what's-it-called? A teacherage, a house where a teacher lives. This always a fantastic idea for a teenager: that teachers have lives.

Mavis takes the short walk on shortening legs back to the pavement that constitutes Crow's main and only street, turns right and continues west. A two-minute walk takes her to Crow's center for information exchange, policy making, philosophical dispute and dialogue, and secondarily, a place to buy groceries (or work boots, Match-Me's, coveralls, fly strips, grass seed, nails, Tampax, .22 shells, or to mail a letter). Fletcher's General Store is a long, narrow building opening with windows and light in the front, then shading toward darkness in the back, where sometimes the men disappear to look for machine parts, nails, barrels of oil, insecticides.

In the back corner is a post office, a place of mystery maybe eight feet square. The Fletcher who looks out from inside the cubicle is formidable and authoritative, transfigured from the good-natured arthritic old guy who occasionally shuffles up and down the store's two aisles, but usually sits by the pop cooler with the other men. On the wall to the right of the partition hover pictures of felons and fingerprints. Only the community's children study the pictures, learning to distrust black men, Hispanics, and white men with beards. Mavis cranes her neck upward in curiosity to study the one picture of an older white woman, who looks so familiar.

Back up front, men sit around the pop machine, a waist-high chest that opens with a lid from the top and in which the bottles hang by the neck until rescued by someone with a quarter. The good stuff is always at the end of the row, so a dozen other bottles need to be slid out and onto other racks in order to get to the cream soda or the cherry pop. Lift the bottle as you slide it out, Mavis reminds herself, or it will jam and one of the men will have to stop talking about politics, rain, cattle, or Little League baseball to come over and help. Women come in, pick up bread and milk, mail letters, correct what's being said, and leave.

Some of the men are waiting for something to be fixed across the street in the blacksmith shop. They try not to leave things there for too long. Items tend to go one step beyond lost in that place; they disappear. It is a large shop, all black inside. Dark with soot, dark with dirt, dark with lack of light through small, dirty windows. The blacksmith himself is dark in a dark cap with no bill. He talks to men sometimes and listens to women with his eyes down, but evidently cannot see children at all. He cannot see Mavis, who, now not even four feet tall, stays close to her father, who is talking to another man in the doorway of the shop. They are standing with the bright sunlight to their backs. Mavis edges forward, keeping her hand on her father's pant leg. The inside looks like a cave. Only a black shape surrounded by flying sparks can be made out.

Mavis wills her father to move on to Crow's last structure, not counting the half dozen or so houses. (It's not a bar, nosiree, not in Crow.) There, beside the railroad tracks, one of the skyscrapers of the plains, the grain elevator with its ramps, scales, grates, trucks, augers, chains, levers, doors, platforms, and an office that seems too bare. The smell is of clean lumber, dry grain dust. Footsteps are sharp and distinct on wooden floors. It is a place of men, and Mavis is in awe.

Mavis is now only thigh-high as she stands beside her father on these wooden floors, trying to stay near and out of the way at the same time. She wants to reach her hand up to run it over the wooden edge of the counter worn smooth by the rough elbows of farmers; wants to tap a knuckle on the metal ticket-and-receipt dispenser that makes such a delightfully hollow sound as the elevator man writes upon it; wants to flip through the crackly papers in the three-ring notebooks in which this man so carefully files the crisp white and yellow copies of the pink ticket that her father folds in eighths and sticks in his breast pocket behind his Lucky Strikes. But Mavis holds herself very still, responding less to her father's unspoken injunction to silence than to the lack of warmth and welcome from the other few men present. These are the same men who, when in the general store a couple hundred yards away or so, smile and joke, but here even when the men laugh they don't seem happy. The conversations she doesn't understand between her dad and the elevator man still include rain and bugs and things like moisture content, but even though her father nods his head and seems to agree with what the elevator man says, his face is closed.

Mavis climbs into the pickup cab and her father shuts the door behind her, then crosses to the driver's side. He shakes his head as he taps his breast pocket, but doesn't pull out a cigarette. Mavis turns to kneel backward on the seat so she can continue to study through the rear window this tall building that pierces the sky. Her eyes fix on the receding shape of a ladder attached to the out-side of the tallest peaked tower. She's never seen anyone on that ladder. What would it be like to be that high? Could she see her house? Could she look past those miles of flatland, over the trees around their farmyard, and into a window that looks in on a drowsing sixty-year-old woman?

Mavis begins the climb upward, effortlessly, feeling the warmth of the sunbathed building next to her and the solidity of the wooden ladder rungs under her feet and hands. She climbs upward, upward, strongly, surely.

Oddly, the roofs of all the buildings below are in primary colors. Bright yellows, reds, blues. And if I go just a bit higher, she thinks, the town below me is only a bunch of bright dots of color against a green carpet. And there it is, there's my house. Mom and Dad are sitting on a blanket under the box elder. It's hard to tell from here which twin which one is holding. I can see in the window that Maxine is lying on our bed reading. And there goes Janice racing around the corner barefoot in shorts and no top, with Judy chasing behind with the garden hose. Dad's getting up. He hands Irene? Isabelle? No, that's Glenn? He's handing Glenn to Mom, who is holding Craig, too. He's walking across the yard toward Frank, holds out his hand to take the bucket of water Frank is hauling into the barn. Frank holds his hand out and I reach over and slip my hand inside his callused grasp. We hold hands while he does chores.

Down the hall, Janie reported to Becky as she returned from a trip to the bathroom which took her by her parents' bedroom, "Grandma sleeps with her mouth open."

22

MAVIS'S DEPARTURE LEFT A GENERAL UNEASINESS IN the kitchen as the women shifted in their chairs. Maxine got up to make a pot of coffee, Jackie absentmindedly turned an empty box of playing cards over and over on the table, and Janice continued to study her lap, occasionally shaking her head slightly or lifting her fingers away from her legs as she carried on an internal conversation.

Peggy, still sitting on the counter, reached into the cupboard behind her to hand the coffee can to Maxine, pretending not to watch the interaction taking place between Judy and Isabelle.

Judy had settled into the chair Mavis had left, tapped out a cigarette from a leather case in front of her, and reached for the slender silver lighter she had placed earlier on the table. Isabelle, too, had rummaged for a cigarette in her purse, which hung off the back of Janice's chair. She reached for the lighter at the same time. When the sisters' hands touched, they both jerked back as if burned. Judy recovered first and cut off Isabelle's automatic scowl with her "Allow me," as she held the lighter to Isabelle's cigarette while holding her gaze even more insistently. Isabelle was strong enough to meet the look. Perhaps it lasted two seconds, long enough for Judy to lift the lighter to Isabelle's cigarette, long enough for Isabelle to inhale. Two seconds were not enough to erase years of hurt. But what both realized in the discomfort, yet determination, of the moment, was that they had spent their adulthood looking away, looking sideways, and not looking at all. And that had made the anger so much easier.

The women expected to sit and talk and drink coffee late into the night, but when Mavis left the room, she left them feeling unmoored. With their shared point of reference gone, they shifted, took on a new structure, became a different entity.

"Mavis is sick, Maxine. How sick? What's going on?" Isabelle asked.

"Honestly, I don't know any more than you do. Obviously, something's wrong. But just as obviously, she doesn't want to talk about it."

"But how can we help if we don't know what's wrong?" Judy asked.

"Help Mavis? Help Mavis?" Janice was incredulous. "Since when did anyone help Mavis?"

"Janice, what are you so angry about? Mavis is sick and she's in trouble. Is that what's making you angry? Or afraid? That's okay, you know. I suppose we're all afraid of losing her someday. She's as much mother as—"

Isabelle was cut off by Janice's explosion. "Bullshit. She is not my mother. We had a mother, if you remember. It's like you've all forgotten her, cooking, cleaning, sewing, baking, canning, working, working, working. But never a word about her. Always 'Mavis this' and 'Mavis that.' Well, I haven't forgotten Mom, even if you have. I was the one who helped her stay in that little apartment she got after you and Irene graduated. I was the one who helped her shop and helped her fix her meals. And I'm the one who took her in when all anyone else could say was 'nursing home.' Oh yeah, Mavis put out money and—and shopped, and—and did other stuff, sure. And you two," nodding at Isabelle and Maxine, "sent money, but it was me who took care of her." Janice emphasized each word with her fingers tapping against her chest as she repeated, "Took care of my mother."

"What did you want from us?" Isabelle asked, defensive again. "If you wanted something, why didn't you ask? Why wait till now to get mad?"

"I didn't wait till now to get mad," Janice answered ruefully, and then looked into her lap again. "I've been mad for a long time."

"But why at Mavis?" Maxine asked, calmer, sitting forward.

"I'm just tired of her thinking that she can take care of everyone. No one can. I can take care of myself."

"So you're mad at Mavis for wanting to take care of us. I don't get it," Isabelle said.

"Of course you don't. You and Irene thought of her as mother. Judy thought of her as a protector. She's Maxine's best friend. But me. What about me? I had a mother. I took care of myself. I didn't need a best friend. So why's she always trying to take care of me? What's she been to me?"

"A sister." Jackie's voice was soft, more statement than question.

Janice looked away from the eyes focused on her. With her mouth set in a stubborn tired line, her shoulders tight and yet beginning to stoop, she looked so much like the mother she championed.

"This time," she said finally, "this time she's done too much."

Jackie popped the top of her third Pepsi. "I don't agree. What everyone is thinking, but only Janice is saying, is that this time Mavis went too far. That when it came to protecting, or avenging—" Jackie raised her eyebrows at the word. "—that at least she should have drawn the line at murder. But Mavis didn't murder anyone."

The women held their breath and watched Jackie.

"What are you saying? What do you mean?" Janice's eyes were feverish, the question asked in rising excitement, anticipation.

"I mean it isn't murder to put a sick dog to sleep. Before it can hurt someone else."

"Jackie, we will all stick by Mavis no matter what she's done . . . or says she did," Maxine said. "But I don't think that means we can ignore the gravity of the action itself. Each of us grieves for Irene daily. And none of us can really know your pain or loss, but I don't know that any of our pain at losing Irene gives us the right to— to . . ." For once it was Maxine who hesitated, unwilling to finish the sentence.

"To kill." Judy jumped at the opportunity.

Maxine continued, "And I myself don't feel that pain alleviated one iota by Jack's death. It just feels like now he's hurt one more of my sisters."

"You don't understand, Maxine. None of you understand." Jackie looked at each sister while taking a deep breath. "I hated my father. I hated him for who he was and what he did to my mother. I hated him when he slapped her. That was easy. Easy to hate. But . . ." Jackie hesitated, started again, but made no sound. She reached for one of Judy's thin cigarettes, and after inhaling went on in a rush: "Over and over I've asked myself, why did it have to be that way? What did I need to do to make it different? What had I done? What could someone else have done?" Jackie stopped, and each woman watched the smoke rise from the cigarette Jackie held aloft in her hand, raised now to keep them from speaking. A Schmidt hand with long fingers, squared fingertips, but here the nails were bitten short. Finally Jackie added, quietly, "But how can you hate and love someone at the same time?"

"Jackie," it was Peggy speaking, "he was your father. You probably have many fond memories of him. That's okay, too."

"No, no, no! Not him! Not him. Why didn't she stop him? Why didn't she do something? Why didn't she take us away? And now she's gone. And I never asked, and I'll never know. And Blair's so fucked up, too."

Jackie was suddenly sobbing, her breath coming to her in rough spasms, the cry entering each woman's chest and filling it with dread. More than the dread of what was about to make itself known in this farmhouse kitchen, it was the dread of what was already known, known maybe for years, but not acknowledged.

Maxine and Janice caught each other's look, briefly. Then Maxine closed her eyes tightly, taking refuge in one of those moments of absolute blankness, which could be held only by the most determined concentration on the void behind the eyes. She knew that with one word the dark would explode into certain knowledge, knowledge that she had managed to hide, repress, ignore, bury. With that explosion much of a cherished past would be rewritten.

Janice, however, was feeling the nausea rise in her gut as she opened herself to accept more pain, more guilt, more responsibility. But more powerful than the nausea was a sense of vindication. Again she heard evil laugh, and again she pulled the trigger.

And Isabelle, her jaw working, was doing the impossible: praying, "Please, no. Please, no. Please, no." Knowing that the "Please, no" prayer is always a reaction, always too late.

It was Judy, lacking the patience for introspection, who spoke almost immediately. "What?" she asked Jackie. "What didn't Irene do?"

"Maybe she just didn't love me enough. Maybe she loved some idea of family more than she loved us," Jackie said through her sobs.

"I don't get it," Judy said. "Are you saying Irene wasn't a good mother?"

Jackie's sobs stopped at once as she leveled a swollen gaze full at Judy, then at the other sisters. All were motionless.

"He hit us all." The words were simple, awful. "And Mom didn't, couldn't, stop it."

Perhaps it would be fair to say that none of the sisters sitting in the kitchen knew exactly what Jackie was talking about. Perhaps it would be more accurate to say that they had always known more than they wanted to realize. The four-way silent echo of "Why?" that reflected from sister to sister did not ask why a man would abuse his children, for that was not the question they were being called upon to answer this evening. But why didn't Irene, their Irene, nurturing, caring, loving Irene, why didn't she do something?

But then, no, that wasn't the question for them, either. Why didn't I do something? Why didn't I?

Jackie was speaking. None of the women tried to stop her or tried to soothe. They were thinking of bruises Jackie, as a little girl, had carried. Thinking about letters they had received from the adolescent asking if she could come visit for a while, maybe for a summer, a year. Thinking about Blair's reclusiveness. Thinking of family pictures where the children seemed clustered around Irene, shrinking away from their father. Thinking of Jackie's too-sudden metamorphosis from shy child to wild adult, her wildness more frenzied than fun, fueled by alcohol and drugs.

"I don't know when it started, to tell the truth. I don't really want to know, but maybe I have to in order to someday get rid of this hate, this disgust. What I do know is that no one stopped it. I had to leave. Run away."

The sisters looked away from Jackie and into the eyes of each other, each of them introduced into a past they'd managed to believe they had never known. Not even their beloved Irene, supposedly safe by virtue of death, could they point to as the one of them who was only good.

"And you want to hear something funny?" Jackie's eyes were unfocused as she directed her gaze out the bay window, perhaps into blackness, perhaps onto the women's reflections. "I hate him most for taking her from me. I just wanted to hear her say it would be okay. She still had time to say it would be okay."

Minutes passed in silence. Janice moved her chair toward Jackie and placed her right hand over Jackie's, clasped in her own lap.

When Maxine broke the silence, it was as if she were speaking to herself, but needed to hear the words out loud.

"Mavis couldn't have known."

"No." Isabelle's voice added emphasis. "Mavis couldn't have known."

"Of course not," Judy put in. "Unless . . ." She hesitated, and then blurted out yet another possibility, one that Maxine and Isabelle were already resisting in their own minds. "Why else would she do what she did? Unless she'd found something out? Saw what the rest of us . . . what we should have . . ."

"I need to think she's acting out of love," Jackie said, not looking up. "I need to believe that she took her love for Mom and Mom's love for me, for us, and put them together, and somehow that's why she's doing what she's doing. That's the only way I can live with all this."

It was Janice now who was finally crying. "But it's too much love. I never asked for this much love. It makes me too . . . too—" She caught her breath, and in a voice almost below hearing, finished, "It makes us all too small."

A full fifteen minutes later Glenn and Craig walked into a kitchen of silent, stricken women.

Peggy looked at Glenn's expression and saw that it matched the women's in tone if not degree.

"What's wrong?"

"Well, you were right about not hearing hail here. As much as I can tell in the dark, the home section looks pretty much okay."

"But . . . ?"

"But the area around Mom's took a beating. There's a path about three miles wide, it seems, northwest of Crow that's probably hailed out. The section around Mom's looks as bare as if it had already been combined. All the windows on the north side of her house are broken, the siding's taken a beating. Linda was sweeping up glass from the windows when we got there. There's not much rain damage inside." His voice was tired, defeated. "I won't know for sure if there's damage on this section until I walk the fields in the morning. With the rain and wind we got, I'm sure some of the grain has lodged. Mom has a lot of limbs down, and the electricity is out."

Craig noticed Isabelle swallowing and pretending not to be overly concerned as she gathered her purse and stood.

"Linda's fine. She said she remembered you talking about heading for the basement during storms, so when she saw the trees bent over during a lightning strike, she hightailed it downstairs." He stopped and chuckled.

"What?" Isabelle demanded.

"She said she waited out the storm in the bathtub. Was that your advice, too?"

Isabelle shook her head and shrugged.

"Will we be able to harvest the beans, Glenn?" Peggy asked.

"No saying yet. Maybe the damage wasn't too bad. You never know how the pods will fill out after something like this."

"Glenn," Isabelle asked, "what does this mean for your year?"

He shrugged his broad shoulders with a heavy sigh and took his gaze from Peggy, who had held it as if she were holding him since he walked in the door.

"We'd already taken up half of the grain crop at Mom's, and I'm guessing the rest is gone there. We'll just have to wait until the morning to see what shape we're in here." He smiled the smile the sisters had all loved on his father, and added, "It means we have some cleaning up to do tomorrow."

"Tomorrow," Craig reminded Glenn, "Mom wants us to go with her to her doctor's appointment."

23

MAVIS BEGAN TO PARCEL OUT INFORMATION DURING Monday's drive into Fargo. This was not her first doctor's appointment. She had discovered a lump on her left breast a bit ago—when asked by Craig to better define "a bit," Mavis clarified with "not that long"—and had seen a doctor this past Thursday when she'd gone in to get her hair done. The doctor had taken a needle biopsy and then sent her to another part of the clinic for a mammogram. Today, she told her stunned sons, she would get the results. That's why she had asked them to come along with her; she may need to make some decisions.

This information broke through the calm Craig had been maintaining in the midst of the family's confusion. Impatient with his mother's reticence and spurred on by his own need for logic, Craig was suddenly intent upon putting together a coherent picture of the past two or three weeks. When, precisely, had his mother discovered this lump, and had she made any other appointments or decisions they should know about? And this shooting: why, just for starters, was she saying she had done it? And where did Jackie fit in all of this? Did anyone know exactly where she had been since leaving the Hazelden? The steadiness of Craig's voice could not mask his anxiety as he all but cried out, "Help me understand what's going on."

Glenn just looked miserable.

"Jackie," Mavis replied, "evidently just grew weary of the Hazelden's timetable for her recovery, and decided to see how well she really was by releasing herself. That shouldn't surprise any of us."

"So where was she, then, from the Tuesday before Jack was killed until yesterday? That's almost three weeks."

"She has a college friend in the Cities who let her use her cabin on Mille Lacs Lake. Jackie spent the first couple of weeks there, just reading and swimming and, let's see, 'chilling out,' I believe."

"Was she straight?" Craig asked.

"What do you mean?"

"Did she stay off drugs? Was she drinking?"

"She says not and I believe her. You've seen her here."

Craig didn't answer, but nodded in agreement. "Then what?"

"Then she called Blair. She'd decided to hitchhike out to see him. Blair told her about Jack and . . . Glenn, Larson's beans really took a beating."

"I see that," Glenn answered, "but look north. The barley's lodged here and there, but it doesn't seem too bad."

"Is Aarstad still farming that land?" Mavis asked.

"No, he rented it out to Ronny Baugh this year."

"That must make, what, six quarters Ronny is renting, on top of what he's farming with his dad. I wonder—"

"Mother." Craig's voice cut in. "We can farm later. Finish what you know about Jackie."

"Well, Jackie was in shock, of course. She said she bought a bottle of whiskey and set it on the end table beside the couch she was sleeping on, and looked at it all night long while she thought and cried and smoked two packs of cigarettes until it was dawn. Then she poured the whiskey down the drain. I think Jackie smokes too much."

"Mother."

"Then she decided it was time to go home, to be with Blair. So she hitchhiked to Brickton—"

"And no one saw her?" Craig couldn't believe it. "She passes through a town of under five thousand where her father was just murdered and the police are looking for her, and no one sees her? That's impossible."

"Perhaps." Mavis smiled. "But if anyone saw her, no one said anything."

"And?" Craig prodded again.

"And that's about all Jackie said. I really haven't had much time to talk with her. She said Blair seemed as upset about our plans for a family reunion as he did about his father's death. So Jackie spent the rest of the week making and freezing casseroles for Blair and then had that alphabet man drive her back here for the picnic."

"Now wait a minute. Jackie showed up at the farm in that hippie van with a ponytailed stranger, and nobody reported it? That's pretty hard to believe."

Mavis raised her eyebrows. "He works in mysterious ways. I'm sure they parked the van in the machine shed and kept that goofball out of sight. It was only for a couple of days."

Glenn entered the conversation with what was not, his

mother and brother knew, a non sequitur: "Jack was one unpopular son of a bitch."

"But the fact remains," Craig said after a pause, "that agents Heyerdahl and Madsen are looking for Jackie."

"I gave her the number for the Wash County Sheriff's Department. She said she'd call today. But surely that is a formality. And in a couple of days she'll fly back to the Cities, she promised, to finish her treatment at the Hazelden, which," Mavis closed with a wry smile, "is also, I expect, just a formality at this point."

The three rode in silence for a few miles, until Craig spoke again. "And the rest?"

Mavis sighed. "The rest of what?"

"Of everything."

"As for the lump"—Mavis spoke the word reluctantly— "let's wait to hear what my doctor says before we come to any conclusions."

And then, much to Glenn's relief, Mavis once again turned the conversation to last night's storm, to the ditches running with water and the battered fields that pushed against the double ribbon of straight, flat Interstate 94. With Craig now silent in the backseat, and Glenn's foot increasingly heavy on the gas pedal, Mavis directed her sons' attention sideways into the open farmland, as if to resist the trajectory of the car away from the country, toward the city, the clinic, and the doctor who had no investment in the secrets and plans of a sixty-year-old farm widow.

Mavis's physician hadn't needed to read the biopsy results to know that her patient would be in surgery within the next few days. Still, the malignant word needed to be spoken before others about choices and decisions—lumpectomy, modified radical, percentages of recurrence, reconstruction—could be dispensed. Assuming that the carcinoma (now that word had been spoken as well) was growing rapidly, Mavis's physician had made arrangements for her to check into the hospital that day. But Mavis said no, the day after tomorrow would have to do. So blood was drawn and schedules set, and Mavis stepped once more into the post-rain sunshine of a clear summer day, accompanied by her two silent sons, who did not know that they had just heard the other shoe drop because the unspoken word, "cancer," was drowning out all else.

The few necessary errands in Fargo and the drive home were completed in silence. Both Mavis and Craig, she in the front seat again, he in the back, sat with their heads tilted against headrests, eyes closed. Glenn noticed in a sidelong look how pale and tired his mother had become. Through the rearview mirror he could see that Craig's color wasn't much better.

Craig was not asleep; rather, he was studying his reaction to the day's news. His mother had breast cancer. She would go into the hospital on Wednesday in preparation for surgery on Thursday. And yet the images he watched from behind closed eyes were of a rally he had attended one summer weekend in 1987 outside the capitol building in Olympia. He and Rob had been there to join the cry for more state and federal monies to be directed toward AIDS research and health care, and had gone away offended by a small group of women in the midst of the crowd who held a banner that read: 42,000 BREAST CANCER DEATHS PER YEAR! WHO CARES ABOUT WOMEN? Like many of the men and women trying to heighten an awareness of the need for AIDS support, he was furious, not by the women's issue, but by their timing.

Gathered over margaritas later than evening, he and his friends were further incensed to see the television reportage of the event situated in terms of men versus women, as if only men got AIDS, as if, by insisting on more government recognition of and involvement in the disease, AIDS activists were suggesting that other diseases did not merit attention.

"It's exactly that 'us versus them' mindset," Rob had insisted with typical fiery vigor, "that the government and the religious right loves. Set up a false dichotomy, play one disenfranchised group off another, and get them to start pointing fingers at each other—and the real issue, the right of *all* people to adequate health care, conveniently disappears."

There had been six of them scattered about the living room that evening, tanned and fit and young. The numbers they had heard at the rally were terrifying, the predictions almost beyond belief, but death remained an abstraction. In the year that followed, however, it became specific, charting a harrowing trajectory of weight loss and exhaustion, night sweats and purple lesions, and fuzzy white fungus that circled fingertips and clung to the roof of the mouth. Three years later two of those six young men were dead, and Craig was alone. Yes, Craig thought, in our anger and our terror, in hospitals and sterile bedrooms, in those last hours, it has become us versus them, because death's focus is always only inward, and we are dying.

The hint of a song entered Craig's consciousness and he opened his eyes and looked at the back of his mother's head. And watched the boundaries of "us" and "them" dissolve, then reconfigure. And knew, We are dying here as well, but here we are dying of breast cancer.

Just then Glenn began to sing the song Craig had sensed, "My hope is built on nothing less than Jesus and his righteousness," in that tenor of his that had always made Craig want to giggle, it was such an incongruous sweetness coming out of all that bulk.

"Well, was that it?" Glenn demanded of his mother

next to him, who although she had her eyes closed and head back as if sleeping, was now humming just loudly enough to be barely audible, but not loudly enough to allow her sons to name that tune. She'd done this all the boys' lives, and while it soothed Craig, it made Glenn silly with curiosity.

"No," Mavis replied without opening her eyes, then continued to hum just a few decibels lower, to where her sons had to turn all their attention to her.

"Just tell me, then. Is it a tune I know or are you making it up?"

"Um-hum" was the reply, which brought the first simultaneous smiles of the day to mother and sons.

The smiles were lost quickly enough in Mavis's kitchen. Janice and Norton had driven back to Fargo the night before, after the storm, but Judy, Maxine, and Isabelle were gathered around the table for a report. Linda held herself just outside the table's circle, sitting at the counter that separated kitchen from family room. Maxine poured the coffee, and the sisters held their cups and listened and swallowed Mavis's news, which was news, but not really. It explained the way she'd been looking so rough lately, and maybe it explained more, but the sisters couldn't put any more together just yet, because it is possible to be stunned by news that isn't news. Something in Mavis's voice made Isabelle and Maxine trade a look that asked the other to verify a question each was still unable to formulate.

In response to most of her sisters' questions—When did you feel the lump? When did you first see a doctor? How long have you felt tired? Is there pain? What happens now?—Mavis was vague, less out of reticence than the determination to decide what was useful information and what was just dwelling on the subject needlessly. Although the sisters' voices were tight, this wasn't a family that appreciated tears, and each felt, accurately, that Mavis would prefer their calm as they talked about what the next few days would hold. Isabelle's features were more sharply defined as she clenched and unclenched her jaw, finally loosening it to ask if Mavis was sure her doctor knew what she was talking about—how could a woman have a lump in something that barely existed in the first place? It was a weak joke and the smiles were small. But they were passed around gratefully nonetheless.

With the tension broken, the conversation shifted to the storm the night before. How much rain. How much hail from here to Fargo. Reports of damage in different counties. What Glenn had seen on his own land that morning before the Fargo trip. And on and on, with plans made for cleaning up after the storm. After about twenty minutes of farm talk, Mavis said she was going in to lie down for a while before supper, but she'd call Janice first, from her bedroom.

MAVIS

"IF YOU NEED TO TELL SOMEONE, THEN TELL GOD. BY all means, talk to God, but Janice—hear me now—let me finish this."

It had been a short call, but perhaps the hardest of all, and Mavis knew her voice was wrong, all wrong. Even to herself she sounded too hard, too patronizing, too strict. "Don't do anything, Janice, just don't do anything," she heard herself repeat over and over. And echoing her insistence came the unspoken reply, I never do anything, you know. Then, strangely, hearing Janice's frustration and confusion and pain come through a voice muffled by sniffs, she felt as if maybe she should sing to this sister.

"When we hang up, Janice. Don't go anywhere. Please. Just sit for a while."

"I just got home, Mavis. I've been on my feet all day. Now you tell me . . . this. Where would I go?" Then came the question Mavis had no intention of answering, perhaps not even completely to herself. "How long have you known? Mavis? Mavis? What are you doing? What will you do?" But they both heard her say, What will we do?

"Stay put. Stay calm. It will be okay." The reassurances, the direction, the hope that wasn't accepted but was repeated until the good-byes, and Mavis, sitting on

the edge of the bed looking at the phone, thinks to herself, Can my meadowlark sing for me today?

She lay back on the bed, surprised to find her own tears
for the first time in weeks as her words to herself tore in
her chest: I *am* singing. I *am* singing. Daddy, this is how
I sing.

24

THE NEXT MORNING IT WAS MAXINE, NOT MAVIS, WHO
was the first one up to put on the coffee. Recently risen
from the couch she had moved to so that Isabelle and
Linda could take over the upstairs guest bedroom,
Maxine sat at the kitchen counter intentionally keeping
her mind blank by repeating over and over to herself the
words she had awakened to in her head: I like to see it lap
the miles, I like to see it lap the miles. Maxine stirred
half-and-half into her cup and remembered sitting with
Mavis on the edge of a winding coulee that typically neither lapped nor gurgled, but barely trickled through most
of the summer, and only with the spring's melt-off of
dirty winter snow came close to resembling the coursing
waterway of their imaginations.

We would have been, what, in our early teens, I

suppose, holding carefully the volume of poetry we had been given together for Christmas. It said: "1945, Merry Christmas from Mom and Dad." Dad had never laid eyes on it until we unwrapped it in front of him on Christmas Eve, and Mom had bought it only after we took her to the used bookstore. There we had passed it back and forth so gently because of the tissue paper on the frontispiece and the leather beginning to split on the spine. Such authenticity, we marveled, hushed in the midst of so many words, all musty and solemn and dark. And how we delighted in the book's misspelled original inscription— "Too Hattie, with love, Elmer"—captivated by the romantic excess attributed to the original recipient.

When spring finally was more potential than possibility, we could hardly wait for that first weekend when we could slip out the door, still wearing our white Sunday dresses from church. We had searched the bureau drawer for the matching white gloves that otherwise were worn only on Easter morning. Oh, we could just see ourselves. We'd been sharing the vision without speaking directly of it for the last three and a half months of winter and early rough spring: we would spread a blanket by the stream, and the wind would rustle our flowing white dresses, and we would read the poetry of Emily Dickinson.

But not exactly.

Mom wouldn't let us out of the house in our good clothes. So we put on our sweatshirts and dungarees, and then we couldn't find just the right spot by the creek because it seemed like everywhere the banks were all squishy where the cattle had walked into the water to drink, and there were cow plops everywhere, and when we did find a place, it wasn't long before the dampness had seeped through the old quilt and our noses were running in the cold. But we were determined by the picture of ourselves, reading poetry on the banks of the gurgling stream. And then, I read "I like to see it lap the Miles," and we got the giggles when Mavis said that the dashes were pauses to sniff back our runny noses, and we hooted when I got to "neigh like Boanerges," which was me blowing my nose. So we gave up and went back to the house, our butts wet from the ground, but Mom had made hot chocolate for us, and even the little ones had their warm cups, too. And the twins in their high chairs. All of us in the kitchen with Mom at that huge old stove. I wonder where that volume got to. Maybe Mavis knows. Maybe she'd like hot chocolate for breakfast instead of coffee. Maxine smiled to herself, and then felt her chest tighten as she heard Mavis begin her morning coughs from her bed. The coughs seemed longer today, fuller, junk breaking and cracking and snapping in her lungs. A smoker's cough in a woman who never put a cigarette to her lips.

In the guest bedroom separated from Mavis's by the bathroom, Linda and Isabelle lay side by side, not touching, also rigid with discomfort at the sounds of Mavis trying to catch her breath between coughs. They had come awake quickly with the sound, Isabelle finding herself, as usual, wrapped in Linda's arms. But she had disengaged quickly, as if she needed to give all her attention to the sounds next door. Linda knew better than to reach out for Isabelle's hand. Isabelle would take no comfort now, as if to do so would somehow not give the severity of Mavis's discomfort its due. Isabelle was wondering, once again, how she, an experienced nurse, had completely blocked out Mavis's symptoms up to this point. Now she was intent on the sounds, accepting the diagnosis that she knew had registered in her heart long before her brain.

After two or three minutes Isabelle slipped out of bed and reached for the bathrobe on the floor beside her. A deep breath and she was Isabelle Schmidt, R.N., going in to see if a patient needed her. The coughing woman in the bed was just Mavis, Isabelle was startled to see. Somehow yesterday's news and this morning's abrupt awakening had fast-forwarded her imagination to the point where she expected to find one of the skeletal patients she had nursed when she had been up on the wards.

"Can I help you?"

Mavis held up a hand, Kleenex to mouth, and coughed a few more times, caught her breath, blew her nose, smiled, and got out a negative. "You and Linda use the bathroom first. Then I'll get up. I'm okay."

She wasn't, of course. And wouldn't be. It was unclear to the others if they had just been unreasonably blind to her obvious ill health and had subconsciously managed to ignore the unhealthy looseness of her skin, the sudden oiliness of her forehead, or the frequent beads of sweat on her upper lip. And had she been going into another room, or outside, to cough this past week? Or had they somehow willed themselves not to hear the crud gurgling and snapping within her lungs? Did her hands shake the day before yesterday when she poured coffee, cut bars, held children at the picnic? Or had the reunion's end and the next day's doctor's appointment been the line of demarcation she had set up for herself, choosing the moment when the disease inside her body was allowed to register on the outside?

And now they were each profoundly uncomfortable. Not because they were unwilling to nurture. Not because they didn't know how. But because they didn't know how to nurture now. Judy wanted to talk about doctors and hospitals. In the midst of her own fear she had latched onto the notion of the Mayo Clinic in Rochester as the solution to all medical problems. The word itself brought her reassurance that everything could be okay, and as the day wore on, her references to the Midwest's most famous medical mecca—where, according to local wisdom, you went if you were either very rich or very sick—were more and more frequent, more determined than frantic, but unsettling nonetheless, because of the urgency behind her hope.

Maxine had been able to sidetrack Judy's refrain for a moment by reviving a conversation Judy had begun a few days earlier about a young friend who was about to have a baby. It was a completely artificial moment for Maxine, who teetered between amazement and irritation at Judy's habit of carrying on long conversations about complete strangers. But when Isabelle began to grind her jaw at Judy's insistent repetition of the miracles of the Mayo, Maxine put down her book and nudged Judy into repeating the information about her friend, her marriage, her difficulty in getting pregnant, and now the added news that the baby appeared to be positioned to come out feet first.

"What should I get the baby when it's born?" Judy then wondered.

To which Isabelle immediately suggested, "Shoes?"

Maxine hid her smile, gave up, and went back to her book, and Judy, uncomfortable with silence in general, returned to her campaign for Mavis's treatment in Rochester.

It wasn't long before Isabelle felt flushed out of the truce she had silently made with Judy, interjecting with more fatigue then venom, "The Mayo, the Mayo, the

Mayo. Just give it a rest, for Christ's sake. Maybe that's not the answer. Maybe it is. But could we please go a couple of hours without hearing that word again?"

Before Judy had a chance to reply, Mavis spoke from the kitchen: "I'm making up ham sandwiches for lunch, Isabelle. What would you like on yours?"

"Ha ha, Mavis." Isabelle smiled as she crossed over to the refrigerator to get Cokes for Glenn and Craig, who were busy replacing hailed-out windows with the panes they'd picked up in Fargo the day before.

"Let me make lunch." Maxine set her book down again and rose out of the easy chair next to the couch where Judy was now pouting while she worked on the day's crossword. "You sit down."

"I've been sitting all morning, Maxine. You can keep working. What are you reading?"

"A book by a French psychoanalyst named Jacques Lacan. I'm considering early retirement so I don't have to finish it."

"Well, if you want to make the sandwiches, go ahead. I'll go tell my children how to do what they're already doing. If Jackie calls, tell her I'll be down there this afternoon."

"You should take it easy, Mavis," Judy called, and then added, "What's a five-letter word for 'beat'?"

"Easy? I'll take whatever I can get. Strike."

"Five letters, and it starts with a P."

"Spank," Maxine offered.

"It starts with a P."

"Thump."

"Shape." Mavis and Maxine raced to toss out synonyms.

"It starts with a P!"

Mavis hesitated, then gave Maxine her best "I got it before you did" look. "Pommel."

"Nope." Maxine smiled. "Pommel has six letters."

Mavis shrugged her shoulders and was walking to the door when Maxine brightened and called out, "Pulse."

"That's it! I thought you were the crossword wiz, Mavis." Judy smiled.

"Judy," Mavis called back, "when you can't count on me, you can count on Maxine."

25

JOAN MADSEN DIDN'T LOOK UP FROM THE NOTES ON HER lap as Heyerdahl rounded the drive and turned onto the gravel road that quickly led to the county highway. On either side of the blacktop, fields of gold waited for mining. Here was the order, neatness, and sense Heyerdahl had once known as the youngest of four sons on a farm that would struggle to support half that many.

"I wonder what wheat here is running?" Heyerdahl gestured toward the golden blur beyond his driver's window.

"Um-hum," Madsen muttered, circling something she had just written on a yellow legal pad, and drawing a line from this note to a list above it.

"Storms are funny. I believe the hail missed this stretch completely."

"Um-hum."

"Maybe forty-five, fifty bushels an acre."

"Maybe."

Madsen had yet to look up from her notes, and Heyerdahl wondered for the moment if she could really see this land, these people at all. Certainly she knew what it was like to wait in a warehouse, a side street, behind a car door, with weapon drawn, knowing that lives depended on her split-second decisions. But could she fathom the patience called upon to wait for the spring rains to release the fields for planting, or the courage required to see beyond a field leveled by hail or wasted by drought or rotted by weeks of rain, toward the promise of the next year's crop?

It's all here, Heyerdahl thought. The motive behind Carlson's murder, behind Mavis Holmstead's confession, and it, too, will contain its full quota of patience and courage. But murder isn't like farming, because it never, ultimately, makes sense, and that's where it will all break down.

Slowing for a stop sign, Heyerdahl glanced over at Madsen's notepad. "Okay, what have we got?"

"A daughter who seems less than distressed about the death of her father, for starters." Madsen looked up, ready to go to work.

"I have an idea, Joan." Heyerdahl lifted a finger from the steering wheel to return the salute of a stranger in a pickup whizzing by. "Let's just find the person who's sad that Jack Carlson is dead, and arrest him for lying."

"I get your point, but you have to admit it's a little odd, and—" Madsen took a deep breath. "—you should know that I'm uncomfortable with letting her wait until tomorrow to come into the station."

"We got her prints and her statement, neither of which has told us anything for certain yet. And with no witness and no motive, we're not in a position to make an arrest, even if we were convinced that she murdered her father." Heyerdahl's tone was both reassuring and respectful, but his younger partner wasn't satisfied.

"Nonetheless, Jackie Carlson's our principal suspect . . . Ed." Their recent transition to first names still caused Madsen to stumble, unsure as she was whether it marked informality or intimacy, and typically embarrassed by either. "We certainly have enough to bring her in for a more—" Now she searched for the right words, wary of criticizing the senior agent. "—for a more formal interview."

"Jackie Carlson will be at the Fargo police station tomorrow morning to sign her statement, as she agreed. We'll have plenty to do by then to go over today's tape and get her prints to the lab in Bismarck. If by some miracle we have reason to make an arrest, we can do it tomorrow."

"Assuming she shows."

Heyerdahl did Madsen the favor of a short nod. Then he looked over his left shoulder as he merged onto the empty four-lane interstate that would put them in Fargo in under an hour.

"You've met the whole family now, Joan. Have you gotten the impression that there's a one of them that won't spend the day in the waiting room in Dakota Hospital tomorrow?"

"Ordinarily, no. But some of the members of that family appear to have gotten awfully unpredictable of late," Madsen replied, holding her ground. "She seemed a whole lot more shaken by her aunt's tumor than by her father's death."

"Perhaps Mavis Holmstead has been a bit nicer to her than her father ever was," Heyerdahl mused, and then added, as if he had not changed the topic, "What was the name of Carlson's brother again? Ted?"

Madsen studied Heyerdahl's profile for a minute, thinking that just now he looked like one of her father's golfing buddies. There was something about his approach to the investigation, the first they'd worked on as the lead team, that she found disconcerting. Whereas her own inclination was to quickly zero in on the most likely suspect and then to meticulously sift through each detail of that individual's involvement, Heyerdahl seemed to float among the possibilities in a sort of willful indeterminacy. He seemed most comfortable keeping several theories in the air, dealing with them as they dropped, willy-nilly, into his attention. So one minute Heyerdahl was focusing on Jackie Carlson, and the next she was as good as forgotten as he studied Carlson's debt records, which were then put aside as he made the rounds of area cheap motels. And how had he come back to the brother whom no one knew, or cared about, but was last seen on the other side of Montana?

Madsen was well aware of Heyerdahl's impressive record of arrests resulting in conviction, but this investigation was beginning to remind her of a game she had played as a child at the Minnesota State Fair. There, armed with a soft club, she would whack away at plastic moles that popped out of the table in front of her in no predictable pattern, so that just as she went to bop one mole, it would disappear back down its hole and another would pop up elsewhere. It had not been a satisfying experience.

Just now, Madsen thought, we should be ignoring any other moles that pop up, waiting with the club poised over Jackie Carlson. She thought Heyerdahl had come to that conclusion as well. Although random acts of violence did occur, Mavis Holmstead's confession certainly suggested that Carlson's murder struck closer to the family bone. And Jackie Carlson, with an erratic history of alcohol and drug abuse, and evidently some history of disaffection from her father, was as yet unaccounted for at the time of his murder.

So Madsen was a little taken aback by the gentle, almost apologetic nature of Heyerdahl's questioning of the young woman this morning and his practically informal invitation to stop by the station in Fargo tomorrow to "tidy some things up." And when Madsen had attempted to get a better sense of Jackie's past relationship with her father, Heyerdahl quite obviously steered the questions in another direction.

"There's got to be some reason for the daughter's coldness," Madsen said, torquing the discussion back to Jackie after she and Heyerdahl had ridden in silence for a few minutes. "But there's no police record of any domestic violence or child abuse."

"I'm not sure there would be, but we have school records to check, neighbors and teachers to see. And there's our talkative young Blair to visit again."

Madsen gave a shake of her head that only temporarily tossed the hair out of her eyes. "She actually smiled when we talked about her father's death."

"And lost the smile in a hurry when we mentioned Mavis." Heyerdahl ran a hand over his own bristly scalp.

"It's odd that Mavis hadn't said anything before this about her lump."

"Is it?" Heyerdahl asked the highway in front of him, and the agents slipped into their separate silences.

Heyerdahl knew his partner felt a little stung, even a

little embarrassed just now about Jackie Carlson. But she'd done a first-class job in tracking her, and it certainly wasn't Madsen's fault that the daughter had turned up of her own accord before Madsen could close in. She'd done some damned good work back there in Minnesota, moving from information garnered at the Hazelden, to the college friend nobody knew Jackie had kept in touch with, to the cabin at Mille Lacs Lake, doing in just five days what the Minnesota special agents hadn't accomplished in over two weeks. And even if the trail had gone cold there, she'd been able to get a positive ID from the vacationers in the neighboring lake cabin, although unfortunately, Jackie had already been at the cabin when they showed up to begin their own vacation, so there was still no confirmation of her whereabouts on the night Jack Carlson was murdered.

Heyerdahl tapped the steering wheel in a counter-rhythm to the finger-drumming Madsen had begun on the legal pad until she took the hint and stopped. She was smart and she was tenacious, and when she learned how to wait as well as she attacked, she'd be pretty good.

Heyerdahl was glad he'd been there early this morning when the sheriff's secretary had casually mentioned to Sheriff Hansen in their presence that Phyllis Gottschaulk had dropped by the Carlson place yesterday to take young Blair a tuna noodle casserole (the ladies of the Brickton Busy Bee Homemaker Club were taking turns getting him some decent food), and wasn't she surprised to find him at the table eating a plate of cold fried chicken. So she'd asked him which of her neighbors had dropped that off, since of course whoever it was had provided out of turn, and Blair had just shrugged. Now granted, Phyllis thought (and Lila had to agree), Blair had unfortunately picked up some of his father's bad

manners since Irene's passing, but that did seem odd. But
not as odd, Phyllis had added (and Lila repeated as she
stirred her Nescafé into a steaming cup of water), as how
clean the kitchen was. Why, it looked for all the world
like Irene had come back to life to scour it spotless, and
there were only a few dirty dishes in the sink. So Phyllis
said to Blair, "I see you've been doing some cleaning,"
and he just looked a little offended at the suggestion, then
shrugged again. So Phyllis just said, "Well, I'll put this
casserole right in the freezer, then, and you can bake it up
later," and wasn't she surprised to find the freezer
stacked with labeled Tupperware, dinners to last a
month.

Then Lila had stopped and smiled at the sheriff, who
looked a bit sheepishly at Heyerdahl, who was watching
Madsen get ready to blow a fuse.

"Has there, or has there not been a patrol car, either
yours, your deputy's, or a town cop's, out at the Carlson
farm twenty-four hours a day, as we clearly specified?"
Madsen had half growled, half spit the question that had
just been answered and was about to be further verified
by the deputy's timely exit from the rest room with his
Field and Stream. When he announced to the silent room
that he guessed he'd better get back to the Carlson farm
to keep a lookout, Heyerdahl had quickly suggested that
the deputy look after some of his other duties. He and
Agent Madsen would go out to the farm.

There, her mood had not improved upon discovering
that while she had been traversing Minnesota and Heyerdahl had been traveling from town to town in eastern
North Dakota and in northwestern Minnesota talking to
motel clerks and bartenders, Jackie had actually been
keeping herself out of sight right there on the farm. And
although it didn't make much difference now, it didn't

help that a few neighbor ladies at Rosie's had probably been speculating on Jackie's presence in the area for a couple of days now, or that Heyerdahl had himself insisted that disrupting the Schmidt family reunion with their presence this past Sunday was unnecessary.

So it was only too perfect that when they'd arrived at Glenn Holmstead's late this morning, they'd been met by Jackie's innocently apologetic announcement, "Oh, I've been meaning to call you."

Heyerdahl snickered to himself as he pulled into the Fargo police station parking lot. He would tell Madsen that she'd done good work, to take the afternoon off and then get a good night's sleep, that they'd get back at it in the morning. Before he could push the gearshift into park, Madsen turned toward him with a question.

"Shall we listen to the tape first?"

26

EARLY THAT AFTERNOON, JACKIE CALLED MAVIS FROM Glenn and Peggy's with the news that she had spent the morning in the company of agents Heyerdahl and Madsen, who had shown up on Glenn's doorstep just as

Jackie was about to make the call to the Wash County Sheriff's Office that she had promised to make the day before. As usual, there was little to glean from Mavis's end of the phone conversation, which consisted largely of a series of "yeah, uh-huhs," and ended with an "I'll be right down."

When Mavis left, leaving her sons to finish fixing the windows without her advice, Maxine, Judy, and Isabelle settled around the kitchen table to play three-handed pinochle. Linda had been invited to make up the fourth, but had declined, choosing to put in a full workday in the rec room in Mavis's basement, where she sat at the wet bar with her notebook computer and wrote letters and memos about a manuscript she'd finished reading that morning.

Upstairs the mood was solemn, but soothed by a sense of camaraderie. Judy had eased up on her Mayo refrain, and Isabelle, in return, was practicing her newfound, if tentative, restraint. As they bid, declared trump, and made disparaging remarks about each other's skill at cards, they talked about Mavis, murder, malignancy. Unable to make sense of what had preceded their return, they were increasingly bewildered by what followed. Clearly they had been summoned by Mavis. Once home, they helped prepare for the reunion, all the while waiting for whatever it was that would come next, for reality according to Mavis. They had no idea what that reality would look like, because this time the contradictions were complete. Mavis didn't lie; if she said she shot Jack, she shot Jack. But Mavis just wouldn't do that.

If, for a brief moment on Sunday night around a kitchen table in a thunderstorm, Mavis had made sense of their return by making sense of them individually, in relation to her, and in relation to each other, that peace had been quickly shattered by Mavis's more mundane news the next day.

Isabelle advanced her theory that the shooting wasn't the reason for the summons at all, but that Mavis's health was somehow why they were all gathered. The other sisters accepted that as a possibility, "But," Maxine cautioned, "what makes us think it's either this reason or that reason?"

"There has to be a reason," Judy replied. "Usually a family reunion is something we talk about doing ahead of time, so everybody can get here. I know my Chrissie would have liked to have been . . ."

"Here. I'm not saying there wasn't a reason at all. I'm saying that somehow it all might fit together."

"How could the shooting and Mavis's . . . be related?"

"Not causally, necessarily," came Maxine's measured response, "but linked nonetheless."

"I wonder what Mavis and Jackie are talking about?" Isabelle asked her cards after the women had been silent for a moment. When she looked up, Maxine met her eyes and the two women continued their questions silently as Judy looked from one to the other as if she were watching a tennis match.

Finally, feeling left out of the silent conversation, she broke in with, "Well? What? I'm not Kreskin. What are you two thinking? Jackie's thoroughly bummed with her life, and needs to talk to someone like a mother, so she wants to talk to Mavis about—about, well, probably about, well, what she was talking about Sunday night. You know." Noting that her speech had brought new looks of concern to Isabelle and Maxine, Judy hurried on. "Although that would be hard news for Mavis to hear, if Mavis doesn't already . . . so maybe she won't talk about that. Maybe she needs to say more to Mavis about her not hating Mavis for, well, you know, doing what she did. Although I don't believe that—"

"Don't believe what?" Isabelle cut in when it appeared that this time Judy wasn't going to leave a pause in her speech. "Don't believe that Jackie's not angry, or that Mavis did what she did, or that that's what they're talking about?" Isabelle laid her cards down on the table, the game forgotten.

Judy started to respond as if Isabelle's were an easy question, but got no further than, "That she . . ." Now Judy entered into the silent conversation, as they wondered together what assumptions they were about to solidify.

It was Isabelle who took the leap.

"It occurs to me that Jackie has been—and rightly so— one angry young woman. At all of us. Except maybe not at Mavis. At Irene, surely. At Jack. The question is . . ." Isabelle took a deep breath, licked her lips, reached for Judy's cigarettes but scowled and chose to tap the lighter on the table instead, the tapping emphasizing her words: "How mad at Jack was she? Did she hate him? I would. I do. Did."

Judy's response was excited. "Do you think she . . . ?"

Maxine's words, however, added another layer of questions. "Then why did she go to Mavis? Why would Mavis say she did it? Are you suggesting that this is something they planned together? I will not believe that." She held up her hand to stop Isabelle's startled reaction to her words. "And if that's impossible, then how could we think that Jackie, who for years wouldn't even sit in her own living room because there was a gun over the mantel, picked up a rifle and pulled the trigger on her own father?"

"Self-defense, maybe."

They had been so intent on their discussion around the card table that they hadn't heard Linda come up the stairs. She hesitated at the door that entered into the kitchen. Clearly, this wasn't her discussion unless invited in, but just as clearly, she had an opinion to offer.

"There's coffee in the air pot," Isabelle said, noting the empty mug in Linda's hand. "And I don't see how that could be. Even if, and it's a big if, Jackie . . . was the one who did it, she didn't live at home, hadn't for years, and Lord knows when she'd last even seen her father, since Irene's funeral. And then it seems she made sure, except at the church itself, to never be in the same room he was in. So I don't see how it could have been self-defense."

Linda filled her cup as Isabelle spoke and brought the pot over to the table to refill three half-full cups. With a sigh that signaled her own hesitancy about what she was about to explain she set the pot back on the counter and climbed up on a stool behind the food bar. "Well, maybe not exactly self-defense as we usually think of it, but something like it." Linda hesitated, but then, slipping into the professional voice that Isabelle loved, continued.

"Last year I went on business to a battered women's seminar. One of the speakers I met there was an attorney who, herself, had been a battered wife. The statistics are terrifying, really," Linda digressed. "She said that between twenty to twenty-five percent of the adult women in the U.S. have been physically abused at least once by a male intimate. Did you know that the United States lost thirty-nine thousand soldiers in the line of duty during the Vietnam War, while during those same years almost eighteen thousand women and children were killed by members of their families? And it's estimated that in this past year alone—" She stopped at Isabelle's loud throat-clearing, intended to get Linda back on track.

"Linda, Jackie wasn't a battered wife. She was knocked around as a child. And besides, the point is, that was a long time ago."

"I know. But I think that psychologically the trauma might be similar. One of the things this woman talked about was the battered-woman syndrome. And here, finally, I'm sorry I got sidetracked, is my point. She says that battered women—usually that means wives and girl-friends, but I suppose it could also mean children—suffer from a post-traumatic stress syndrome, like pris-oners of war or hostages or someone who's so severely traumatized that she feels like her life is in danger at all times, even if the man isn't beating on her at the moment."

Linda stopped, totally dissatisfied with her explana-tion. She'd gotten used to having this discussion with women who either already knew what she was talking about or were anxious to believe what she said. Although Isabelle had come a long way from the North Dakotan's "If it isn't in my experience then it doesn't exist" way of approaching the unknown, and certainly Maxine's edu-cation had brought her into contact with a variety of opinions, just now Linda was looking at three uncon-vinced faces.

The sisters were silent, Maxine tapping an index finger on the card table absently as she watched the goldfinches busy at the bird feeder in the yard. Isabelle held Linda's eyes, and Judy swung her eyes back and forth at the two, more intent upon their relationship than the import of Linda's speech.

"Granted, that could . . ."

"That doesn't explain . . ."

"I don't see . . ." The three women broke the silence at once all together. Then smiling, stopped. Isabelle picked up the conversation's thread.

"That would shed light on Jackie's actions, if—let's remember we're still talking *if*—if she were still living at home, if she felt like she were still in danger. But she'd escaped, I guess you could say, although for Jackie it's always been out of the frying pan and into the fire. I mean, she wouldn't have felt physically threatened by him anymore. She wouldn't any longer be a battered woman."

"Well, maybe not physically," was Linda's quick answer, to Maxine's agreeing nods, "but perhaps psychologically. That's partly what this woman was saying— that just because the physical abuse is absent, that doesn't mean that emotionally someone is no longer a battered woman."

"So, psychologically, she needs to get rid of the battering man in order to extricate herself from her role as battered woman?" Maxine's question was directed to Linda, although her eyes, unblinking, continued to study something outside the window. Isabelle looked at her sister, knowing that she was as likely to be studying infinity as the swirl of yellow around the bird feeder.

"I don't know about that," Linda backed off. "I didn't really mean to present it as a hypothesis as much as just a piece of a possibility to think about."

"Well," Judy found her entry into the discussion, "it doesn't make sense to me that she'd up and leave the Cities one day and hitchhike to Brickton to shoot Jack, no matter how pissed-off she's been for how many years, thinking all the while that she was doing it in self-defense. When you get right down to it, if Jack beat on Irene and Jackie, then he's probably messed with Blair, too, so maybe Blair's the one—"

"Oh dear God." Maxine looked up over her glasses at her sisters. "This just gets more and more horrible. Here we are trying to make sense out of something that is inherently senseless, murder. But then, the murder of someone who did the unthinkable, abused his children and his wife, and instead of being unable to find someone to slip into that impossible position, we have too many possibilities. Thinking about Jackie doing that is hard enough, but Blair? He's just a boy."

"He's a young man." Judy was wide-eyed and on the edge of her chair, and suddenly Isabelle was angry.

"Stop, then. Just stop. This isn't a game of Clue we're playing here. The truth is we don't know anything. And I think the police would have found out by now if Blair had been involved. As for Jackie, sure there's a couple of days between the time Jackie left the clinic and when Jack was killed, but what does that prove? Nothing. What we keep forgetting to ask is just what role is Mavis playing? Because you know, and I know, that Mavis just didn't get tired of watching *Wheel of Fortune* one night, so she decided to go out and murder someone. So what's she doing? Clearly, she thinks she's protecting somebody. 'We need to take care of our own.' 'God helps those who help themselves.' 'Blood is thicker than water.' So what blood is she protecting? And is she doing it because she thinks she's going to . . . Does she know she's going to . . .'"

27

THE MOOD AT GLENN'S WAS MUCH CALMER. GLENN AND Craig had returned late in the afternoon to find Peggy, Mavis, and Jackie sitting side by side on the front porch steps shucking sweet corn for dinner. Peggy was over-dressed for the occasion, having just gotten back from a long day in her office. She would spend the better part of this week and the next doing administrative work in preparation for the upcoming school year, which would shortly be under way. As the brothers joined the women, Glenn asked Peggy where the girls were. Becky, Peggy was sure, must certainly be on the phone, and Janie was down by the creek resenting the end of summer. "But she did take a book with her, so perhaps this year's transition will be smoother than usual," Peggy added.

"Was it a book of poetry, by any chance?" Mavis smiled wistfully as she asked the question.

"Double Trouble for Rupert."

"Great book," Glenn asserted, "although the sequel, *Triple Trouble for Rupert*, is a little better."

"My scholar." Mavis patted her son's thigh as she reached for another ear of corn.

Craig leaned back against his cousin's knees, closed his eyes, and listened to the small talk while Glenn broke off the ends of the husked cobs passed to him. Together the sons, the daughter-in-law, the niece, and Mavis constituted a moment that differed from so many other moments in their everyday lives only in their determination to keep it ordinary. When Peggy announced that the mosquitoes had found her so she was going in, Mavis got up to leave. Glenn asked her what time she wanted to get going tomorrow, and Mavis replied that right after noon would be fine. There were some kisses. That was sort of unusual. And Mavis was gone.

She drove home under one of those dramatic purple prairie skies with royal-blue clouds swirled on the horizon, the kind accurately represented on canvas in only the worst paintings. If Frank had been sitting next to her in the car, Mavis thought, he would say, "Would you just look at that sky," no matter that he'd told her to look at that sky a thousand times before. Suddenly Mavis felt a lightening, a lifting, an excitement of anticipation in her chest, as if she were a young woman again about to meet a special date. Frank. Shaking her head and smiling in wonder to herself, she tapped the steering wheel with her palm, said thank you to God, and added her own dust to the sunset as she skimmed over the gravel roads.

She got home as Maxine was frying bacon for BLTs. Judy was slicing tomatoes and tearing lettuce. Linda and Isabelle were in the basement making phone calls home. Supper was a piecemeal affair with sandwiches eaten as the toast popped out of the toaster. The women were quieter than usual, the mood fragile. The only reference to the next day was a question from Maxine about who was going in and when.

After supper Mavis went into her room to lie down "for a short nap" while the other sisters cleaned up, took twilight walks, read, watched TV, waited for Mavis to wake up and rejoin them, and generally looked for excuses not to separate for sleep. Finally, around ten-thirty, Maxine got out the bedding for her couch. Linda had gone to bed a half hour earlier, and Isabelle was about to join her. Judy, with a complaint about everybody going to bed with the chickens, was headed toward the stairs when she interrupted Maxine's "Good night" with a raised hand and a "Shhhh." She answered Maxine's raised eyebrows with a question: "Is that the TV on in Mavis's room?"

"I think so," came Isabelle's reply as she walked out of the bathroom that shared a wall with Mavis's bedroom. "I'll see."

A minute later she returned. "It's *The Quiet Man*!"

"*The Quiet Man*!" Maxine smiled. "I love that movie. It's been, oh Lord knows, how many years. I still think he was one handsome man."

"Who?" Judy asked.

"John Wayne."

"John Wayne! What a dud. What's the name of the . . ."

"*The Quiet Man*," Maxine and Isabelle answered in unison.

"I've never heard of it."

"And who's the woman?" Maxine asked.

"Maureen O'Hara." Isabelle was smiling.

By the time this conversation was over, there were four grown women in, on, and around one bed.

"You may have the controls, Mavis," Maxine stated, putting a pillow behind her head, "only if you remember to mute during the commercials."

28

WHEN MAVIS WENT INTO THE HOSPITAL, THE SISTERS set up a whist table in the corner of her room. During Mavis's surgery the sisters played pinochle in the waiting room. Mavis's surgeon had explained that the procedure would be long and involved, but she couldn't say just how long or how involved because she couldn't be sure of what she'd find. As it turned out, the surgery wasn't long at all. Not because there was little to remove; rather, since the doctors weren't in the business of excavation, they had almost nothing to do. The cancer had metastisized to the lymph system, and had spread to Mavis's lungs as well. There would be no mastectomy, no reconstruction, no recovery, no cure. There would be some radiation treatments, because it is the nature of the medical profession to try something, always; there would be some drugs, for the pain. And there would be, the surgeon explained to Glenn and to Craig, and to Maxine, and to Judy, and to Janice, and to Isabelle, very little time. They had been called home for neither a picnic nor a trial, it appeared, but, if only they would be a little patient, for a funeral.

Of course, no one said anything out loud about waiting for Mavis to die. Isabelle called her hospital administrator, and then a few nurses on her staff, explaining that she would be extending her leave and adding, unnecessarily, that she hadn't had a real vacation for six years and that anyone who wanted to give her a hard time about this extension could get creative with a laryngoscope. She encouraged Linda to go back home to California now, and Linda agreed to leave soon. Maxine decided only that she wouldn't decide just now when she would return to Chicago. Her classes were to begin the day after Labor Day, which was three weeks away. As for preparation, well, it just didn't seem very important, and her freshman advisees could be shunted on to someone without the seniority to refuse. Judy, who would have liked nothing more than to show her devotion to Mavis by moving heaven and earth to make it possible for her to stay, was dismayed that no such heroic gestures were necessary. There was simply no reason why she couldn't stay indefinitely. No one to call to ask for an extended leave. No one who really cared when she came home. And Janice continued her long days of work, the only sister without the leisure to take time off, and for this she was grateful.

Slowly the sisters realized that the surgery's purpose had really been symbolic, a formal marker of the end of seeing the world as they had known it. From this moment on they would look into a world in which Mavis was dying. Even now there was no way to envision a world without her at all.

29

TUNNEL VISION. IT WAS THE INVESTIGATOR'S CARDINAL sin, and she was guilty. Throughout her short conversation with the technician from the crime lab in Bismarck, Madsen's mind had raced to explain the lack of evidence she'd been expecting, to find something, anything, that would let her believe that she hadn't just hit a dead end. She hated being wrong, but this was worse because she'd allowed herself to be convinced in part by her determination to be right. Now she had to admit that she could stare at that hole with her club poised until the cows came home, as Heyerdahl would say, but no mole would pop up to accommodate her.

Heyerdahl. Damn, damn, damn. Madsen lifted her head from the hand that still rested on the phone's receiver and turned toward her partner with a deep breath.

And saw, with some amazement, that he appeared to be sleeping. By pushing the conference table that filled most of their work space in the storeroom flush against one wall of shelves, the agents had created a pathway in which to move on the opposite side. Heyerdahl even had enough room to tip his chair back against the shelf behind him so he could rest his feet on the table. It must be more comfortable than it looks, Madsen thought, noticing that the photograph he'd plucked from the table almost an hour ago still rested on his lap.

Madsen was about to take this opportunity to delay her news when Heyerdahl startled her with a shorthand version of what she'd just learned from her phone conversation.

"Nothing, right?"

"Right . . . nothing."

Madsen waited for his next comment, then began to tap the table beside her to break the silence. After about twenty unanswered taps, she spoke.

"I would have put my money on Jackie Carlson. I just can't believe she's not involved in some way."

"Maybe she is," Heyerdahl mused. "But she doesn't appear to have pulled the trigger."

"We've wasted a lot of time."

"Oh, I'm not so sure about that. We do have her back at the Hazelden, where they're more likely to keep a better eye on her now until she finishes her program. She might just come out of this okay."

Madsen opened her mouth, then thought better of the reply she wanted to make and busied herself for a moment straightening the pleats of her khaki slacks, which she had decided this morning were quite presentable and not at all too casual for work. That would be just dandy if we were social workers, she thought, but as investigators of a murder without a suspect, things seem a bit less sunny.

"What have we missed, Ed?" Madsen spoke aloud.

Heyerdahl finally looked up from the photo. "Maybe we need to take another look at Mavis's confession."

"Are you saying that you believe that she really could have killed Jack Carlson? That she was out for his blood because he caused her sister's death? Ed, none of that checked out."

"Not out for blood, but looking out for blood. That much, at least, I think we've been right about."

Madsen realized as she looked her partner in the eye that he was teaching now, and she was getting ready to resent it. She'd read Mavis Holmstead's statement a dozen times, could practically recite it verbatim, and no matter how many times she scrolled it though her memory, it just didn't add up to much more than a canned speech, presented without emotion, complete with a retroactive motive that . . . Madsen's eyes suddenly widened. Then, to the steady nod of Heyerdahl's head, she said, " 'My sister is still young' . . . 'This I can do for her' . . . present tense."

"Yes, yes, and yes."

Heyerdahl dropped his chair back to the floor and reached for a black felt-tip pen on the table in front of him. With a quick motion he drew a circle on the photograph that had been taken at the Schmidt family reunion a little over a week ago, and handed it to Madsen. She looked at the photograph for a fraction of a second, and then looked back up in question.

"Why?"

"That's exactly what we need to find out. And Joan," his tone was now all authority, "we'll go slowly. We gain nothing by spooking her now."

30

MAVIS WAS IN THE HOSPITAL FOR ONE WEEK AFTER THE surgery. During that hospitalized week of recovery, she grew somehow smaller instead of stronger, reinforcing Isabelle's privately held theory—totally at odds with her life's work in medicine—that a body punctured by surgery releases some buoying, ineffable essence. It wasn't a theory she'd ever aired, although she knew that there were probably a few of Linda's acquaintances, crystal-carrying holistic health nuts, who would not find such a notion odd. Indeed, she acknowledged to her rational self that for the most part she was attributing wrong cause to effect, that people who were operated on for a cancer usually looked like hell afterward, and never got around to looking better before they died quite simply because surgery is hard on a body and a progressive cancer is harder. Nonetheless, she couldn't shake the certainty of seeing shadowed death accompany each post-surgery cancer patient she'd nursed. As a good nurse on the wards she had assured countless men and women, pre-surgery, that their doctors were absolutely right and that a proactive course was certainly the best strategy against cancer; to herself, she swore to never let a scalpel crease her fragile casing. As a result she was the only sister who didn't need to comment at least once on "what on earth could Mavis have been thinking about" to have let it go this long. She was thinking about remaining intact, Isabelle supposed.

So it was a smaller Mavis who came home from the hospital. A smaller Mavis who played whist, although a no less competitive and no more patient Mavis. A smaller Mavis who prompted Vanna into motion—"second letter to the right, dummy"—sitting now with an ever-present afghan tucked around her knees, despite the warmth of the mid-August weather that had not yet begun to cool toward September. A smaller Mavis who at first told Isabelle, once again the nurse, that she would take any medicine Isabelle gave her, but since she didn't see the point in all the drugs just now herself, she wasn't going to worry about remembering them on her own. And it was a further diminished Mavis who soon surprised herself by watching the clock for the hour when she could take something more for the pain.

Because the pain made her smaller yet. Although Mavis had never chosen hardship for its own sake, she had always felt charged, enlivened, fortified by challenge, loving the quickness a conflict brought to her senses. Those who responded otherwise were, to her mind, decidedly inferior. Hard work and early poverty, she believed, had strengthened her and made her always capable. But this was different, this was something that admitted neither heroism nor stoicism. This was a constantly increasing nauseating pain that left no room for an element of blank because it could be replaced by only two options: yet more pain, or the terrifying disorientation that increased in direct proportion to the drugs taken to counteract that pain. It wasn't a bracing pain to be striven against valiantly or a noble pain to be ignored. It was a persistent, wretched, debilitating pain indistinguishable from the persistent, wretched, debilitating nausea it caused. So that within two weeks of her return home, all food frying stopped because the smell brought the bile into her throat before she was even aware of which sense had been so viciously assailed that she had time only to turn her head before she vomited. Soon thereafter all meats were banned: fried or not, the smell could not be tolerated. The question of how, then, to prepare Mavis's food was short-lived, because by day twenty Mavis was getting all her nourishment from cans of Ensure and the occasional milk shakes, supplemented by whatever Isabelle could think to safely put in them, carried in by Judy and cleaned up by Maxine.

Mavis's dietary restrictions placed little hardship on whomever else happened to be rotating through the house. Now that this was a place of dying, it was no longer a place of eating. Hot meals were served at Glenn and Peggy's house, into which the silence and waiting of Mavis's had crept.

Becky spoke softly on the phone to her friends about football games, cheerleading, classes, and homework— her life continuing apace, quieted but not slowed by a dying grandmother. She visited Mavis when Peggy suggested it—about twice a week. She stayed and chatted with, then at, an old lady she recognized less each visit. An even older lady asked fewer questions, then asked the wrong questions or called her the wrong name, and finally just returned the pat on the hand in recognition.

Janie, on the other hand, was obsessed with the drama before her. Invariably her first words after being dropped off by the school bus formed a question. Can we go see Grandma now? If the answer was yes, Janie would sit on the corner of Mavis's bed and babble, filling her grandma's ears with everything that had gone on that day, and more. She made lists for Mavis: "What I like most about summer"; "Names of the pets and animals we have ever had"; "Presents I got for every birthday"; "All the people I know"; "Places to hide." Mavis joined her list-making on occasion, but more and more often fell into what were restless sleeps from which she would wake not knowing she had slept, unable to distinguish between dream and reality, and equally suspicious of her family's attempt to separate her reality into categories of past and present.

Mavis's sleep, occasionally accompanied by groaning exhalations, did not stop Janie's lists. When Peggy stepped in the room once to find Janie silent and wide-eyed in the corner, her pencil and paper on her lap, she resolved that this was enough. Janie's vigil, or whatever it was, had to end. But the next day when Peggy got home from school to find Janie waiting in the kitchen, her list of Christmas ornaments they put on their tree each year already begun, she was moved by her daughter's stunned reaction to the suggestion that she not see Mavis that day. But her grandma would miss her! So Peggy capitulated, and wondered what fruit her ten-year-old's death watch would bear.

The traffic was thus steady in and out of Mavis's bedroom. Children and grandchildren sat on the side of the bed, whereas neighbors did their visiting from a straight-backed chair placed at the foot of the bed. They came and told some stories and talked about the cooling weather and left. But Maxine and Judy and Isabelle stayed.

Linda had been gone for some time now, having said her good-byes just two days after Mavis's release from the hospital. The plans for a cross-country drive with Craig had quickly become obsolete, and Linda already had been away from work for two weeks and could justify no more—to herself or to the publishing house. More to the point, Isabelle wanted her to go, wanted to be able to hold on to the notion of a Linda there, in their home there, in their life there. Because for Isabelle the here was Mavis, and would be everything now.

Isabelle and Linda had driven into Fargo the night before Linda was to fly home, in time for supper at Janice's. Mavis's parting with Linda had been warm and sincere. It *had* been a pleasure. She *would* take care. "You take care, too," Mavis finished, "and take care of our Izzy."

Supper had been a quiet affair. No one joined Norton for a drink. The roasted chicken was juicy and pungent with rosemary, but offers of seconds were refused. Isabelle even skipped the seconds of potatoes and gravy which ordinarily would have constituted the bulk of her meal. Both Isabelle and Janice were fatigued by depression, and Linda felt no compulsion to try to lighten their moods with pleasant conversation. The best she could do, she thought, was to keep the conversation going with Norton and thus allow the sisters their silence. Only politics remained to be discussed, it seemed, after the weather was covered. But Linda's politics differed so radically from Norton's—as would Isabelle's from Janice's, had they paid any attention—that this topic, too, was dropped in embarrassed silence once they realized that the warmonger Linda feared was George Bush, whereas Norton had assumed she meant Saddam Hussein.

Even Norton's news, introduced with some pride, that agents Heyerdahl and Madsen had been around to his work that day, didn't get the response he had hoped for. Once Mavis's cancer surfaced, the sisters relegated Jack's shooting to the status of yesterday's news, something they had only been peripherally involved in, something of little import. Mavis; Mavis was the thing.

So Norton, prompting himself with a little help from Linda, explained how the investigators seemed most interested in finding out where he'd been on the Thursday night that Jack was killed.

"Well, there was no problem remembering my bowling night, especially that night 'cause—remember, Janice?—it was my turn to drive, and you'd taken the car to the shop and didn't get back in time. So Morrie had to pick me up, and you'da thought he had to drive a hundred miles out of his way, the face he was wearing."

Norton stopped and waited for a comment. When no one picked up the conversation, he continued. "And here's the kicker. Those agents wanted to know where I *typically* spent Thursday nights, up to over a year ago!" Norton grunted. "Now that might be a problem for some folks to say, but not me. I been bowling at the West Fargo Lanes every Thursday night for the last five years, by God, I told them. They never need to look for a sub for me."

"Can we assume then, Norton, that you didn't kill Jack?" Isabelle was shaking her head at the story.

"Isn't that something?" Norton agreed. "That Agent Heryerdahl said that with his busy schedule, he'd never had the nerve to ask his wife for one night a week out with the boys. He said I was pretty lucky to be married to someone who didn't mind. So, to be honest, I told him that there was a time when Janice wasn't all that hot about my Thursday night out bowling, but that ever since she started taking the occasional night off for herself— what was that, a year or two ago?—to go out to a movie now and then, that I'd been off the hook. Remember that, Janice? Well, Heyerdahl says, that's a great idea. So he's going to suggest that to his wife. Isn't that just something?" Norton asked again, this time looking at Janice.

"Something." Janice got up to clear the table. "I've got maple nut ice cream if anybody would like dessert."

With the table cleared, they played one dreary game of

whist, Linda still confusing her high and low invites and
Norton watching a sitcom while he played, and Isabelle
and Janice saying little but coming back after each
silence with something about Mavis. It was an evening
of incomplete sentences and heavy sighs, and finally
the cards were tossed into the middle of the dining room
table and good-byes were passed around.

"Janice doesn't look well, does she?" was Linda's first
comment to Isabelle once they were back in Mavis's
Cadillac and headed toward the Town House Motel,
where they would spend the night and where, both
women secretly hoped, the desk clerk had changed in the
past two weeks.

One snicker out of that pasty face, Isabelle thought,
and I'll probably throw something. But to Linda she
answered, angrily and unfairly, "She works too hard, her
home life is, shall we say, unfulfilling, and her oldest
sister is about to die. She looks like shit. What else would
you expect?"

It was an old pattern of Isabelle's, and one Linda was
thoroughly tired of after nine years together. It was
something they were going to have to work on—
together—to change, but not now. Now Linda would
accept Isabelle's misdirected anger, let it wash past her,
let it sweep her up with the rest of the world that
offended her lover, help to channel it away from what
they were together, so that finally Isabelle, temporarily
emptied of the rage that would soon enough begin to
build again inside her, would be able to see her clearly as
the ally, the partner, the friend. Linda knew now was not
the time to put her foot down, to say, "No, I refuse to let
you not only include me in your rage, but to use me as
the buffer against which your disgust, anguish, and dis-
content gets directed until you're nurtured back to sanity.
Because it just flat wears me out." Just when the time

would be right to make this stand, she didn't know. But
what they had was too important to be worn down by
misplaced aggression. And, Linda thought, since we're
headed toward some sort of, let's say, new understanding
about how she uses alcohol, the two issues should
probably be dealt with at once. But it's more than I can
do alone. Isabelle in therapy. With or without me, that's
going to be some trick.

"Well?" Linda's silence was more than Isabelle could
tolerate just now. She would have liked to stop for a
drink, but didn't want to give Linda the moral upper hand
in the fight she was about to pick.

"I'm sorry, Isabelle, I was thinking. Well, what?"

"Well, doesn't it make sense that Janice should look
like hell? What else would you expect?"

"It makes perfect sense. I think you should all look like
hell."

"And what's that supposed to mean?"

"Isabelle. Sweetheart. What do you want?"

"I don't want anything. You just made a comment and
I was carrying on the conversation. That's all."

"I think you're tired, Isabelle."

"Of course I'm tired. For Christ's sake, I've spent
every waking moment thinking about how I'm going to
nurse my sister who will be dead soon no matter what
anyone does, and I'll be doing it in a house with
everyone looking at me every time I walk out of that
room as if maybe I should have something good to
report. And then there's Judy yapping at us for not
forcing Mavis to go to the Mayo Clinic, as if that would
accomplish one goddamned thing except to make her die
in a hospital far away from home, so in her lucid
moments she could feel even more isolated and guilty
about keeping people from their lives. And you're right.
Janice looks terrible. This is eating away at her in a way

more than I expected." She stopped for just a moment before adding, "But Maxine. This will break Maxine's heart."

"And your heart?"

Isabelle was silent as she waited for the light at the intersection of Main Street and I-29 to turn green, all the while watching the cars to her left head north on a highway that once led to her twin. Her anger had subsided as her last speech wound down. Now she answered quietly after a moment's thought.

"My heart will hurt. A lot. It will hurt more than when Mom died, and even more than when Frank died, although in some ways that was like losing a father, a big brother, and a best friend all in one. But losing Mavis . . . I don't know. I'm crying now. I'll cry then. I'll feel empty. I'll feel afraid, and alone, and mortal, and all of that. And if my heart breaks, then it will get better. My heart will be okay, Linda. Because we are . . ." She searched for the word and decided on, "Just because we are. But Mavis is more than just my big sister. She's this family."

Again Isabelle drove in silence, although Linda knew by her lover's changing facial expressions, as well as her slight gestures on the steering wheel, that Isabelle had continued the conversation to herself.

When they pulled into the motel parking lot, neither made any move to get out of the car. Isabelle sat with her hands on the steering wheel and looked straight ahead, as if she were reading a script from the windshield.

Finally she spoke out loud: "When I lost Irene, *I* lost Irene. I know that for her children the loss was incomparable, that the rest of my sisters were heartbroken, but I have never really been able to think about how they miss her. She was my twin. She was my loss. She *is* my loss." Isabelle stopped and took her hands from the steering

wheel in order to get a Kleenex out of Linda's purse.
"And I'll tell you something else. I'm damned tired of
crying and blowing my nose. Why are you looking at me
like that?"

"I'm thinking that if I ever leave you, it will be
because you put your used Kleenexes back in my purse.
But go on."

"Well, Mavis is the hub. She always has been. I guess
I'm afraid that without her we'll all, what's left of us, go
flying off into space, away from each other. It's just too
much to lose."

When they lay down in bed, Linda automatically lifted
her left arm to allow Isabelle to curl into her, and wondered for the hundredth time how Isabelle ever managed
to get to sleep alone. But instead of settling in, Isabelle
slid on top of Linda so that her legs matched the length of
Linda's, the tops of her feet pressing against the soles of
her partner. Lifting herself just off Linda's chest so that
their breasts kissed, Isabelle lowered her head to reach
the mouth of her surprised lover. Linda knew Isabelle's
moods, and Isabelle sad, silent, and pensive was not
likely to be Isabelle the lover. Linda had expected her to
take gentle comfort, but to allow nothing more. She
returned the kiss, but took care not to let her own kiss ask
for more, and then said, "Are you sure?"

"Please." Isabelle's look was steady, refusing to hide
her own feelings. "I need your life now. I need to feel
mine." And then the kiss again, harder and more insistent.

Isabelle did not intend to make love. This was not
about the giving and taking of pleasure simultaneous
with the giving and taking of vows and declarations,
spoken and mute. This was not about shared passion. It
was not about Linda, really, at all. Linda knew that
Isabelle needed just sex now. And she knew that the

distinction Isabelle was about to make in her own mind between having sex and making love was at best arbitrary and, for Linda, impossible, because without Linda's love, the sex Isabelle intended, needed now, would have been impossible. Would not have been allowed. It didn't matter that Isabelle did not mean to make love to Linda. Linda, in releasing all claims to control, made love to Isabelle.

Isabelle was not gentle. She was not tender. But for a while she was nowhere else. A body inside another body, feeling nothing but Linda's body close around her, suck her in, want her, want more. Tasting nothing but Linda's warmth and welcoming wetness. Smelling nothing but the hot spice that Linda, aroused, was bathed in. Seeing nothing but Linda's angled jaw arching away from her, her tongue sliding over full lips, her mouth forming the O from which would come the growl that preceded the orgasm and cautioned Isabelle not to stop. And then hearing nothing but Linda's spiraling calls which she knew by heart and which Linda herself had never heard.

Then the quiet, with breaths subsiding, until Linda's right hand began exploring Isabelle's inner thigh. But Isabelle caught Linda's hand, saying softly, "No. I just want to feel you."

Within minutes Linda was sleeping, now in Isabelle's arms. Just as quickly the banished world, filled with death and disease, returned to share Isabelle's night.

31

By the fourth week of Mavis's steady decline at home, Maxine, Judy, and Isabelle had settled into an unarranged arrangement which kept them rotating through the house. Two sisters would stay and care for Mavis while the third spent a few days with Janice or at Glenn's, taking time out from the demands of death. One morning Isabelle returned from Fargo after spending the evening before first with Janice and Norton, and later alone in a Fargo movie theater, and still later even more alone in a nondescript downtown bar. She was surprised to find Mavis sitting in a lawn chair outside in the sun.

Just a few days earlier Mavis had woken from a restless night filled with pain and coughs that brought tears to her eyes and cupfuls of phlegm from her lungs. She had made the rough passage from tormented and interrupted sleep to the cruelty of her body's waking, morning's victory without the reward, to find Glenn sitting next to her, drinking coffee and humming.

"Coffee smells good." Mavis turned her head toward her son, who registered yet again how quickly the jaundice of his mother's eyes was seeping into her skin.

"Good morning. Would you like a sip?"

"I can't, but it's the one smell I still enjoy. What are your plans for the morning?"

289

"Making hay while the sun shines. Craig will be up in an hour or so."

"Open the curtains for me, Glenn. Were you humming just now?"

Glenn answered by singing, "Softly and tenderly Jesus is calling. Calling for you and for me," as he pulled the curtains open.

"Go on."

"I don't know the next line." Glenn smiled, and then repeated the first line to the tune of the second, before moving on to, "Come home. Come home. Ye who are weary come home." Once again he hesitated, and then finished with, "Softly and tenderly Jesus is calling, calling . . . oh sinner, come home."

"Where did you get that voice, Glenn? Your father always said he knew he had a lot of good music in him, 'cause none of it ever got out."

"I got it from you, I suppose."

Mavis closed her eyes and they were silent for a moment. "What's the weather like? It looks so nice."

"It's a beautiful morning. No wind. Going to be a nice day." Glenn hesitated, then asked, slowly, "Would you like to sit outside?"

Mavis's response was surprisingly emphatic: "I sure would."

"Then let's."

Isabelle had been called in to help Mavis with morning toiletries while Glenn went outside to place lawn chairs in the sun. Then, leaning heavily on Glenn and making slow progress, Mavis went outside for the first time in over a week.

As they crossed the threshold into the expanse of blue sky and flatland, Mavis hesitated with an "Oh!" as if she had been slapped, and Glenn felt her fingers tighten on his arm. Taking one step at a time, they descended the

front steps and crossed the few feet to the chairs. Glenn
tucked the afghan with its multicolored crocheted flowers
around his mother and then sat, leaning his head back on
his chair, closing his eyes, and feeling the morning sun
warm his face. He sighed, enjoying a now-rare moment
of relief in his mother's company, and opening his eyes,
turned to comment yet again on the weather. Mavis's
expression and posture, however, startled Glenn back
into silence.

Hands gripping the arms of the chair and feet planted
squarely in front of her, Mavis leaned slightly forward,
not as if she were about to get up, but rather, as if she
were using what was left of her weight to push her chair
and herself back down to the earth. The yellowing skin
was covered now with the oiliness of an unnatural sweat,
and was stretched around the increasingly prominent
teeth bared in a smile of fright. Her eyes were wide. Then
Glenn noticed that she was trembling.

"Mom, are you okay?"

"Hold on to me. I think I'm going to fall."

"It's okay. You're sitting. I'm right here." Glenn
pulled his chair closer and laid a big hand on her arm.

"No. I'm spinning. It's too big. Glenn. Glenn. I can't
see where it ends. I'm going to fall."

With words of "It's okay. It's okay. I'm here. I'll
take you inside. It's okay," Glenn picked his mother up,
stumbled for just a moment with the ungainliness of her
long limbs, and carried her inside, to her bed. Then, sitting beside his mother, his large calloused hand anchoring
her to the earth, Glenn watched as Mavis drifted into her
ragged sleep, her expression now a mixture of relief
within the sanctuary of her bed and a remnant of confusion over what had made itself known to her in an open
yard in the prairie under a cloudless sky. It's too big.

Glenn thought she was asleep when he heard her wonder, again, "I can't see where it ends."

Through his own tears he looked past the bed, through the window, past the yard with its short hedge, beyond the stubble field, toward the horizon toward infinity. It calmed him. It always calmed him. This expanse, this space, this land without boundaries where he knew he could walk, arms outstretched, and touch nothing more than the sky itself.

He looked at the old woman in the bed and saw her, young again, walk precisely that way, down a gravel road, head up, arms raised, with him trotting behind. What was it she would say? "Stay in the open, son. It will make you strong."

Did it? he wondered. Or did you need to be strong to stay in the open in the first place? It didn't make any sense, for Christ's sake. How can it be frightening to sit in your own yard and look out across the fields? When had the security of limitless space turned into a terrifying vertigo?

Then, with a sigh that pushed back his fear, the fear of a son at any age seeing his mother afraid, Glenn put the cap he'd been turning in his hands back on his head. As he passed through the kitchen, he both lied and spoke truthfully to himself and to Isabelle, who was washing the morning's few dishes: "I don't see where it ends."

Well, Isabelle thought as she now walked across the yard toward Mavis, we only err when we underestimate her. I would have bet money that she would never set foot outside again. Then Isabelle gave a guilty snort. We always give up before she does.

Isabelle noticed that Mavis's glasses were in her lap and the *Fargo Forum* lay unread on the grass beside her. She approached quietly. But Mavis was wide-awake, had watched, in fact, Isabelle's dust cloud approach the farm for several miles.

"I'm glad you're keeping my car in racing form these days, Izzy." She spoke softly, but the intensity remained behind the yellowed eyes. "We wouldn't want the neighbors to think the roads were safe just because I'm out—" Mavis held up her hand to stay Isabelle as her body convulsed into a series of coughs that left her struggling for a breath. With eyes watering and hands shaking, she reached under her chair for the plastic cup half filled already with slugs of phlegm. Turning away from Isabelle, she coughed, gagged, and spit. Waited. Coughed, gagged, and spit. She set the cup down, leaned back in her chair, and continued. "—out of commission."

"It's good to see you back out here."

"Not, I'll not, carrion comfort, Despair. Etcetera. Etcetera. Tell me where you've been."

Isabelle pulled another lawn chair beside Mavis and sat down to take up the conversation. She'd had a nice dinner with Janice and Norton. Sure, Janice seemed okay. Had Mavis taken her medicine? Had Glenn and Craig been up this morning? What were they doing today?

These few questions, however, caused Mavis to quickly tire, so Isabelle made an excuse to get up, leaving Mavis to the quiet Isabelle suspected she preferred. As Isabelle began to walk away, Mavis spoke, to no one in particular: "I can smell the fall today. I'm glad."

Inside, however, the atmosphere was decidedly chilly. Maxine and Judy were standing at opposite ends of the kitchen counter, each holding a half full coffee cup as if about to fling the contents at the other at the count of ten. Judy ignored Isabelle's entry; Maxine greeted her with an exasperated look which seemed to ask Isabelle if she could believe it. Whatever the "it" may be, thought Isabelle, I don't want to know, and yes I can.

"Don't go throwing those eyebrows around on account of me, Maxine," Judy growled. "And don't try giving me a Mavis-look, either. You're not Mavis. And don't *you* say anything, either," Judy finished with a caution for Isabelle.

Isabelle shrugged, happy not to be invited into the fray, and headed silently for the bedroom to change her clothes. The lawn could almost use mowing, and it would be nice to sit on a tractor and listen to nothing but a motor and blades.

"Where do you think you're going?" Maxine said, calling her back as if speaking to a recalcitrant teenager. "Just come back here and listen to this!"

Isabelle stopped, amazed at Maxine's tone, but mostly amused at just how foul Maxine's mood must be for her to assume such condescension toward a forty-six-year-old. Wisely, she hid her smile. "Okay," she said, turning. "I'm listening, but remember, I just walked in the door. I'm not the one you're mad at."

"Go ahead, Judy. Tell her."

Judy turned full on Isabelle and challenged her with her words: "I've decided to go home. I'm not doing anything here. I don't care what you say. Mavis is going to die and there's nothing we can do about it, and I can't . . ." She stopped, waiting for someone to finish her thought, but Maxine was stonily silent. So Judy continued, "I can't just sit here and wait for her to die. I can't see any reason to hover. If there was something I could do, I'd do it. But there's nothing I can do. I don't live here. I want to go."

"That's probably a good idea."

"What?" Maxine turned toward Isabelle. "Are you out

of your mind, too? Leave? Leave Mavis now? I can't believe what I'm hearing."

"Maxine, I'm not leaving. I need to be here. And you need to be here. But Judy doesn't feel like she does. It's up to her. And maybe having all of us ministering angels hovering around *is* tiring Mavis out?"

"Thanks." Judy's tone showed that she was as surprised by Isabelle's response as Maxine was indignant.

"I just think you need to be sure of two things. One, why do you want to go, and two, how will Mavis feel about you going? If it won't hurt Mavis, and," turning to Maxine, "I don't think it will . . . When you get right down to it, Maxine, I think *we* need to be here now more than she needs us. . . . If it won't hurt her, then you," Isabelle's eyes swung back to Judy, "just need to know why you want to go."

"I don't know what you mean," Judy replied, closing down.

"Well, so much for that conversation." Isabelle turned back toward the bedroom, then stopped and looked to Maxine. "I did my part. May I be excused now?"

"No." Maxine's tone had lightened a shade, but she wasn't through with the conversation. "I can't believe that if Mavis didn't want us all here she would have called us home."

"Maxine," Isabelle countered, "Mavis called us home for the family reunion. We had it. We were all together. Mavis couldn't have foreseen this . . . this day . . . exactly. I don't think she's running the show anymore."

"Exactly," Judy added. "It's just day by day now for her, like for the rest of us, and . . ." Judy stopped.

"Yes?" Isabelle prompted.

"Okay, you want to know why I'm going home. Partly it's because I can't do anything here. I'd stay if I could. But you've got the nursing to do, and Maxine's taken over the house—" She stopped Maxine's interjection with a raised hand. "—and no one really wants to hear my advice anyway, although I still think we should have gotten her to the Mayo for the surgery. But me, I just don't need to be here, and . . . and, well, go ahead and laugh, but I want Mavis to think I've got something to go home to."

"What do you mean?" Isabelle was no longer edging out of the room, but was now perched on the arm of the recliner.

Judy took a sigh, and looking at the back of Mavis's head out the window, went on, "She's asked me twice in the past two days if Jed and I are serious. We'd had this conversation when I got here before the picnic. I told her then that Jed and I were about kaput. Then she asked me yesterday again, and it was clear she hadn't remembered that first conversation. I told her again that it looked like it was over with Jed. Then this morning she asked again. I didn't know what to say, but she looked so worried that I said that yes, I thought we'd be together for a long time. Fat chance, but, well, she looked so relieved. I guess she worries about me, and I don't want her to have to worry. Now."

Judy stopped and waited for a response. When none came, she directed a "Well?" toward Maxine.

Maxine sighed and studied her cup. "Then you'd better talk to Mavis this morning while she's still clear. Take some juice out to her. And put that sweater back around her shoulders."

"Well?" This one was directed at Isabelle.

"You've already had my blessing, although I don't see why we have to vote on each other's actions as if this were some kind of women's club. And, hey Judy, this doesn't mean you *have* to get this Jethro or Jasper or whatever his name is to marry you."

When Judy closed the door behind her, Maxine turned to Isabelle. "You realize, of course, that Judy just gave us one-half of her reason for deciding to go, although I'll grant you that that one-half was about ten times more introspective than I'd ever expected from her."

"Don't pick on Judy, Maxine, that's my role. So what's the other half? Jed wants his car back?"

Maxine ignored Isabelle's joke. "Clearly Mavis has always taken care of Judy, watched over her and made her safe. She can't do that now, and it probably has Judy pretty scared."

"She's taken care of all of us, Maxine. We're all pretty scared."

"But it's taken on a momentum of its own, hasn't it? I don't feel like I'm making any decisions anymore, or that I can. I even waited for my chair at the university to suggest that I take this semester off before I made the decision about when to go back." Maxine hesitated. "We really are just waiting for her to die now, aren't we?"

"Yes."

The sisters were silent for a moment. Then Isabelle added, "But it feels more like we're just hanging on to each day, along with her. It doesn't matter. You and I will stay until it's right to go."

32

EARLY THE NEXT MORNING JUDY'S BAGS WERE PACKED in the newly tuned-up Mercedes, which was covered with a light coat of dust despite the washing it had been given by Becky and Janie earlier in the week. Mavis was sitting up in bed, her Carnation Instant Breakfast beside her untouched. It was a short good-bye, both sisters embarrassed by, but allowing, their tears.

"I love you, you know," Judy said, and then added, "you old bat."

"I know you do, Judy. I know," Mavis responded, giving Judy exactly the words she needed to hear, and then asked as much as added, "You'll be okay. You'll be okay."

"I'll be okay," Judy said, handing the necessary words back to Mavis.

They held on to each other. Judy, amazed at the lightness of the body she cradled and unable to locate the substance of her iron-strong big sister within Mavis's fragile embrace, felt as if she were holding loss itself in her arms. Finally, Judy got up and walked to the door. As she was about to pass through to the other room, Mavis added in a distant voice, "On your way out, check on the twins. They're awfully quiet. No telling what they're into now."

Startled, Judy turned quickly to look at Mavis. But

Mavis did not see her confusion. With her eyes closed, she had sunk back into the bedding with a heaviness that belied her diminishing frame, pulled down by a force stronger than gravity.

MAVIS

MAVIS'S EYES WERE CLOSED. HER LIPS BARELY MOVED and no sound came out. Our Father who art in heaven, hallowed be thy name. Thy kingdom come, thy will be done on earth as it is in heaven. Give us this day our daily bread. And forgive us our trespasses, as we forgive those who trespass against us. And lead us not into temptation, but deliver us from evil. For thine is the kingdom, and the power, and the glory forever. Amen. Not asleep yet, Mavis thought. Those drugs usually work so fast. Again. Our Father who art in heaven. Hallowed be thy name. Thy kingdom come will be done on earth is in heaven . . . Give us this day our daily bread . . . Forgive trespass against us . . . Lead us into temptation . . . evil . . . Our Father who art hallowed thy kingdom come, kingdom come, kingdom come come now come soon I'm coming I say I can't believe it and Yes, yes, yes he says oh how embarrassed we both are we never talk not like that and then the barn impossible stubble hay against my back calling out impossible and he says yes, yes, yes and we are embarrassed but we are. That smile a rough cheek. When he comes in after chores I'll have to tease him about it his ears so red from the cold, cheeks red, nose running. So cold out there, even for a big Norwegian like him who art in heaven who art hallowed by thy name Mavis Margaret Schmidt Mavis Margaret Schmidt Holmstead Homestead Mavis Margaret Mavis Margaret I'm coming, just hold your horses. Big with feet the size of dinner plates and faces as long as your arm eating us out of house and home with icicle beards and yellow teeth. Sure they're only two, you say, and sure they're no good for anything, but they've worked long days, and hard days with my Father who art in heaven and now they can live in this pasture barn and wink when the tractor goes by, old Chub and Ethel and you and Dad standing there touching them like you would touch yourself reaching through the mirror and say Good Boy, Good Big Brute that you are. You are, you are, you are, you are the best big brute and look God isn't winking and he doesn't watch us at all when you lift me up and laughing lay me down and we laugh and laugh and you say I'm a good egg and you dammit all the twins have forgotten to wash the eggs again. So angry you say this will be done before you use the car again you can bet this will be done, thy will be done thy will be done on earth because the land is everything you tell me singing the song about the gophers you made up while haying. Sing to them while you and Glenn are waiting with that .22. Just a whistle then. And there's a head, over there! Frank! Watch out he's grabbing for the gun. He has a knife. Down Magnus, that's no way to jump up on our father who art in heaven hallowed be thy name will be my name and thy people my people. What's good for the goose is good for the gander. Tweedledee and Tweedledum, Frick and Frack, one for you and one for Irene. Keep your fingers out of the frosting I see what you do, Izzy, upstairs with your new friend. Don't be angry Irene don't cry. You're not alone. Don't cry. We can get you out. Get her out! Get her out! Don't cry Irene. I know it hurts. Put it out Frank. Put it out! I'll do it. I'll shoot the son of a bitch. I can shoot like father who aren't in heaven, aren't in heaven, in heaven.

"PUT IT OUT! PUT IT OUT!"

"Mavis, wake up. Mavis. It's okay, Mavis. You're having a dream. You're okay. It's okay. Mavis. Take a deep breath. You're awake now. It's okay."

"Irene? I'm so sorry, sweetheart. I'm so sorry it hurt. Have I been dead long? Are we in heaven?"

33

MAVIS'S WINDOW WAS OPEN TO THE WARM BREEZE that moved the curtains around and carried inside the comfort of Indian summer. Somewhere in the near distance a meadowlark repeated his song, a whistled note that leapt an octave, followed by the meticulous trill back down the scale to start again. The breeze should have been soothing and the birdsong pleasant, but all Janice could feel as she stood by the window, her back to the bed, looking out on space and then more space, was emptiness. She inhaled deeply at the window, and was rewarded with the acrid smell of medicines and bed-clothes and something else she chose not to identify that the breeze had stirred. And then, spotting the splash of yellow on a fence post by the barn, surprised herself by saying out loud, "Oh, shut up!" Her voice brought the bed behind her into motion, and Janice silently repri-manded herself as she turned to watch Mavis fight herself awake.

It was a struggle the sisters now knew well, even Janice, who, for the most part, was able to get out to the farm only on the weekends, but who tried to get out more often in the attempt to diminish the horror of finding her sister so drastically altered from visit to visit—so that she thought if only three days passed instead of six or seven, then maybe she wouldn't be able to track so clearly the loss of weight, the increasing jaundice, the transforma-tion from body to skeleton.

She wanted to help Mavis awake, to touch her on the arm, to talk her into the present. But they had discovered that the confusion and terrors of Mavis's sleep gripped her too strongly within the dual vices of a capricious cancer-induced dementia and the drugs that were now the only way she could tolerate the pain of a body simultane-ously atrophying and growing out of control. There was no way of knowing if Mavis could distinguish a soothing touch from the hot hand of guilt and remorse that gripped her unconscious. For if Maxine or Isabelle or Janice or Glenn or Craig reached out to touch Mavis before she made that increasingly infrequent trip to complete consciousness, they ran the risk of setting off a frenzied and frightened response that too quickly fatigued her back into tormented sleep.

It was a wrenching moment to watch, unseen and unheard, helpless as Mavis's body fought against her invisible demons, her eyes flashing open but unseeing. More horrible than witnessing the desperate gasping for air, more anguishing than the realization by the sister or son leaning over Mavis that she or he had been mistaken within Mavis's disease-chewed mind for someone or something to be feared, were the words that accompanied the struggle. For each word of Mavis's opened the door a crack onto her pain, allowing the family an unbidden look into her horror at her own guilt.

Because guilty she knew herself to be. A murderer she believed herself to be. And the most harrowing remorse brought her no relief from the image that filled her sleeping unconscious, the image that Janice had unwittingly provided: a face flying apart into bones and blood with the impact of a thirty-ought-six bullet. Mavis had placed herself at the other end of the rifle she would carry with her into eternity. She knew what everyone else knew: she did not lie. She could feel the cool of the summer night against her bare arms. She could hear the crickets in the grass, unseen, as she waited. She could feel, burning in her chest, what must have been the anger and the hatred that would make her do such a thing. Again and again and again she heard the explosion that made it impossible for her to catch her breath. She was choking, surely, on guilt.

She believed. And because she believed, she was damned. So that more and more frequently the words "Please forgive me" punctuated her sleeping moans directed toward the God she had created in her own image, loving but stern, willing to give some leeway to sinners, provided those sinners sinned with common sense, but holding fast to a few unbendable rules, including Thou Shalt Not Kill.

When Janice realized that this time Mavis would win the battle to wake, she moved quietly to the chair that had been placed by the bed. Some of the pain that creased the skin tightening over Mavis's skull gave way to an open-eyed look that combined apprehension with curiosity. Mavis had been able to explain not too long ago that it was like waking in the dark and not knowing where you were, but knowing that there was something possibly dangerous nearby.

Finally Mavis's eyes fixed on Janice's face. Mavis smiled and spoke, forcing her helplessly foul breath toward her sister. "Janice. How long have you been on patrol?" She lifted her hand with effort to lay it on Janice's hands folded in her lap. Both women noticed how long Mavis's yellowed fingernails had become.

"Good Lord, that looks awful, doesn't it?"

"I'll take care of it." Janice smiled and patted Mavis's hand. "Where do you keep your manicure stuff?" Janice asked, getting up, and then, seeing the surprised confusion on Mavis's face, hastily added, "Never mind. I'll find it."

While Janice held Mavis's left hand over a page of the *Capper's* spread beside her on the bed, she began trimming and filing Mavis's nails, which seemed to have hardened and strengthened in inverse relation to Mavis's weakening. When did it stop being *Capper's Weekly*? Janice wondered. And who has time to read page after page of homey anecdotes, to try the recipes, to cut out sewing patterns?

"Mavis. Listen to this joke in the *Capper's*. Why do muskmelons have church weddings?"

"Because they cantaloupe." Mavis's voice was a rasp. "That joke isn't really still around?"

"It's right here! Amazing. What goes around, comes around." Janice took a breath and made small talk about her children and grandchildren as she worked on Mavis's hands, forcing herself to speak about life continuing and life beginning for Mavis's sake, and Mavis clung to the words for Janice's.

When both hands had been manicured and Mavis had declined the offer of a shampoo with a "No thanks, I don't think I'll be out in society today," Janice took a deep breath and plunged into territory that haunted her as thoroughly as it did Mavis.

"Mavis. Listen. I want you to stop saying you killed Jack."

The pain that statement brought to Mavis's face was doubled in Janice's heart as she looked on. Mavis closed her eyes and did not answer.

"Mavis? I know you don't want to talk about it, but I need you to stop. I need you to stop saying that."

Still Mavis was silent, although Janice noticed now that her lips were trembling.

"Mavis?"

"That's just the way it is, don't you see?" Mavis's eyes found Janice. "I don't know why I did it, but I did, and now I need to accept what's been done. What will be done. Thine will be done."

"See what?" Janice insisted.

When Mavis's expression changed to angry exasperation, Janice realized that Mavis *had* answered her, but wasn't aware that she had done so silently.

"Say that one more time," Janice quickly added.

But exhaustion and pain were once again claiming Mavis. Janice watched her go rigid with the slicing intensity of an agony that required all of her attention. Mavis turned her head to the PCA pump that held the morphine which drained into her veins.

"I need more. Ask Izzy. Tell Izzy I need more *now*."

Janice didn't need to ask. At this stage Mavis herself was the indicator. If she couldn't stand the pain, if she were willing to substitute drugs for lucidity, then it was time for the medicine. Janice crossed to the other side of the bed to manipulate the apparatus just as Isabelle had demonstrated.

As usual, the morphine worked quickly. The two women were silent, one waiting for the opportunity to speak again, the other falling away from speech into the drugged sleep that could no longer mask the pain from her body which continued to register the cancer's remorseless attack through grimaces and moans.

Janice couldn't wait for their next visit to make herself heard. "Mavis. I want you to stop saying you killed Jack. Please. I know you've been protecting me. I know why you thought you could. But I was wrong to let you."

"I was wrong."

"No, you were taking care of me as usual, and I love you for it. But no more. Please. It's just wrong."

"Take care of me. I love you. It was wrong." And Mavis drifted off into her litany of "forgive me's."

Janice returned to her chair and just as insistently, if softly, answered each "Forgive me" with "You did not shoot Jack."

"You did not shoot Jack," Mavis murmured in response.

"You are forgiven."

"You did not shoot Jack."

"You did not shoot Jack."

"Forgive me."

"Let her sleep, Janice." Maxine's voice from the door startled Janice away from this battle of wills with her all but unconscious sister.

Still watching Mavis, Janice shook her head stubbornly, but answered softly. "She can't hear me say this when she's awake. Maybe I can get it through to her while she's sleeping."

Again Maxine spoke, but this time more tenderly: "Let her sleep, Janice. Let her rest. Let *it* rest."

"You don't understand, Maxine. She really thinks she killed Jack. And it's tearing her apart. She's so scared, can't you see. She thinks she's about to face God with blood on her hands. I can't let her suffer like that. I can't let her believe that."

"Janice. Janice. That's not up to us, not now at least, and probably never was. That was between Jackie and Mavis. Whatever they decided is between them. And even if it were someone else's business, it doesn't make much difference now anyway. Changing Mavis's mind in the best of times was hard enough; you're beating your head against a wall now."

Janice's expression had gone from stubborn to confused to incredulous during Maxine's brief speech. Sitting straight in her chair, all her attention now directed toward Maxine, she asked slowly, "What's Jackie have to do with this?"

Now Maxine was hesitant. "I thought that you probably thought, too, that Jackie probably, or at least certainly could have . . . well, was the one . . . and Mavis is covering for her. Not that I know that to be the case. I don't know any more than you do. It's just that, well, Jackie being basically unaccounted for at the time, and knowing, now, about her abuse . . ." She hesitated, and then, irritated by Janice's open-mouthed disbelief, added, "Listen. I don't know what happened and I don't care. Jack Carlson hurt people until someone, whoever, put a stop to him. And if Mavis wants to say she did, well then, as far as I'm concerned, *she did*."

Suddenly Janice was moving. With an "Oh my God," she stood and brushed past Maxine, who, after taking a minute to check the PCA pump, reached the living room window in time to see Janice churning up the gravel drive as she sped out of the yard. Janice drove six miles of gravel road at seventy-five miles per hour before she fishtailed to a stop to turn onto the blacktop that led to the interstate. That's when she realized that she was still clutching a wadded-up newsprint page in her hand. At the stop sign she rolled her window down and tossed the wadded *Capper's* onto the road. But she was unable to drive on, and laughing humorlessly at herself, got out of the car, muttering "I can murder, but I can't litter." She picked up the paper ball, and shaking it open, watched the yellowed fingernails float to the earth, where they would cling to the roadside grass.

34

"WHAT ARE WE WAITING FOR, ED?" JOAN MADSEN USED both hands to push her hair back behind her ears as she waited to see if her question had registered with her counterpart, who appeared intent upon a breaded veal cutlet covered with tomato sauce. His horn-rimmed glasses had slipped down to rest on the end of his fleshy nose, causing Joan Madsen to wonder for the hundredth time if he reminded her of her high school physics teacher or her postman.

"Ed?"

Heyerdahl looked up as if he were about to answer, but instead flagged the passing waitress in orange and brown who carried a coffeepot in one hand and with the other tugged at her skirt's waistband, which cut her at the middle.

"I'll take a little more of that coffee, please, and maybe you should tell me about your pies."

When the middle-aged woman with immovable hair and thick support hose moved on with a "Sure, hon" after Heyerdahl's dessert order, Madsen couldn't help but note, "That isn't coffee."

"Sure it is."

"And that's not food, either." She gestured toward her partner's plate.

Ed Heyerdahl looked down lovingly at what was left

309

of his breaded cutlet, then gestured across the table with his fork. *"That's* not food."

"No," the young woman agreed, moving the iceberg lettuce around in its wooden bowl, "but it's closer." After a moment she said again, "What are we waiting for?"

"Hot apple pie and cinnamon ice cream," he said, smiling again at the waitress who handed him his dessert.

"Funny. Now here's what we know"—Madsen held up her left hand, palm inward, about to tick off items with her right, but then added, parenthetically—"and what we have known for some time now."

"Go ahead."

"Jack Carlson had a habit of leaving home on Thursday afternoons and getting back early Friday mornings. Jack Carlson also had a habit of never having quite enough money in his pocket but of being pretty free with his American Express card."

Madsen stopped and looked at the credit card her partner had just pulled out of his wallet to place on the table. She shrugged and added, "Not that that in itself is a crime. But it's given us a pretty good idea of how he spent those Thursday nights." She stopped again, and asked, "Why always on Thursday, do you suppose?"

"He didn't like to bowl?" Heyerdahl smiled.

"But he liked to sleep with women who weren't his wife."

"Also not a crime."

"Even if for a while one of those women is your wife's sister."

"Which is where it gets harder to believe?"

"Which is where it gets harder to stomach. But positive IDs of Janice Berg by night clerks at both the Midway and Stagecoach motels don't leave much room for doubt."

"And do you think that would hold up in court? Hundreds of couples pass through those motel rooms each year. How could those clerks be absolutely certain, over a year later, mind you, that the woman they remember was Janice Berg?"

"Because she stood out, because she didn't look right. Because she—" Madsen stopped to pull a small notebook out of the pocket of her cotton blazer hanging on the back of her chair, flipped through a few pages, and read. "—looked too nice and too tired, like a middle-aged housewife, to be fooling around with some drunk for a couple of hours. End quote."

Madsen waited for Heyerdahl to reply, but he seemed more intent upon pushing the last piece of pie crust around his plate to mop up the melted ice cream.

"And there is a direct correlation between calls from Carlson's home to Janice's work on those nights," Madsen prodded.

"Okay, so Janice is probably guilty of an extramarital affair, but not one, as far as we know, that lasted past a couple of months at most. And certainly not one that continued past her sister's death, which means she may not even have seen Carlson for a year."

Madsen was silent for a moment, turning her spoon over and over in her hand, rubbing the concave, convex, concave surface against her thumb. To the table she said, "The guy was really an asshole."

"So?"

"So nothing. But Janice strikes me as someone likely to simmer for a long time before boiling over."

"You may be right, but that's not the kind of information that gets arrest warrants signed." Heyerdahl gave the young woman across the table one of his expressionless looks, and then added, with a slight smile, "You're going to rub the finish off that spoon."

"And probably leave some fingerprints. Ed, I understand that you want to have all your ducks in a row before you interrogate her. But what more do you need? There was another set of prints, other than Carlson's and Thorson's, all over that gun. It's way past the time to see if they belong to Janice Berg. We know she didn't work that night. We have motive and we have opportunity. Ed, you know we have probable cause." Agent Madsen hesitated, and then added deliberately, "And we *should* have more by now."

"Just say it, Joan."

"Okay, why are you dragging your feet on the information from the loaner car? I've been bugging the crime lab techs in Bismarck for weeks, and this morning they finally tell me that you told them that this was *not* a top priority. Not a top priority, Ed? For a murder investigation?"

Ed Heyerdahl's sigh was long as he shifted his gaze away from his partner's face, over her shoulder, and out the windows lining the front of the Highway Host. When he began to nod his head, Madsen turned in her seat to see what was holding his attention behind her. But there was nothing out of the ordinary, just cars picking up speed as they passed by on Main Street, about to merge into westbound I-94. She didn't speak, but began to drum the table with her left index finger.

Finally Heyerdahl spoke, but as if to no one in particular.

"I talked to Dr. Finn, Mavis Holmstead's oncologist, this morning. She says Mavis is unlikely to live beyond the week."

Madsen waited for a moment, then said, "That's too bad. There's something about her I couldn't help but like. But—"

"A remarkable woman, I'd say."

"Some of that 'remarkable,' Ed, constitutes giving false information to the police, at the least, and more likely impeding a felony investigation. Although—" Madsen's voice trailed off. "—I guess that doesn't matter much now."

"No greater love . . ."

Madsen studied the nondescript older man across the table from her. Finally she said, "Nonetheless."

Ed Heyerdahl brought his gaze back to the young woman. "Joan, Janice Berg is not going to do anyone else any harm and she's not going anywhere. And we have plenty of other work to do for a week." He hesitated and looked back out the window. "We will get the lab report on the loaner car, we will get Janice's statement and prints, and we will arrest the murderer of Jack Carlson. But first we will go to a funeral."

35

GLENN WAS AT THE STOVE MAKING FRIED EGG SANDwiches for Isabelle and Craig. Young Donny Nordstrom had already bolted the first two sandwiches and headed back out to the field to continue working the stubble. With the small-grain harvest finished, Glenn was spending the day servicing the combine in preparation for the edible beans, which would soon be ready. It was not a three-person operation by any stretch of the imagination, but Glenn welcomed the company of his brother and aunt, who together were almost doing the work of one hand. With these two around, Glenn found himself turning the tractor and disk work over to young Donny, while he lingered over the hot dish he heated up or the hamburgers he fried for the noon dinner. So that the only one dissatisfied with two extra hands was young Donny, who was working harder than ever.

Fried egg sandwiches and beans and wieners and Glenn was in heaven, Isabelle was perfectly satisfied, and Craig was amazed at his own appetite for the stuff.

"There, see." Glenn pointed out with his fork. "You just needed to do some real work to get that appetite back and put on some weight. Farming is good for you."

"Don't start, Glenn." Craig began to shake his head.

Glenn turned to his aunt. "Isabelle, talk to this man. The two of us would be great farming together."

Craig didn't wait for Isabelle's opinion. "This is your life, not mine, Glenn. You and I both know I'm no farmer, and you certainly don't need to add someone to your operation to subtract from your income."

"We could do okay on what we have, plus a few more rented quarters until you got your feet under you and started buying in. Mom would like it, too."

Isabelle's "uh-oh" was simultaneous with Craig's interjection.

"Now wait right there, big brother. I think it's great that you'd like to have me back on the farm. I also know that it would be a mistake. I'm a computer nerd, for Christ's sake."

"You keep saying—" Glenn interrupted, but Craig interrupted back, "And as for what Mom would like, she's pretty much done liking anything. Don't get that look on your face. I'm not being disrespectful. But truthfully, do you really think, at this point, that she could care if I take up farming?"

"I think she'd like to hear it."

"No, Glenn—it would make you feel good to be able to say it."

There was silence around the table, which was particularly difficult for Isabelle, who agreed, without hesitation, with Craig. She knew he was right and she also knew that Glenn was searching for a way to fill the void he anticipated with Mavis's death. But she didn't worry. Glenn was not the type of man to stand still in grief. He lacked patience for the introspection that caused more thoughtful people than he to exchange a pleasant-enough reality for the dark cliché of "What does it all mean?" Glenn would feel the loss of his mother keenly; he would miss her company, her approval, her advice. Her death would slice away at that which he valued most, family. And he would heal the wound with just that; Peggy and his girls would keep him moving forward into the future and into life. No, Isabelle thought, Craig would be an average farmer at best, with no heart for the routine. What's more, by moving home, he would be making the decision to be alone for the rest of his life.

Craig pushed his plate toward the center of the table, reached for the coffeepot behind him on the counter, and broke the silence: "So I suppose this is as good a time as any to let you know that I've called my manager at Boeing to say that I'll be back at work this coming Monday."

"But . . . Mom?"

"If Mom could, I'm sure she'd say 'go.' I've been away from work for six weeks already. My job's secure, but only up to a point. There are projects I'm way behind on."

"Your job? Projects? For Christ's sake, Craig, Mom's dying!"

"I know!" Craig raised his voice to match Glenn's, then hesitated, and continued evenly. "I know. And if I thought that staying here would give her life, or even pleasure, I'd say 'Screw the job.' But Glenn, we're just waiting now. And I'd rather not. Six weeks ago she was playing softball with us. Three weeks ago she was explaining gift and inheritance taxes and investments to us, and how she had set aside money for Blair's education. But two weeks ago she couldn't beat you in Scrabble. And last week she thought I was Dad. It's happening fast now, and now we're ten years old or twenty, or we're Dad, or we're who we really are . . . but she's already let go of us, I think. And I just don't want to watch anymore."

"Well, I'll be damned." Glenn stopped, and tried again. "I'll be damned." Shaking his head, he tried another variation on the preface and got out, "Well, I'm damned if I understand how you could go now, but I guess that's your business, then. Will you come back for . . . Will you come back?"

"No. I'll say good-bye before I go."

"Well, I'll be damned . . . Isabelle! You're staying, aren't you?"

"Yes, I am. But you both should know that I can't take care of Mavis much longer at home. Maybe through the weekend. Monday we'll need to take her to the hospital. I know, I know, Glenn. We promised we wouldn't, and she does seem calmer, finally, than she has been." Isabelle hesitated, then added, "But she'll need the hospital equipment to make these last days even bearable."

Now both sons were defeated, but whereas Craig's

defeat would keep him glued to his chair, held down by thoughts, Glenn was projected away from what distressed him. Anything to keep from sitting there with the same thought tracking back and forth across his mind: we promised her we wouldn't let anyone take her to the hospital. "That's no place to die," she had said.

On his feet and heading for the door, Glenn spoke as he pulled his cap onto his head. "You know best, Izzy. Do what you have to do. I'm going out to spell young Donny. I'll be up to Mom's after supper tonight." And he was out the door.

"He's not really mad at you, Craig. He probably knows better than he admits that you need to go back to Seattle . . . and stay there."

"Sure."

"But?"

"But no matter what my reasons are, I'm not going to feel too good about myself for a while."

Craig stood to load the few dinner dishes into the dishwasher. As he closed the dishwasher door he looked up at Isabelle.

"Last night I had a dream where I was in the movie *E.T.* I knew it was a movie and that I was the extraterrestrial. But I didn't know my lines. And then the little boy, Ell-i-ot"—Craig said the name in an E.T.-like nasal gurgle— "said not to worry, he knew the lines and he'd prompt me. And then, I can't really remember exactly how, but somehow the little boy was Mom and she looked terrible, even worse than she does now. She was still prompting me, but she was more than just sick, she was covered with purple sores and her skin was white and wrinkly and then *she* was E.T. and I was the little boy. I've been thinking about that dream all day. I suppose this is really sick, but I almost feel guilty about my own health. I know Mom was worried about me even though she wouldn't let herself ask about it. And . . . oh hell. The bottom line is, there's no spaceship coming for her."

"I wouldn't be so sure of that, Craig. Only she'd probably call it a chariot."

Craig studied Isabelle's half smile for a moment, and then added his own. "Whatever. Let's prove to Glenn that we're really shitty farmers and quit for the day."

"Sure. I should get back to check on Mavis, anyway."

MAVIS

I WONDER IF THEY'VE CALLED THE UNDERTAKER YET? I'll have to remind Maxine. She's probably got her nose stuck in one of my books somewhere. But I can count on her to see that the others get to school on time. Judy's been staying out too late. When did I see her last? She's getting as hard to get anything out of as Janice. So sad and works too hard. Always doing laundry. So many stains, she says, so many stains. Don't you do it, she says. I'll do it. I'll do it for you. I'll tell her she's done a good job. And what will we do with the twins? Maxine can take care of them, too. She's so good with them.

Boys can be a handful. Especially two at the same time. Maybe Craig would like to come with me. But where was it I was going? I'll ask Maxine. Maxine, are you there? Could you get that fly? It's been buzzing in the window all morning. Open the window, Maxine. It's time to let it go.

36

THERE IS A SOUND THE PRAIRIE MAKES. IT IS A SOUND that alters in pitch and intensity with the changing of the seasons, but not with the generations. It is the sound of clarity in the winter, brittle, defining the distinction between safety and danger: the one, warm and enclosed, inside; its opposite, changeable and bigger than all precautions, outside. A sound tensile and determined, like that of icy snow whipping straight across a flat country road, hurtled unchecked across the empty miles by a blizzard come to full force in less than an hour's time, forcing drivers, their hearts pounding with the acknowledgment of human helplessness, to creep their vehicles along the road, hoping that the shadow guiding them on the right is the side of the road, fighting the blizzard-induced vertigo that could lure them into that ditch, or into the path of another creeping car. When the blizzard calms, the replacing hush holds within its memory the howl. Then begin those nights of iron fragility when the expanse of the pitch-black sky with its diamond lights mirrors its negative below: mile after mile of flat frigid white, dotted by black stars of stubble breaking through the icy crust.

Winter moves slowly, reluctantly, into spring in North Dakota. The sting of winter's tension eases but its force remains as raw Canadian winds sweep the plains, washing the remaining snow with dirt. Now a faint percussion of farmers at work insinuates a background rhythm to the incessant wind, as they hammer, pound, fit, weld, dismantle, and reassemble machinery in anticipation of those days that must come when spring wins the tug of war. Suddenly, what was raw wind becomes a breeze, a chinook whose sound is a wasted admonition to the awakening world to quiet. Sometimes this breeze only means to tease these plains' people, because not only March, but April, and even May can come in like a lion, so that the lamb exits directly into the hum of summer.

It is a hum without the tension of winter and the insistence of spring. It is the steady buzz of activity, of motors, tractors, cars passing on a blacktop that promises shimmering pools of melted tar always just beyond. And just above, more felt than heard, the hum of the high line wires stretches between huge headless skeletal women wearing skirts of steel girders. It is a hum that yokes the swish of the swather, the whack of the baler, and the growl of the truck, with the whine of the grinder that throws sparks around the sharpened blades of the sickle mower. And mixes with the rhythmic munching of the hedge trimmers and lawn mowers, and the whump of the clothes dryer, and the sporadic gurgle of the sump pump. In the distance the hum separates into the calls of dozens of birds. There's the endless cry of "killdeer" by the long-legged prairie actors running as if broken-winged along the ground when approached and then, suddenly, screaming in mockery as they take off in flight; there's the hammering flicker, and the rich music of the meadowlark and the redwing blackbirds, and the gentle questioning of the mourning doves, and the raucous laughter of the crow. Closer to the earth is the gravelly hiccup of the frogs in the coulee, and closer to the ear is the whine of the mosquito. A hum. A buzz. Constant. Not noises to escape, because they have no boundaries, no walls, and no dimensions. Like the space of the prairie itself, the hum encloses, includes, the voices of men discussing rain received or absent, commiserating over market prices, and giving directions on which field to spray next to sons and the occasional daughter, and, if no one else is around, lifting those voices in song or prayer.

And the voices of women.

Ordering parts over the phone, yelling for children to hurry up and get in the car, mumbling to themselves over a grocery list of items to be picked up after work. Or making a phone call to a university in Chicago, saying she will be returning spring semester, but not saying, just yet, not out loud, that yes, she will take early retirement, and that, yes, she will move back to North Dakota. To live. Or making a phone call to California saying, "I'll be home soon. You are my home."

Or opening the door to two BCI agents, the older one standing back quietly, the younger one pushing the hair out of her eyes, looking hungrily at the woman who is saying, "Please come in. I've been expecting you."

Women talking and doing and talking and talking—at work, in the store, over coffee, at a picnic, their voices the engines, the pumps, the songs, and the cries reaching out in concentric circles to spread over the plains, to touch everything and everybody. To go on and on.

Then, slowly, the hum quietens. Augers churn the last of the wheat into granaries and aluminum bins. Combines roll into machine sheds for servicing between the summer and the late fall harvests. Huge cylinders of hay rest behind feedlots. Smaller rectangles are stacked in hay mows. Harvest halts, if only temporarily, while row crops sway and dry in the breeze—beans almost ready now for picking, sunflower heads hanging heavier each day, cornstalks drying away from green toward the brown they will be by the end of the month. The prairie takes a breath, stands still for just a moment, and then releases its sigh. It is no longer the sigh of the man-high prairie grasses that once hushed the passing wind. It is the sigh of a people who have worked and now will rest before they work again.

It is the sigh of autumn. A time of bounty that holds within it the contradiction of death. A gathering in and a gathering together before the bounty is spent.

There is a sound the prairie makes in its fall. Like the Sunday sigh that parts the lips of the dying with that last breath, so full of unsuspected vigor, expelled with unexpected force as if to say, "There, that's done now." Followed by the eyes snapped open to interrogate a space that holds no flowered draperies and no earthly beings, so that the others in the room, if that last breath should be witnessed, feel themselves to be ethereal, invisible. The eyes, bright and intent after weeks of steady dimming, bear witness to an amazement beyond description. Amazement at what, who could say? Perhaps at the vision of something heretofore unseen and undreamt of. Perhaps simply at the final and greatest surprise of all: that there will not be another breath.

And in the absence as intense as the dead woman's presence had been, the sigh of autumn, impossibly, returns.

JANE SMILEY
has crafted a body of work of uncommon depth
and strength.
These classics belong in every library and are
available in your local bookstore.
Published by The Ballantine Publishing Group.

A THOUSAND ACRES
by Jane Smiley

Winner of the Pulitzer Prize
and the National Book Critics Circle Award
and soon to be a major motion picture

An American family raised upon the fertile, nourish-
ing earth of a prosperous farm learn that wealth and
comfort cannot stay the hand of tragedy. This is the
intense and compelling story of a father and his
daughters, of sisters, husbands and wives, and of the
human cost of a lifetime spent trying to subdue the
land and the passions it arouses. A riveting, heartbreaking story of contemporary American life that is
destined to be read for years to come.

MOO
by Jane Smiley

"Delectably entertaining . . .
An uproariously funny and at the same time
hauntingly melancholy portrait
of a college community in the Midwest."
—*The New York Times*

In the heart of the Midwest lies Moo University, a distinguished institution of higher education devoted to the art and science of agriculture. In an academic atmosphere rife with devious plots, mischievous intrigue, and lusty liaisons, a remarkable cast of characters struggles to maintain tenure and their collective sanity. Here is a wickedly funny comedy that is also a darkly poignant slice of life.

BARN BLIND
by Jane Smiley

*The auspicious debut novel
that established Jane Smiley as a writer
to be reckoned with*

The verdant pastures of a Midwestern farm have the lyrical charm of a landscape painting. But the horses that graze there have become the obsession of a woman determined to win, no matter what the cost. Her ambition is the galvanizing force in this complex and elegant tale of work, love, duty, and the dark side of the pursuit of excellence.

"Jane Smiley is a born storyteller."
—*The Washington Post*

ORDINARY LOVE & GOOD WILL
by Jane Smiley

Two finely crafted short novels from one of the foremost writers of her generation

In *Ordinary Love*, a reunion with her grown children forces a woman to confront long-ago choices that changed all of their lives forever. In *Good Will*, a man discovers that even the right choices have unexpected, sometimes heartbreaking, consequences.

THE AGE OF GRIEF
by Jane Smiley

A stunning collection of five short stories and a novella confirms Jane Smiley's place as one of our most gifted writers

In the title story, a man struggles to save his marriage even as he is certain that his wife has fallen in love with another man who has spurned her. A meditation on the vagaries of love and life, THE AGE OF GRIEF is a true cause for celebration.

DUPLICATE KEYS
by Jane Smiley

They were six friends from the Midwest who moved to New York City to pursue success in the music industry. Although the dream had faded, they had all remained friends. Or so it seemed until one of them was murdered and they all became suspects. DUPLICATE KEYS tells a riveting story of the emotional aftermath of a violent death and the shocking secrets that lie between even the closest of friends.

THE GREENLANDERS
by Jane Smiley

In rich and fascinating detail, Jane Smiley delivers a riveting tale of life in fourteenth-century Greenland. This is the story of Asgeir Gunnarsson, a proud landowner, and his rebellious children. The willful and passionate ways of his daughter will send her into exile while his son's quest for knowledge will change all of their lives forever.

You won't want to miss even one!
Published by The Ballantine Publishing Group.